THE FURY
BEFORE THE FIRE

BILL PERCY

Black Rose Writing | Texas

ISBN: 978-1-68433-646-3
PUBLISHED BY BLACK ROSE WRITING
www.blackrosewriting.com

Printed in the United States of America
Suggested Retail Price (SRP) $20.95

The Fury Before the Fire is printed in Palatino Linotype

*As a planet-friendly publisher, Black Rose Writing does its best to eliminate
unnecessary waste to reduce paper usage and energy costs, while never
compromising the reading experience. As a result, the final word count vs. page count
may not meet common expectations.

Editing: Lorna Lynch
Proofreading: Kim Cheeley
Cover Design: David Levine
Author photo: Bruce Fischer

Books in the
Monastery Valley Series:

For Michele Brooks and Sue Haasis, the best first readers an author could have, and for Freddie Manton, former host at Brit's Pub in Minneapolis, Minnesota, where some of my best work has been written.
May he rest in peace.

ACKNOWLEDGEMENTS

Writing a novel is a team thing. Sure, crafting sentences and paragraphs, building a well-structured and well-paced tale from the original idea through the final revisions can be solitary work. But a *book* won't emerge from that unless it's supported by a team. In *The Fury Before the Fire*, you'll find that teamwork is one of the themes, and here I want to thank my teammates.

Tim Gift, a retired Captain with the Phoenix Fire Department, was a career firefighter and paramedic who during his twenty-five years on the job worked on engine and ladder companies, brush trucks, ambulances, and airport crash trucks. I asked him to read the scenes relating to the "fire" in the title with the goal of helping me get it right.

After Tim read those scenes during the summer of 2019, when we met, his first question was, "Tell me, Bill, how close to reality do you want this to be?" I knew he had a lot of feedback to give! As invaluable as his feedback was in dragging me closer and closer to the reality of what firefighting can be like, his "show and tell" was just as helpful. For example, he brought Nomex suits and showed me the difference between what structural firefighters (the ones who go into burning buildings) wear—about a thousand pounds of clothing, it seemed—and what hotshots facing wildfires wear (much lighter and less protective shirts, pants, jackets. Thanks to Tim's advice and knowledge-dump, those scenes in the book are much stronger now.

Next up, my editor Lorna Lynch grabbed hold of the manuscript and did her always-thorough editing, helping me see where the characters or the story lacked consistency and where it needed spice. She was especially helpful in pointing out scenes that were, simply put, boring. One recurring problem was that I'd show a team of deputies and the sheriff planning something they were about to do, and then I'd write a second scene in which they did it. The first scene (talking about doing it) was in every instance unnecessary, and Lorna kindly, but in a tone with no ambiguity, told me to get rid of them. Lorna, my thanks can't say enough.

Kim Cheeley did her always stellar proofreading of the final manuscript (well, okay, there's never really a *final* manuscript, at least not until the final galleys are approved) and did so with an amazing turnaround time. Thanks, Kim. I don't know how you do it!

Finally, thanks to Reagan Rothe and his team at Black Rose Writing, the book has finally seen the light of day. I'm more than grateful for the support Reagan has shown the Monastery Valley Series, publishing all five novels and naming me one of Black Rose Writing's "Signature Authors."

Last, but not least, my thanks to Michele Brooks and Sue Haasis, this book's first readers. After their reading of the earliest draft, their feedback, complete with markup by Michele's famous red pen, set a course for this book that enormously improved it. I hope you enjoy reading about the team at work inside *The Fury Before the Fire* as much as I've enjoyed working with them to bring it to you.

THE FURY
BEFORE THE FIRE

THE FURY
BEFORE THE FIRE

PROLOGUE: FIVE YEARS AGO

It happened during the last tax-conspiracy meeting with the Reverend Loyd Crane. Victor Sobstak wore a wire, hoping to win back Maggie's respect by putting himself in danger. Sheriff Ben Stewart had ordered him to stay in Reverend Loyd Crane's good graces until they got what they needed to arrest him. Deputy Andi Pelton led the team that would go in if Vic got in trouble. Which Vic no doubt would.

The reverend expected Vic to obtain damaging information about the Democratic candidate for Montana governor—a Black pastor—and deliver it to Crane's henchman, Mike, whom Vic called "Stetson," named for the brand of his hat. The day of the meeting arrived.

• • •

Wired, putting on a brave front, Victor drove to the motel and knocked on the right door.

He delivered the information. Then, through their radios, the sheriff's team listened as everything fell apart:

Stetson's voice (angry): "What the hell? You told us this already. This isn't news. What're you—"

Vic's voice: "Well, I'm just sayin'—"

Stetson's voice (cutting in): "Reverend, something isn't right here. This pussy's—"

Vic's voice: "Goddamn, Mike, you quit callin' me that!"

• • •

Loren, the deputy manning the radio console in the station, groaned, "No."

He told Callie, fast, "Get Andi's team in there."

Callie thumbed her mic and radioed. "Sheriff, this is Base. Send them in!" From the speaker, loud rustlings, Vic shouting, sounds of fighting.

Vic's voice (loud): "Hands off, you goddamn—" and then two heavy grunts, and Vic's radio went dead.

• • •

Sheriff's voice (booming): "Go! Go! Go!"

Sounds of loud pounding on a door.

Andi's voice (big, commanding): "Sheriff! Open this door!"

Andi's voice (again, louder): "Open this door or we're coming in!" A loud smashing sound and then:

Andi's voice (shouting): "Drop the weapon!" Shouts, then three loud sounds, pop, pop, pop.

Ben's voice (screaming): "Officer down! Officer down!"

PART ONE

PART ONE

CHAPTER ONE — SUNDAY, JUNE

1

"Andi, line two. Trouble incoming."

Deputy Andi Pelton groaned. Only eight in the morning, the last shift before her honeymoon, and outside the early-June temperature flirting with the upper eighties. *Last thing I need is trouble*, she thought, and punched the button hard. "Deputy Pelton."

"Andi, Vic Sobstak here. Look, some yahoos are camped on the high ridge where I summer graze part of my herd. You gotta get 'em the hell off so I can move my cows up. This heat's killing 'em."

She relaxed. No sweat, moving a family campsite away from the herd. Sheriff Ordrew could handle this one just fine—another reason to be glad she'd lost the sheriff's election last November. She asked Vic, "That's federal land, right?"

"Damn right, and I got me my grazing permit in my wallet."

"How about just asking them to move their campsite out of your herd's way?"

"They won't be doing that, Andi. Seriously, you gotta come out."

"Why, Vic? There's gotta be plenty of room up on that benchland for some campers and your herd."

"No way. I counted more'n thirty pickups, four RVs, a bunch of towed trailers, and maybe thirty, forty guys up there. God knows how many I *didn't* see. They've got them vehicles circled like a spooked wagon train. Lord, it's a damn fort."

She sank back into her chair. "You're kidding."

"Nope. Hand on the Bible I ain't."

Damn. "All right, Vic. The sheriff and I'll come out to talk to them. The road up's decent, right? A squad can make it up, if I remember."

"I'd use a pickup. Them yahoos tore up the road pretty bad."

"They *what?*"

"Chewed 'er all to hell. That old road ain't built for traffic. Potholes deeper'n some lakes."

Andi, emptying out like a pricked balloon, envisioned the airline tickets waiting on the kitchen table, her honeymoon suitcase already in Ed's truck, the naughty lingerie she'd ordered from Victoria's Secret tucked among her undies. Thirty-plus vehicles and forty guys were no innocent family to be politely talked off the ridge.

Maybe the sheriff will still let me leave.

And maybe a grizzly would let go a rodent because it squeaked. "Vic, wait for us. We'll be there in a half hour. We don't know who these people are, so let us take the lead."

"Andi, hell, it's my herd and my grazing permit. I ain't—"

"Vic," she interrupted. "What you're describing sounds serious. This's nothing you can do alone. Wait for us."

A long silence. "All right, Andi. But hustle your buns. I got me some dry and hungry cows to cool off up there."

And I have a honeymoon to take and a sweet little teddy to drive Ed crazy. She ignored the clench in her gut.

2

Vic Sobstak was waiting where his driveway reached the highway, rifle cradled on his arm. He yanked open the door and climbed into the back of the department's crew cab before it'd come to a stop, already chattering. "You took your damn time getting out here. I need—"

Sheriff Brad Ordrew turned, glared him quiet. "You need to go back to your house and put that firearm in the gun safe. I'm not taking a civilian up there armed and looking to get hurt."

Vic scowled. "I ain't going up there without this." He tapped the rifle barrel affectionately. "I'm a Montanan, Sheriff, and you know us Montanans."

Andi chuckled. She knew Vic, all right; they'd been shot side by side in a failed sting operation five years before. Mostly, his mouth ran ahead of his brain. She said, "You willing to be a *dead* Montanan?"

His eyes widened. "Well, hell, didn't quite think that one all the way through." He leaned toward the front seat. "I'll leave her here in the back when we get up, but that's the best I can do."

Andi looked at Ordrew, gave a tiny nod. The sheriff turned and looked up the highway. "Where are these campers?"

Vic pointed out the window to a cliff rising a thousand feet at the distant edge of his winter pasture. "Up on top."

"Okay. Show me how we get there."

"Drive north." A mile and a half later, they turned onto a dirt road at the far end of Vic's winter pasture; it was early June, but the grass was already August-brown. Vic got out, saying "I got the gate."

After he'd opened it, Ordrew drove through. He whispered to Andi, "Not sure I'm happy taking this guy up there."

"He's okay, Brad. He's the one got shot when I did. He grabbed the shooter's gun barrel before he could get off another shot. Bullet tore through his hand."

His eyebrows bobbed. "Him? My mistake. I pegged him as all wind and no rain."

Vic had closed the gate behind them and climbed back in. "Damn hottest and driest spring I can remember. Cows need to get up on the benchland, where it's cool and the grass is green." A herd of perhaps ninety cattle grazed on the brown grass beside the pasture road.

They looked at the herd, spread out, necks bent to the dry grass. Ordrew said, "It's hot all right. Mid-eighties already." He moved the pickup along the road ringing the pasture until they reached the base of the cliff and turned south. After fifty yards, the road began to climb up the mountainside. The ruts and potholes jostled the truck, bounced them around.

"This road's in shit shape," the sheriff muttered.

"I told you, they tore it up."

3

As the sheriff eased the truck over the ridge, Andi gasped, then held her breath. Even from two hundred yards away, the camp loomed, formidable. Ordrew whispered, "God help us," as he stopped the pickup.

A circle of pickup trucks and RVs, each with a trailer, had parked nose-to-tail in a wide ring around a big RV in the center. One truck-length had been left open facing the access road, an entryway of sorts. Through it, Andi could see into the inner space. Tents were scattered around the ground inside the ring.

In the middle of the high meadow where the camp had been set up, there were no trees and no shade against the heat. Awnings had been put out from the RVs, and other free-standing awnings had been set up beside several pickups, lawn chairs clustered under them. Men moved around, all in shorts and sleeveless camo t-shirts and military-style boots. Most were sweat-dark, though it was cooler up here than down in the valley. American flags and yellow "Don't Tread on Me" flags hung limp from many of the vehicles. Many of the men wore rifles slung across their backs, despite the heat; other weapons—lots of weapons—rested against the sides of RVs and pickup trucks. Stacks of olive-drab military ammunition boxes stood beside the weapons.

"Christ," she whispered. "It *is* a fort."

She flipped on the dashboard DMI.

Vic's voice startled her. "What's that thing?"

Her finger hit the wrong button. *Damn.* "Distance measuring instrument," she whispered, again. She found the right button. The display flashed.

"Two hundred ninety yards to the RV in the center of the ring," she whispered.

Ordrew grunted. "Stop whispering." But his voice was low, too. She adjusted the DMI, took another reading. "So to the nearest pickup beside the entryway, it's two hundred ten yards. If the RV's in the center, that circle is . . ." She stopped to calculate.

Ordrew murmured, "One-sixty in diameter."

"Looks like the vehicle ring is midway between this granite edge we're on and the mountain in the back."

Ordrew looked back at Vic. "What's this mountain?"

"Roberts Mountain. Real steep behind the camp, but when it gets to this benchland—" He gestured north, then south. "—she flattens right out. Little creek runs through a couple hundred yards south. Perfect pasture land."

"Is there any way we can sneak in behind them?"

Vic grimaced. "Doubt it. There's an old road down at the south end, but it ain't any good for vehicles."

"So," Ordrew said, "this road we just came up is the only way down, unless they walk out—and I doubt they'd leave all their vehicles and gear." He resumed the pickup's forward creep.

Andi ensured her Glock's safety was off.

Ordrew said, "Mr. Sobstak, behind your seat there are external armor vests. Please pass two up here. You'll wait in the truck."

Andi stiffened. "Due respect, Brad, we want to keep this low-key, friendly. We've got our soft armor on, and we don't know what they're up here for, maybe—" She stopped. As they rolled closer toward the entry, she watched two men armed with AR-15s step out from behind the vehicle on the left side of the opening and take up a position in the gap. They watched the sheriff's vehicle warily. Inside the camp, men were running toward the entry, all carrying rifles, many of them AR-15s or AK-47s.

Andi said, "God, they look furious."

Ordrew looked at her. "Hard armor, Andi."

"Got it."

Ordrew drove as slowly as he could, but kept approaching. He let it roll to a stop about ten yards short of the entry and surveyed the situation. "You're right, though, about keeping it friendly."

Vic protested. "The hell, Sheriff. Get them down off this benchland. This damn heat, my cattle ain't got enough good grass and water down below."

Ordrew kept his eyes front. "Mr. Sobstak, I need to find out what this is before I do anything."

Andi's shoulders loosened. Good, no show of force, no thunder. She pulled on the vest with its steel plates, clasped it carefully. *More guns in there than this vest'll stop,* she thought. "Brad, how about we call for backup?"

He nodded, studying the circle of vehicles and trailers. "Call Callie, send everybody out who's available. Have them come up the road to just below the ridge and wait."

Andi shivered. She clicked on her portable radio.

Ordrew looked across at her. "Use the truck radio."

"Testing my portable. Just in case." She tried not to think about what "in case" implied.

She radioed Callie Martin, weekday receptionist and dispatcher, told her what was happening, and relayed Ordrew's order. She clicked off her portable. "Radio's good."

The fifteen-minute wait felt like an hour. Andi wondered how the men were interpreting their waiting in the pickup. Then the radio crackled. "Sheriff, backup here. We're in place below the ridge. Backup over."

The sheriff replied, his voice low. "Backup, Sheriff here. Stay clear unless we call. We'll see what this is all about. Sheriff out."

Ordrew nodded again. "Okay. Let's see who came to this party."

They got out and walked toward the entryway. The two guards stepped forward to block their way, AR-15s pointed down and to the side.

Ordrew cleared his throat. "Gentlemen, I'm Sheriff Brad Ordrew of Adams County. May I ask what your business is up here?"

The guy in front of Andi said, "Ain't none of yours, Sheriff. Just climb in your truck and go back down the hill so nobody gets hurt." Andi stilled herself. She began counting the men gathering behind the guards.

Ordrew smiled. "Afraid not, guys. But let's not get off on a bad foot. I'm Brad Ordrew, and this is Andi Pelton, my lead deputy."

Andi nodded at the men, and resumed her count. Ordrew said, "And what'll I call you?"

"You'll call him fucking nothing," the other guard barked. "You're the problem here, the damn government."

"Ah. So, you're here to make a statement about the government?"

"I'm here to keep you out."

Andi saw his weapon waggle and stopped counting. She concentrated on his eyes, but avoided resting her hand on the grip of her gun.

A tall, rangy man came out from behind the RV on the left, and stepped into the space between the guards. "All right, I'll take over," he said. Andi recognized him. *Carl Jenkins.* Slender, big calloused hands. A local rancher. She'd met him last November during her campaign for sheriff, and he'd made clear his dislike. "Hey, Carl. We meet again."

"Deputy." He turned to Ordrew. "Sheriff, I'm Carl Jenkins, one of the leaders here."

Someone in the group behind him called out, "We got us *one* leader, our Lord and Savior Jesus Christ!"

Andi felt a chill. *Damn. Guns and religion. Pour some alcohol on this and watch how high it blows.* She kept her smile steady.

Ordrew said, "Carl, I appreciate your coming forward. I'm Brad Ordrew."

"I know. I voted for you."

"Well, thanks for the support. I'm sure we can sort this out."

Jenkins nodded. "We'll see. Just, uh, don't try force against us. We can talk, but if you try force—" He turned and looked back at the crowd of armed men. Andi finished her count. Forty-two men. All armed, except Carl. What about others she couldn't see?

Beside her, she sensed Ordrew going tight, but his voice stayed calm. "I take your meaning. We don't want violence any more than you do, Carl."

At that moment, a man in the group, a different one, yelled, "Of course you do, liar. You're nothin' but a front for the guv'ment."

Jenkins swirled and found the man who'd yelled. His voice was low, but it carried. "We agreed I'd do the talking, and I'd appreciate you shutting up."

"Well, then, do some real talkin'."

Jenkins turned back, but Ordrew spoke first. "You men are on federal land. Either you show me your permit to be here, or you'll have to leave."

"Not happening like that, Sheriff. We're here to make a statement."

Andi thought Jenkins's voice sounded hesitant. He continued, "But we're not prepared to do so at this time."

Waiting for the media, Andi guessed. She shifted her weight to the other leg. At the movement, the guard facing her raised his weapon toward her. She froze. Carl Jenkins caught it, looked her in the eye. Without turning to the guard, he said, "Lower it, Quinn." The guard glared, but obeyed.

"What *are* you prepared to tell us, Carl?" Ordrew asked. He gestured around the circle of trucks. "Your camp looks like you're ready to do more than make statements."

For a moment, Jenkins, his eyes still fixed on Andi, said to Ordrew. "Sheriff, I'm prepared to tell you to come back tomorrow. We'll make our statement then."

Ordrew's face flared red. Andi saw it, cleared her throat. Ordrew straightened, took a long breath. *Don't argue*, she thought. *Let him win this one.*

As if he'd read her thought, Ordrew said, "Sounds like a plan, Carl. Tomorrow. We'll be here in the morning, nine sharp." His voice was pleasant. "One thing before we leave." His voice raised. "If any of you men come down off this mountain, for any reason, you will be arrested for trespassing on federal land. Unless you've got a permit, the only safe ground for you is right here inside your camp."

The man who'd hollered earlier yelled again. "You're threatening us?"

"No, sir," Ordrew said. "You men came up here on this mountain to make a statement. That's what you're going to do, and that's all you're going to do."

Andi cleared her throat again, and this time Ordrew looked at her, nodded. She turned toward the truck, and he joined her. As they walked side by side, he whispered, "Your throat clearing trick saved me. Otherwise, I'd have arrested that prick in a heartbeat."

She flinched, but said nothing. After a moment, he grunted. "And got us both killed."

But when they got in the truck, Vic angrily demanded that the camp be removed. Ordrew looked out the rear window as he put the truck in reverse and backed around. As he did, he glanced at Vic. "Sir, did you count the men in there and see the weapons they're carrying?"

"I don't give—"

"Yes, you do. If I turn this violent, I'll have to bring in the FBI or the Bureau of Land Management and the state police. The fight will spill down this road onto your ranch, and your house and your wife and your cattle will be right in the middle. That what you want?"

Vic looked startled, then sheepish. "Sorry, Sheriff. Just running my mouth. Worried about my stock. Too damn hot for 'em down below."

"Let's not make it any hotter." Ordrew finished backing around and drove over the ridge onto the access road. Andi looked back to smile at Vic, but through the rear window she saw that the crowd of men had moved up to the entry of the camp, weapons ready. In their midst stood a tall man with silver hair, one who hadn't been there before. Was he familiar? Another shiver climbed up her back.

4

Ordrew drove onto the access road. About twenty yards below the ridge, at a wide spot, three deputies stood beside the department's other crew cab pickup. Ordrew pulled up and rolled down his window.

"Everything copacetic up there?" Pete Peterson, a tall, muscular man with sandy hair, asked. Pete was Ordrew's other senior deputy.

Ordrew shook his head. "We got serious trouble on our hands. Looks like a demonstration or protest." He turned to Andi. "How many did you count?"

"Forty-three. I counted forty-two, but I caught sight of someone who hadn't come out till we were leaving."

Ordrew said to Pete, "Forty-three. They're anti-government and heavily armed." He looked at the other two deputies. "Lanny, you and Felix follow us down. Park across the base of this road. Nobody goes up without my okay, and anybody who comes down, arrest them. Trespassing on federal land. Pete, ride with us. We've got some planning to do."

Pete climbed in beside Victor and shook his hand.

The pickup bucked and rattled on the ruts and potholes. Andi thought about her honeymoon plans, the new swimsuit she'd bought, the expensive surprise for Ed. But when she slanted her head enough to see the muscles bunching in Brad Ordrew's jaw, as if he were gnawing a bone, her chest tightened.

• • •

As they approached his driveway, Vic said, "You can drop me here, Sheriff. A little walk'll settle my stomach."

Ordrew pulled onto the highway shoulder across from Vic's drive; the rancher grabbed his rifle and climbed out. After driving back onto Highway 91 toward Jefferson, Ordrew said nothing for ten miles. Andi waited for it. As they approached the edge of town, he cleared his throat. "Your vacation starts tomorrow."

Here we go. "Actually, tonight. My honeymoon. We take off at 8:20 p.m." She started to talk about their plans, but he interrupted.

"You're flying out of Missoula?"

"Yeah. To New York, then Florence."

"Italy?"

"Italy."

His jaw clenched again.

This conversation's not done.

He fell silent again, pulled into the lot behind the station, and turned off the engine. She side-eyed his jaw, its muscles tight as a fist.

He gripped both hands on the top of the steering wheel. "Ah, man," he sighed. "Don't make me say it."

5

In the station, she dialed fast and held her breath as it rang.

Ed picked up on the third ring. "Honeymoon Central, Husband-in-Chief speaking."

"You sound happy." She hated this.

"Going on a honeymoon with my new wife. What's up? You need extra sunscreen?"

Just say it. "Something's come up."

A long silence. "Huh." All the lilt in his voice had drained out. "How did I know that would happen?"

She described the encampment and flinched at his sigh. She said, "Ordrew will just have to assign Pete to this. I've earned this vacation."

"Ordrew'll want you."

"He can't force me to stay as long as there are deputies available." She knew she was putting off the inevitable.

"Maybe not, but he can *ask* you to stay, damn it." Ed's voice rose, then cut off, as if he'd left the call.

Andi waited him out.

His silence stretched. Finally, "And you'll say yes."

She visualized the anger, or perhaps hurt, on his face. She bristled, then pushed it aside. She closed her eyes, wishing she could be with him, touch him, let him know she loved him more than the job. "I don't know, Ed. Nothing's decided yet. We'll talk. I'll keep you posted."

Another moment's quiet, though she could hear his breathing. His struggle almost brought tears to her eyes. Finally, he managed words. "Yeah. Keep me posted." His voice was dull, distant.

She was just hanging up when he called her name, "Andi!"

"I'm here."

"Uh, just stay safe, okay?"

• • •

Ed didn't need it spelled out. When Andi had told him what they'd found on Robert's Mountain, he'd known their honeymoon was up in smoke. Another case swooping into their lives and shoving everything off the rails, just like the murder case with that sex trafficking cult leader, the Bishop, did last fall.

"She won't cancel the trip," he muttered to himself. "But she'll postpone the damn thing."

He reined in his resentment. *Be fair.* Given what she'd described up on Vic Sobstak's summer pasture, big trouble was descending on Monastery Valley. National media-fodder trouble. This wasn't personal. Things happen.

He thought about that. He wanted to feel supportive. It's Andi's job, crises happen. He could yell at her, get past it that way, but what good would yelling do? Things are what they are. He could sulk, pile on the guilt. But he hated himself when he did that.

He started unpacking their suitcases, still mulling his reaction to the news. When he came across the sexy new teddy Andi had hidden amid her underwear, though, he hatched a plan. For the first time since she'd called, he smiled.

6

Grace came into the bedroom where Ed was unpacking. "Northrup, what's going on? On the phone, you sounded like a pissed-off boyfriend."

Ed frowned. "You're right, I *am* a pissed-off boyfriend." He piled Andi's underwear in her drawer.

"Why are you unpacking? You're going on your honeymoon in a few hours."

"That's why I'm pissed." But was he being fair? Hadn't Andi sounded apologetic? He stooped over the suitcase.

"Come on, Northrup. What's going on between you and my new step-mom?"

Ed straightened. "She just caught a case, something big. I'm guessing the sheriff's going to tell her to stay." He paused. "Correction: I *know* he will." He shook his head. "And she'll stay."

"So, you're mad."

"Pissed as hell. It's our damn honeymoon, for Christ's sake."

Ed saw the shock on Grace's face. "Northrup, you haven't said *pissed, hell, damn,* and *Christ* in the same sentence since you adopted me."

"So now you're watching my behavior?" The minute it was out of his mouth, he regretted it. *Dial it back, pal.*

She blushed. "Well, I figured a year of college under my belt gives me some cred as an observer."

"Given your many life-expanding experiences."

Grace frowned. "Don't use sarcasm, Northrup. It diminishes your argument. Besides, college life *does* have its life-expanding moments."

"Such as?"

"Not on your life, Daddy." She giggled. "I'll brief you when I'm on my own and your credit card no longer supports my lifestyle. Till then, imagine the worst, but keep the money flowing." She flashed a coy smile.

Ed found a chuckle. "I'm sorry, Grace. No need to take my anger out on you." He stopped, surprised. "Believe it or not, part of me wants to support her. How's that for being of two minds?"

Grace waited a moment. "Just two?"

He shook his head. He realized that deeper than the anger were the worries. No, the fears. Fear she'd be harmed somehow, shot by a crazy or . . . He sighed. *Stop. That's old news.*

Grace said, "You should call Andi, talk it out with her. Like you told me to do when Zach broke up with me."

"She has enough on her plate right now."

"You always tell me if you have a complaint, complain. Andi can take care of herself."

Even though he knew what she said was true and meant kindly, he experienced a wash of shame—he didn't *want* to talk about it, not yet. Even if Andi *could* take care of herself. Even if she didn't need him to take care of her.

What he didn't want to do was face the fact that she didn't need *him* at all. She needed the *job*.

7

Except for Felix Maslow and Lanny McAlister, who were manning the roadblock below the camp, all the deputies sat with Ordrew around the big conference table. At the far end, Ben Stewart, former sheriff and now a consultant to the Department, sat alone.

Ordrew was saying, ". . . know who owns that benchland? Sobstak said he has a grazing permit. From who?"

Pete Peterson said, "All the benchlands along the Washington Mountains are Bureau of Land Management land, except the one that holds Magnus Anderssen's house."

"That's no good." Ordrew rapped his pen against the edge of the conference table. "I don't want interference by the BLM or the FBI. We'll settle this our own way, which means doing it by the book."

Ben Stewart shook his head. "The Fibbies *wrote* that book, Bradley. From what you're describin', you ain't gonna control that camp without all the help you can get."

"The feds'll take over, and they'll be as eager for a fight as—" He stopped, looked around. "You're right, damn it." He turned to Andi. "Your thoughts about calling the FBI?"

"We've got you, Ben, and nine deputies. They've got forty-some armed men—and could be more we didn't see. If we want to pin them up there, that'll tie up at least two deputies every shift closing the road. I agree with Ben."

Ordrew said, "Pete?"

"I'm with Ben too. But like you say, the last thing we want is a firefight, and federal agents aren't known for backing down from one. There's Waco, Ruby Ridge . . ."

Ben shifted in his chair. "I know the field supervisory agent in Missoula, guy named Greg Haney. He's good, and he ain't one to step on your toes. Remember, it ain't just him. He's got agents and a SWAT team at his disposal, and another SWAT team in Bozeman. You call 'em, they'll be here in three hours."

Ordrew nodded. "Okay, let's move on. I'll call FBI Missoula when we're finished. Now, goals." He glanced at some notes in front of him, read off four objectives: prevent violence; end the protest quickly; arrest the leaders; and hand them over to the FBI. No one objected until the last one. Pete said, "Protocol is, we call the BLM and hold the fort till they get here. Not FBI."

Andi knew Pete had said "protocol" intentionally. Brad was a stickler for protocol.

"Sure, fine," Ordrew said. "So we'll make the arrests—with the FBI's help, I suppose—and then we'll call BLM to pick up the perps. I don't want BLM interfering." He looked around the table, as if daring someone to challenge him.

Andi sensed the tension in the room. *He's not listening.* Ben weighed in. "You maybe got you a problem there. I ain't doubtin' the campers called the media before they got here. The BLM'll turn on their TVs and see what's goin' on."

"Ah. The media." Ordrew frowned, but nodded. "Odds are, you're right."

Andi said, "Another problem. The weaponry up there will make arresting anybody big-time risky. Safety's priority one."

Ordrew chewed his lip, his eyes darkening. "So they trespass on federal land and we don't make any arrests?"

Andi said, "Well, the leaders, sure. But we'll never arrest the other 40-plus without violence." She watched his face; he was listening. "The FBI can help, Brad. Let's get them over here."

Ben stood. "Want me to phone up Greg Haney in Missoula? Get him movin'?"

Andi watched the sheriff's jaw working. He rubbed his eyes. "I'd appreciate that, Ben. If he needs me to say it, just get me—I'll be in my office." The others started to get up. He said, "Guys, another minute, please."

When Ben left, he said, "Everybody's on deck for the duration. I want two deputies at that access road, four-hour shifts around the clock until the FBI gets here. Andi, you're with me."

Objection boiled up, but she tamed it. "Brad, my vacation?"

Ordrew looked at her a moment, visibly uncomfortable. "All right, I'll beg. I need you here." After a silence, he added, "Please?"

She wanted to say no, but knew he *did* need her. "Okay. But you owe me one."

Ordrew let out a long breath. "Thank you," he said. "Pete, keep yourself plus one deputy down here for regular calls, then rotate the others on the access road till the FBI takes over. Nobody goes up or down without my approval, twenty-four/seven. Park the department SUV across the road. I know it'll be rough duty till the FBI gets here, but we'll handle it."

Again, he looked at Andi. "You and Pete write up the duty schedule we'll use till Missoula gets here."

She nodded, but kept still.

"Last thing." He looked around the room. "If I'm not available, chain of command is Andi for anything regarding the camp, Pete for everything else. Until further notice, whoever's not on duty is on call, and just one day off a week. If you're on call, have your phones on and charged, and be prepared to get in within fifteen minutes of a call. Understood?"

Andi sighed. *Understood. Goodbye, honeymoon.*

8

"Victor, calm yourself." Maggie hadn't seen Vic this upset since her breast cancer, but then he'd been loving-upset. Now he was about-to-be-stupid upset.

"Don't argue with me, Maggie. I don't give a good goddamn who those crazies are, my cattle are hurting. Eighty-eight damn degrees today, and in the nineties the next week, and there ain't enough green on the winter pasture down here to make a dollar bill. The hell with Ordrew, I'm moving 'em up tonight."

"Vic, just stop. You said yourself, those men up there are armed. If you—"

"I'll move 'em up the back trail. We'll keep 'em way down at this end of the bench, not in nobody's way. Don't tell me how to protect my herd, Maggie. It's twenty degrees cooler up there and green as Ireland."

"Vic, look, I—"

He'd already grabbed the phone and dialed, turning his back on her. "I'm calling Buddy." He kept his back turned while the bunkhouse phone rang, ignoring Maggie's protest. "Bud," he said, "round up the guys. We're taking the herd up to the bench. . . . Yeah, damn it, now. Everybody meet in my yard in a half hour. We'll take 'em up the old trail, soon's it gets to dusk."

Maggie's anger surged, but she knew it was useless. When her man got a notion in his head and welded it in with that Sobstak stubbornness, he became a bull with a tight flank strap on. "Promise me one thing, Victor."

"What?"

"Don't go near that camp. The herd'll do fine at this end of the benchland for a few days."

He squinted at her. "All right, that's fine. And you promise *me* one thing."

"What's that?"

"Don't go calling your friend Andi Pelton."

CHAPTER TWO — MONDAY

1

Morning briefing crackled with tension. Andi and Pete had given up their seats at the head, joining Ben Stewart at the far end of the table. Chip Coleman and Frank Renata, manning the roadblock, had called in on speaker phone.

At the head of the table, two new men sat with Ordrew, who tapped his knuckles on the table. "Okay, people, let's work. First, let me introduce our colleagues." On his right sat a tanned man with curly salt-and-pepper hair, a strong chin, an easy smile. "This is Supervisory Special Agent Greg Haney, from the FBI's Missoula field agency. Greg'll be consulting with Ben and me as this unfolds." He glanced at the former sheriff, who smiled at Greg and nodded.

Andi decided stress laced Brad's voice, not hostility.

Turning to his left, he introduced the other agent. "Special Agent Joe Mitchell is a hostage negotiator with the FBI, also from the Missoula resident agency." Joe, who looked ten years younger than Greg Haney, was runner-slim, had a trim beard, and wore thick glasses. He waved politely. "Joe'll help negotiate with the crazies when we get to that stage." He turned back to Haney. "Greg, anything you want to say?"

"Just to say Joe and I are here as consultants. If Sheriff Ordrew thinks a change is in order, we will let you all know, but for now, we are here to advise, not to take charge. Your local chain of command is operative. I'll shut up and start getting up to speed on the situation."

Ordrew thanked him, then opened the floor. "Questions?"

Lanny McAlister said, "Yeah, Brad, uh, Sheriff. What do those crazies want?"

"Who knows what the idiots want, Lanny."

Joe Mitchell leaned forward. "Mind a suggestion, Sheriff?"

Ordrew looked surprised. "What?"

"Not a big deal, but I'd suggest we all use the word 'protesters' to refer to the men in that camp. Negative words like 'crazies' can get lodged in the mind and lead to unconscious attitudes that may hinder progress. Just a thought."

Andi watched Ordrew's face as Mitchell was speaking. He kept it neutral, but she saw the muscles tighten around his eyes and a light flush cross his cheeks. But when Mitchell sat back, he thanked him. "Got that, guys? *Protesters*. No negatives."

Andi's cell phone buzzed quietly. She glanced at the screen, then excused herself. She mouthed, "Sobstak" to Ordrew as she left the room.

· · ·

Outside, she kept her voice low. "Maggie? What's going on?"

"Trouble, Andi. Vic moved the herd up onto the benchland last night, and Buddy Alsop just called Vic to tell him six of our cattle were shot during the night. Vic's in a fury. He says he's taking his rifle up to confront those men."

Andi caught her breath. "Is Vic there?"

"In the mud room, putting on his boots."

"Put him on the phone."

When Vic came on, he snapped, "They killed four cows and two calves. Don't give me grief, Andi. If it's one cow, maybe I think accident or illness, or stress from the damn heat. Six, Andi, and all shot, for God's sake. I'm going up."

She kept her voice even. "Vic, don't be foolish. Wait for Sheriff Ordrew and me to get there. What's one man against forty or more?"

"My foreman and two hands are up there. That's four."

She kicked the chair. "Give us a damn half hour, Vic. Don't risk your men's lives too."

"The hell, Andi." He stopped.

Maggie's voice sounded in the background.

Vic said, "All right. Twenty damn minutes."

"Thirty. We need a half hour."

"Twenty-five. Then I'm going up."

•   •   •

Maggie followed Vic to the barn, where he started the four-wheeler. It sputtered a few times; he swore. Then it caught and roared. Maggie yelled over the noise. "Vic, you can't drive that up, they'll hear you."

"I'm going up the back road, and the pickup won't handle that. I need to see the cows before I do anything."

"You promised Andi you'd wait."

"Changed my mind."

"Victor, think! You take this machine up the back way, they'll know there's another way down. You're not wanting them coming through our yard, are you?"

Vic deflated. "Aw, hell, Maggie, you're right, damn it. I'll take the pickup 'round the front way. But I'm going." He snapped off the machine and dismounted, glared at her, then headed for the door.

Maggie shadowed him. "And I'm going with you."

"Now just wait a minute, you're . . ."

"I'm what, Victor? A woman? You helped me with the cancer, and I ain't about to let you get yourself killed over a couple of cows." She put on her sternest frown. "I need a minute to pee."

"Well, get on with it. I ain't waiting."

Inside, she called Andi and told her Vic was heading to the access road, then went outside and climbed into the pickup.

Vic snarled. "You call Andi?"

"Darn right, I did. I ain't looking to be a widow."

Vic slammed the pickup in gear and sped up the drive to the highway. "Don't matter, woman. We'll be up there before the sheriff's halfway out."

•   •   •

Back in the conference room, Ordrew was running through the day's ordinary issues.

Andi interrupted, heart racing. "We've got trouble. Vic Sobstak took his herd up to that benchland last night, and somebody shot six cattle during the night. Vic's in a rage—he's going out to confront the protesters."

Ordrew paled. "Didn't we have people stationed at the foot of that road? Somebody's going to lose his job—"

Chip Coleman's voice barked out of the speaker. "No way, boss. Me and Frank relieved Lanny and Felix at eleven. Nobody came by on their shift and nobody on ours, either."

Ben Stewart slapped his forehead. "Christ in a Chevy, I forgot all about that back way. Starts out behind Victor Sobstak's second barn. Kids use it for lovers' lane when the one by the river's too buggy. Bet he took 'em up that way."

Ordrew barked, "Damnation! Xavier, you and Loren grab a squad and seal off that back road. Pete, you take over down here. Bud, you stay with Pete and help with any calls." He leaned toward the speaker phone. "Chip, you there at the road?"

"Yessir, boss. Me and Frank."

"Vic Sobstak's on his way to your position. Don't let him through. Arrest him if you need to. Interfering with a police investigation."

"On it, boss."

"The rest of you guys follow me in one of the SUVs. It'll handle that access road if I need you up top." Ordrew turned to Greg Haney. "You guys coming?"

The agent nodded. "Wouldn't miss it."

"Okay," Ordrew said. "Come with Andi and me in the crew cab. Everybody carry hard vests. Let's go. Fast."

"Sirens?" Lanny McAlister asked.

Ordrew turned to Greg Haney, who shook his head.

The sheriff ordered, "No sirens. Lightbars, though, on the highway."

His confidence, his rapid-fire thinking, reassured Andi. As they all ran out to the vehicles, Ordrew shouted, "My pickup goes to the camp. Everybody else come most of the way up, but don't show yourselves. If I need you, I'll call."

Climbing into the pickup, he muttered, "If we're lucky, Frank and Chipper'll contain Sobstak before he starts a war."

2

As Vic Turned off the highway, he looked across to where the access road began its climb. "What in the holy hell?" he muttered.

"What's wrong?" Maggie said.

He pointed. A sheriff's squad stood astride the access road, blocking the way.

When they got there, Chip Coleman raised his hand and came over to Vic's door, making a sign for him to lower the window. As Vic did that, hot air boiled into the car.

"You can't go up, Mr. Sobstak. Sheriff's orders. Nobody goes up, nobody comes down."

"Damn it, Chipper. I got me dead cattle up there."

Coleman wiped his forehead—the heat had him sweating, though it was only seven-thirty. "I'm sorry to hear it, sir. But nobody goes up till Sheriff Ordrew gets here."

Vic got out and walked around the squad. He stood, rough hands on his hips, studying the clearance. He spit on the dry grass. "Damn truck won't fit through."

Maggie joined him, with Chip right behind. Vic's look traveled up the road. *About a mile and a half hike to the top*, he calculated. *Half an hour on a flat road.* He turned to the deputy. "You say the sheriff's on his way? How long before he gets here?"

"Dispatch called me—" He glanced at his watch. "Eight minutes ago. They should be here—"

Vic finished for him. "—Seven minutes." He turned on his heel and walked back to his pickup, announcing, "We're waiting," as if it had been his plan all along.

3

The Sobstaks and the deputies watched the sheriff's vehicles approaching along the pasture road. The sheriff's crew cab pickup nosed up within a foot of Vic's. Ordrew, Andi, and Greg, the lead FBI agent, got out. "Chip, what we got here?" Ordrew flashed a quick but cold smile toward Vic and Maggie.

Vic didn't let him answer. "We got us some dead cattle, Sheriff. I'll appreciate it if you tell your boys to move their damn car so I can get through."

"Vic, here's the story. We go up first, you follow. You stay unarmed. I do the talking. You stay out of it. Am I real clear?"

Andi wondered how Vic, never one to take orders well, would respond. "Depends on what you're planning to say. You don't get my answers, I'll do my own talking." Maggie put her hand on his arm, but he shook it loose. Andi thought, *Not good.*

Ordrew frowned. "You took your herd up without my authorization." He paused, as if he were pondering how to handle that. "I'm tempted to arrest you for impeding our investigation of these protesters."

"Pardon my French, Sheriff, but that's bullshit. I got me my permit to graze, and that's all I'm doing. Arrest the damn campers for killing my cows, not me."

Andi saw Ordrew's shoulders stiffen, but his voice stayed even. "How do you know the protesters killed them?"

"Well, ain't it the best explanation? All six, four cows and two calves, were fine last night when we moved them. Your men were parked right here all night. All six, shot in the head this morning."

The sheriff said to Chip Coleman, "You hear any shots overnight?"

Chip looked at Frank, who shook his head. Chip said, "No, but we dozed off a lot. Could've happened."

Ordrew signaled Andi and Greg Haney, and they walked away a dozen yards. "What do you think? We take him up or keep him down here?"

Andi said, "I'd let him go up, as long as he follows your orders. We'll need the community on our side for the long haul, and I can't see pissing Vic Sobstak off. He's a talker, and the ranch people trust him."

"Greg?"

Agent Haney said, "Andi's right about keeping the community on your side. If he's under control, I can't see a downside."

Ordrew looked at her. "So controlling Sobstak's your job."

4

When their vehicles crested the ridge and rolled toward the camp, Carl Jenkins came and stood in the entrance, arms folded, flanked by the same two guards. They were sweating already. The protesters assembled behind them, many shirts dark with sweat. Except for Jenkins, all cradled their rifles in the crooks of their arms, or rested them on their shoulders, pointing at the sky. The guard named Quinn licked his lips. Andi couldn't tell whether he was dry or scared. Decided Quinn didn't look like a man who scared easily. He looked like a man accustomed to fury.

Ordrew climbed out and led the way toward the entrance, followed by Andi and Greg Haney. Behind them, two truck doors slammed. She glanced back, froze. Vic was out of his truck, carrying his rifle. She whispered, "Brad?"

Ordrew stopped. Andi kept her voice low. "Vic's got his rifle. Give me a minute to disarm him."

She walked back to Victor and Maggie. "Vic, put that back in the truck."

"Not happening, Andi. Just step aside."

She didn't. "Vic, in ten seconds, either you and your rifle are back in your truck, or I arrest you."

"Damn it, Andi! Damn it to hell! These are my cattle we're talking about!"

Andi sensed the gazes of the camp on her back. "And it's your wife's life we're talking about, too. You think those men in the camp will shoot at just you?"

Vic looked stricken. He swung to Maggie. "See, damn it?! I told you not to come up here." Back to Andi. "Now what?"

"Now you and Maggie get in your truck and stay there. Let Sheriff Ordrew and me handle this before you get us all killed."

Fuming, Vic stalked to his truck. Maggie whispered, "Thank you, Andi. I'll keep him there."

"Good." She turned, rejoined Ordrew and Greg Haney. "Contained."

"For now," Ordrew murmured.

When they got to the entrance, Carl Jenkins said, "Sheriff. You're an hour early. You specified nine o'clock."

"We have some business that's more important than your statement. The rancher in the truck is Mr. Vic Sobstak. He—"

Jenkins nodded. "I know Victor well."

Maggie called, "Victor! Stop!"

Vic stepped around from behind the sheriff's group. He was carrying his rifle, cradled like those in the camp. "I'm damned angry, Carl. And you know why."

Ordrew stepped between them. "Mr. Sobstak, stow that rifle in your pickup, or I will arrest you."

"All due respect, no, sir. It's my right to carry it and it's my cattle got killed. I'm wondering how a citizen of this valley gets rougher treatment than a bunch of yahoos?"

Andi stiffened. Vic was boxing them in. No way Ordrew dared back down from Vic in front of the protesters. She said to Ordrew, "I've got this." She moved over in front of Vic, her back to the camp. "Cool it, Vic," she whispered, looking hard into his eyes. "This can't work. You buck the sheriff in front of these guys, he loses any chance of getting them out of here anytime soon, much less of protecting your cattle. Give me your rifle." She kept her eyes locked on his, saw the fury in his eyes. They darted around, his fingers twitching on the gun.

Maggie, too, whispered. "Please, Vic. Let the sheriff do his job."

"Damn it all to hell!" Vic shouted, jerked back, lifted his rifle, fired a shot into the sky.

5

Instantly, rifles rose throughout the camp. Jenkins turned, lifted his hands, yelled, "Hold your fire!"

Another voice, deeper, resonant, and more powerful, rang out from behind the armed men. "Stand down!" Warily, the men began lowering their weapons, but all glared furiously at the sheriff's group.

A figure emerged out of the crowd, tall, tan, silver-haired. Andi and Vic gasped together. Her face flushed, hot.

The man, in his fifties, athletic, commanding, entered the crowd, which parted to allow him through. Obviously in command, he moved toward them. His gaze took them in; a smile that gave Andi chills played across his lips. Vic muttered, "Good goddamn. It's that bastard, Loyd Crane."

Andi shuddered, relived the pain from Stetson's bullet in her shoulder.

Crane stepped around the guards and came out to face the sheriff. "Sheriff Ordrew, my name is Loyd Crane. The Reverend Loyd Crane. Congratulations on your electoral victory." He held out his hand to Ordrew, although he looked straight at Andi.

Andi saw Ordrew's face go white. She remembered Crane backing Ordrew — anonymously — in the election, and recalled Crane's vicious ads defaming her and the Department. Ordrew, before the end, had found his conscience and repudiated Crane's support. Now, he refused Crane's extended hand.

Crane pulled his hand back, shrugged, and turned to Andi. "Ah, Deputy Pelton, Victor, we meet again. To what do we owe the pleasure of your visit to our camp?"

Answering, Andi knew, would weaken the sheriff's standing. She narrowed her eyes and said nothing.

Ordrew spoke instead. "You're on federal land, Crane. Have you a permit to camp here?"

"Good for you, Sheriff, cut to the chase. The federal government steals the land from the people, then requires you, as county sheriff, to enforce that theft by demanding permits to use land that belongs to the people in the first place."

"I'm not here to argue about that. Do you have a permit to camp here?"

"How fitting you should demand a permit. We're naming this project Freedom Camp. Freedom from government regulation, freedom from government seizure of our lands, freedom from *permits*. And you—"

Ordrew spoke over him. "Cut the crap, Crane. You're on federal land. Without a permit, you're trespassing and have to leave."

"I think you'd do well not to be unneighborly, Sheriff." He turned and surveyed the crowd of angry men, their weapons ready. "I'm the leader of these men, and they listen to me. Are you and Deputy Pelton going to force us to leave?" A few men smiled; the guard named Quinn barked out a laugh.

"Or is Mr. Sobstak your backup?" Again, laughter.

Beside her, she felt Vic tense, but when Andi brushed his arm, he settled. Ordrew, his voice thick, gestured at the camp. "Is this the project you told me you'd be bringing to the valley? The project you wanted me to 'turn a blind eye' to?"

Crane smiled. "With a few variations, yes. But I hadn't anticipated such a reunion." He looked at Vic, then at Andi. She returned his gaze, knowing and not caring that her welling hatred showed in her eyes.

Vic spoke. "You killed six of my cattle, Crane. I want—"

"You have no proof of that accusation, sir, so what you want is immaterial. What *we* want—" He pointed back over his shoulder at the men behind him. "What we want is at issue here." He turned back to Ordrew. "Sheriff, this man fired into the air above my camp and put my men at risk. I want him arrested for reckless endangerment."

A silence came over the camp. Andi stiffened, wary. Crane had a point. Vic had indeed endangered them, and the first violence had erupted on their side, making the sheriff look weak. Andi wondered how Ordrew would respond.

He turned to her. "Agent Haney and I will talk with Mr. Crane. Take this idiot—" He glared at Vic. "—to the station and book him. Reckless endangerment." He lowered his voice. "Get his keys and have Ms. Sobstak bring them to me. We'll drive his pickup to the station when we're done here so she'll have a ride home."

Vic burst. "Hell, Sheriff, you can't—"

Quickly, Andi stepped up very close to him, and put her hand against his chest. "Shut up, Vic." She pitched her voice low, but fierce. "This could turn very bad very fast. Come with me. We'll sort it out later." She grabbed his elbow, and looked over his shoulder at Maggie, who looked stricken. "Help me?" Andi said, softly.

Maggie nodded and took Vic's other elbow. "We'll figure it out, Victor. Let's just get the hell out of here."

Vic looked stunned, defeated. His wife never swore. "Okay, Maggie." For a long moment, he just looked at her, then turned and walked between the two women, his back straight, to the sheriff's department pickup.

Andi put him in the back seat and his rifle in the bed of the truck. Maggie sat up front. As Andi climbed in behind the wheel, Maggie turned toward Vic and spoke through the grill. "Trust Andi, Vic. She'll take care of it."

Andi's stomach tightened. *And just how do I do that?*

6

As she drove over the granite ridge onto the dirt road down to the pasture, Andi swore under her breath. Facing them, twenty-five yards below the granite ridge, was the department SUV, with three men waiting in it, Special Agent Joe Mitchell and two deputies. She said to Victor, "Sit tight and keep your mouth shut." She rolled her window down and waved the driver over.

Deputy Bud Gilman came around to her window. "What's up? We heard a shot."

She rolled her eyes. "Victor Sobstak lost his temper, fired into the sky."

"Jesus," Bud said, leaning down to peer into the back seat, shaking his head.

"Yeah. Look, I'm taking him to the station." She pointed down the road a hundred yards. "Can you back down to that wide spot so I can pass you?"

Bud nodded. "No sweat. I'll pull in tight to the cliff. You should be able to get by me there."

"Got it."

They pulled off the maneuver. Andi relaxed, headed down toward the valley floor.

Maggie asked, "What's going to happen?"

Vic must have recovered his anger. "Yeah, damn it. Am I being arrested? You got no right—"

Andi interrupted him. "You're here because you fired your weapon at a crowd."

"Bullshit, Andi, I fired straight up into the air."

Andi adjusted the rear-view so he could see her scowl.

"What?" he said.

Maggie said it. "What goes up comes down, Victor. That temper of yours makes you dumb as a sack."

• • •

On the highway to town, Vic repeated his demand. "Andi, you know I ain't the one who should go to jail. I'm pissed that—"

Andi held up her hand. "Can it, Vic."

Vic stopped.

"In any other situation, you fire a weapon in the air over a crowd, you go to jail. But arresting you while those protestors stay free will cause real blowback from the community, and there's some in the valley who'll take things into their own hands. That could mean a real shooting match up there, which could kill a lot more of your cows." She locked eyes with him through the rearview. "So, I'm not going to arrest you. But you're going to wait in the station with Maggie till the sheriff gets back and I can talk him out of filing charges. Any more crap from you, though, he won't back down. If you want to sleep with Maggie tonight, keep your mouth shut."

Vic started, "I won't—"

Andi said, "Starting now."

7

A half hour later, Sheriff Ordrew and the others piled into the station. When Ordrew saw Vic sitting with Maggie in the conference room, his face reddened. He said to Andi, "In my office."

After he'd slammed the door, he snapped, "You haven't arrested him?"

"Brad, if we arrest Vic for firing a shot, but don't touch the protesters for killing the cattle, how do you think the other ranchers in this valley are going to react?"

"Don't ask questions, make your damn case."

She took a long look at him. *He's under pressure. Cut him some slack.* "Look, Brad, just so you know, I'm not happy about losing my honeymoon, so don't push me too hard." She waited. He didn't reply. "Okay, my case: We'll have a range war on our hands. There're plenty of guys who'll pump each other up to storm that camp with their own assault rifles."

"So, I just let Sobstak go? Just enforce *some* of the laws? The ones I want?"

"Not at all. Don't arrest him, so that if anyone in the valley asks, we can say he wasn't arrested. Let Crane believe he's been arrested—don't tell him anything, one way or the other."

"He'll demand to know."

"It's none of his business. Then when this is done, Vic makes a generous contribution to the Sheriff's Department, say, just about the same amount as he'd get fined for the reckless endangerment."

Ordrew shook his head. "Jesus God. You people . . ." Ordrew had joined the Department three years ago, after being fired from the

LAPD; he'd always claimed the Montanans were lax. Rummaging in his pants pocket, he took out the keys to the Sobstak's pickup, and tossed them at her. "Leave me. Send the bastard home."

8

"Long day," Ed said, sympathetically. He sat beside Andi on the porch swing, sweating in the stifling evening air.

She rested her hand atop his leg. "I'm sorry about the honeymoon."

"I called our travel agent. The trip insurance means we can re-schedule for another time."

Relieved, she said, "Thanks for not making this a problem, Ed."

"Who says it's not a problem? You know I'm disappointed."

His leg had tensed. She pulled her hand away. "Disappointed? That all?"

He shook his head. "I've got a ton of feelings about it. Mostly, I'm angry, I'm disappointed, I'm afraid, and I'm worried about you. You name it, I feel it."

She knew Ed's worst fear was that she'd get hurt in the line of duty. "Well, just don't hate me."

"How about I hate you for a day or two?"

She searched his face, decided he was letting it go. "Okay." She looked beyond the porch at the fading light. "I get it. I'm disappointed too. I had a nice surprise for you." She thought of the teddy, blushed.

Ed arched an eyebrow. "I know. Found it when I unpacked your suitcase. I've got a plan for you redeeming yourself."

"'Redeeming' myself?" Curiosity defeated annoyance. "How?"

"Go put the teddy on and we'll pretend we're in Italy."

"Now?"

"Now."

But Grace's pink Volvo was coming up the drive. In a moment, it crunched into the yard and parked in the third spot on the gravel, beside Andi's SUV and Ed's pickup. Ed had bought the vehicle for her high school graduation, and within minutes, she and her girlfriends had named it the Pink Vulva. Andi grinned. "Saved by the PV."

Ed whispered, "You're not escaping my clutches that easily."

Before Grace joined them, Andi whispered back, "I love your clutches."

"Hi, newlyweds," Grace said, bouncing up the porch steps. "I'm bummed you're not on your honeymoon."

Andi said, "We are too. Real inconvenient time for an occupation by crazy—uh, protesters."

"Yeah, I was looking forward to two weeks of college-style carousing, parties every night, seducing Jen's and Dana's new husbands, that sort of thing." She gave an elaborate sigh. "Guess it'll be normal-level chaos now."

They laughed, and Grace sat down across from them, fanning herself. She said, "Seriously, you must be really bummed."

Andi shook her head, glanced at Ed. "Yes and no. The occupation has me in its grip now. I'm focused. And your dad's being understanding about it." She patted Ed's thigh. Up high.

"Good for you, Northrup," Grace said. "I knew you were up to it."

Ed, thinking about the teddy, smiled.

Grace turned serious. "Lots of people are talking about going up and forcing the campers to leave."

Andi stiffened. "That's the last thing we need. How serious are they?"

"I don't know. Jen and Dana's husbands are doing most of the talk, and I think they're serious."

"Do me a favor. Ask around. Try to find out what they're planning—if anything. And if there's a leader. And a timeline."

Grace grinned. "I knew it'd happen someday."

Andi tilted her head, puzzled. "What?"

"You're *deputizing* me."

"Well, kind of."

"So, the real question is, how much do I get paid?"

9

When Grace went inside, Ed chuckled. "How about a little foreplay talk? What's the plan for the occupation?"

She laughed. "That's foreplay talk?"

"I'm betting it's the only thing you want to talk about at the moment."

She looked at him. *I'm forgiven.* "You'd win that bet, bucko." She told him about how Vic's shot almost drove them into the ditch and how she'd persuaded Ordrew to let it go.

Ed smiled. "You ought to be the negotiator."

"No, Brad's claiming that job." She sighed. "I wish he'd let the FBI negotiator take over."

"Brad's not up to it?"

"Wound up way too tight."

"He's been sheriff, what, six months and he's handed a major crisis, with national implications. As soon as the media get here, the whole country will be watching. I bet he's petrified."

"The media's already here. He's corralled them at the foot of the access road. They're furious."

Ed said, "What do you mean, 'corralled'?"

"We rented a big tent and a generator and a bunch of tables and chairs, and told them it's their office-away-from-home. Brad won't allow anybody up at the camp." She stretched. "You're right that he's acting spooked, and that worries me more."

They gazed out at the evening. The sky was darkening across the valley, although light glowed behind the high peaks in the west. She realized she hadn't told Ed. "Say, you'll be shocked to know who's running the protest."

"Anybody I know? Somebody from here?"

"One that we know of, Carl Jenkins. But the real leader is Loyd Crane."

Ed's mouth fell open. "You're—"

"Nope. It's him. He showed himself today."

Ed ran his fingers through his hair. "Man, that ratchets this thing tight, doesn't it?"

"Tighter than sex in an airplane restroom."

Ed grinned. "Hmm. Knew we'd get there." He stood. "You ready for that teddy?"

"Rev up those clutches, cowboy."

CHAPTER THREE — TUESDAY

1

At six-thirty next morning, Andi stepped into Ordrew's office for the day's first team meeting. Ben followed her. A few minutes earlier, they'd cooked up a plan to persuade Ordrew to let Joe Mitchell negotiate.

After everyone sat, Ordrew said, "Okay. Our first negotiation is at nine this morning. They were going to give us their statement yesterday, but that bozo Sobstak fucked that all to pieces. I need a plan."

Andi turned to the FBI negotiator. "Joe, what's reasonable for a first sit-down?"

"Well, first thing, don't expect a sit-down. Standing you up at the gate puts them in control, and I can't see them giving that away. Second, today's all about what *they* want, what their agenda is. We'll get our turn, but first we have to find out what they're after."

Ordrew ran his fingers through his thick brown hair. "They're breaking the law. Why should we play nice?"

Andi glanced at Ben. His face was calm, unrevealing. She opened her mouth to speak, but caught Ben's soft head-shake.

She saw it coming. Ordrew snapped, "They break the law, they get all the patience we can give them, we let them make demands, and we just smile and eat their crap?"

Joe nodded. "Seems like that for a while, Sheriff. Just for a while. Once we get them off the land and their gang's broken up, we arrest the leaders. They know as well as we do that's how these things work, unless somebody starts shooting. Our job's to keep them calm and under control till they're ready for the next chapter. We'll win in the end."

"God, I hate that. I don't know that I've got it in me to grovel to those crazies, uh, protesters. I—"

Ben cleared his throat. *Now*, thought Andi. She lifted her hand. Ordrew glared at her. "What?" His tone would pierce steel.

"I'm like you, Brad," Andi said. "I'm too mad to be any good with what Joe's talking about. He's a pro. What about letting him do the negotiating?"

Ben piggy-backed. "Andi's on target: We oughta leave the talkin' to the pros. Like Joe here."

Ordrew shook his head. "No, I'm sheriff in this county. It's my job."

Ben in turn shook his. "Disagree, Brad. The sheriff's job is overseein' the troops, settin' strategy for 'em. It ain't doin' their work. You don't ride patrol or investigate crimes; you leave that to your deputies. Same way, you ain't the one to do the negotiatin', either. You got a skilled and trained FBI negotiator right here. Use him."

Andi held her breath.

Ordrew seemed to shiver, as if he was taking off some piece of clothing that protected him, kept him warm and safe. Losing something. Andi watched his face.

He turned his head to her. "You agree?"

She let out her breath. "I do."

Ordrew looked up at the big wall clock. Abruptly, he stood. "Okay. Seven o'clock. Time for morning briefing. This meeting's done." He ushered them across the hall to the conference room, where the other deputies waited.

2

At the entrance to the camp, Rev. Loyd Crane stood with Carl Jenkins, legs spread, arms folded against his chest. Crane wore a long-sleeved shirt, but despite the heat, he looked cool, commanding. *Doesn't break a sweat*, Andi thought. The same two guards, Quinn and the unnamed one, flanked Crane and Jenkins, and behind them armed men stood shoulder-to-shoulder; some held their rifles down, others aimed them toward heaven. The sheriff's team walked toward the camp, stopping ten feet away from Crane and Jenkins.

Crane looked at his watch. "Nine-oh-seven, Sheriff. You promised nine o'clock. Is this a sign of what we can expect when you give us your word?"

"Good morning, Reverend, Carl. What's on the agenda this morning?"

Andi, surprised, glanced at Joe Mitchell. His face was neutral, but his eyelids dropped subtly. Ordrew had handed Crane the initiative.

One man behind Crane and Jenkins shouted, "Your guy tried to kill us!"

Crane turned and stared him quiet, but said nothing.

Ordrew shouted back. "He fired straight up in the air. Nobody tried—" Andi moved beside him, so that her shoulder touched his arm softly. He stopped.

Crane stepped closer, and lowered his voice. "Sheriff, let's keep this between us. My men fear your townspeople will assault us. We require a guarantee of safety from you."

Ordrew matched Crane's softer tone. "Under the circumstances, I suppose I can understand their fear, although . . ." He paused, looking hard at the weapons in the protesters' hands. "I understand it, but I can't ignore the fact that your people killed a half-dozen cattle, which is a crime here."

"Sheriff, you have no proof it was any of us."

Ordrew narrowed his eyes, then said, "Please, sir, don't insult my intelligence." He paused another moment. "I will guarantee the safety of your camp and your people, provided you do the same on your side."

Andi saw Joe Mitchell's eyes light up. The first *quid pro quo.*

Crane turned away, huddled with Carl Jenkins, whispered something. Jenkins nodded. Crane turned back to Ordrew. "I will ensure your people's safety here at Freedom Camp."

Ordrew paused a moment. "And I can guarantee that if any of your people leave this camp without my authorization, they will be arrested for trespassing on Federal land."

He's pushing too hard, she thought, but Ordrew surprised her. "Reverend, I'd like to introduce our negotiator, Special Agent Joe Mitchell."

Ordrew gestured for Mitchell to step forward. Andi hid her surprise.

Crane's face hardened. "FBI? We don't deal with the FBI."

"I didn't ask you to deal with them, I said I'd like to introduce Joe."

Mitchell said, a laugh in his voice, "Actually, guys, my name's not Joe, it's George. I go by Joe because, uh, my dad always called me 'Gorgeous George.'" He spread his hands as if he'd been caught red-handed.

Andi laughed. They all frowned at her, including Crane, who squinted. The sudden jut of his jaw was reptilian.

Crane said, "All right, *George.* Come over here."

Mitchell extended his hand. Crane looked like it was used toilet paper, but Andi guessed Joe was trying to do what he'd said. "You help the other side get a little more comfortable, or you get nowhere." But Crane refused the offered handshake.

Ordrew stepped back. Joe said, "I'm curious about your movement, Reverend."

Crane's eyelids lowered slightly, as if he were calculating something. Andi thought, *Ah. If Crane answers, he loses face by talking to the FBI. If he refuses, he risks shutting down the negotiation before it's even started.*

Crane seemed to decide something. He said, "We're the Church of Jesus Christ of the American Promise. An affiliate of the Posse Comitatus."

Andi shuddered. The name conjured an image of the small motel room where Crane's "church" had met to plan the tax-evasion conspiracy and where she and Vic had been shot.

Crane kept talking. ". . . in Idaho, but we now are associated with the nationwide Posse. Along with the Bible, we revere the Constitution, and we are exercising our constitutional rights here. We insist that these lands be returned to their rightful owners, the people of Adams County. The federal government stole these lands, and if this unlawful taking isn't reversed, it will lead to war among the citizenry. This is our effort, an effort of peace, to guarantee that war between the government and the people never comes."

"So you're here to protest federal ownership of this land?" Joe spoke very politely.

"You weren't listening. We're here to see this land returned to the people."

"Uh-huh. Thank you." He paused a moment, as if thinking. "Sir, I'm told that Mr. Jenkins . . ." He nodded to Carl Jenkins, who looked surprised. "That he's a rancher here in the valley. Who are some of the other ranchers from around here in your group?"

Crane turned toward Carl Jenkins. The rancher's head moved slightly, like a twitch, to one side. Was he shaking his head no? Andi couldn't tell. Crane addressed Joe Mitchell. "I do not discuss my men with the FBI, *George*." He turned away. "We're done here."

Brad Ordrew stepped forward. "Reverend, one more thing."

Crane turned back, warily. "What?"

"I think we have a lot to discuss. I'd like to meet twice a day until we can settle this."

"At what times?"

"Nine in the morning, three in the afternoon. Starting this afternoon."

Crane snorted. "Or, perhaps, nine-oh-seven and three-oh-seven?"

Andi could tell from his eyes that Ordrew's smile was forced. "Well, yeah. That range."

Crane rubbed his chin. "I'll agree, with two conditions."

"Which are?"

"That we have unlimited access to the media, here."

"And your second request?"

"Not a request, Sheriff. It's a condition you must meet. I speak only with you, the county sheriff, the highest legitimate governmental authority the Posse recognizes." Without looking toward Joe Mitchell, he said, "We do not recognize the authority of the FBI, and I will not speak with this federal trash again."

Ordrew's lips tightened; Andi sensed an explosion. But the sheriff, restraining himself, said, "I will consider both of your *conditions*, Reverend. You'll have my answer this afternoon at three."

Back in the pickup, he muttered, "We'll be back at three-fifteen. Fuck him." Andi glanced at Joe, who rolled his eyes.

3

At two, Ordrew called the meeting into session. "Let's win this time." When they were all settled, he turned to Greg Haney. "Tell me what I do at this point."

Haney said, "Joe, you take this."

Joe Mitchell nodded. "Like I was saying this morning, active listening is the first step. Crane told us what they want: that land reverted to Adams County. Don't argue with them, just show you're interested. Empathize, let them know you understand."

Ordrew looked pained. "Can you do that?"

"Sure. Just part of the job."

Ordrew shook his head. "I sure as hell don't think I can, but they won't talk to you."

Ben said, "How about Ed? He's a good listener."

Ordrew looked at Andi. "Your boyfriend?"

"Husband," she corrected. Last night and the teddy popped into her mind. She had a quiver of arousal.

"Will he do it?"

"I'll ask. He's always helped in the past."

"Okay, do it. I don't imagine he'll be free in—" He looked up at the clock. "—forty-five minutes?"

"I'll call him." She left the office, tapping Ed's cell number, but the call rolled over to voice-mail. She wondered where he was—couldn't be working, he'd cancelled all his patients for the honeymoon. To his voice-mail, she said, "Ed, can you get free at three this afternoon to go up to the camp? We need your help. Call me." She was opening the conference room door when her phone buzzed. It was Ed. "Sorry," he said. "I didn't pick up in time. What's going on?"

The team looked up at her entrance. She said, "I'm going on speaker with Ed," then touched the *Speaker* button. The team waited.

"Okay," she began, "we—"

Ed interrupted, "You were hot in that teddy last night. How about a replay tonight?"

She swiftly re-tapped the *Speaker* button and hurried back into the corridor. She enjoyed the laughter behind her, although her face burned.

"Not now, Ed. The issue is, we need your expertise in the negotiations. You free this afternoon?"

"Well, not really. I'm on my way out to Magnus's—we're going fishing. How's trout sound for dinner?"

"Fine. How about nine o'clock tomorrow morning?" she asked.

He agreed. She ended the call and returned to Ordrew's office. "He can't get here in time," she told them, "but he'll help us tomorrow."

Ben grinned. "Ain't all he said."

She blushed again.

Ordrew nodded. "Okay, I'll handle it this afternoon, and we'll get Ed on board tomorrow morning."

Ben, still smiling, sobered. "What're we thinkin' about Crane's other condition, the media?"

The debate centered on the First Amendment, and seemed unresolvable until Andi made her suggestion. Ordrew listened, but he said nothing for a long time. She waited for the outburst. None came. "All right," he muttered. "We'll do that. Meeting's adjourned. Get whatever you need—we leave in ten minutes."

4

Once again, Carl Jenkins and Loyd Crane waited at the entrance to the camp, between the same guards holding AR-15s across their chests. Andi thought, *Acolytes.*

The team approached the entrance. Reverend Crane raised his hand when they were five yards away. "Approach no closer."

Ordrew stopped. "What do you say we meet in that RV of yours. Be cooler, I suspect."

"My men and I aren't here for comfort, Sheriff, though I'm not surprised you are. We're here to restore these lands to their rightful owners, the citizens of Adams County."

Andi tried to sense Ordrew's reaction, but without looking at him, couldn't.

"Well, you're getting ahead of yourself, Loyd. We have our answers to your two requests this morning. Interested? Or did we waste our time coming up?"

"*Conditions*, Bradley, not requests. State your answers."

"Thank you. To your request to negotiate with the county sheriff alone, I'm not a professional negotiator. We both deserve someone with the necessary skills. Our answer is no." Andi watched Crane's face.

Murmurs swept the crowd behind the Crane-Jenkins line. Reverend Crane swung around. "Silence!" The muttering stopped. Crane turned back, looked at Ordrew with darkened eyes. "And our response to that is that we will not speak with the FBI. We're at a standoff."

Ordrew shook his head. "No, we're not. We have a psychologist in town, a man with long experience and the necessary skills, who's willing to negotiate for us. That way, you will have someone whom you can trust."

"You're not being candid with me, Sheriff. The sole psychologist in Jefferson is Dr. Ed Northrup." He paused. "Who is married to your deputy here. I sense a conflict of interest in your, ah, 'man with the necessary skills.'"

Again, murmuring erupted in the crowd of men, but Crane waited, allowing the muttering to continue. Soon, the men quieted.

Andi looked at Ordrew. Saw his shoulders tensing, rising. She moved closer. He glanced at her, then spoke. "Anyone on my team would have the same conflict of interest, as you call it. Take it or leave it, sir. And be aware, my answer to your request for media will depend on your taking it."

Crane's eyebrows lifted. "Having an infusion of courage, are we?" He took Carl Jenkins's arm and the two stepped back and walked around the corner of the camper parked beside the entrance. Ordrew and the team waited, unable to see them. The armed crowd shuffled impatiently.

After a minute, Crane and Jenkins returned. Crane smiled. "Very well, we'll negotiate with Dr. Northrup. I agree with you—he will do a much more skillful job than you're capable of."

Andi realized she'd stiffened with tension; she forced herself to relax. Ordrew seemed to be doing the same. She hoped he'd ignore the taunt.

He did.

Carl Jenkins said, "What about the media?"

Ordrew glanced at Andi. "We will allow one pool reporter and one cameraman, uh, cameraperson to accompany us to each of the negotiations. No one else will be allowed up the road at any time. The pool reporter and cameraperson will cover our negotiations, and after each session—"

Crane erupted. "That is utterly unacceptable. We either—"

Ordrew interrupted right back. "I'm not finished, Loyd. After we leave, the reporter will be available for a press conference. My deputy will accompany the reporter and cameraperson back down to the valley. They will not be allowed to enter your camp." He paused. "Now you may gnash your teeth, *Reverend*."

Entirely the wrong tone, Andi thought.

"And if I refuse?"

"Then we have nothing further to discuss. We'll seal off this benchland and you and your men can starve. Or leave."

Andi held her breath. A declaration of war. She raised her hand. Crane looked at her. "You have something to add?"

"With the sheriff's permission," she said, her throat dry.

Ordrew, looking angry, nodded.

She took a small step forward, then a second, toward Crane, who didn't order her back. "I would suggest that the pool reporter serves your interests. By broadcasting the discussions and the presser afterwards, there'll be an accurate record, which I suspect you do not trust us to provide. All the other media will have to report the same thing, using the same video. Your message will get out unfiltered by different people reporting it—or misreporting it—in their own way." She stepped back, taking meager satisfaction that she'd invaded his space.

Crane studied her for a moment. "It appears that almost dying has transformed you into a diplomat, Deputy." He turned to Ordrew. "Make her your negotiator, Sheriff. I'd love a chance to come up against her." He leered at her.

Her stomach surged; she hoped her expression hid it.

Ordrew shook his head. "Out of the question. Deputy Pelton is valuable to me in many ways, but we will negotiate through Dr. Northrup, or not at all."

Listening to the two men arguing about how she'd be used, Andi kept her face neutral. Barely.

Crane looked away, up toward the western mountains, higher and more rugged than those rising behind him. "This is a beautiful place, Sheriff. Are you sure you wish to risk my men becoming discontented and deciding to come down into your town to take their message to your townspeople?"

Andi watched, fascinated, as Ordrew also turned, also looking up to those mountains. He didn't turn back for a moment. When he did, his voice was soft. "You're right, Reverend. It is a beautiful place." He nodded, as if making a decision. "Very well. I've offered you a reasonable solution to both of your requests. It's in your court now. If you refuse our solution to the media issue, you and your men can wait up here, alone, until you're ready to leave. And no one will leave this mountain until that day."

Crane studied Ordrew's face carefully, and his eyebrows gave a small lift, then settled. "Very well, Sheriff. You'll have my decision at tomorrow morning's meeting."

"We'll wait while you consult with your people."

"You aren't listening, Sheriff. We are finished." Crane turned and stalked away, followed by Jenkins.

5

When Andi drove into the yard a little after seven that evening, Ed had dinner ready—gazpacho with grilled trout. He met her at the door with a glass of ice-cold Pinot Noir. She smiled, kissed him, took the wine, sighed, and held the cool glass against her cheek. "Man, oh, man, I'm roasting. I cranked the AC to max, but it didn't make a dent. This is way too hot for June."

"Not too hot for a certain teddy."

She looked at him sharply. "Whoa. You horny again?"

"What can I say? It's a magic teddy."

"Huh. Let me change into something cool. Something not a teddy."

When they had settled on the porch, Andi asked, "Where's Grace?"

"She drove over to Missoula this morning, shopping with Jen. She'll be home in an hour or so. So, what's this help you need from me? Negotiating with Loyd Crane? I can't imagine speaking civilly to that bastard, much less negotiating with him."

"Well, you're the only person in the valley qualified to do that."

His brows contracted. "I'm not a trained negotiator."

"Joe Mitchell can help you with the micro skills, but you're great at active listening."

"I'm good at active listening?"

"Yeah, when I—" She stopped, grinned. "Got me."

He laughed.

"Well, listen." She described the situation after today's two meetings and told him Crane hadn't yet agreed. "Ordrew is taking the hard line—they accept you as our negotiator and a media pool team, or negotiations are off and we seal the camp."

Ed grew thoughtful. "You need me at nine each morning and three each afternoon?"

"Would other times be easier for you?"

"How long is the round trip?"

"About fifteen minutes from the station to the base of the mountain, then another ten or so to the top. Thirty minutes max one way."

"If it lasts into next week, can we move the times to 8:30 in the morning and 5:30 in the afternoon? For my patients?"

"Don't see why not. Crane will fuss about it, but he'll do it."

"Okay, I'm in." His eyes were dancing. "This sounds almost more exciting than a honeymoon."

Andi sipped her wine, her body reminding her of last night. "How 'bout we give that teddy another workout?"

"You want trout first?"

"After. You're in *my* clutches tonight."

6

A half hour later, on the darkening porch, they ate their trout and gazpacho. Andi handed Ed her empty wine glass. "Sir, a refill for your now-satisfied deputy-wife?"

"Deputy wife? Who's my *head* wife?"

"Figure of speech."

"Ah. Okay, Pinot Noir on the way." He grinned as he opened the screen door. While he was gone, Andi listened as Grace's PV crunched up the long gravel drive from the highway. She parked beside Andi's SUV.

Andi stood up as Grace came up the porch steps. "Gimme a hug, step-daughter."

Grace stepped into Andi's arms. "I liked being your step-girlfriend a lot," she said, "but I gotta say, the word 'step-daughter' sounds awesome."

"How was shopping in Missoula?"

Grace turned and looked up to the mountains. "Isn't it beautiful? I love how the sky turns that gold color after the sun sets. I don't remember that in Minneapolis." She and her mother, Mara, had lived in Minneapolis until they'd come to the valley, where her mother abandoned her—leaving Grace with Ed, who adopted her when Mara died.

Ed came out with two glasses of wine. "Hey, Grace. How was Missoula?"

She said, "A glass of wine for a dry girl?"

"Sure. Grab a chair." He left for the kitchen.

Andi caught a tone in Grace's voice. "What's going on?"

Grace sank into the chair opposite the swing. "Wait till Northrup gets back with the wine."

When they were all seated, Andi said, "So?"

Ed looked puzzled. "What's up?"

Grace sighed. "All right, all right. Jen and I saw that camp."

Anxiety flooded Andi. "*What*? Both roads are blocked by deputies!"

Grace looked miserable. Ed repeated Andi's question. "How'd you go up?"

"Not physically. We borrowed Jen's husband's drone and flew it over the camp." She looked more uncomfortable.

Ed and Andi waited.

Grace shifted on her chair. "It didn't turn out so well."

Andi, now worried, said, "How so?"

"Somebody in the camp shot down the drone. Jen's husband's furious, and now he and his buddies are talking about getting their hunting gear and attacking the camp. They're serious."

Andi, alarmed, pictured the ring of parked vehicles. "There are forty-three armed men in there, or more, and the camp's very well defended. There's no way a bunch of kids will survive that. And we've got deputies on both roads. Nobody's getting through."

"I told Jen that. She said, 'I know, but if I tell him not to try, he'll pout for a month.'"

Ed grunted. "Pouting a month's better than dying forever."

7

Ben Stewart sat on the corner stool of the old mahogany bar in Ted Coldry's Angler Bar, brooding. Sheriff of Adams County for thirty-two years, his father before him another twenty-eight, he'd learned a thing or two about staying in touch with the people. Almost every evening of almost every week for those thirty-two years, he'd sat on the corner stool of one of the bars in town, meeting with ranchers, merchants, firemen, county road workers, doctors and nurses, coaches and cowboys, one per evening, listening to their worries. After Ted and Lane Martin, Ted's husband and the restaurant's chef, had bought and renovated the old Angler, he'd made this grand old bar his headquarters. Many evenings hadn't been fun, but he figured knowing his people's concerns came with the job. When a rancher lost half his herd to a blizzard, Ben would buy him a beer and let him try not to weep on his barstool and then put in a good word with Marty Bailey at the bank for a new stock loan. And every four years, all those evenings paid off. Folks came out and voted.

And now, he groused to himself, *crap on toast. It's over.*

Over or not, he dropped into the Angler every weeknight at six, just like old times, and chatted with the other drinkers, bantered with Ted, drank his two beers, always two, and went home to Bernie, his girlfriend for a year. He smiled. *Bernie's the bright light, and that's the truth.* Tonight, though, nobody else was in the bar except Ted, and banter didn't appeal. "Ted?" Ben said.

Ted turned from the back bar, where he was drying glasses. "Benjamin? Another beer?"

"Not yet, I need information. What're folks sayin' about the protesters?"

"The feelings are hot on both sides. I'd estimate three-fourths of what I hear is anger with the protesters. People feel invaded. Truth to tell, Benjamin, *I* feel invaded. People object to this nonsense being brought into our valley."

"Well, it's here now. People know what it's about?"

Ted took a clean glass from the dishwasher and started drying it. "As you can well imagine, opinions differ. Some believe we're replaying the Bundy standoff. Others think they're squatters, moving here for some reason. A bizarre few are convinced they're illegal immigrants come to steal our jobs."

Ben snorted. "Jesus in a Jeep, what people'll come up with. Well, word'll be out soon enough, if it ain't already. It's a replay of Bundy's 'return the land to the people' show." He sipped his beer. "People supportin' the sheriff?"

Ted hung the dried glass in the rack above him and grabbed another. "To a great extent, Benjamin, but to be frank, sometimes it's lukewarm. A group of young fellows in their early twenties have been in two nights now, carrying on about taking their rifles up and driving the protesters off the bench. The word is, someone from the valley flew a drone over the camp and the demonstrators shot it down."

Ben's hackles rose. "Crap on a cracker! You got names?"

Ted hung the glass. "Sure, Benjamin, but why don't you hang around tonight. They'll be in—we're pouring Chas's new Porter and these young men like it a lot. You can listen in and judge for yourself what to do."

"I ain't sheriff any more, Ted." Ben rubbed his eyes. *That's the nub, ain't it,* he thought. Consulting, trying to gentle Ordrew into being reasonable, at least kept him in on things. But being unable to "judge for himself" grated on him. "But you know what? I ain't hangin' back." He drained his pint glass. "I'll have number two."

"That's my man," Ted smiled and turned to pour.

Ben took out his phone and dialed.

8

The land line rang. Ed went inside to answer it.

"Ed, Ben here. Come meet me on the corner. Bring Andi. We got us some talkin' to do."

"Oh, man, Ben, I've already had a glass of wine."

"So, drive careful. This ain't waitin'."

He hung up and relayed Ben's message. Andi sighed. "Ben's chafing at the bit, I'm guessing. Trying to talk sense into Brad is tough. I'll bet he needs to blow off some steam."

"Didn't sound like venting's on the agenda. And I quote, 'We got us some talkin' to do.'"

Andi sighed. "Okay, but I'll tell you, last thing I want to do is drive back into town."

Grace said, "You think Sheriff Ben would let me come too?"

"Sure. Come along. If he thinks you shouldn't hear things, he'll tell you." Ed looked at Andi, who shrugged. "Of course, you can't drink there, being only nineteen." He left unsaid that Grace could stay home, alone with an open wine bottle.

Grace just shook her head. "Northrup, drinking alone at home isn't half as fun as working with the police."

9

Ben turned on his stool when they came through the old swinging doors into the bar. "You hit a deer or somethin'? It's twenty-five minutes since I called."

Ed laughed. "You in a rush?"

"We got us big trouble. Ted, tell 'em."

Andi interrupted. "Hang on, Ted. We've got some bad news, too." She turned to Grace. "Tell them."

Grace opened her mouth, but Ben raised his hand. "We been waitin' longer. Ted?"

"There's talk of people weaponing up to assault the camp."

Grace frowned. "Hey, that's what I was going to say. Jen's husband and his buddies."

Ted nodded. "Yes, he's one of them. They have a few beers and work themselves up."

Ben scratched his head. "Remind me. What's his name?"

Grace said, "Bobby Place."

"Right, Mick Place's boy."

Ted wiped a glass. "I expect they'll be coming in soon."

Ben lifted his pint glass toward his lips, then held it suspended. "Ain't possible to talk to every damn man, woman, or kid who might want a shootin' match." His glass finished its trip to his lips. He took a long draught.

Andi, anxious, pictured young men with guns attacking the camp—and dying. She said, "We need a community meeting. Get to as many as we can at one time."

Ben grimaced. "The high school auditorium don't hold more'n 500, max. We'd need us at least six, seven meetings, if everybody in the valley comes."

"That's fine. However many it takes."

Grace said, "Is this adults-only, or can I say something?"

Ben swiveled his big butt on his bar stool and grinned at her. "Gracie, you've got the floor."

"Why not put big-screen TVs in the gym and the cafeteria? You can get another thousand people that way. You'd only need two meetings."

Ted clapped his hands. "I love it! Soooo urban." He rubbed his hands together. "I have a friend in Missoula who can supply all the equipment—TVs, video gear, connections, audio, the works."

Ben knocked twice on the bar. "Let's do 'er." He pulled out his phone and dialed.

After a moment, "Bradley, Ben Stewart here. Look, we got us some trouble." He repeated the news of the young bucks and Andi's idea about the community meeting. "We can get 'er all set up for tomorrow evening or Thursday, latest."

He listened, his face clouding over. He shook his head. His lips tightened together. After listening, he said, softly, "That ain't bein' wise, Brad. You gotta stay ahead of the people on this."

After another moment, he ended the call sharply. Ed echoed him. "*Unwise*? From the look on your face, he said no."

"His exact words was, 'I've got protesters to deal with, not the public.' And *unwise* ain't the word I wanted to say. He's bein' dumb as a mule's hind hoof."

Andi said, "Ben, call him back. Sweet-talk him, all the work he's got on his plate, that kind of thing. Then offer to run the meeting yourself. People trust you on both sides of the fence. It'll save him extra work and be a plus for the people."

"Now you're talkin'." Ben dialed his phone again, waited, made his pitch, and again his face clouded over. "Like I said, Brad, you're bein' unwise here." He listened again, then ended the call.

"Christ in a Chrysler," he swore. "The man's lookin' a gift horse in the ass."

Andi looked at her watch. "Okay, everybody, Ed and I have to get up at five-thirty in the morning, but I'll hang around here a while more to see if I can make contact with the young bucks."

Ed sounded shocked. "Five-thirty?! I never signed up for five-thirty!"

Ben grinned. "Buddy, you ain't got no idea what you signed up for."

CHAPTER FOUR — WEDNESDAY

1

Next morning, Brad Ordrew convened the meeting of the group he'd started calling his "executive team." They were meeting in the half hour right before the daily morning briefing. He said, "Let's begin. Ed, welcome." He nodded at Ed, then looked at everyone else. "Ed's going to conduct our negotiations, starting this morning. Greg and Joe will be with us for consultation. If we're not able to resolve this thing in the next couple of days, Greg will bring his SWAT team over from Missoula to support us."

Andi raised her hand. "We have reliable information that some young men are planning to storm the camp. It's more than beer talking. Ben and Ed and I listened in to some of their rants last night at the Angler. When I tried to talk sense to them, they just blew me off. 'Tell the sheriff either he ends this or we will.'"

Ordrew frowned and shook his head. "Does this ever go our way?" He turned to Pete. "I want two guys on that back trail too." He looked around the table. "Thoughts?"

They argued about that. Two deputies against a large group of armed men, whether protesters or valley people? Can't work. Ben suggested now was the time to bring over the SWAT teams—and hold a community meeting. "We gotta get the people's hearts and minds."

"A public meeting isn't going to stop an attack, either." Ordrew's face had reddened. Abruptly, he said, "We're done here. Time for shift report."

Andi, wondering how far this was going to unravel, saw Joe Mitchell tapping on his phone. A moment later, her own phone vibrated quietly. She glanced at it. A text from Joe. *This guy for real? He'll blow this thing up.* She glanced across the table at him, nodded very slightly, then glanced at Ed. Concern was palpable in his eyes.

·   ·   ·

While the others filed out, Ed waited behind. When Ordrew walked toward the door, Ed said, "Brad, with all due respect, I can't accept the role of negotiator under these conditions."

"What? What the hell *conditions*?"

"Your refusal to take good advice from experienced professionals. You need to reassure the people of the valley. Ben's right—you've seen during wildfires how people depend on the sheriff's daily reports. This is the same thing. And I can tell you, Brad, if the people get anxious, bad things happen."

"So, if I refuse to hold a meeting, you won't help me."

Ed nodded. "And if you don't bring in the SWAT teams. I'm sorry, but I won't be part of a disaster in the making."

2

Ed brooded all the way out to the camp. Ordrew had left the door open to a community meeting, barely, but enough for Ed to attend the morning negotiation. Andi, sitting beside Ed in the second row of the department SUV, whispered, "You all right?"

He nodded. "A little nervous," he said, "but I've been nervous before."

They said nothing more, but when they drove over the ridge and he got his first look at the camp, Ed murmured, "Holy shit." He closed his eyes, focused on his breath.

Ordrew, driving, approached the camp. "Are you ready, Ed?"

And then, unexpectedly, he was. "Yep. Tell me the set-up." He saw four men standing in the wide entrance to the camp, the two on the outside holding weapons, the two in the middle not. "The two guys in the center, they the leaders?"

The sheriff said, "Yeah. Crane's the silver-haired one on the right, Jenkins you know. We'll walk toward them and they'll make us stop a few feet away. Crane's the real leader, though he may make you talk to Jenkins. He likes to manipulate."

"I'll consider this a win if I don't rip that asshole's face off," Ed said, and saw Joe Mitchell's look of alarm. "Sorry. Just a little pep talk before the big game."

They walked to the point where Loyd Crane stopped them. Ed whispered to himself, *Showtime.*

Ordrew spoke first. Ed took the time to look around the camp, what he could see of it. The men gathered behind Crane and Jenkins looked tired, hot, and furious. And armed.

"Good morning, Loyd," said the sheriff. "We're here at . . ." He eyed his watch. "Nine o'clock promptly, since you seemed uncomfortable with us being seven minutes late yesterday."

Thanks a lot, Ed thought. *Piss him off before I even start.*

Crane didn't seem put off. He ignored Ordrew and turned to Ed. "Dr. Northrup, I presume. Congratulations on your recent marriage."

The guy does his homework. Ed smiled. "Thank you. I'm a very lucky man." He glanced toward Andi, smiled, then grew serious. "Under the circumstances, I can't say I'm pleased to meet you. But I've often *wanted* to meet you."

A look of discomfort flickered in Crane's eyes. "Hmm. Yes, I can imagine that's so." He turned to the man beside him. "Do you know Carl Jenkins, my second-in-command?"

"Yes, we met last November, during the campaign. Carl?" He put out his hand; Jenkins hesitated, then shook it.

"Sheriff," Crane said. "I must ask you and your team to return to your vehicles while Dr. Northrup and I talk."

Ed raised his hand. "No, sir. You have Mr. Jenkins and two armed guards, and behind you a few dozen armed men. Our team is five people and our weapons are holstered. They stay with me or we all leave."

Crane narrowed his eyes. "I see you have some experience in opening gambits, Doctor."

"I do," Ed answered with a small smile. "And please, call me Ed."

"Very well, Doctor, your team stays." For a moment, Crane said nothing. Ed waited. Then, Crane cleared his throat. "I consider the media pool idea an insult, not merely to our camp and our movement, but to the media themselves, a slur on their objectivity and integrity."

Ed nodded. "I understand that, although I'm not of the same opinion. In any case, it's a ten-minute ride from the valley floor. Shall we call down to have the reporter and cameraman brought up? Or would you prefer to proceed without the media entirely?"

"Neither is acceptable to me."

"So, your preference is no discussions at all?"

"No, it isn't, but your position gives me no choice."

Ed smiled. "Loyd, let's get serious. Sheriff Ordrew has already compromised. You insisted on full media, and he wants none. He's already moved toward you. It's your turn."

Crane waited a moment before answering. "I'm already serious. This proposal is an insult to—"

"Yes, you said that. Look, Loyd, if you say no, we pack up, drive back down the mountain, and seal that road and the other road tight enough a fart won't escape. At some point, your food and water will run out—" He caught a furtive glance from Carl Jenkins, wondered what it meant. "—and there's zero cell service up here, so unless you've got satellite radio, you've got no communication with the outside. Your story won't be told. It'll be the sheriff's story, told over and over to the media down below."

"Eloquent, Doctor." Crane looked at the mountains, then back at Ed.

"Please, the name's Ed."

"Nevertheless, unacceptable."

Disappointment tightened his chest, but Ed again made a small smile. "Very well, then, Loyd." He made a slight turn.

"I will make one small concession."

Ed stopped, waited.

"I will discuss this with *my* team. We will deliver our final answer this afternoon. Three p.m."

Stringing it out, Ed thought, *the jerk. This could take weeks.* All he said was, "Good. We'll see you again at three p.m. For your decision."

3

As they drove down, Andi said to the sheriff, "I'm worried. Suppose Crane refuses the pool reporters. We leave. If I were Crane, I'd spend today preparing for a sudden breakout. We can't stop them if they come down in force against our two guys and a pickup."

Ordrew looked at her. "That's what we want. We *want* them to leave, damn it."

"What *they* want is access to the media and the townspeople. I'm thinking they could come down in force, and the media's right here watching it, hungry to interview them. Then they could go into town."

Ordrew made a fist, hit his thigh. "Damnation. Even if I put all nine deputies on the access road, they wouldn't stand a chance against forty-some-odd fanatics with all that weaponry."

Greg Haney leaned forward from the third row. "You think it's time for our SWAT guys?"

Ordrew stiffened, drawing in a long, deep breath, then expelling it. Andi tensed.

But he took her by surprise. "It's time. You said you can have twenty-five here in three hours?"

"Yeah, two teams, twelve agents from Missoula, thirteen from Bozeman. Driving will take three-and-a-half hours from when I call. Each team will travel in armored personnel carriers—two from Missoula, two more from Bozeman."

Andi asked, "What about food or lodging? The media's bought up all the rooms in town."

"They'll bring tents and field rations," Joe Mitchell said. "MREs aren't fine cuisine, but they'll do."

Ordrew looked at his watch. "They'll need toilets. Andi, you handle that when we get back." He turned back to Greg. "Okay, it's now nine thirty-five. Call them in. If for some reason the teams won't be here by three, we'll come up with some reason to postpone the meeting till we can secure the road."

Haney, who'd pulled out his phone, cleared his throat. "One thing, Sheriff. This commitment from the FBI means I need to take command of this operation. I won't do anything without talking to you, and I'll still operate more as a consultant to you, but if the chips go down, I'm in command. Agreed?"

Ordrew grew very still. "What constitutes the 'chips going down'?"

"If we need to deploy the SWAT agents, I give the orders and manage the deployment."

Ordrew's scowl spoke loudly. After what must have been a dozen heartbeats, he said, "If I were you, I'd do the same thing. Your team wants you as their boss. But Greg, don't blindside me again."

Greg nodded and held up his phone. "Let me call now—I want them here in time."

Ed added, "Let's pray we don't need them."

4

When they returned to the station, Ed walked across the hall to his office to call Lynn Monroe.

"Hey, Ed. I thought you were in Italy."

"Hi, Lynn. Nope. I assume you're aware of our occupation?"

"I saw a quick report on the news, but they didn't know much. What's going on?"

"Posse Comitatus members. They've taken over a summer pasture north of town. The sheriff asked Andi to stay. They want Adams County to take over the land from the federal government."

"Like those guys in Oregon?"

"Yeah, and Nevada." He made his pitch, asked her to take on a few additional clients for the duration. Whenever he'd needed her before, she had never hesitated. She'd always said that getting a private practice had been her life-long dream; Ed had given her the chance.

She surprised him. "Can I ask why?" Her voice sounded tentative, guarded.

He gripped the phone hard. *Why is she hesitating?* "I'm going to be the negotiator with the protesters. I don't know how long this'll take, but judging from Oregon and Nevada, it could be a while. I need to free up a couple hours first thing in the morning and the late afternoon."

Last year, Ed had invited Lynn to join his practice part time. In his plan, she'd work up to full time and take over the practice, or at least reduce his work load considerably. He joked that she was his retirement plan.

Now, Lynn didn't answer. The silence stretched, and Ed's anxiety rose.

"Lynn, you there?"

She cleared her throat. "I'm sorry, Ed. I don't think that'll work."

"Really? I know you're booked full on Tuesdays, but Fridays you've got one client. Couldn't—"

"No, Ed." She sighed. "Rachel hates me being gone so much. I promised her that when my Friday client is done, I won't take any more."

He jumped up, started pacing. "What?" He hesitated. "I thought we'd agreed you'd build up your practice down here, not cut it back."

"You're right, we did. But Rachel's totally unhappy with this. During the school year, I'm gone four evenings a week." Lynn was the high school counselor in Jefferson. "It's putting a strain on our marriage."

Ed strode to the south window, looked at the Coliseum, the glacial cirque gouged high on the side of Mt. Adams. *Stay calm*, he told himself. "That's not good." Should he ask? Had to. "Uh, you'll be keeping Tuesday, at least?"

He held his breath.

"I don't know, Ed. All I'm sure of is I don't want to lose Rachel."

"How do *you* feel about this, Lynn? Private practice is your dream."

Another silence. Then, "Frankly, I'm angry. I love her, but she's using my love against me."

"I'd like you to reconsider, Lynn. Not about seeing some of my patients while this thing is happening, but about cutting back to one half-day. I need you. And you have your dream."

"Rachel's part of my dream too, Ed. Would you give Andi up to keep your job?"

"Andi wouldn't put me in that position." He thought about the lost honeymoon. *Not the same thing.* "We support each other."

"Ouch."

Ed turned back to his desk. A couple deep breaths didn't slow his heart rate. "You're right, that wasn't called for." He sat. "Look, will you think about it for a few days? I don't want to lose you."

A long pause. Then, "I can't see much chance I'll change my mind."

Stop before you make this worse. "Think about it. I'll call next week." He punched the *End* button on his phone, then sat staring at his darkened computer screen. *His* dream of working less began to slip away.

5

Ed climbed out of the department's SUV at three p.m. and walked to the point that Crane had indicated this morning. On the drive from town, he'd struggled with Lynn's refusal. Since they'd spoken, his anger had mixed with disappointment, distracting him from what was about to happen. The rest of the team got out and stood a few feet behind him. He tried to sound friendly. "Afternoon, Loyd. How'd your deliberations turn out?"

Crane peered into the sheriff's vehicles, the SUV that carried Ordrew's team and a department crew cab pickup driven by Xavier Contrerez, with Joe Mitchell beside him and two people in back, the reporter and the cameraman. Crane focused on Ed. "You brought the media. You're expecting my answer to be yes."

"Hoping, yeah. The sheriff wanted to speed things along. If you say no, we'll leave." *And maybe you will too.* He thought of the two SWAT teams deployed below, wondering if the protesters had found out about them. Decided Crane would bring it up if they had. "Do you want the pool media to film your answer?"

Crane ignored the question. "As far as I'm concerned, you can leave." He looked over Ed's head toward the mountains. Ed, alert to the tell, waited. *He hasn't said his real decision yet.*

The tension had taken Ed's mind off Lynn's betrayal and centered it squarely on Loyd Crane's decision. His focus was back.

Crane turned back to him. "But my team thinks otherwise," he said. "They believe that our story will not be honestly communicated unless we accept your plan. I would much prefer to have all the media here."

"In your shoes, I'd want the same thing, Loyd." He turned and waved the pool team out, flashing a quick thumb's up at his group. The reporter and her cameraman scrambled out of the pickup, retrieving their equipment from the rear of the vehicle. It took a few moments to get everything organized, then they trotted over to where Ed and Reverend Crane faced off.

Ed introduced them. "Reverend Crane, this is Katie Glauber, senior reporter for KEMT in Missoula. Her cameraman is Jay Gersich, also of KEMT. They'll be the pool team for the duration, elected by the media people gathered down below."

Crane said nothing to Katie and Jay, although he waited till the light on Gersich's camera blinked red. He composed himself. "I think it's time that we discuss the issues, Doctor."

"Look, just call me Ed. It's tense enough up here, and being less formal might ease things." He'd harbored a profound bitterness toward this man who'd almost killed Andi, so he surprised himself by meaning what he'd said.

"No, Doctor, we're not just two men. I represent a movement larger than either of us, and you represent the repressive force of the American government. We'll use our titles."

Ed kept his face neutral. "I don't represent any repressive force, Reverend. I'm here because the sheriff wants to work with you."

Crane's laugh was dagger-sharp. "I know how 'working with us' goes, Doctor. First, all is sweetness and light. Then come the guns."

Ed nodded. "We've seen it. Ruby Ridge. Waco. Let's you and I avoid that road, shall we?"

Crane looked at him, as if he were calculating. "Very well, Doctor. What do you propose?"

"May I suggest that we start with what you're asking of Adams County?"

"We are not asking anything of Adams County, Doctor." He faced the camera. "We're demanding that the federal government return all the lands they've confiscated in Monastery Valley. We expect these lands to be placed in the control of the sheriff of Adams County. As you know, the Posse Comitatus considers the sheriff the highest legitimate authority under the Constitution. I'm sure that Sheriff Ordrew will be happy to receive these lands."

"You want the sheriff put in charge of all the federal lands in Adams County?"

"We want *all* federal lands put under the control of the local sheriffs, but we're practical men. We're *starting* with Adams County."

"May I ask why you've chosen us?"

"Our choice of venue is irrelevant to the discussion, Doctor."

"It's not irrelevant to the people of the county, Reverend."

"I'm not interested in what the people find relevant."

A mistake. Ed waited a moment, watching Crane's face redden. "I see. Even if it were possible to carry out your proposal, it would be expensive for the county's taxpayers—but you're not interested in how the people feel about that." He paused again, because several men in the armed crowd were muttering angrily. The camera swung toward them.

Crane turned and silenced his men.

The camera turned back, and Ed said, "How do you envision this transfer of control happening?" The steadiness of his own voice pleased him.

"That's not our business, Doctor. Your sheriff will negotiate that with the Bureau of Land Management, which has misused and mismanaged the public lands for generations."

Brad Ordrew spoke up from behind Ed. "I have no damn authority to negotiate with the BLM about anything. And even if I did and even if the BLM transferred the federal lands to the county, the taxpayers of Adams County would bear the burden. Do you think we're fools, Crane?"

Crane's eyes darkened. "I'm speaking with your designated negotiator, Sheriff. Please remain silent."

Ed picked it up quickly. "Reverend, the sheriff is correct. His authority does not include negotiating about the lands with the federal government. You'll have to—"

"I don't have to do anything. We're occupying this land in the name of the people of Adams County and until the *people* tell us to leave, we demand that the sheriff do his constitutional duty. Indeed, a founder of our movement believed that if the sheriff shirks his constitutional duty, he should be hanged."

Ed cocked his head, but decided not to react to that. He said, "We will discuss this further among our team. We're not in a position to make any response until we do."

Once more, Crane looked toward the mountains. He said nothing for a moment. "Your sheriff mentioned the taxpayers of Adams County. Adams County will be enriched when the sheriff takes control of these lands. They can receive the revenue that now goes to the federal government for grazing permits. They can sell mineral and timber rights. This will be of great benefit to your taxpayers."

Ed surveyed the benchland on which they stood, the long stretch of emerald grass, the steep mountain rising behind the camp. He chuckled softly. "The grazing permit for this land amounts to around twelve hundred dollars for the season, Reverend. I don't see any trees on this benchland, and the minerals on this side of the valley are, well, common rock." He pointed to the forest rising up the mountain. "That mountainside is state land, not federal. Not much profit in any of that. I doubt any Adams County folks will think twelve hundred dollars much of an enrichment."

Crane snapped, "As I said, the thoughts of the Adams County citizens are of no concern to me."

Annoyed, Ed waited a moment before speaking. "And I imagine you can suggest incentives the sheriff might offer to the Bureau of Land Management to help them decide to make this transfer?"

From the crowd of armed men in the background, one, a grizzled old man, gray stubble on his cheeks and scalp, shouted, "Here's your fucking incentive," and fired a half-dozen rounds from his AR-15 into the air.

Crane pivoted. "Stop!"

Ed had flinched, but put a neutral look on his face and started to speak. But Brad Ordrew stepped up beside him. The camera locked on him. "Crane," the sheriff said, "you demanded that I arrest a citizen for this same act. I insist you hand that man over to my deputies."

Crane sneered, "I suggest you put that on the agenda for your *negotiator*, Sheriff. He and I will discuss it in due time."

"That man endangered everyone here," Ordrew said. "You guaranteed the safety of these proceedings, and I expect you to keep your word."

Ed watched Crane, wondering how he'd respond.

Crane's eyes blazed. "Then we are finished here. We will continue this discussion tomorrow."

Ed started to speak, but Ordrew overrode him. "There's nothing to discuss, Crane. Turn over the shooter. Now."

Crane turned and walked toward his RV in the center of the camp.

The sheriff called after him. "When we return tomorrow, I expect you to deliver the man who fired his weapon. If you fail, there will be no further negotiations, and no media coverage, until he's in custody." Ordrew turned back to the vehicles. "We're going down." To Katie and Jay, he said, "You too. No press conference until the shooter is under arrest."

As Ed walked toward the pickup, Andi joined him. She whispered, "I despise Crane."

He nodded. "He's not winning my heart either."

6

Below the mountain, where the access road leveled onto the already-brown pasture, the scene had changed. In addition to the large tent the county had rented to shelter the media folks from the blazing sun, a long motor home was parked in the dry grass beside the road. Beyond the motor home, three large military tents had been erected; between those tents and the media tent stood two large armored personnel carriers and the black SUV Greg Haney and Joe Mitchell had driven from Missoula. A third armored truck had been parked across the access road. Ordrew stopped the sheriff's vehicle a few feet above it, waiting while one of the SWAT agents moved the APC out of the way.

Seeing the sheriff at the wheel of the SUV, all the media came running toward him, wiping sweat off their faces, calling out questions—which nobody in the SUV could understand. They kept the windows up.

Ordrew turned and spoke to Greg Haney in the back. "I assume the tents are for your SWAT team, but what's the motor home doing here?"

From the third row, Greg Haney said, "No idea. It's not ours."

"It's Mack Anderssen's," Ed said. "He and I were fishing yesterday, and he offered it for a command post."

Ordrew's head snapped around. "What? You accepted his offer without my authorization?"

Ed tilted his head, puzzled. "I thought it'd be a good idea. You don't want it, Mack'll move it off."

"How much will it cost us?" Ordrew demanded.

"A dollar a day."

The sheriff backed off. "Better."

Ordrew parked beside the motor home. Before getting out, Ed looked at Andi briefly, shook his head.

One of the media, a heavy-set man wearing a sweaty T-shirt that read "PremierNews Media," yelled, louder than the other reporters, "Sheriff, why won't you allow media up at the camp? You're violating freedom of the press."

Ordrew said, "Give me five minutes with my team, then I'll be with you."

All the reporters started shouting questions, but Ordrew ushered the team toward the motor home. Magnus Anderssen waited by the door. "You folks need a place to meet closer to the action. It's yours until this is over." He looked at the tents. "Those tents are going to be awful hot—your men won't get much sleep. I've arranged for a big generator and a bunch of fans, which should be delivered within the hour. It'll be noisy, but bearable." He looked at the blazing sky, a coppery yellow. "I hope."

Greg Haney introduced himself. "Thank you, sir. I'm told the south access road is impassable for vehicles, so I've positioned six men and one personnel carrier there, with their own tent."

"Yeah, that road's been grown up in brush for years. You might get a four-wheeler up, but not trucks or cars. I'll get a generator over there too." Magnus smiled. "In high school, we called that old road 'Make-out Mountain.' I'll wager the kids still do."

Everybody laughed.

Ed didn't. "I'm concerned about those armored trucks."

"The APCs?" Greg asked. "What's your concern?"

Ed said, "Well, the protesters can look down here with binoculars. I don't like waiting for *them* to find the SWAT teams." He looked at the media, who had stopped shouting questions. "It's all over the TV, and if Crane has a satellite phone, chances are someone's notified him already. Let's tell them up front and use it to our advantage, show them we're not hiding anything."

"Shows good faith," Joe Mitchell agreed. "If the time comes that we need them up above, we can bring them with us."

The hair on Andi's neck prickled. She shuddered. "If that time comes, we've lost."

CHAPTER FIVE — THURSDAY

1

Next morning, Ed wasn't prepared for Crane's opening. No one was.

Without preliminary, he announced, "As of tomorrow, I demand the sheriff's department provide food and water for forty-four men. Unless you do, there will be no negotiations."

Startled, Ed shook his head. "Our agenda this morning is the man who fired his weapon yesterday."

"The agenda just changed, Doctor."

He regrouped. *Active listening.* "You're saying your men are already short of food and water?"

"Our situation is not your concern, Doctor. Meeting our demand is."

He tried again. "Reverend, your demand is *about* your situation. We can't negotiate it unless you tell us the extent of the problem you expect us to solve."

"We have no problem, Doctor, as long as your sheriff agrees to our demand. Until he does, our negotiation is finished." He turned and spoke to the video camera. "The sheriff publicly guaranteed the safety of our camp, but he refuses us access to town for supplies. This makes our camp unsafe and violates his guarantee. We cannot negotiate in unsafe conditions with a sheriff who breaks his word."

Ed let his annoyance subside before he spoke. "Be realistic, Loyd. Your demand has no specifics. Do you need one meal for forty-four men, or twenty meals, or fifty? Our team can't consider your demand without more information."

"I'm not asking you to 'consider' our demand. I'm asking for your commitment to provide Freedom Camp with food and water. Then we will inform you of what you need to provide."

"And you're suggesting that unless we agree to that, with no idea what we're agreeing to, you won't talk."

Crane's smile was contemptuous. "Don't play the good listener, Doctor. You demean yourself. I'm not *suggesting* anything. I'm informing you of a new fact on the ground. If you need a few minutes to talk with your people, we will wait."

The sheriff stepped forward. To Katie and Jay, he said, "Turn your camera off and return to the valley." To Crane, he said, "We will not discuss it here. We're going back to town."

"We have a right to a press conference with the media."

Ordrew's anger showed, but he said nothing. Ed said, "The sheriff said there'll be no conference until yesterday's shooter is in custody. If you want a presser, turn over the shooter."

Crane pivoted and walked toward his RV. Carl Jenkins looked at Ed as if he wanted to speak. Ed caught a hint of fear in Carl's eyes before he turned away, following Crane.

2

Ed climbed up the steps to the command RV. The team crowded in behind him. Inside, the heat was brutal. Ed switched on the air conditioner. "I doubt this old machine is going to make a lot of difference. I'll call Mack to send a guy." He grabbed his cell phone, tried to open it. "Damn, battery died."

Greg Haney tossed his phone to Ed. "Satellite. Until the AC's repaired, let's meet in a tent outside."

Ordrew said, "I have to talk to the media. Andi, tell them I'll be ready in fifteen minutes. We can meet now."

• • •

When Andi came into the tent, she noticed that Joe Mitchell was smiling. He said, "Lost that round, didn't we?"

Ordrew snapped, "Don't look so damn pleased about it."

"I'm not pleased, but it happens. And we learned a thing."

"What? That Crane is a snake? We already know that."

"No, we learned he's not sure how to handle his shooter. He doesn't want to hand him over, but he's stuck—everybody knows he insisted that you arrest Sobstak. If he refuses, he's on tape operating with a double standard. He loses credibility. His demand for food and water is a stall."

Andi said, "Suppose he's serious. What if they do need food and water?"

Ordrew banged his fist on the table. "Fuck him. Let them starve. I'm not going to be bullied into . . ." He sputtered to a stop.

"On the other hand," Ed said to Ordrew, "providing them with water, but not food, lets you keep the upper hand—and you call his bluff. Healthy men can go thirty days or longer without food, but only three or four without water, so we're being fair, even compassionate. After that, if he refuses to turn over the shooter or to talk, we shut him down and starve him out. But with the camera recording it all, you offer him water for ongoing negotiation."

Ordrew slammed his hand against the table again. "No, damn it! I said, they get *nothing*. If it makes us look *uncompassionate*, screw it." The sheriff looked around the group, defiance on his face. No one spoke. "Okay. Talk me down."

Andi said, "I agree with Ed about withholding food. Water, you supply."

Greg agreed. "Hunger's a good weapon. Use it."

Ordrew relented, a bit. "Okay. Water, but only when they beg, not before."

Ed said, "Or we offer water, in return for handing over the shooter."

Joe shook his head. "The deal he's proposing is food and water in return for *talking* about the shooter. If we offer water for talk, it'll get us to the shooter issue."

Ed nodded. "Logical."

"And he did win this one."

The sheriff turned to Ed. "Go see Crane. Tell him to fuck himself. We'll consider his *request* and answer tomorrow. Use those words."

"You serious, Brad? 'Go fuck yourself'?"

"Deadly damn serious."

3

The brutal sun was pounding the valley when Ed climbed into the department SUV and Xavier Contrerez began the drive up the road. Andi, Greg Haney, and Joe Mitchell sat in back. When they reached the pasture on top and rolled to a stop, Ed looked at his watch. Five minutes before noon. The air was cooler up here, but not much.

The guards weren't at the entry. Ed waited beside the SUV until Quinn hurried to his usual spot, followed moments later by the other one. To Quinn, whose eyes reflected fury, he said, "I'd like to speak with Reverend Crane."

"It's not your time."

"I have word from the sheriff," Ed said.

"Stay there," Quinn said, then walked back toward the big RV, which Ed decided must be the HQ. The other guard, taller than Quinn, but hairless and skinny, and not as muscled as Quinn, moved into the center of the entrance.

"I'm Ed Northrup. Your name is?" Ed said, conversationally.

The guard said nothing.

Carl Jenkins came around the corner of the big RV, followed by Quinn. Ed again caught something troubled in the man's eyes. "This isn't a negotiating session," Jenkins said, his voice uncertain.

"I know that." Ed took a breath. "You're from the valley, Carl, but I haven't seen anybody else I recognize. Are there any other ranchers from here in your group?"

Jenkins looked at the ground. "I'm not free to say."

"All right, I understand. Look, I have two messages from Sheriff Ordrew. The first is that we now have twenty-five SWAT agents from the FBI down below. They'll remain there, both to ensure that you remain up here until you agree to leave, and to protect your camp."

Jenkins's eyes narrowed. "We can protect ourselves."

Ed eyed the weaponry scattered around camp. "No doubt, but there is mounting talk of a citizens' attack. We're committed to keeping you safe, and that's one reason we called the SWAT team."

Jenkins stared at Ed for a moment, then said, "I'll inform the reverend. What's the second thing?"

"About your request for food and water: The sheriff's remark on that was unkind."

Jenkins's head tilted. "I can guess. Something like, 'go fuck ourselves.'"

"To that effect." Ed shrugged. "Still, he's agreed to supply water when you notify us yours has run out. In return, you guys keep talking with us."

Jenkins lowered his voice. "I appreciate that. But we need food. Tell the sheriff I'm doing my best up here to keep things from exploding, but it's not good. Most of the guys from the valley have plenty of food—we knew how isolated this place is."

Ed noted the slip: There *were* other valley men up here. "The outsiders didn't bring their own supplies?"

Jenkins shrugged. "They thought they'd be able to go into town for groceries. That's how Bundy's occupation was handled in Oregon. They're trying to get us to share our food now. If we do, *we'll* need food real soon."

"How bad is your situation?"

Jenkins shook his head. "I can't talk about it. Just tell Ordrew it could turn ugly. There's already a few of the outside guys talking about fighting our way out. I'm trying to talk them down, but Crane riles 'em up. They're not like valley people, Ed. They're mad, they're hungry, and they want a fight."

4

At three, Ed and the team arrived at Freedom Camp. Ordrew had stayed behind. "I said I wouldn't talk until we get the shooter. You talk for me."

Ed was surprised when Crane appeared. "I'm not sure what you're here for, Doctor. We are not going to talk until you agree to provide food and water. Was I not clear?"

Ed nodded, thinking quickly. The team had decided to act as if negotiations were still on, and despite his harsh talk, Crane *had* come out and *was* talking. *Why?* Ed wondered. *Ah. He's under pressure. What about? Food. We already offered water, so it's gotta be food.* Ed got it: The have-nots were angry with the haves and it could explode into civil war with all those weapons. "No, Loyd, you were quite clear," he said. "I'm here to talk about our negotiations. We will exchange water for negotiations, provided that—"

"You said there'd be no food, and I said there'd be no negotiations. You're fortunate I'm even standing here."

"Yes, thanks for that. I realize that having too little food and water is a pressure point for you. We can help with water, and we may decide later to be more helpful." He waited a beat. "But if you won't negotiate, there's nothing we can do."

"Nonsense, Doctor. You can agree to supply food for the camp."

"Not without negotiating. We need to know the scope of your need, and we need to develop some trust in you. We need to be confident you're not manipulating us to add to your food supply so you can prolong your presence here. We need to know what we will get in return for providing food." He paused to let Crane speak, but got only silence.

Ed said, "What we need in return for providing water is negotiating, first for the arrest of your shooter, and later, perhaps the food issue—and that requires that you, Carl, and I talk. We're willing to consider anything, but not without trust and not without understanding the scope of what you're asking us to do."

"I fail to see how your knowing all that is necessary. You either supply food and water, or you don't."

Ed changed focus. "I assume Carl made you aware of the two SWAT teams closing the two access roads."

Crane's eyes narrowed to a squint, but he gave a curt nod.

Ed continued, "They're there for three purposes. First, to ensure that you and your men won't be coming down to go shopping in town. Second, to ensure that no angry citizens—and there are many—will be coming up to storm your camp. Third, to escort you off the mountain and out of Monastery Valley." Again he paused, and again Crane said nothing.

Ed shrugged. "Meanwhile, you need water from us, and you're not naïve enough to think that we'll provide it in return for nothing. We realize you're under a lot of pressure from the members of your group who didn't bring food. We're willing to discuss helping you with that pressure, but only through good-faith negotiations—water for negotiation about the shooter, and later about food, if there's trust. *Quid pro quo.*"

Crane turned around, looking back into the camp. Jenkins, standing at his side, caught Ed's eye and gave a single slight nod. Crane said, still looking away, "Your sheriff sent me a message. He said I could go fuck myself."

Ed cringed. "An unfortunate choice of words, I agree. Do you want an apology?"

"No." Crane turned back to Ed. "No. Tell your sheriff he can do the same."

5

Ordrew exploded. "I should 'go fuck myself'?" He paced the small space in the command RV. "Give me a minute. I'm pissed, I'm not rational, and I'm not ready to make wise decisions. But goddamn it, this asshole occupies federal land, does all this shit, then tells me to fuck my*self*?"

Bad sign, Ed thought. *If Ordrew's going to lose it this soon . . .*

Greg Haney said, "Brad, let's dial it back and see what our next move should be."

"Our next move? I'll tell you our next move." The sheriff caught himself. "Okay. You're right, I should've expected something like that. Hell, I'm the one started it." He rubbed his eyes. "Talk to me."

Ed admired Ordrew's shift. "Okay," he said. "Crane's under pressure over the food situation. Jenkins tells me the valley men brought plenty of food and the outside group didn't. There's a split in the camp over it. I think Crane *had* to tell us to fuck off, make a show of strength for his people."

Joe said, "There's also the shooter. Crane could also be in a bind about that."

Ordrew sat with his eyes closed for a moment. "Maybe." His eyes opened. "We don't know squat for sure."

"Yeah, we're speculating," Greg said. "Could be it's food, or the shooter, or even the usual power struggle groups like this get into. But either way, if Crane's weakened, I think if we play it smart, we could decapitate the camp."

Ordrew grimaced. "Decapitate the camp? How's that happen?"

Andi jumped in. "Crane's keeping the shooter. Obstructing justice. We arrest Crane himself and cut off Freedom Camp's head."

Ed looked at her. "How the hell do you arrest him with forty-three armed men against you?"

Ordrew frowned. "Easy. We fuck ourselves, just like Crane told us to."

CHAPTER SIX — FRIDAY

1

At eight-thirty in the morning, under an already overheated sky, Sheriff Ordrew walked toward the gathered media. Heavy clouds hung low, aggravating the sultry humidity. The crowd of reporters stood apart from one another, as if praying that a breeze would circulate in the spaces between them.

Including Katie and Jay, there were twenty-three media folks. The video cameramen stood in front, focused on the microphone with its speaker on the ground beside it. The SWAT team had just started its hike up the access road. Distant thunder rolled across the valley.

"Sheriff," CNN shouted. "Why are the FBI going up? Are you going to raid the camp?"

"No, we're not. One of the campers fired his weapon and endangered everyone, and I intend to arrest him. The SWAT team's purpose is to keep the situation under control."

The PremierNews Media's reporter, wearing the same sweaty T-shirt, repeated yesterday's question, his voice demanding, angry. "Why are you violating our first amendment rights?"

"We're not. You're free to report anything you observe or learn. What I'm restricting is your freedom to go up to the protest in person. My job is protecting public safety, including yours, which I swore an oath to do."

He pointed to another reporter, but PremierNews shouted over her question. Ordrew cut him off. "Sir, I answered your question. These other folks have the same right you do. Next."

The woman PremierNews had interrupted asked about the camp's food and water problem.

"We've offered water in return for negotiations, but the protesters haven't agreed yet."

PremierNews yelled, "But they want food, too! You're being inhumane."

Ordrew ignored him and replied instead to the woman. "Men can go without food for a month or more before hunger has serious effects on health, but without water, only a few days. So, we're offering water now, then food if it becomes necessary. But they need to agree to keep talking." He glanced at his watch. "Just a minute, folks." He waved Andi over, spoke quietly. "Get the pool reporters ready to go. Oh, tell them not to broadcast on the way up, so the protesters don't find out about our guys below the ridge."

"You think they've got TV reception up there?"

"Don't know, but I don't want anything to wreck our plan."

"Got it."

He turned back to the reporters. "Sorry, folks. Next question?"

Andi walked with Katie toward the van. "The sheriff wants you ready to go up with us when he ends this presser. You're going to see things happen. Stay out of the way so you'll be safe. Please, don't reveal anything you see before this is over, and don't let Jay video the FBI guys on the way up. Okay?"

Katie grimaced. "I can't do that, Andi. Our colleagues elected us to cover this, so we owe them *complete* coverage." She looked up the road. "Is it true the FBI's only for protection?"

"Yes, they are, and just if things get out of control. We wouldn't allow you to go up into danger. Look, I appreciate your ethics. But we don't know if they have satellite access to your coverage. If they do and you broadcast the FBI positioned on the road, they'll know something's going to happen. People could get killed."

"I'm sorry, Andi, but Jay and I can't violate our colleagues' trust."

Andi liked Katie, but this annoyed her. "Look, Katie," she said. "You and Jay are elected to provide pool coverage of the negotiations. That doesn't include the FBI's position. If you won't abide by the conditions of your being allowed up there, I can't let you go. Lives might be at stake."

"Including my own." Katie shook her head. "Our journalism is about the story, Andi, not just the negotiations. All of us interview agents and deputies and people in town. The FBI's action is as much a part of the whole story as any of it."

Andi got that. "Damn. Give me a minute." She walked fast to where Ordrew was answering a question, and stood ten feet back. When he finished, she said, "Sheriff, a word?"

He came to her. She related the exchange with Katie.

Ordrew shook his head. "Screw it. I'm forbidding coverage. They stay down here."

Joe Mitchell, who'd been standing behind Ordrew during the presser and had followed him over, said, "If the media don't show up as usual, the protesters will know something's different."

Ordrew shook his head in disgust, but said, "What's the bigger risk?"

Andi said, "The camp having TV is a *maybe* risk, but if the media aren't up there, tipping our hand's a *for sure* risk."

The sheriff nodded. "All right. We bring them up."

2

At five minutes to nine, the mid-morning air was a stew of heat and moisture. Heavy black clouds hung over the Monastery Range; gray veils of rain drifted under them, evaporating high above the valley floor. Far-off thunder rumbled. The SWAT team was in place on the road twenty-five yards below the ridge. Andi carefully inched the SUV past them, Ordrew beside her, Ed and the two agents in the second row, Katie and Jay in the rear. Xavier and Felix followed in the department's pickup. Andi glanced in the rearview as they passed the SWAT team's position. Jay raised his camera to film them as they drove by. She sighed. They'd know if the camp had TV in a minute. Perhaps in a hail of bullets.

Greg Haney's radio sounded. "Haney, south team here. We're in position. South over."

"South, Haney here. Copy. Haney over."

"Haney, south here. Any new orders? Over"

"I'll be in touch if we need you. Out." Haney leaned toward the front. "Sheriff, you heard. The Makeout-Mountain team's in place."

Andi's gut tightened further. She wished Ed wasn't going to hear this: "Brad, what if you and I, uh, can't direct the action?"

"Right." Ordrew turned. "Greg, if Andi and I go down, you're in public command. I'll radio all my guys with that. That good with you?"

As he spoke, Andi glanced in the rearview at Ed. Her heart sank at the pallor of his face.

Greg said, "Got it." He turned to Joe. "Stay on the radio with the team till it's done. Call 'em up if I signal you." He paused. "Oh, if I'm taken out too, you're next in line."

Andi looked at Ed again. His face was hard. She tilted her head slightly, mouthed, *Love you.*

Ed took a deep breath, then nodded.

3

"We ready?" Ordrew asked. Andi flinched. Something was bothering her, but she couldn't name it. They'd planned this operation quickly; what had they forgotten?

The others all said they were set to go.

As Andi drove the final yards, Joe said, "Sure as hell hope they don't have any TV reception up there. Every reporter's hair's on fire about the SWAT team going up, and I'll bet they're all on the air with it. We could be in for a shit storm and not even know it."

Andi couldn't shake a nagging worry. "Something's wrong." She braked. They had almost reached the ridge.

Ordrew said, "What?"

A flash of lightning distracted her, but then she got it, and her alarm ratcheted higher. "When we're marching the shooter to the squad, our backs'll be turned and Ed'll be alone with the guards. He'll be exposed." Thunder rolled over them.

Ordrew let out a harsh breath. "Good catch. Okay, Ed, the minute you hear the word 'arrest,' get back in this vehicle, fast."

Ed nodded. "Got it."

Andi looked at him, her stomach tight. *If anything happens to him . . . .* A warm wash of love for this man brought tears to her eyes. She brushed them away.

Ordrew said, "Go. Anything looks wrong, shout it out."

4

They made their usual approach. Crane did not appear, but Carl Jenkins did. Andi studied his eyes, but he wouldn't meet her gaze. "The Reverend is indisposed today," he said, almost too softly. Then his voice rose and he turned so the men behind could hear. "I'm authorized to speak for the camp, but we will not negotiate unless you're prepared to provide food."

Andi thought, *He's talking to the camp, not us.* She held her breath. *Is our plan screwed?* She thought fast—arresting Jenkins wouldn't decapitate the camp.

Ed cleared his throat. When he spoke, his voice was calm. "Loyd would want to participate in this session. I'm sorry he's not able."

Despite her tension, Andi almost smiled. Ed had diminished Crane's status, translating Jenkins's "indisposed" into "unable."

Ed was saying, ". . . considering modifying our stand on food, but I'm permitted to negotiate that only with him."

Jenkins hesitated, looking wary. "I'll tell him."

Everyone waited. Thunder cracked, closer. The protesters shuffled restlessly, looking at the sky. A dense hot breeze brushed Andi's sweaty neck. Many minutes passed.

Ed said to Quinn, "Will you please let Reverend Crane know that in five minutes, we will leave. He wants food, so he needs to come out, or we'll go."

The guard named Quinn left. A skeletal man stepped into his place, his face angry. He angled his AR-15 down and toward the front. Not quite threatening. Not yet.

Another man yelled, "Double-talk. You're going to starve us." Weapons shifted throughout the crowd.

Andi glanced at Ordrew. His face was red, and his jaw was working, but he stood very still. After a pause, Ed held up four fingers. "Four minutes, folks."

The guard Quinn came back. "He's coming out. Fucking wait."

After a moment, as Ed looked at his watch, lightning flashed. Ed held up three fingers. "Three minutes." Thunder echoed across the valley.

Someone yelled back, "The Posse don't meet the timetable of tyrants." A chorus of murmurs followed, then quieted. Guns moved in people's hands.

Ed ignored it all, held up two fingers. "Two." The hair prickled on the back of Andi's neck.

As Ed held up one finger, the crowd parted and Reverend Crane came forward, followed by Jenkins. He walked solemnly, a deep frown on his face.

"I'm informed you will provide food."

Ed looked at Carl, standing behind Crane's left shoulder. Jenkins gave a tiny shake of his head as lightning blazed, turning the camp white under the dark clouds.

"Sir, perhaps I wasn't clear with Mr. Jenkins. I said we would *consider* modifying our position on supplying food. But we have one condition." The clap of thunder startled everyone.

Crane looked at the darkening sky. When he answered, his voice was low. "Name your condition."

"You will turn over the man who fired into the air. Now."

The crowd erupted into jeers and angry cries, shifting their weapons toward Ed. Crane swung around, raised both hands high in the air, fingers spread wide, roared, "Stand down." The protesters backed off, but only partially. Weapons still pointed dangerously toward the front.

Crane lowered his arms, turned back. "I will never do that."

"You insisted that we arrest the man on our side, and he was taken." Glancing at the pool camera, Ed raised his voice. "You have no ground to stand on, Loyd."

Crane shook his head. "I will not allow you to terrorize my men. He has my protection, and you cannot have him."

Swiftly, Ordrew stepped forward, took Crane's arm, said, "Loyd Crane, you're under arrest for obstruction of justice." Andi moved fast to Crane's other arm. They pushed his wrists together and snapped on a zip tie.

Over his shoulder, Crane called out, "Jenkins and Dolan are in charge until my release. The Church will post bail, and I will return."

Andi and the sheriff pulled Crane toward the squad car. Xavier started the engine. Felix waited at the open rear door. Andi hoped Ed was moving. Marching Crane, she wondered, *what's going on behind—*

A shot rang out. Sheriff Ordrew jerked forward, his body slamming into the ground.

PART TWO

CHAPTER SEVEN — JUST AFTER

1

Swiftly drawing her weapon and tightening her grip on Crane's arm, Andi swung him around to face his people. Dozens of guns were leveled at her and at Ed, who'd stopped running toward the pickup when Quinn yelled "Stop or I shoot!" She pulled Crane close against her, a human shield. Andi said to him, "Call them off. My gun is at your back." She pressed it against him.

Crane said, quietly, "This is your doing."

"Call them off. *Now*, damn it." She jammed her gun into his kidney.

He grunted, then called out, "Men, stand down. We are not here for violence."

Many rifles lowered. But they heard a shout. "I fucking am, Rev." The old buzzard who'd fired his AR-15 into the air stepped out of the crowd. "They started it. I'm finishin' it!"

Crane roared, "Stenborg, *stand down! Now!* They will use this as an excuse to destroy us and Freedom Camp. *Stand down*, damn you."

Stenborg shook his head. His AR-15 lifted toward them. The two guards didn't lower their weapons. Andi swept the scene with her eyes. Ed was badly exposed. She looked down at Ordrew, bleeding on the grass. *We're not getting out.*

She nudged Crane again with her gun. "Stop him."

Crane grunted again, but before he called out to Stenborg, another protester swung the stock of his rifle down on the old man's neck. He yelled, then fell forward, and his AR-15 flew from his hands, landing at Crane's feet. Crane moved as if to pick it up, but Andi jerked him back. "Greg! Get it."

Haney took it into custody. But too many guns stayed locked on Ed and Crane, Andi behind him. Another shout: "Reverend, what do you want us to do?"

Andi said to Crane, "I have sixteen men just below the ridge, and another twelve on the south road. If you don't settle this, it will turn very bad. Disperse your men into their vehicles."

"Release me, then."

"No! This isn't a negotiation. Disperse your men into their vehicles. If this blows up, you'll face the full fury of the state of Montana and the FBI." She glanced down at Ordrew's body, face down in the grass. *I've got to get him help!* She saw blood on the back of his uniform shirt. To Crane, she barked, *"Now!"*

Crane hesitated. "I, ah, don't have complete control of everyone at this moment."

"The hell with that! Disperse them. *Now.*"

"Men!" he bellowed. "No more violence. The world will blame us. Get into your vehicles before anyone else is hurt."

Slow motion. Men looking at one another, weapons lowering. A few moved toward vehicles. Then, more. The guards lowered their rifles.

Andi's stomach unknotted a notch. She called, "Ed, into the SUV. Now." Were the men entering their vehicles, or lurking behind them? She kept the gun hard against Crane's back, watching as Ed climbed into the vehicle. Out of the corner of her eye, she caught Jay, filming, too close. She yelled, "Get back, Jay. *Way* back."

Crane tried to pull away. "Don't move a goddamn muscle, Crane."

"Or what, Deputy? You'll kill me?"

"Don't tempt me." She called, "Joe, Xavier, Felix to me."

They came to her side. She glanced into the camp—no one was visible except the two guards, weapons lowered. "Xav, Felix, put Crane in the squad and take him to the jail. Book him, obstruction of justice."

Crane struggled to turn. "I demand—"

Andi jammed her gun hard into his back. "Shut up! One of your men may have murdered my sheriff. You're demanding nothing." Xavier and Felix grabbed Crane's arms and dragged him to the squad car, thrust him into the back seat.

To Greg and Joe, she said, "Get Brad onto the second row of the SUV." She yelled at Quinn. "We're moving the sheriff. Then I want to talk to Jenkins. This is not finished."

Together, they lifted Ordrew into the second seat of the SUV. He was breathing shallowly, making gurgling sounds. She opened the driver's door, glanced in. *Keys in the ignition.* Ed leaned over. "You okay?"

She shook her head. "No, I'm pissed." She climbed in the back with Brad. "I don't see any blood in front. Bullet must be inside. He's breathing, but it sounds bad."

She got out. "Ed, I need you to climb back here and help Brad. You're CPR certified, right?"

"Yeah. Took the refresher just a year ago." He took Andi's place on the floor, facing Ordrew. She pulled the first aid kit from under the front passenger seat, set it beside Ed on the floor.

"Joe," she said, "you drive the SUV toward town. I'll call the station, have them send EMTs to meet you on the highway, fast. Go!" She looked at Greg. "Will you stay with me?"

"Of course. I'm calling up the SWAT team."

Andi surveyed the inner space of the camp. Everyone except Quinn and the other guard were in vehicles. "Wait. I think we're safe for the moment. If we bring them up, it could inflame the protesters."

Greg frowned. "You have a plan?"

They moved out of the way so Joe could swing the SUV around.

"First, get EMTs on the way. Then, talk to Carl Jenkins. And arrest the old man when he comes around."

Greg nodded. "Okay. I'll leave my team below. For the moment."

Facing the camp, she punched the mic on her shoulder radio. Felix, riding down in the squad, answered. She told him, "Call Callie to order EMTs up the highway to meet our SUV." On the ground, the old man, Stenborg, was moving, moaning. Andi said to Greg, "Keep an eye on him. If he tries to get up, take him into custody. Reckless endangerment. And get his rifle."

"It's in the back of the SUV. Best I could do."

Inside the camp, Andi saw no one except the two guards, and Stenborg lying on the ground, still moaning. The guards raised their guns as she approached.

Holstering her gun, she said, "No one's threatening you. Please lower your weapons as our vehicle leaves." She glanced back. The SUV was rolling onto the access road. The guards kept their guns on her.

The guard with no name began to lower his AR-15, but Quinn barked. "Don't obey!" The first guard raised his weapon again.

Alarmed, Andi said, "Please, let's not let this get any worse." She held back the threat she wanted to make.

The guard who'd first lowered his weapon looked at Quinn and muttered something. Andi watched Quinn chew his lip. Finally, he nodded, and both men lowered their weapons, but held them ready. She glanced at Stenborg, still lying on the ground, moaning louder. "I need to talk with Carl Jenkins."

Carl Jenkins stepped out from behind the RV where he'd hidden himself when Crane ordered them into the vehicles. He held an AK-47, aimed at Andi's chest.

2

She froze, heart pounding. "Carl, I'm trying to protect you and your men. Two FBI SWAT teams are deployed on both access roads. If you and I can finish this peacefully, they will stay away." She breathed deep. "If you or your men start shooting, your camp will go up in smoke." She pointed at Stenborg. "Your man may have murdered Sheriff Ordrew. If you help me, you might be able to preserve some degree of public support."

"Nobody here trusts you, Pelton." But his voice faltered. His eyes met hers, then darted away.

"Neither of us trusts each other, Carl. But it's already bad for you. You can't expect the valley people to support you after one of you shot

Sheriff Ordrew." She glanced at Jay, Katie beside him. They'd backed away, but Jay had kept filming. Jenkins followed her eyes, and looked sick. "Yeah," she said gently. "It's nationwide now. Making it worse by shooting me will not help you."

The AK-47 wavered. Andi was about to continue when a small group of men came out of hiding behind the headquarters RV, all armed, weapons leveled. *Jesus*, she whispered to herself. Immediately, the remaining men in the camp left their vehicles and lifted their weapons.

She raised her voice. "Men, I just told Carl there are two groups of FBI SWAT agents within yards of us. If there are any more shots, they will respond. Do you want that?"

Angry murmurs swept the crowd; Carl looked hesitant. "No." He turned. "Lower your weapons."

They did, slowly. "Thank you." She spoke quietly so the crowd wouldn't overhear. "Carl, I need the man who shot Sheriff Ordrew."

In turn, he lowered his voice. "Look, Pelton, you can tell the position I'm in. I didn't see who fired that shot, but even if I did, if I turn him over, I'd lose any authority I have." The men stirred restlessly. One of them yelled, "Why're you talking, Jenkins? Kick her ass out of here before we do it."

Andi turned to face the one who'd shouted, found him, a large man with angry eyes, fifties, unshaven, the chest of his camo T-shirt stained black with sweat. She glared at him, wrestling with an almost unbearable urge to shoot him. She focused on the man's eyes until she regained control of herself, then looked back at Jenkins. Made a quick decision. She spoke loudly. "Carl, if you refuse to give him up, I'll leave for now." She paused. "But we'll be back in force for him."

"Hey, Carl, she's going. You fucking won, man!"

Carl waved his hand impatiently. He muttered, "Like hell I won."

Andi added, still loudly. "And when we're back, we'll bottle you up here so tight you won't be able to breathe."

"You'll kill us."

"Didn't say that. But we'll shut you off from the world, including the media. You already asked for food and water. Eventually, you'll starve." She looked around Freedom Camp. "Not to mention needing toilets when the heads in your RVs fill up."

Stenborg stirred himself, rolled up onto his knees and waited on all fours a moment, then stood, shakily. His old-man voice was raspy, but his eyes were red and cruel. "I shot him, and I hope he dies. Arrest me, bitch. Give us our day in court." He searched the ground for his weapon. "Where's my damn rifle?"

Greg shook his head. "It's in our custody."

Andi said, "Your name's Stenborg?"

"Leroy Stenborg." He spat it out. "Give me my gun back."

"Mr. Stenborg, you're under arrest for the attempted murder of Sheriff Ordrew." The man stepped toward her. "We'll keep your weapon—and any other weapons on your person."

The other men raised theirs. "No one's taking his weapons," one man snarled. Carl Jenkins shouted, "Knock it off. Stenborg asked to be arrested and . . ." He looked at Andi. "Why do you need his gun?"

"The ballistics will show whether his rifle shot the bullet that's in the sheriff. If not, you'll get Mr. Stenborg and his weapon back."

She locked Stenborg's eyes with her own. "Turn around."

"Like hell. I don't take orders from women."

Greg Haney stepped behind Stenborg and cuffed him. Andi raised her voice to the other protesters. "I suggest you discuss among yourselves the wisdom of leaving. This camp is already responsible for five serious crimes. If you leave now, only Crane and Stenborg will be charged. If you don't leave, we'll have to discuss what the next steps will be. I guarantee they will be fair on our side." Her body tensed like a too-tight string. "No more second chances, though. Any more violence will be met with force."

No one spoke. She pushed Stenborg toward the access road, Haney on his other arm. She called to Katie and Jay. "No presser today. You're hiking down with us. You go first. We'll meet you below the ridge."

Sensing the anger radiating like heat lightning behind her, she wondered if any of them would make it to the road alive. Thunder echoed off the mountains.

3

She and Greg were still alive when she goaded Stenborg down onto the access road. The old man gasped when he saw the FBI team and the deputies lined up along the cliff face, weapons ready. Wearing armor, the men looked terrifying. Andi knew they were sweltering.

"Shit," Stenborg said, recoiling. "You rats are set to kill everybody."

"Shut up," she hissed, dragging him along.

Greg Haney, holding Stenborg's other arm, ordered two of the SWAT team members to take custody of Stenborg and march him down the access road. Then he ordered the full team off the mountain. "It's too dangerous here. If the protesters come to the ridge, they could start firing down on us."

Andi looked up at the cliff top. "Rats in a barrel."

The march down was hot and dirty; twenty-three people moving fast raise a lot of dust. At the command post, the agents stuffed Leroy Stenborg into the back seat of an Adams County squad. She saw the media crowd rushing toward her. Chip Coleman was getting into the driver's seat. She asked him to keep the media at bay for five minutes.

She climbed into Magnus Anderssen's RV. Ed was waiting. She leaned into his arms.

4

She and Ed rode back to Jefferson in the FBI van. As the driver signaled his turn into the department parking lot, Andi jerked alert; she'd been absorbed, reliving the shooting. "No! Take us to the hospital first. I'll check on the sheriff, then I'll walk back to the station."

Doc Keeley met her at the ICU nursing station. "He's in critical condition. He'd lost a lot of blood before he got here. Fortunately, we were able to get a line in." He shook his head. "That's about it for the good news. The bullet missed his heart, but his pulse rate's sky-high. His right lung's seriously damaged and he's got a traumatic pneumothorax. It'll need—"

"Which is what?"

"Sorry, collapsed lung due to the bullet. He's going to lose part or all of that lung. Anyway, on X-ray, the bullet is too close to the heart, so he's beyond what we can do for him here. He'll be airlifted to Missoula for surgery within the hour. He's got a chance there."

"How big a chance?"

Keeley grimaced. "I wouldn't use the word 'big.'"

Andi leaned her elbows on the counter of the nurses' station, covering her eyes with her hands. The sharp sound of the shot echoed in her mind, the jerk of Crane's body as Ordrew, still clasping Crane's arm, fell. The weapons pointed at her. Ed's hands in the air. She straightened, left the hospital. Ed was waiting outside. "What do you need, kid?"

As she slid into his arms, the shaking began. She managed to whisper, "To know this wasn't my fault."

5

They walked back to the station. The hot air was sultry, thick, hard to breathe. She hadn't heard any more thunder. At first, as they walked, she tormented herself, blaming herself for Brad Ordrew's being shot. Ed tried to coax her away from that, but after a few tries, he gave up, gently held her arm, and listened.

She told him the sensation of Crane almost being pulled from her grasp when Ordrew fell. How she pushed her gun into his kidney to get him to disperse the men. How she flinched when the protester clubbed Stenborg. How she thought, seeing Ed stopped with his hands raised, "We'll never get out."

Ed was holding her arm. He stopped walking outside the Department's front door, so she stopped as well. "But you got us out."

She pulled closer to him. "Thanks," she whispered.

Ed opened the door.

She sighed. "Some honeymoon, eh?"

"Hey, who wants to spend time staring at dead painters' masterpieces?"

• • •

The station was abuzz. When they walked in, Callie hit the intercom. "Andi's back!" Within seconds, deputies were swarming her, questions flying. "How's Brad?" "What do we do now?" "You okay?" "Are you Acting Sheriff?" "You bringing more FBI in?"

She raised her hands. "Hang on! I'm not the one to be answering all those questions. We need to see who the commissioners appoint as Acting. Till then—"

Pete Peterson had joined the group. "We already know. I called Jack Conrad and they just met. It's you."

Her chest tightened. She willed herself to breathe. Looked around at her friends. "All right, then." She looked at her watch. "Twenty to eleven. I've got two calls to make, then I want a meeting of Brad's— sorry, I mean, *the* executive team at eleven. After that, an all-staff meeting over lunch, starting at noon. Callie, two things: get enough sandwiches from Alice's for all the deputies, for Greg and Joe, and for as many dispatchers as you can round up by noon. Oh, for Ben and Ed too."

Callie was scribbling. "You mind a couple suggestions?"

"Please."

"Half the order to Alice's, half to the Angler. Spread the wealth."

"Do it. What's the second suggestion?"

"Order a sandwich for yourself."

6

She convened the meeting at eleven. For a moment, she looked down at the notes she'd jotted.

"Okay, number one. I've spoken with the commissioners and they've approved my request to add a new deputy to the team."

Pete's eyebrows jumped. "Who, Andi?"

She looked down at her notes, enjoying the moment despite the tragedy. "His name is . . . let me look. Oh, Benjamin Stewart."

She smiled at him. The look on Ben's face was priceless. His jaw had dropped open and his eyes were wide. He cleared his throat roughly. "Ain't sure I saw that comin'."

"Assuming you want to come back to the department."

Ben took a long, shuddery breath. "Ain't nothin' on this green earth I want more."

Pete was beaming, and everyone started to clap. When the applause died, Andi told Ben she needed him for two things: to mentor her—show her what she was forgetting, point out what she could do that she wasn't doing and to whom she should talk—and be her eyes and ears with the valley people.

"Everybody trusts you. Find out what they're thinking, about the protest and our response."

Ed grinned. "You're back on the corner, Ben." Everyone laughed.

She looked at her notes again. "Okay, next item," she said. "From now on, Greg and I will decide strategy together, with your input. Greg will be in command at the camp, but Ed and I will deal with the protesters, since they won't talk with the FBI. Questions?"

"Same chain of command for everyday policing?" Pete asked.

"Yep. You're in charge of that. Anything else?" She glanced around the room. Heads shook.

"I want to ask Magnus Anderssen—" She paused to explain to Greg and Joe who Anderssen was to the valley's people. Their leading citizen. For many, a benefactor. The richest man and largest employer in the valley. "I want Mack to join us as an advisor, and to be my *voice* with the community, like Ben will be the department's eyes and ears."

Ben slapped the table. "If that ain't a righteous idea, there ain't no such thing as righteous."

But Andi saw Greg's wary glance at Joe. The agents raised a concern: Could Anderssen be trusted with their plans? "Civilians aren't trained in keeping things under wraps like we are."

Ben shook his head. "Mack 'n me go back to when we were kids. He ain't broke a confidence in all that time, not once. We say, 'no leaks,' he'll be the Hoover Dam."

Greg nodded. "Then I think it's a good idea." To Andi, he said. "You're going to need somebody beside yourself to meet with the media and with the community when you can't. Think he'll do it?"

Ben spoke first. "Ain't a doubt in my mind. He'll step up."

Andi seconded that with a nod. "Good. Okay, last item. We'll meet again at two this afternoon to prep for the meeting with Jenkins and that other guy Crane named."

Greg said, "Dolan."

"Right," Andi said. "Meantime, I need your feedback about something. I need to know how these people think, what their motives and beliefs are, how they might react to our plans. I want to find somebody in the valley who shares the protesters' ideas."

Greg held up his hand. "Whoa. To get a fair read on how the protesters might react to a plan, we'd have to reveal it to this guy. How will you know he's not calling one of them on a cell phone as soon as he's done talking with you?"

Ben added, "Ain't thought this through, but why would a guy like that be willing to help us?"

"I haven't thought it through either," Andi allowed. "Let's let it percolate."

Ben grunted. "One good thing though, there ain't no cell phone service up on that ridge."

7

At two-twenty, as Andi hurried across the county building's parking lot, thunder again echoed across the heat-soaked air. She drove fast up Division Street to the sheriff's office, and ran into the station, sweat running down her back. This thunder would bring no rain, no relief from the heat.

The executive team, along with Magnus Anderssen, were filing out of the conference room. "Sorry I'm late." She was breathing hard. "Had a meeting with the commissioners."

Pete chuckled. "They do talk, don't they?"

"Eternally. Okay, everybody, thanks for meeting without me. Pete, how about you and Greg come into my cube and fill me in on what I missed." Her breathing was slowing.

Pete said, "Don't you think we should meet in the sheriff's office? You're sheriff now."

She recoiled. "*Acting* sheriff." She thought of Brad Ordrew lying unconscious in Missoula. "Too soon. Let's use the conference room."

While Greg and Pete took their seats, she walked to the window and stared toward Mt. Adams. She saw a lightning bolt lash the ground south of town, and waited for the thunder, counting. When the sound rumbled over town, she said, "Eleven miles south."

She joined the men at the big table. Pete briefed her on the department's part of the meeting. A community-wide gathering would be held in the high school auditorium on Sunday evening, and Magnus would see to the arrangements. A press release about Sheriff Ordrew's shooting had to be written and emailed to Bud Groh at the radio station. The only witnesses who'd seen the shooting were Greg, Xavier, and Felix, who were responding to a traffic call. So Greg had volunteered to write the press release if Callie could set him up on a computer.

"That's it on the department side, Andi," Pete said. "Greg can fill you in on the protest."

"We covered three issues," Greg said. Just then, closer thunder startled them. "Man, I hate these dry lightning storms."

Andi nodded. "Makes me think of wildfire." She stood again and looked out the window. The clouds loomed darker, closer to the ground. "Go ahead, Greg."

He filled her in. Mostly, they'd agreed to stay away from the camp till after the community meeting and he mentioned that BLM-Missoula wasn't coming. "A new policy, I guess. Let the locals do the dirty work."

She watched the darkening clouds, roiling in the sky. The wind was rising.

Greg told her Magnus Anderssen had a contact who could provide water and portable toilets to Freedom Camp, and suggested they request a Critical Incident Resource Group team from the Salt Lake FBI office. He doubted they'd send more than twenty, if that many. "But even twenty from CIRG will even the odds."

As they talked, lightning flashed outside, followed in no time by the thunder's crack. All three jumped and moved to the window. Wind whipped the trees on Jefferson's too-dry streets, tearing off flights of parched brown leaves. No rain fell.

Pete looked at the tumultuous sky. "We need a storm to knock down this heat." He shook his head. "But this one's not it."

8

Lightning flashed across the valley all evening. Thunder rolled from deep inside heavy clouds, but no rain came. The humidity worsened the heat. Andi and Ed sat exhausted on the porch swing, watching lightning dancing above the trees. The dead dark air was oppressive, dense, hot. Grace was indoors, reading in front of a fan.

The buzzing of her cell phone sounded through the screen. Andi sighed. "Grace, will you answer that for me? I'm not moving."

"Sure," came the answer. After a moment, Grace came onto the porch and handed her the phone. "It's Doctor Keeley."

"Damn," Andi said. "At this hour, it can't be good news." She took the phone. "Doc? Hi."

She listened, her head bowed. "God, John. Do you think he'll make it?"

Grace and Ed watched her intently. She was shaking her head. After a moment, she said, "All right, John. Thanks for the news. Keep me posted, okay?"

When she ended the call, Ed said, "Bad?"

"Brad's in grave condition, no change. They're thinking he'll lose his right lung—if he survives, which they're not sure he will."

"Ouch. If we lose him . . ."

"I'm sheriff till the next election." She sighed. "Once upon a time I thought I wanted that."

Ed said, "I never liked Brad, but this is wrong. I don't want him to die."

"Yeah. *So* wrong."

Grace's cell rang inside; she ran to get it. Andi heard her voice, but couldn't make out what was said. After a couple minutes, Grace came to the screen door. "Andi, that was Jen. She says Bobby and his buddies are getting drunk in their garage, talking about going up to the camp to get revenge for the sheriff."

"Jesus. Are you still on the line with her?"

"No."

Andi's own phone rested on the arm of the porch swing. She grabbed it. "Jen's number?"

She tapped it in. "Jen? This is Andi Pelton. Can your husband come to the phone?"

She waited. Then, "Hi, Bobby. It's Andi Pelton. I'm told you and your buds are talking about going up to the protesters' camp. That right?"

She listened, rolling her eyes. "Boy, I get that. These guys have no right to come into our valley and cause trouble. I—"

More listening. "Yeah, I agree. So, look. We're having a community meeting Sunday evening. How about you and your friends come and raise that question, and we'll be able to let the whole community know what we'll do about it. You good with that?"

Again, she listened, and rolled her eyes more than once. Finally, she said, "Okay, good. I'll be sure to call on you and let you have your say. Meantime, keep it cool, all right?"

Listened. "Got that right, Bobby." She ended the call, shook her head.

Grace said, "You okay?"

Andi shrugged. "Just say we dodged a bullet that'll probably be fired at me Sunday night."

Ed groaned. "That's one lousy metaphor, Andi."

Lightning flared behind him. Thunder blotted out her answer.

CHAPTER EIGHT - SATURDAY

1

Next morning, a little past six, Andi and Ed were finishing coffee on the porch. Andi savored the quiet; the heat at night had made her sleep restless. Her cell phone buzzed. She looked at the screen. "It's Doc. This can't be good, not this early."

She pressed *Talk*. "Hi, John. News about Brad?"

"Yeah, bad, I'm afraid," Keeley said. "He had two cardiac arrests overnight. They revived him, but his rhythm hasn't stabilized. Removing most of his right lung's on hold until they can assess and treat the degree of heart and brain damage."

"God. *Brain* damage?" Andi saw Ed's frown.

Doc said, "Cardiac arrest patients often stroke, and about eighty percent go into either a natural or a medically induced coma afterward."

"A medically induced coma?" She froze.

Ed's eyes narrowed.

"When an arrest survivor doesn't regain consciousness, therapeutic hypothermia is the best treatment. Lowering body temperature prevents worse inflammation."

Andi leaned against the counter. "Doesn't look good, does it?"

Doc Keeley was quiet. Andi waited, her hand rising. She pressed her fingers against her neck, searched for her heartbeat, found it. Doc said, "Cardiac arrest's never a good sign. Still, the best predictor of survival without brain damage is getting the heart beating quickly, and each time he was resuscitated within sixty seconds. But we won't know for a while."

By now, Ed was standing beside her, his hand on her shoulder. She looked up at him, eyes sad, shook her head. "Well, thanks for the news, John." She ended the call, told Ed what had happened, then whispered, "Can't see how this gets anything but worse."

2

Since they'd postponed negotiations until Monday at the earliest, the team met later than usual. Andi began with the news. "Doc Keeley called this morning. Brad's not doing well." She relayed what she'd learned.

At first, no one spoke. After a moment, Ben grunted. "Got me half a mind to walk over to that cellblock and beat the crap outta both those monsters." He cleared his thickened throat. "If I ain't been made a deputy again, I'd do it."

The door opened. Greg Haney and Joe Mitchell stepped in. Greg, who looked rumpled, took in the somber mood. "Bad news?"

Andi filled him in. Greg looked around the table. "Terrible. I'm very sorry to hear it." He sat back. "Perhaps we should meet later?"

"No, let's get started. Everyone all right with that?"

"Sittin' here mopin' ain't gonna do Bradley no good," Ben said. "Let's work."

"Okay, then," Andi said, aiming for brisk. "Greg, what's going on up top?"

"Not much. It was a miserable night. The heat never let up." He nodded at Magnus. "Your fans blow plenty of air. Hot air. My guys didn't get much sleep." He yawned. "Sorry. Like I say . . . This morning, we notified them we're not coming for a couple of days. Quinn and the other guy met us at the camp's entrance, and a few guys backed them up, but we didn't see much activity inside. I doubt they slept any better than we did."

"Okay, thanks." Andi looked at her notes, then up at the team. "I've got one thing. Anybody else have anything?"

Magnus raised his hand and gave a quick update on the community meeting tomorrow evening.

"Perfect," Andi said. She paused, then repeated yesterday's question about finding an anti-government type to get feedback on what the protesters might be thinking.

Ben disagreed, agreeably. "We know damn well how they'll react to any plan we got—*bad*, every time."

For a minute, they went back and forth about whether the protesters could communicate with the outside, and if so, might Andi's source betray them. Joe pointed out that given their lack of food and water, he doubted they were good planners, but since Crane claimed a connection to a nationwide group, perhaps his RV had a satellite dish.

Magnus said, "I've got a fellow who works on my logging crew who's a neo-Nazi. Or was. He did bombings and very rough stuff back in his teens and twenties. He served eighteen years in federal prison, but he's worked for me nineteen years now. He's a hermit, built his own cabin on the side of Hunters' Peak. He's still a fascist, but he keeps to himself, and in all those nineteen years, he's been no trouble of any kind. I'm pretty sure we can trust him, if I can talk him into cooperating. Shall I give him a go?"

"What about communicating with the protesters? Can we trust him not to?"

Mack smiled. "Ad Schaefer doesn't own a cell phone or a computer. Like I said, he's a hermit, with nothing but an old rotary phone. I doubt he'd know how to use a satellite phone if I handed him one."

Ben rapped his knuckles on the table. "Son of a gun. You're talkin' about old Adolf Schaefer. Forgot all about the old coot." He looked at Andi. "If you want a quiet Nazi, Ad's your guy."

3

Ad Schaefer, chief bucker on Magnus Anderssen's logging crew, straightened up and stretched his sore back, aching from working the heavy chainsaw. *Getting old sucks*, he thought. But he enjoyed the work in the woods, not to mention the long soothing views out across the valley from the mountainsides where they harvested trees. Now, he was looking south, toward Mt. Adams, thinking about the monastery on its upper slopes.

As he pulled the cord to fire up his chainsaw, he spotted Magnus Anderssen climbing up from the logging road below. Ad liked two things about the boss: he paid well, and he left his workers alone. Him marching upslope toward the work site gave Ad a pit in his stomach. Davey Houlihan, the crew chief, climbing beside Anderssen, called out, "Stop work! Visitor on site!"

Shouts passed the command up the mountain. The buzz of chainsaws stopped. Ad shut off his own. *Hope to hell this visit ain't with me.* But Houlihan and Anderssen changed course and headed toward him.

When they reached him, Ad nodded to the crew chief, then to the boss. Anderssen held out his hand. "Ad, it's been a while."

"Yessir." He shook the boss's hand. "Long time."

Anderssen turned to the chief. "Thanks, Davey. I'll find my way down when Ad and I are finished. You can resume work, we'll be safe over here."

When Houlihan left, Ad ventured, "When we're finished? What're we doing?"

"We're talking, Ad. I have a proposal for you. The sheriff's department needs your help."

Right, and you're gonna name me in your will, he thought. *Sheriffs arrested me plenty, but they ain't never wanted my goddamn help.* Ad kept his face straight. He'd been at war with the American government all his youth, and his opinions hadn't changed with age. And he knew how trouble smelled.

He trusted Anderssen, though. The boss knew Ad's record and his views. Never made a fuss about them.

"How many years on my crew, Ad?"

Ad screwed up his forehead. A long time. *Longest damn job I ever held.* And Anderssen knew it. Knew everything about him. The violence, the bombs. The prison time. The tattoos. And didn't seem to care. Of course, Ad had mellowed. Being fifty-eight makes jail time less appealing, truth to tell. But *helping* the sheriff's department? "I reckon it'll be going on twenty-one, twenty-two, boss."

Anderssen laughed, shook his head. "Twenty-one years ago you were still in prison. It's nineteen." He paused, and put his big hand on Ad's shoulder, squeezed. "Nineteen years I'm very happy with, Ad."

Now there's a goddamn surprise. "Well, thank you, boss."

"So, when the sheriff asked me to find a trustworthy fascist who hates the federal government to help her, your name came to mind right off."

This floored him. *The sheriff wants a Hitlerite to help her? And 'her'? First damn things first.* "I thought the woman deputy lost the election."

"Long story short, a group of protestors have taken over some federal land up above Victor Sobstak's ranch. They killed six cows. When Sheriff Ordrew arrested their leader, one of them shot him. So, Deputy Pelton took over as acting sheriff."

Ad thought that over. "Shot the sheriff, eh? Somebody sung a song 'bout that, back in the day. What kinda help we talking about here?"

"She wants to ask you what they might be thinking and how they would react to things she plans to do. Using your experience. Politically, they're not unlike what you used to be."

"Still am, boss. These days, people'd call me a terrorist. Just don't *do* no terror no more." He squinted into the distance for a moment, savoring the long view, the forest sweeping up the sides of the mountains, but not liking the direction this conversation was taking. "I ain't big on helping sheriffs, boss."

Anderssen laughed, a deep hearty laugh. "Don't I know it." He turned serious. "Look, Ad. She's a good one. Her goal is to end this standoff with no more violence on either side. She wants to ensure justice is done for Vic Sobstak. And she's keeping the FBI under control."

"Victor. Hell, him and me go way back. What's he need justice for?"

"The six cows were his."

Ad frowned. "Boss, you know me. I ain't got no pendings on me anymore. I ain't done no actions since I come to work for you, *nineteen* years, nor the eighteen years in the joint before that. I still got my ideas, and you know 'em, but I keep 'em to myself and I don't want no trouble."

"You'll get no trouble from Andi Pelton. She'll tell you what she's thinking and ask your opinion about how those protestors might react. That's it. You're a consultant."

That took the cake. "A consultant, you say?" Ad chuckled. "So, I get the big bucks now?"

Anderssen shook his head. "Nope. Just the reward of serving your country."

Ad laughed. "The same country I'd as soon burn down?"

"The same."

Something Anderssen had said echoed: Victor Sobstak. *Good guy. We used to have a beer or two together.* "You said these protesters killed Victor's cows."

"Six. No reason we can figure out."

Huh. "I have time to think about it?"

"Well, sure, but we could use your answer as soon as you can give it. This situation could turn violent any time."

"And it blows up, we get plenty more government pigs in the valley, don't we."

"We do. FBI. Homeland Security. National Guard. State troopers. You name it, they'll come."

Ad looked around at the forest, felled trees waiting for bucking, other growth standing, waiting for the faller's saw. *Used to hide from the pigs in woods like this.* "We get all that ruckus down here, folks like me are the first to lose. I've been safe working for you. Happy, even. Those fights we had when I was a kid, they were fun, but the quiet's what I want now." He paused and looked around again. "These woods are home now, Mack." He paused again; first time he'd called the boss by name. After nineteen years.

Magnus put his hand again on Ad's shoulder. "Can you give me your decision by tomorrow morning, my friend?"

Ad shook his head. Magnus pulled back his hand. Ad figured the boss thought he'd say no. "No, boss. I can give it to you right now. I'll help. But on one condition."

"Name it."

"I'll talk to you. Only you. Not to the sheriff."

Magnus extended his hand. "You've got a deal, Ad." They shook and Magnus asked, "What persuaded you?"

"Boss, I ain't got no time for people who kill my friend's cattle."

4

Grace watched Ed stare at his dinner. He hadn't said anything since coming home after the team meeting at the sheriff's office. Now, his eyes were down, as if he were absorbed in studying his food. Which he hadn't touched. "Northrup?"

He looked up at her, and gave a narrow smile. "I'm not much fun, am I?"

"Is something wrong with the pasta?"

"No, no, it's good."

"How do you know? You haven't tasted it."

Ed sighed. "Busted. Yeah, something's wrong, but it's not your pasta." He swirled pasta and sauce on his fork and chewed on it for a bit.

Grace waited.

He paused, gathering his thoughts. "It's a few things. I'm worried about Andi. This occupation is a ton of pressure."

"She seems okay to me."

He nodded. "So far, yeah. But it's going to get worse before it gets better. We've got the SWAT teams, but we need more help, I'm afraid." He grimaced. "And I'm worried about Sheriff Ordrew."

This confused her. "Why?"

"You know he got shot, don't you?"

"Sure, but I heard he was going to be all right."

Ed shook his head. "Unlikely. He had two cardiac arrests and now he's in therapeutic hypothermia."

"Hypothermia? Like what I had when I got lost in that blizzard? How's that 'therapeutic'?"

"The doctors control it. They cool his body down about ten degrees to try to minimize brain damage that might have happened during the cardiac arrests."

She took that in, piecing it together. "So, you're worried he won't be able to come back." Another piece fell into place. "And if he can't, you're worried Andi'll be stuck in the job and that might be too much for her."

He smiled thinly. "Bingo. I am worried she'll get stuck in the job, but not that it'll be too much for her. I'm just afraid it'll be hard on our relationship. You know how devoted she is to law enforcement."

Aha. "Are you still mad about cancelling your honeymoon?"

He looked at her fondly. "Very perceptive, kid. But no, not mad. Disappointed. Not mad."

"You sure?"

He chuckled. "You sound like me at work. You take a psychology course this year?"

"Nope, just my inborn skill." She enjoyed his praise.

He laughed, and then his face changed. Grace thought he looked like he was realizing something.

"It's something else, too. You know Lynn Monroe's been working with me this year."

Grace knew Lynn well—she'd been her high school counselor. "Yeah, she's your retirement plan, right? You want her to take over your practice so you can go fishing with Andi." Then it hit her. "Oh. But if she's sheriff . . ."

"No, not that. Lynn called me a few days ago and said her wife is unhappy with the arrangement and wants her to cut back. She may pull out altogether, so she *was* my retirement plan. Emphasis on '*was.*'"

"Wait. You said, 'wife.' Is Lynn lesbian?"

He nodded. "You didn't know?"

"Despite my well-tuned intuition, nope. It never dawned on me. What's her wife's name?"

"Rachel."

"What's Rachel upset about?"

"The current thing is that Lynn's away from home four evenings a week. But the bigger problem is Rachel's got a wellness consulting business in Missoula. It's still very small, and they need more income from Lynn. So Rachel wants Lynn to stay in Missoula and go back to the jobs she gave up to come here."

An idea tickled Grace's mind. She gave it a moment, letting it take enough form for her to recognize whether it was good enough to say out loud. After a few seconds, she decided it might sell. "What if Rachel started doing what Lynn is?"

His eyes widened, looked shocked. "What? Join my practice?"

"Why not? You always say therapy works better if the patient's lifestyle changes. There's nobody in the valley who's doing wellness stuff, is there? What if Rachel did that here, and expand what you can offer people. It'd help your retirement plan even more, because you'd have to get out of your office and go fishing to make room for Lynn *and* Rachel. And she'd get her evenings with Lynn back—not at home, but why not?" She folded her arms, feeling triumphant.

Ed said nothing. Grace waited. Was he thinking about it? Dismissing it as naïve? She unfolded her arms. Finally, she said, "Come on, Northrup, react. Don't just sit up there at sixty thinking this nineteen-year-old's dumb as a Barbie."

He shook his head, a smile spreading across his lips. "Just the opposite, Grace. I couldn't decide whether to tell you you're a genius now, or save it for later."

5

Back at the station, the evening heat was still relentless. She wondered how long this weather could last. She finished the last of her paperwork for the week and stood to go home.

Her intercom rang. "Call on line 1, Andi. Magnus Anderssen."

She sighed and punched the button. "Hi, Mack."

"Evening, Andi. You sound tired."

"Heat-beat more than anything. The air conditioning in this building's not so great. What's up?"

"I spoke with my guy and he agrees to work with us, including keeping our conversations to himself. He made two conditions: He'll only talk with me and I'm not to give you his name. Are you good with that?"

"Sure. I already know his name, but it's irrelevant."

"Good. I'm sitting in his cabin. What do you want to know?"

She asked two questions, and told Magnus to call her at home.

• • •

At home, she sank onto the porch swing. Despite the heat, Ed and Grace had gone for a walk. They'd acted like conspirators, but fatigue defeated her curiosity. Grace had left some pasta warming in the oven, but even that didn't draw her from the swing. The dense hot air was thick and still, as if last night's lightning storm had exhausted it. She rubbed the tightness in her neck.

What must Freedom Camp be like tonight? Even if all those pickups had air conditioning, would the protesters risk draining fuel to run them? They claimed they're already short of water, and the camper toilets had to be getting full. Were hunger and tedium and loneliness gnawing at them? With no family sounds around, no spouse to rub the stress out of their shoulders, were tempers rising? What was the real situation with the food?

The hot yellow of the evening sky mirrored her mood—too intense. She wished Ed would get home, would sit beside her, comfort her about the siege. Now that the protest had become her responsibility, it seemed that way, as if *she*, not only the protesters, were under attack.

Her cell phone rang. She sighed. *What now?* She picked it up and touched *Talk*.

"Andi, Mack here. Two pieces of news: First off, I'll have water and portable toilets for forty men for a week. Both'll be delivered tomorrow afternoon."

She snapped, "Let's let them wait another damn day. They just shot our sheriff."

Magnus was quiet a moment. "Okay, if you say so."

"Am I being vindictive?" *Of course I am*, she thought. "Don't answer that. They shot Brad."

"Monday afternoon it is. The other thing is, Ad Schaefer's given me his thoughts about your questions. Are you in a spot to hear them, or would you prefer we wait till morning?"

Her shoulders ratcheted tighter. "No, Mack, let's do it. Ed's on his way home and he and I can process what you tell me."

"Good. So, your first question was what the protestors will think if you meet their demand for water and throw in toilets unasked. He says they'll think you're weak, just a woman, someone they can manipulate. I asked him what if you *aren't* weak. He said they won't believe it; they'll try to figure out who's behind you. He said they'd think Ed or the FBI was running things and you were window dressing."

"Huh. Window dressing, eh?" She thought about that. "Could be a good thing if they underestimate me." She thought about that a moment. "Okay. I also asked what he thinks they'd do if Crane doesn't come back. He answer that?"

"He said he didn't know, but that in his day, they'd take their guns to town and raise holy hell."

6

After their walk, Ed and Grace climbed onto the porch. Ed gave Andi a soft kiss. "I'm sweaty. I need a quick shower. Mind?"

"Not at all. I'm not moving from this swing."

While Ed showered, Grace dished up the pasta and brought it to the porch. Andi smiled. "Thanks. I was too beat to do it myself."

Grace said, "How's it going, solving the invasion?"

"The 'invasion'?"

"That's what everybody's calling it now."

Jesus. "The young guys still itching for a fight?"

"More than ever. Bobby Place said you guys have this meeting tomorrow night, and he and his boys are giving you one shot at talking them out of their plan. If you don't, they're going up."

Andi's gut tightened. "Do they realize we'll arrest them if they try to do that?"

"I don't think they care, Andi. Or that they think that far ahead."

"If Bobby and his friends go up, people who agree with the protesters will march up too and that civil war will last a generation. And it'll start on my watch." Her neck muscles twisted tighter.

Grace shook her head. "No way, Andi. You'll set them straight."

Andi inhaled, tried to relax.

"Can I tell you what I think we should do if you can't talk them out of going up there?"

"We?"

She outlined a plan conjured up by her girls at last evening's party. A women's march on the camp. Ladies—moms, grandmothers, daughters—all lined up in front of the protesters. A counter-protest, a demand the protesters leave the valley.

"These guys are fanatics, and they're armed. They've already killed cattle and shot Sheriff Ordrew. The one person who might've controlled them is in our jail, and I have no idea whether Carl Jenkins can keep them peaceful." The longer she thought about it, the worse this got. "Grace, listen. Those men could take you all hostage, unless we bring the SWAT teams up to protect you, and that'll only make everything worse. I can't allow a women's march on that mountain."

"Please, Andi. Give us a chance to help. It's our valley too."

Andi forced herself to stifle a reply. She knew Grace wanted to be a part of things. "Look, I have an idea how you and the women can help, and it's more valuable to us than marching. And a hell of a lot safer."

"What is it?" Her eyes betrayed her.

Andi saw the hurt. "Since they got here, the FBI guys have been eating MREs, which are boring. We need—"

"What are MREs?"

"Meals Ready to Eat. We need to set up a food operation to take better care of them. I'd like you to organize your friends and their moms and grandmas for me. To provide good food."

A long silence. Then, frowning, Grace said, "Women's work, eh? Let's not allow the ladies to expose themselves to danger, but they can cook and feed and do dishes for the men. And clean their tents, maybe?"

Give me a break. "I don't need a lecture on feminism, Grace. This could be a way you guys could help."

Another long silence. "I'm sorry. It's just . . ."

"You wanted to make a difference, and I get that. But the difference we need isn't the one you wanted to make. Think your friends might be open to this?"

"I don't know, Andi." Disappointment drenched her voice. "But," she said, "I'll talk to them."

Chapter Nine - Sunday

1

Andi was writing notes for the community meeting—Magnus was coming at nine to plan it—when her cell phone buzzed. The screen said *Grace.*

"Andi, I'm so excited! Jen and Dana talked about your meal idea with their moms and everybody likes it. A lot. Jen's mom's going to announce it at her church this morning and ask for volunteers."

"Fantastic, Grace. I'll call on you during the community meeting today and you can ask for volunteers there too."

"Oh, man, that's perfect. I'm all over it, Andi. And I came up with a name."

"A name?"

"'Operation Square Meal.' What do you think?"

"Perfect. Go for it, girl."

2

Grace sat at the kitchen table, a pad of yellow paper in front of her. Tapped a pencil on the pad. Fifteen minutes ago, at the top of the page, she'd printed big block letters: "Operation Square Meal." The rest of the page was blank.

After calling Andi, she'd danced around the kitchen. But that excitement had dimmed. How do you organize something like this? She doodled. At least swirls and curlicues kept the yellow space at bay.

A name came to her, and she wrote it under the lowest doodle: *Luisa Anderssen.* The excitement rushed back and she ran to the phone. Dialed. Luisa Anderssen answered, *"Hola. Buenos días."*

"Hey, Luisa. *Como está?"*

"Muy bien, thank you. *Y tú?"*

It came out in a rush. "Andi's the sheriff now and she asked me to organize volunteers to feed the FBI and I was thinking you'd know how to do that and could help me."

"Again, please? My *inglés* is good, but a little slow."

Grace repeated it, slower this time.

Luisa said, "Yes, of course. Shall I come to your home?"

Another thought struck Grace. "I'm going to ask the Ladies' Fishing Society to help us. I'll call you back when we figure out where and when."

"Very good. Thank you for thinking of me, Grace."

· · ·

Twenty minutes later, Grace dialed Luisa again. "Luisa, I just talked with the—" *Too fast.* She slowed herself. "I talked with the Ladies' Fishing Society and they suggested meeting at the Angler when it opens at eleven, because Lane Martin's a member."

Luisa was quiet for a moment. "Tell me again this society's name."

"The Ladies' Fishing Society."

"But Lane is a man."

Grace shrugged. "I guess it doesn't matter. Andi says all the Ladies' do is gossip, eat *hors d'oeuvres,* and drink wine. No fishing allowed."

3

After the older women ordered wine at the Angler, Grace smiled up at Ted Coldry. "I'll have a Pinot Noir, thanks."

Ted smiled and waited, his pencil poised.

Grace sighed. "All right. Coke, please. But if a little rum splashes in it, I won't tell."

Ted laughed and left to pour the orders.

Lane Martin joined them from the kitchen. "This idea of yours is splendid, Grace. Let's get to work on plans."

Their plan took shape in half an hour. They would use the Angler's kitchen for food prep and cooking, Lane would order from his distributor—wholesale prices would help a lot. They settled on eight crews per day, four each for lunch and dinner: food prep, meal set-up, meal tear-down, and dishes. As Grace was asking how many volunteers they'd need for those teams, her cell phone beeped. "It's Andi," she told them and left the table. Before she got very far, Lane called after her, "Ask Andi whether the FBI will eat here or out at their camp."

"How's it going, kid?" Andi asked.

"It's awesome. Everybody's helping and we've got most things figured out already. I'll tell you all about it tonight." She asked Lane's question.

Andi said, "I just got off the phone with Greg Haney and I told him about your idea. He said he doesn't want his men to leave the camp for meals. Can you bring the food out there?"

"I don't know, but I'll bet we can. I'll go ask the team."

"The team?"

"I asked the Ladies' Fishing Society for help and they're all here. Plus Luisa."

"Ah. Great. Say hi to them for me. And don't forget the community meeting at seven. You can ask for volunteers then."

"Got it. See you."

She returned to the table. "Andi says they want to eat out at their camp. Can we do that?"

"Certainly, not a problem," Lane said. "But we'll need a transport team for lunch and dinner to take the food out and bring leftovers and dirty dishes back."

Grace asked, "Did you figure out how many volunteers we need for the teams?"

Bernie snorted. "You betcha, child." She picked up her calculator. "Adding the fifth team brings the total to . . ." She tapped the keys. "One hundred sixty, forty each day for four days. Each team'll work every fifth day."

Grace knew her alarm showed on her face. "We'll *never* get that many."

"Darlin'," Callie said, "you just watch."

4

In the hiatus between year's end at the high school and summer school's start, anyone who knew how to turn on the auditorium air conditioning was out of town. People coming into the auditorium for the community meeting took it in stride, although one joker interrupted Magnus Anderssen's introduction. "You keepin' 'er hot so's we'll leave quicker, Mack?"

After the laughter, Magnus wrapped up his introduction and Andi took the podium. She glanced down at the front row. Grace's friend Jen sat beside her husband, Bobby Place, whose face was beet red. *Heat? Or anger?* She saw a bulge under his jacket—in fact, why was he wearing a *jacket* at all? She scanned the others in that row. All were Bobby Place's age, all wore jackets in the oppressive heat, and she saw bulges under those jackets.

They're armed, damn it.

She welcomed everyone, then outlined the situation briefly. Doc Keeley updated the crowd on Sheriff Ordrew's condition, after which she introduced the FBI agents and mentioned the FBI SWAT teams and their role. She looked down toward Bobby Place and his pals, and smiled. "The SWAT teams are here to keep the peace, to protect you folks from the protesters—she paused a beat. "—and to protect the protesters from you."

She listened to the laughter with relief. But Bobby's face was redder, and she saw sweat on his forehead.

As she described the killing of Vic Sobstak's cattle, tension replaced the good humor. Furious mutterings ran through the crowd like fire through dry grass. Most of the valley people worked with cattle, or in the various small businesses catering to the ranches, and many hadn't heard of the killings.

She looked up at the rest of the audience, who had quieted and were looking expectant. "I don't blame Vic for his frustration, and the sheriff and I decided he shouldn't be charged with anything. Except stubbornness." As the crowd laughed, sweat trickled down her back. She glanced again at the young men in the front row. They all sat stiffly, looking straight ahead, not at her. Not one laughed with the crowd. Or even smiled.

When Bobby Place looked up, their eyes locked. He eyed her defiantly. She looked over the crowd again. "So far, with FBI's help, we've got the protest well under control. We don't want any surprises or reasons for the protesters to have a legitimate grievance. So, we need the support of *everyone* in the valley." She looked again, right at Bobby. "And that means everyone."

She moved on to the negotiations, told them about the food and water demands and the plan to provide water and toilets tomorrow. "Doc tells us that adult men can live a minimum of four weeks without food, if they have water. We won't provide food until the situation turns life-threatening. Leaving aside the health hazard, depriving anyone of water and toilets is inhumane. It's not how we do business in Adams County. The protesters are armed, they're dangerous, and their mission is hopeless. But as wrong as they are, they're human beings, and we intend to treat them as such."

Toward the back, a man raised his hand.

Andi pointed to him. "Yes?"

He stood, a tall sun-browned man with thick white hair. "I'm thinking my ideas might be closer to the protesters' than yours, but you pulled me up short when you said that about them being human beings. If you can hang onto that all the way through, I think we'll come out of this all right." He sat down, and applause spread through the crowd.

"Thank you. I'll be holding press conferences with the media every afternoon going forward, and you'll get the main points on the evening news." She picked up her water bottle and took a drink. She was about to ask Bobby Place for his statement, but before she could swallow, he leapt from his seat.

5

Bobby swung around toward the crowd and shouted, "Damn it, we have a right to protect our land. That bench belongs to us, and I say no outsiders should be allowed to come in and dictate to us." He swung around and yelled at Andi. "Why won't you let us go up and deal with this problem once and for all?"

Another set of cheers, harsher now, angrier, came from different places in the room. Bobby turned again toward the crowd. His friends started a chant, "Save . . . Our . . . Lands! Save . . . Our . . . Lands!" New yells of "No violence" clashed with his friends' chanting. Andi heard a few voices in the larger crowd joining the chant. When Bobby turned back to face her, she raised both hands. After a few moments, the crowd settled. "Bobby, I'm mad about the occupation too. And I agree with you. We have a right to defend our valley. But as sheriff, I'm responsible for protecting *everyone's* safety, and that doesn't mean just you and your friends. I have to protect the protesters too." She paused to frame what she wanted to say next.

Bobby shouted at her, "You're *not* protecting the valley. You're doing nothing. We're ready to act and you won't let us."

She shook her head. "Wrong, Bobby, we're not doing nothing." She raised her voice. "We're keeping the protesters up on the ridge. We're negotiating. Eventually, they'll get hungry and leave. But we will not, repeat *not*, start a fight with those men. They have a right to make their ideas known, but the sheriff's department has a duty to keep them— and all of you—safe."

A shout. "Don't let her sweet-talk you, Bobby. We need to take back our country!"

A few rows back, a man jumped to his feet. "Let me talk!"

Andi pointed to him. "Go ahead, Will."

He was gaunt and angular, with short gray hair, but his scrawny shoulders were unbent. "I'm seventy-five damn years old, and us

Montana union guys've seen it all. Men get angry, they throw some liquor on the fire, no time at all they're shooting, the police move in, and men die or go to prison. We figured this stuff out a long time ago. Montanans decide these things by voting, not shooting."

Another man stood, his red face framed by a long white beard. "This is just what a 'well-regulated militia' in our Second Amendment is for. When there's a threat to our county, our militia—which I say means these boys who're ready to fight for the rest of us—should take over. I say, let 'em go up."

Andi held up her hand. "Forgive me, but this argument doesn't bear on my duty, which is to end the occupation and prevent violence. It's up to the legislature and the courts to decide what constitutes a militia, and that's where voting comes in, as Will reminded us. Meantime, the buck stops with me about the safety of Adams County." She looked at Bobby Place, then out over the audience. "Let me be real clear. Anyone who attempts to go up either access road will be arrested for crossing a police barricade. I understand your passion for defending our county and I appreciate it. Please, *help* me defend it. Don't make yourself *another* problem I need to deal with."

Bobby, still standing, was glaring up at her. Jen, sitting, gripped his hand. Finally, he nodded. "All right, screw it," he said loudly. "But when the time comes when you need us—and it will come—there will be a price." Sporadic weak cheers echoed. The crowd was otherwise silent.

Andi took a good look at Bobby. *A price?* She shivered.

6

When Bobby sat, she gazed over the crowd. "I have one more thing and then we can get out of this oven." This roused cheers. Andi searched the faces and found Grace. "Grace, would you come up and tell the folks about Operation Square Meal and our need for volunteers?"

Grace ran onto the stage and outlined the plans. "We've got quite a few volunteers, but we need more." She called out to Luisa and

Maggie to stand. "If you'd like to help feed the agents that are protecting us, please see me or Luisa or Maggie after the meeting—" She showed the audience her clipboard. "—or call the sheriff's department."

She skipped back down and took up a position in front of the stage, and was soon surrounded by women—and a few men.

Andi smiled. *Beats hell out of a women's march!*

7

Driving home, Ed turned to look at Andi, whose eyes were closed, her head lying back against the headrest. She looked exhausted. "Andi?"

"What?"

"You okay?"

"No."

"Tell me."

But she lay her head back again and said nothing more.

She's stressed, he told himself. *Hell, we're all stressed.* Neither spoke till they reached the long drive up to the cabin. As he turned onto the driveway, she roused herself. "How do you think the meeting went?"

"You wanted to convey the facts and defuse tensions. I think you did both."

"How about handling Bobby Place?"

"I saw he was carrying."

"I did too, but I overlooked it. So, what about my question? How'd I do with him?"

He squeezed the wheel. "He's backed off, for now anyway. Time will tell."

"That's it? 'Time will tell'?"

Ed looked at her, then back at the driveway. "I'm on your side, remember?" He parked in the yard. "Let's have a glass of wine and relax."

"I'm too damn hot to relax and I've got a headache."

Ed scratched his chin. "Huh," he murmured.

"What?" Andi demanded.

He shut off the engine and looked at her. "I'm trying to avoid a fight, but you seem to want one. What's going on?"

"Nothing's *going on*," she snapped. "I'm hot, I'm tired, and I'm—" She stopped. Grew very still. She reached over to him, took his hand. "Ed, I'm scared."

8

After signing up the last volunteers, the Ladies' Fishing Society reconvened at the sheriff's station. Grace arrived first. Marla, the weekend evening dispatcher, said, "Girl, I've got thirty-three names."

Grace grinned. "We had twenty-two before the meeting, and I got nineteen more tonight. I don't know what Maggie and Luisa got; they're on the way."

As Marla handed her the list of volunteers, the console lit again. "Adams County Sheriff's Department. How may I direct your call?" She listened, then started writing, mouthing *Another one.*

Maggie, Callie, and Louisa came in, and Grace led the way to the conference room. They began assigning crews.

Bernie said, "People, we want church supper ladies for crew chiefs."

"Why?" Grace asked.

"Sweetness, church supper ladies know all there is to know about squeezing work out of volunteers."

"Oh," Grace said, and wondered why the others were laughing.

Every fifteen minutes, Marla handed them another list of names. By ten-fifteen, they had one hundred thirty-four volunteers. Grace cheered. "We only need thirty-six more!"

They hit that number at nine minutes after eleven.

Grace yawned. "Well, this is awesome. And I'm sleeping in tomorrow morning!"

"No, you ain't, dear." Callie said. "Tomorrow morning, everybody right here, eight o'clock. We start calling."

"About what?"

Bernie yawned too, but chuckled through it. "Dearie, we gotta give people their assignments and write out a good dependable schedule so everybody knows what they're doing. Making the crews is just the first step."

"Oh. How many steps are there?"

"Child, things like this, the steps never end."

9

Midnight. Andi nestled under Ed's arm; her eyes closed. Her fear had subsided into a calm sense of inevitability. Ed had said something banal, something like "We're in it together, babe." The words comforted her. They'd been sitting like this, silent, for a half hour. The air still lay heavy with heat, but the darkness soothed her.

Grace's PV drove up the drive and parked fast, scraping up gravel under the tires. As soon as she hit the porch steps, she started to gush about the volunteer turnout, but in the yellow porch light caught the lingering redness in Andi's eyes. "Oh. What's wrong?"

Andi nodded. "Nothing. Everything. I've been better." She pulled away from Ed's arm, sweaty, and sat up wearily. "We should start organizing the volunteers for Operation Square Meal."

"It's all done! We got all the volunteers we needed tonight, and tomorrow morning we'll assign them to crews and make a schedule and then call the crews." She stood a little taller and squared her shoulders. "There are lots of steps to something like this."

Andi's eyes misted. When her throat opened, she managed a very soft "Thank you, kiddo."

Grace went indoors and her bedroom door closed. Andi pulled Ed's arm back around her shoulders, despite the heat. They rested close beside one another. She sighed. "Sorry about being a bitch in the pickup. I was afraid you'd ask me for sex, and decided no more of that till this is over." She sighed again. "You think I'm being too rigid?"

"As opposed to me being the one who gets rigid?"

She mock-punched his shoulder.

He looked at her. "Are you saying you're being rigid because you feel *guilty* or because you feel *horny*?"

"Neither one, bucko. I need a few minutes of being close and safe and warm with somebody I love and who loves me. Simple."

"I can get with that," Ed said, a smile in his voice. "The warm part, especially."

She nestled closer to him. Her cell phone buzzed.

"Damn," she muttered, fumbling in her pocket for the phone. "Hello?"

She listened. Then, "Okay. I'm on my way." She punched *End* and stood. Ed's arm dropped to the porch swing. She told him CIRG had arrived—early—from Salt Lake City. They'd sent ten agents, not the twenty-four they'd promised. "And their gear won't arrive till morning, so they've got no tents to sleep in. Haney planned to arrange that in the morning. I've got to help them get settled in the high school gym."

"Do *you* have to do it?"

"I'm sheriff now." She smiled. "Do me a favor?"

"Name it, Sheriff." His voice had a chuckle in it.

"Keep the bed warm."

He grinned. "Hell, woman, it's still 84 degrees. That's going to be easy."

CHAPTER TEN - MONDAY

1

Crane's preliminary hearing proceeded smoothly—until it went to hell. After Irv Jackson's opening statement outlined what had happened, Crane's lawyer, Craig Anwalt, called the arrest "a political stunt designed to deprive my client of his First Amendment right to free expression."

Judge Richard Flure—Dickie to his friends—waited while Anwalt said more of the same. After a couple of minutes, he interrupted. "Counselor, save your wind for trial, this is just the probable cause hearing, as I imagine you understand." He looked at Irv Jackson. "Witnesses, please." Ed testified last, but all the prosecution witnesses recalled the scene and what was said in the same way. Crane's attorney cross-examined no one. Judge Flure turned to the defendant's table. "Mr. Anwalt? Witnesses?"

The lawyer rose. "I object to this whole proceeding, Your Honor. My client has more than forty witnesses to this travesty of an arrest, but the Acting Sheriff refuses to let them attend this hearing. Not only is my client being deprived of his First Amendment right to free speech, but his Fifth, Sixth, and Fourteenth Amendment rights to due process as well. We refuse to go along with this travesty." He sat.

The judge turned to Irv Jackson. "Prosecutor?"

Irv said, "May we have a brief recess while I confer with Sheriff Pelton?"

"You have ten minutes."

• • •

They talked in the corridor outside the courtroom. "He's not serious?" she asked Jackson.

"Very. And he's right, I'm afraid. Crane's entitled to his own witnesses."

"Jesus. Forty of them?"

"No. Describe the set-up for me again."

She described the four men—Crane, Carl Jenkins, and the two guards—facing Ordrew, Ed, and herself on the front line, Greg and Joe close behind. "The nearest men were at least ten yards back."

Irv said, "Good. I'll argue that he should have the witnesses in the front line—the two guards and Carl Jenkins, who can be assumed to have heard correctly. The others were far enough back we can't assume that."

• • •

A few minutes later, after Jackson made his argument, Judge Flure asked him how long it would take to deliver the witnesses to court. "After Mr. Stenborg's hearing, they can bring them down in sixty or seventy minutes, unless something happens to delay them."

"Mr. Anwalt, is that satisfactory to you?"

"Not at all, Your Honor. Mr. Jackson assumes that the rest of Reverend Crane's associates could not hear the conversation. I see no reason whatsoever to make that assumption, so I insist that we have at the very least the same number of witnesses that the prosecution had."

Irv stood. "With all due respect, I am not arguing that they could not *hear*. I'm arguing that at their distance we cannot assume that they heard *correctly*. Mr. Anwalt might wish to consider the difference."

Anwalt started to react, but Judge Flure said, "Enough. You two'll have every opportunity to argue your heart out at trial. I'm ordering the Acting Sheriff to bring to court—" He glanced down at his notes. "—Carl Jenkins and the two guards involved in the conversation at the time of Mr. Crane's arrest. We'll reconvene at one p.m. for their testimony."

2

At one p.m., Judge Flure ascended the bench and looked around the room. "This continues the probable cause hearing for Loyd Crane, on the charge of obstruction of justice. Acting Sheriff Pelton, I ordered you to bring three witnesses. You brought Mr. Jenkins but not the two guards. Explain, please."

Andi told him Quinn and the other guard had refused to leave without their weapons. "Facing forty armed and angry men, I didn't think it wise to force a confrontation over guns. I told them about your order and they said you could, quote, 'shove it.' They also indicated a possible location."

Flure, cranky on his happiest day, glowered. "We'll hold them in contempt of court another time. Let's get this done."

Crane, at the defendant's table, snickered.

After Jenkins was sworn in, Anwalt approached him on the witness stand. "For the record, please give us your name and occupation."

Andi grimaced at the word *occupation*. Jenkins said his name and added, "I'm a rancher."

"And you're from?"

"Right here in Monastery Valley." He glanced at Andi, sitting in the front row of the gallery, right behind Irv Jackson. His look puzzled her.

"Thank you. Were you present on June eleventh at the Freedom Camp protest led by my client, Reverend Loyd Crane?"

"Yeah, I was."

"And what was said just before the Reverend was arrested?"

"Uh, best as I can recollect, we were talking about food."

"Food?"

"Yeah. Some of us are short on supplies, and we'd asked the sheriff to bring us food. He, er, well, Dr. Northrup, who's their negotiator, was saying they might consider it."

"I see. And then what happened?"

"All of a sudden, the sheriff walked up to the Reverend and him and Deputy Pelton handcuffed him and walked him toward their squad car."

"And did the sheriff or the deputy say anything?"

"Something about arresting him for obstructing justice."

Anwalt nodded. "Thank you. No further questions, Your Honor."

Judge Flure nodded at Irv Jackson.

Irv stood. "Mr. Jenkins, may I remind you that you're under oath to tell the truth and the whole truth. And that perjury is a serious charge."

Carl Jenkins looked stricken. "I'm not lying."

Jackson nodded. "Good." He waited a moment. "So. Did a man in your camp fire his weapon into the air during a previous meeting?"

Jenkins's eyes widened, and he looked at Andi. His eyes seemed desperate. Finally, he whispered, "Yeah."

"Louder, please."

"I said yes."

"Thank you. And before arresting Mr. Crane, did Sheriff Ordrew or Doctor Northrup mention that?"

Jenkins's shoulders slumped. "I think so." He glanced toward Crane. Andi followed his look, and saw sheer hatred on Crane's face. No wonder Jenkins looked afraid.

"Which man mentioned it?"

"The doctor."

"Can you recall his exact words, please?"

Jenkins, with another glance toward Crane, who'd turned away, shook his head. "No, not exact."

"Your Honor," Jackson turned to the bench. "May I ask the court reporter to read the words from Doctor Northrup's testimony, starting with—" From his table, he lifted his notepad. "'I told him the sheriff offered to consider bringing food. . .'?"

Judge Flure nodded. "The reporter will read it."

Finding it took her but a moment. Then she read, "'I told him the sheriff offered to consider bringing food to the camp under one condition, and Mr. Crane asked the condition. I said Crane would need to hand over the man who fired in the air. Crane said he'd never do that. I reminded him that he had insisted that we take custody of Mr. Sobstak for doing the same thing earlier, which we had done, and then asked Crane again to surrender the man. The reverend said, "He has my protection and you can't have him," and Sheriff Ordrew immediately arrested him for obstruction of justice.'" The reporter looked to the judge.

"Thank you," Irv Jackson said to her. "So, Mr. Jenkins, between the discussion of your food shortage and the moment Sheriff Ordrew arrested the defendant, did the sheriff ask him to surrender the man who'd fired his weapon into the air?"

"I guess so."

"You *guess* so? Remember, you're under oath."

Anwalt stood. "Objection, harassing the witness."

"Sustained." The judge frowned at Irv. "No more reminders, Mr. Jackson."

"Thank you, Your Honor. Mr. Jenkins, are you guessing or do you know?"

Jenkins's voice came out small. "He asked it."

"And did Mr. Crane answer as Doctor Northrup testified?"

A long silence. Then, "Uh-huh."

"You're testifying that, Yes, Crane answered as Doctor Northrup testified?"

This time, Jenkins looked defiant. "You know what I said."

Judge Flure interrupted. "Carl, 'uh-huh' is vague. We need clear answers."

"Okay, Dickie." The men had been friends since high school. "Yes, Northrup said it right." He glanced at Crane, who'd turned his head away.

"No further questions, Your Honor."

The judge looked down at his old friend. "You're done, Carl. Go sit in the gallery next to Acting Sheriff Pelton till we get finished. Then she'll take you back." He scratched his thinning hair. "So, considering the testimony, I find there is probable cause for a charge of obstruction of justice." He tapped his gavel. "Now, on the matter of bail, firstly, in consideration of Mr. Crane's previous harm to this community five years ago, both by recruiting its citizens into a tax evasion scheme and proximately causing the serious injury of both Deputy Pelton and Victor Sobstak, a citizen; and secondly, in light of his interference in last fall's election; and lastly taking note of the fact that his current protest has already resulted in the shooting of Sheriff Ordrew and the killing of six cattle belonging to Mr. Sobstak again, I am denying bail on the grounds that he poses a danger to our community, pursuant to *United States versus Salerno*. Trial is set for—" He thumbed his calendar. "July 18, nine a.m. Pre-trial motions will be entertained on July fifth at the same time. We stand adjourned." He banged his gavel.

Anwalt jumped up so fast his chair fell backwards. "Wait, Your Honor! I object—"

Flure glared down at him. "We're done, Counsel. In the words of your client's colleagues, you can shove your objection up the location of your choice."

3

The teams deployed at the south access road. Andi approached the media area and found Katie. "Why don't you and Jay head up and set up your gear. We're delivering water and toilets, so you'll want to cover it." She sent two deputies up with Katie and Jay.

Andi told the other reporters what was going on and answered questions while they waited for the delivery trucks, which had been ordered for three-thirty. They arrived on time and Andi ended the presser.

After the department's pickup left, carrying the two deputies and the reporters, Andi joined Ben and Greg Haney and they waved the drivers out. The portable toilets were driven by a thin young guy in his twenties with long blond hair, the water tanker by a fat, bandy-legged teamster with a ragged gray beard, who introduced himself as Tony. Andi pointed at Ben, said, "Deputy Stewart will ride up with you, Tony. Follow his instructions and you'll be safe. Got it?"

"Yes, ma'am," the older driver said.

Andi cringed. *Ma'am?*

The young guy said, "Is it, uh, dangerous?"

Andi nodded. "They're armed. Armed men are dangerous. Just do what we tell you and you'll be safe."

She turned back to Tony. Magnus Anderssen's brand was blazoned on the tanker's doors. "You'll be leaving the truck up there. Is someone coming to pick you up, or do you need a ride back to the Double-A?"

Tony shook his head. "Naw, my buddy's on the way. He stopped in town to pick up a six-pack for the ride down to the ranch."

Andi grinned. "Drinking while driving's illegal."

Tony grinned back. "I ain't driving."

"Right answer," she said, then clapped her hands. "Let's do this."

4

Of course, nothing followed the plan.

The usual group—Andi, Greg, Joe, Ben, Ed—was backed up by four deputies who'd driven up behind them. The deputies waited at the SUV. Carl Jenkins was standing beside a different man in Crane's place. Unlike Carl, who was rangy and thin, this man was round and short, with a thatch of white hair and beard, a ruddy face, and a big belly. He smiled broadly. Andi thought, *Santa.* He introduced himself. "Jack Dolan, Sheriff. Pleased to meet you."

"Good to meet you, Jack." They shook hands. "This is Ed Northrup."

Ed shook Dolan's hand. "You're one of the camp's leaders?"

"Just helping out," Dolan laughed. "From Burr Ridge, Illinois." He put an "s" at the end of the state's name.

Andi smiled. "Small world. I'm from Chicago. Worked for Cook County Sheriff for twenty years before I came out here. I know Burr Ridge well."

"Wow, small world, no? Quieter out here, I'll bet."

"Usually, unless a campful of protesters arrives to enjoy our solitude."

Jack Dolan laughed, a genuine guffaw, but then sobered. "Jeez, 'scuse my manners. How's your sheriff?"

"Critical. They medevacked him to Missoula. I called just before we came up here. They're taking it 'hour-by-hour.'"

"Okay, then. What are you charging Stenborg with?"

"At the moment, attempted murder, but that changes, of course, if the sheriff doesn't make it."

Dolan nodded. "I 'spose. Well, you heard it here, it *won't* happen again, unless you people set the ball rolling."

"That makes things easier," she said, relaxing slightly. But she told herself, *Don't trust him*. She glanced at the crowd of men gathered behind Dolan and Jenkins. She spoke louder. "We're bringing water and toilets, as we promised. But before the trucks arrive, the SWAT teams are going to come up to keep everyone safe."

Angry murmurs spread through the camp. Jack Dolan's eyes turned dark. "Whoa, there, Andi. We never agreed to that. I won't—"

Ed interrupted him. "Jack, we don't know you and you don't know us. We understand that asking you to trust us poses a risk to you. But after the cattle and the shootings, we need to ensure nothing hostile happens, and that poses a risk for us too. If you're going to get the water and toilets you need, we have to trust each other for the next hour or so."

"Holy cow," Jack said. "We talk five minutes and already we've got a standoff." He looked away. "All right, bring the Fibbies up." Again, angry murmurs from behind. Jack swirled to face the men. "Wait a minute, here! You want water? You want to stop shitting in a hole in the ground?" The crowd quieted.

"The agents will be here shortly," Andi said. "We're keeping our promise."

"Gotcha, but far as that goes," Dolan said, "we've been thirsty, waiting for you to keep your promise."

"Our promise didn't anticipate attempted murder," she said. "We're here now, Jack. We'll deliver the water and toilets and tomorrow we'll resume negotiations for—"

The distant rumbling whine of the APCs came from below the ridge. Andi saw the protesters' hands tighten on their weapons.

Carl Jenkins said. "We can't see resuming negotiations until the Rev returns."

The Rev? "Carl, you and Jack may not know any of this, but Loyd Crane has a long history of causing trouble here in the valley." She watched their faces. Carl looked suspicious; Jack's eyes narrowed. "He's responsible for the death of one man and the serious wounding of two other people five years ago." She didn't mention that she was one of the wounded. "He was responsible for what may have been criminal interference in Sheriff Ordrew's election, as well as the rape of a young man here many years ago."

Carl Jenkins's face reddened. "You expect us to believe that? Reverend Crane's—"

She interrupted fast, wanting to finish this before the APCs, which were louder and closer, arrived. "I'm not asking you to believe it, Carl. My point is, Judge Flure remembered it, and he denied bail. Crane's not coming back before his trial is over and he finishes his sentence when he's found guilty." Andi paused, letting that sink in. "So, I think you might want to reconsider talking with us before you're trapped up here in the snow."

Jack looked at Carl, then nodded. "We'll discuss it. Come back tomorrow morning for our decision."

Just as he spoke, the first APC rumbled up over the ridge and onto the grass. It moved to the right of the access road, and the second APC followed and drove to the left. Jay Gersich was filming everything.

5

Andi turned and watched the SWAT teams climb quickly out of both vehicles and form a long line. Their handguns were holstered, their rifles slung on their chests.

When they were in place, she turned back to Jack and Carl. "Okay, the water should be here in a few minutes. I need to ask that your men get in their vehicles while we put everything in place."

Carl frowned. Jack said, "That doesn't happen, Andi."

"Because?"

Dolan pointed at the two APCs and the SWAT agents. "We climb in our vehicles, what's to stop you from ordering those soldiers into our camp?"

"I get that. Not a surplus of trust on either side, is there?"

Jack grinned a Santa grin. "You got that right."

Andi wondered if his apparent good humor was an act. And if he had displaced Jenkins. She turned to Jenkins, "Are you in charge, Carl?"

Dolan spoke first. "Carl and I are sharing the leadership. Look, we need food, Sheriff. Water by itself is unacceptable."

"So, you want me to send the trucks back down?"

"Of course I don't." His smile dimmed. "But I need assurance that you'll provide food."

Sounds like he's taking charge. "Men can live without food far longer than they can without water," she said. "We may be willing at a later point to talk about food, but that requires that you folks show good faith."

His smile vanished. "For cryin' out loud, without you assuring us we'll have food, could be I can't stop my men from taking things into their own hands. And we outnumber you, right?"

She waited a moment, annoyed at the distraction, then nodded to Ed, who said, "Threats don't show good faith, Jack. We're here to deliver water and toilets, not to negotiate about food. That may come later, if you cooperate now. Without a credible guarantee that the civilian drivers of the trucks will not be harmed, the sheriff will send the trucks down and close the access roads."

Dolan said nothing. Jenkins looked miserable.

After a minute, Andi said, "I'm leaving, Jack. With the trucks."

Finally, Dolan nodded. His smile returned, though it was not as bright. "Well, then. I'll get the men in their vehicles." He paused. "But Carl and I and eight other men stay out here with you."

She nodded. *To take hostages if anything goes wrong,* she thought.

Dolan said to Quinn. "Pick seven men and bring them to me." He turned and faced the crowd. "Except for the men Quinn selects, the rest of you get in your vehicles. They won't deliver until the yard is clear. Jenkins and I, and Quinn and the seven others he selects will keep an eye on things."

The men were angry, but no one shouted as they had before. *Too thirsty*, she guessed.

Still no one moved. Jack stepped closer to the men, but Andi overheard. "Look. She's taking the water and toilets back down if we don't cooperate."

A man in front, AK-47 cradled in his arm, yelled, "We ain't here to cooperate, damn it. We're here to take back this stolen land from the guv'mint."

Dolan raised his hand. "Hold your horses, Lester. There won't be any taking back the land if we don't get water damn soon. Get in your vehicles."

Another man said, "Don't push us around, Dolan. The Rev may have left you in charge, but we're not all happy about that."

Andi thought, *Good sign: dissension*. She recognized the dissenter — a rancher from the northwest corner of the valley, Jenkins's territory. Alan something. Jack Dolan was quiet a moment, then shrugged. He surprised Andi — and, she supposed, everyone — by laughing.

"Fine with me, guys. It's not me turning the water and toilets around and driving 'em back down the hill. You've got a choice: Water and toilets, or your pride."

Andi watched fury gather in the men, like a storm cloud darkening.

No one budged.

Andi turned away, faced her team. To Haney and Mitchell, she whispered, "Tell your men to be ready for trouble. I'm going to send the trucks away."

Greg grimaced, then spoke into the radio on his shoulder. Behind them, the FBI troops shifted slightly.

She turned to Ed. "Back in the SUV." Behind her, Andi heard Jack Dolan say her name. She stiffened. *My guys can see Dolan. He isn't going to shoot me.* Holding her breath, she turned to face him.

6

"Give us a few minutes?" Jack Dolan asked.

Looking sincere, she thought. "Five minutes. Then we leave." She looked at her watch.

Jack nodded and turned toward his men. "Let's talk." He pointed to the far side of the camp, and said, loud enough that it carried to Andi's team, "Privately."

The men gathered, angrily, around him. Speakers kept their voices low. Andi said to Greg, "I wouldn't want to be Dolan right about now."

He nodded. "I don't much like being *us* right now, either."

After no more than two minutes, the men in the camp began to move toward their vehicles. Dolan came back to the entry and beckoned Andi close. Though he smiled, Andi saw tension around his eyes. "See there? Cooperation," he said. "Water trumps talk."

The water tanker lumbered onto the ridge as he spoke, and moved in between the APCs. The truck carrying the toilets followed a moment later. When the inner yard was empty except for Jack Dolan's ten, Andi beckoned her deputies over and they all walked to the Double-A tanker. Tony's window was open, his arm hanging outside the door. "Where you want me to put 'er?"

She pointed at Crane's RV inside the ring. "Park parallel to that RV in the center."

He craned his neck, looked where she'd pointed, nodded. "No problem."

She introduced him to four deputies who'd joined them. "They'll go inside with you and make sure you're safe. Two men from the camp will come over and you can show them how to get water. Then you and the deputies walk straight out. Take the tanker's keys with you. Don't talk, don't linger. Got that?"

"Hell, Sheriff, I got beer waiting at the foot of the hill. I won't be but five, six minutes, unless those goons can't understand how to turn a spigot." He climbed into the cab. "Let's do 'er."

Jack Dolan and Carl Jenkins waited at the entry, with the two guards and six other men behind them. Dolan refused to step aside.

"No way, José. I can't allow your deputies inside the camp." Two of the protesters caressed their rifles.

Shit! "And I won't leave my driver unprotected." She thought for a moment. "All right." She pointed to the right side of the entry portal. "We'll leave the tanker out here, beside the entry."

Jenkins shook his head. "That leaves us vulnerable when we come outside for water."

Andi bit back her annoyance. "Vulnerable to whom, Carl?"

"To whoever the hell is hiding below the ridge, spying on us."

"Unless we're up here talking to you, no one waits below the ridge. We did that when we intended to arrest Stenborg, because we expected resistance. They stay on the valley floor, unless we need them for security. You want the water or not?"

Jack wiped the sweat from his forehead. "I 'spose. And the toilets go behind the camp?"

"Yes." She looked at her watch. "They should be unloaded and ready in twenty minutes. The SWAT teams will stay up here with the delivery truck, for the driver's and the media's safety, and they'll accompany them both down. Katie and Jay will do a presser with you during the wait." She paused. "We'll be back tomorrow morning. Be ready to resume negotiations."

• • •

On the way down, Greg said to her, "You're assuming they'll agree to resume negotiating."

"Damn right I am. And the first thing they'll demand is food."

"Which you said you won't negotiate."

"Not till I can see Santa's ribs."

7

When the SWAT teams, the media pool, and the two deputies left Freedom Camp, Carl Jenkins touched Jack Dolan's arm as the older man turned to go back into camp. All the men had come out for the press conference, and Dolan had taken all the questions. Jenkins said, "We have to talk about authority, Jack. The Rev left me and you *both* in charge, but you're doing all the talking."

Dolan pulled his arm away and looked at Jenkins intently. "Jeez, did you I say anything about you not being in charge, Carl? The one in charge doesn't have to be the spokesman, too. Think division of labor."

"When the Rev was here, he was in charge and he was the spokesman." Jenkins's voice rose.

"Carl, settle down. You've never taken part in an action like this, and I've been involved in the Reverend's projects for a long time. I know how to stay on message and forward the mission." He looked at a small group of men who were watching curiously. Most of the others had gone back to their lawn chairs. "My men and I aren't rookies at this business, so just step back and let me do what I do best."

Jenkins's face reddened. "And me and the valley men are *rookies*? That what you're saying?"

Dolan snapped, "Hey, there, Carl, it's a figure of speech." He started to move away. "Come into the Rev's RV. We have to discuss the negotiations."

"We haven't decided whether we'll be negotiating."

"Well then, Carl, I have. If you want to be in charge, you'll just have to go along to get along. Come." He started walking toward the RV. To the group watching them, Dolan said, "We're resuming negotiations in the morning. And our goal is to give the media something to write about."

8

Andi pulled into the yard at about nine-forty. The sun had set, and the sparse western clouds glowed with inner light. Ed hardly noticed, though he was staring up at them. Instead, he was mulling over how upset Lynn Monroe's announcement had left him. It surprised him that he was still reacting, after, what? Five days? What was it she'd said? *I can't see much chance I'll change my mind.* He sighed. Grace's proposal had given him reason to hope, but he wondered how Lynn would take it. More the point, how Rachel would.

Andi came up to the porch, looking weary. "Hi, pal," she said.

"Hey," he said back.

"What's wrong? You look a million miles away."

"Nothing. Just a little problem. Nothing to worry about."

"Damn it, Ed, tell me. I've got too much going on and if you've got something on your mind, tell me so I can get past it."

"So you can *get past it*? What the hell's that mean?"

Grace's PV drove into the yard and parked, too fast, as usual. Little mounds of gravel fronted her parking space. "We can finish this later."

Ed didn't answer. *No need to bark at her.*

Grace bounced across the yard and up the steps. She grinned. "Operation Square Meal is cruising! Today, lunch was Lane's burgers and dinner was angel-hair pasta and shrimp. Those agents are saying it's the best food they've ever had on a job."

Ed pushed past his irritation with Andi. "What's on the menu in the morning?"

"The usual: cereal, toast, coffee, fruit, that kind of stuff. It's all self-serve. Maggie Sobstak and one of the church ladies set it up and tear it down, but the guys serve themselves." Grace leaned down and gave Andi a hug. "Thanks for giving me this job, Andi." She looked at Andi, then at Ed. "What? You two look mad."

"No problem. Just talking," Ed said. He couldn't hide the strain in his voice.

Grace lifted her eyebrows. "If you say so." She turned to go inside.

Andi said, "What time does breakfast happen?"

"Same time every day, six-thirty. Agent Haney wants it to be done by seven-thirty when he gets back from your meeting in town."

"Good. We have to go up to the camp at eight-thirty." She turned to Ed. "You're going with us, right? We're hoping to find out if they'll resume negotiations."

His annoyance flared again. He'd scheduled his first patient at ten-thirty, but she was taking him for granted. "Could you have given me a bit more notice? I didn't know you were planning to start again."

Why am I being petty about it? He thought. *I organized my appointments for the negotiations.*

Andi was quiet. After a moment, she said, "Could be you negotiating isn't going to work. I'll see if Ben can do it."

"Damn it, Andi, I'm available. But don't just take me for granted, okay?"

"Well, sorry," she said. Ed heard, *Get over it.*

Grace said, "You sure you two aren't fighting?"

He looked at her. "I guess we're close to it. Lots of stress."

"Not quite a honeymoon, eh?"

"Huh." *That too.*

Grace said, "How about you two kiss and make up."

Both Ed and Andi looked hard at her. "All right, all right," she held up her hands. "Parents to Grace: M.Y.O.B."

Ed forced a chuckle, trying to ease the tension. After Grace had gone inside, he said to Andi, "You're right, I'm bothered about something and I've tried to tell you, but you're so absorbed in this occupation, I can't get in." He paused. "Sorry, that sounds whiny."

"Tell me."

He told her about Lynn's refusal to help.

"When did she tell you?"

"Five days ago."

"Why didn't you tell me?"

"I tried. It was obvious you were focused on the occupation. I didn't want to add—"

"Don't patronize me, Ed. I'm a big girl. What's being married good for if you won't let me support you?"

For a moment, he looked at her, figuring how to answer that. Decided on humor. "Regular sex?"

She shook her head. "Jesus," she muttered, and went inside.

"Wrong answer," he whispered to himself.

CHAPTER ELEVEN — TUESDAY

1

Quinn and the other guard, whom Andi, to herself, called Nameless, met the team at the usual place. Eight-thirty in the morning and the temp down in the valley topped ninety already. Here, higher, it hung in the low eighties. Greg and Joe stood behind Andi, Ed, and Ben. Everyone was sweating. Andi glanced into the inner yard of the camp, saw piles of garbage and beer cans scattered around. *Looks like they didn't forget beer*, she thought. "We're here to learn what you folks decided about negotiations. Can I speak with Carl and Jack, please?"

Without answering, Nameless turned and slow-walked to the RV. He knocked three times on the wall, and returned to his place.

Andi smiled. "Thank you. Efficient communication device." She made a mental note: *Is that a clue they don't have electronics?*

Quinn scowled.

In a moment Dolan and Jenkins came around the RV and joined them. Dolan started, "Good morning, Andi, Doctor." He looked at Ben Stewart. "Well, you I've seen, but we haven't met."

Ben said, "Deputy Ben Stewart." Ben offered his hand, and Dolan shook it. Ben turned to Carl. "Mornin', bud." Jenkins nodded, then looked away.

Andi waited a moment, then asked, "So, what's the verdict?"

Dolan started to speak, but Jenkins broke in. "Before that, the men and I want to thank you for the water and privies."

"You're welcome." She studied Jenkins, struck by how miserable he looked. She wondered if he'd already lost weight. "So, are we resuming negotiations?"

Dolan nodded. "Our decision is to talk. First, about food, and then about you taking over these lands for the people."

Ed held up his hand. "We do have questions about the food issue, but we're only willing to negotiate at this time about a peaceful end to this occupation. If that goes well, we will consider immunity to trespassing charges. Nothing else at this time."

Dolan shook his head. "Holy cow, sheriff, that's unsatisfactory. I—"

Jenkins again interrupted. "Jack, he said, 'Nothing else at *this* time.'" He spoke to Andi. "So, you may be willing to talk food later?" Dolan glared at Carl, not looking like a jolly old Santa.

"Ed's still our negotiator," she said. "But yes, I said that." She turned to Ed. "Go on."

He nodded at Dolan. "One of our questions is, how many more days' food do you have?"

Andi knew this would be a tough question for Dolan to answer without risking the loss of whatever command he had of the occupation, but they'd decided it was important to get it answered.

Jack shook his head. "You don't need to know that."

"Frankly, I do. You keep demanding we talk about food, but you won't tell us anything about your food situation. Answer my question, please."

Jenkins reddened. He interrupted. "They have enough for two more days. Maybe three, but they're already rationing." Behind him, men had moved close to listen, and now were murmuring angrily.

"Shut up, Jenkins!" one called out. "Don't tell them shit. They'll use it against us."

Andi wondered why Carl had phrased it that way: *They* have enough for two days. *They're* already rationing. Who is *they*?

Ed caught that too. "Who's the 'they' who have enough for two or three more days, Carl?"

"Well now, wait just a damn minute," Dolan said. "We're not discussing that. If you won't commit to providing food, we're not about to tell you anything."

"Adult men," Ed said, "can go thirty days without food if they have plenty of water. You'll have plenty of water. And thirty days is enough time to end this without anyone else getting hurt and without any of you going to jail."

"You're going to starve us." Dolan said, his ruddy cheeks ruddier. He turned to Jay's camera. "Did you get that on tape? The sheriff intends to—"

"Ain't what he said," said Ben. "Drop the phony outrage and pay attention."

Ed said, "If there is no further violence from your camp, and if we aren't able to end this sooner, after four weeks we'll consider supplying basic rations."

Jack crinkled his nose. "'Basic rations'? What the hell's that mean?"

"Same food as troops in combat zones get when they're not on base. MREs and water."

Dolan looked straight at the camera. "There you heard it: Four weeks she plans to starve us." Dolan turned to Andi. "And if we reject your inhumane terms, what happens?"

Andi nodded to Ed. He said, "We talk about an end to this protest. And if you won't do that, we'll go down, the FBI will seal off this ridge until you *are* ready to leave, either one at a time or as a group."

The angry murmuring escalated.

One protester yelled, "You can't arrest us all, not if we come down in force."

In her mind's eye, Andi pictured them coming down on foot, rifles firing. Or driving down, all twenty-six vehicles in a long and lethal line. She shivered. *Should we back down? Are we going to provoke them into violence?*

Ed said, "The sheriff has committed to granting immunity from the trespassing charge when anyone leaves. That stands."

She stepped closer to Dolan. Quietly, she said "Jack, I gather you've taken over as the spokesman, and—" She glanced at Carl Jenkins, who looked away, though his eyes were angry. "And the leader. Am I right?"

Dolan nodded.

"Talk sense into your men. We'll be back at five-thirty this afternoon for your decision."

She didn't wait for an answer. Turning, she nodded to Katie and Jay. "Presser time."

2

After the press conference, men, still armed, grabbed lawn chairs and gathered in a wide circle in the shade of the Reverend Crane's big RV. That shade made the heat almost bearable, but even a thousand feet above the valley floor, the air was too warm, thick with humidity. The forest that climbed up the mountain behind the camp was silent. Even the birds seemed worn down by the heat. Dolan, standing with Jenkins in front of the circle of protesters, watched the eleven men from Monastery Valley clustering off to the side. He whispered to Jenkins, "Your friends aren't joining the group. Something I should know?"

Jenkins nodded. "They don't like how you pushed me aside. The Rev left me—"

"—in charge." Dolan moved in front of Jenkins, his back to the gathering men. "Yes, I know." His whisper was fierce. "Face facts, Carl, you don't have the experience, and you and your friends are outnumbered thirty to twelve. Don't be a fool."

Jenkins, equally intense, whispered back. "If Reverend Crane were here, he'd—"

"Oh for cryin' out loud. He's not here and he's not coming back. Come on, either you and I work together or this fucking camp goes up in flames." He turned and faced the men, leaving Jenkins in his shadow. Jenkins stepped to the side, then walked away. He made his way around the circle of lawn chairs and stood behind the men from Monastery Valley, seething.

Dolan addressed everyone. "The sheriff has left us two alternatives. I—"

A man stood. "Dolan, we've been through this before. She's going to starve us till we're weak, then she and her FBI killers are going to take us out. Now, we're armed and we're real dangerous. I say we act now."

Dolan sighed. "Hang on, there. Act how, Roger? Walk down shooting? They've got armor, we don't. We'd be target practice. Drive down shooting out the window? All it'd take is for them to disable the first vehicle and we're all trapped on the goddamn road!"

One of the valley ranchers, a tall lanky guy wearing cargo shorts and a muscle shirt, yelled, "Who the hell picked this goddamn trap? Has the Rev lost his mind?"

Suddenly, arguments broke out. An outsider jumped out of his lawn chair and pointed his finger at the guy in the cargo shorts. "You goddamn dare disrespect the Rev, you got me to answer to!"

Dolan shouted, "Whoa Nelly! Knock it off! If we start arguing among ourselves, we'll never get out of here alive. Listen to me." He waited for the arguing to stop. "We gotta discuss this like civilized men. How we gonna win any support if we act like a bunch of pissed-off teenagers?" He glared at the crowd.

One guy raised his hand. "You made your point, Dolan. So, what do *you* propose we do?"

Dolan took a moment, thinking fast. "As for that, if we accept her conditions, we get some traction. We get time. We have the press here to get our message across. If we stall and keep the negotiations stretching out, supporters will be making their way to this place. Then she'll have enemies at her back. I think—"

"What about food?" one of the valley men called out. "Four weeks without food ain't workin' for me."

"It'll be tough. But most of us have gone through shit for the mission." He glanced at Jenkins's men. Their faces were stony. *Tough tomatoes*, he murmured to himself.

Aloud, he said, "So, what do you say? Do we accept her conditions, negotiate for food sooner than four weeks, and drag out the negotiations on ending the occupation? Or do we risk getting ourselves killed or jailed?"

Carl Jenkins spoke. "No. Let's get the hell outta here. The Rev told me everything would be peaceful and that Ordrew would be easy to work with. Well, he was wrong. This place is a trap. I say we leave."

The men from outside the Valley erupted. They leapt out of their chairs, shouting obscenities at Jenkins and the Monastery Valley men, who also jumped to their feet, roaring back. Dolan tried to call out louder, but there were too many voices screaming. He pulled his handgun and fired it in the air. The camp fell silent, men looking around, eyes wide.

"Enough!" he yelled into the quiet. "I won't tolerate fighting among ourselves. Any man who wants to leave Freedom Camp is free. Go. We need no weak people or cowards in our midst, and we will not fight among ourselves!" He holstered his gun and looked hard at Jenkins, challenging him.

Jenkins frowned. "I'm not weak, and I'm not a coward. I want us to include the alternative of ending the occupation in our thinking."

Dolan decided to concede the point; he knew how his men would go. "I agree, Carl. Our discussion *should* include all the alternatives. So, we have three. First, we accept Pelton's conditions, negotiate for a shorter timeframe for food negotiations, and stall on ending the occupation. Second, we refuse her conditions and see what happens. Third, we end the occupation. Discussion?"

"Enough goddamn chatter!" one of the outsiders shouted. "Vote, for Christ's sake."

Dolan said, "Carl, come over here and count the votes with me."

The two men counted the raised hands for each choice. Ending the encampment got eleven hands, all of them the hands of valley men. Refusing the sheriff's conditions got one vote, Quinn's. Dolan announced, "With my vote, accepting Pelton's conditions but stalling the negotiation has thirty votes." He looked at Jenkins. "Your vote?"

Carl Jenkins, looking defeated, said, "End this farce."

Dolan grinned. "Well, that gets you twelve to our thirty. We win."

3

Andi glanced at the big Howard Miller clock on the wall of her office. *Close to noon.* Her intercom line buzzed. Callie said, "Andi, Doc Keeley on line 1."

Andi grimaced. She lifted the receiver and punched the button. "It's Andi, John. How is he?"

"Bad. They raised his body temperature and he didn't regain consciousness. They're becoming more certain he's sustained significant brain damage."

"Oh, man, that's . . ." *Brain damage.* She wished she could lay her head on Ed's shoulder and cry. Or hike into the forest and scream. She said, "What's next?"

"There's a slim chance they're wrong and he'll come out of it. All they can do is keep him alive and see what happens."

"Not hopeful, is it?" The first faint hint of grief, like the scent of ozone before a storm, brushed her heart.

"No, I'm afraid not. I'll stay in touch."

She replaced the receiver and rubbed her eyes, then held her face in her hands.

She waited a few moments, composing her message. *Buying time,* she thought. She punched in Callie's extension. "Callie, I need you to get a message out to all the guys."

Callie didn't respond for a moment. Andi heard her taking a ragged breath. "So. What'd Doc say?"

"Tell them this: 'Andi wants you to know, Brad remains unconscious and his doctors are concerned his cardiac arrests may have caused brain damage. That's all we know at this time.' Got that?"

Callie said, "Writing it down. I'll pass the word. You want me to email or call the other dispatchers?"

"If you don't mind."

"Lord, some days this job ain't nothing but sorrow."

4

After the media pool had set up, Andi, Ed, and Ben Stewart approached the entry to Freedom Camp. Greg and Joe had their backs. Jack Dolan was waiting; Carl Jenkins was standing behind him. "Do you have a decision, Jack?" she asked.

"We voted," he said. "We'll accept your terms for negotiations, on one condition."

How'd I know there'd be a condition? She unclenched her teeth, nodded to Ed.

He said, "Which is?"

"We insist that your four weeks without food be shortened. To one week—to give you time to make the arrangements."

Someone behind him shouted, "No! Food now!"

Andi saw a few of the others nodding. Thinking about yesterday's dissenter, she wondered whether Santa's leadership was in trouble.

When Dolan faced the shouter, Jenkins made eye contact with Andi, lifting his brows. No one else raised his voice. Dolan turned back to Andi, his round red face taut.

She made a quick decision, turned to Ed, and whispered, "Tell him, in two weeks, if there's no more violence, and if they've been negotiating in good faith to end this, I will consider shortening the remaining time."

Ed made that announcement. Dolan's face loosened. She thought he might smile, but he didn't. "Consider this," he said to Ed. "Some of our guys are older, and a few have chronic illnesses. You might be endangering them if you starve us for even two weeks."

Ed smiled. "Playing to the camera, Jack? We're not starving you. If you came here unprepared for a long stay, it's not our fault, and feeding you is not the sheriff's job."

Dolan turned to the camera. "You see what the sheriff is doing. Rather than negotiating humanely, she's playing the hard line, planning to starve us out. If—"

Ed broke in. "Nonsense. We want to negotiate an end to this much sooner than four weeks from now. You put yourself in this situation, so you can't expect us to solve your problem. Let's get serious."

Dolan focused again on the camera. "I'm deadly serious. And so are my men."

"Good," Andi said. "We'll be back tomorrow morning. Eight-thirty. Don't bother asking for food for two weeks. I'm not budging and you'll just burn more calories. As Doctor Northrup said, your chance of getting food sooner than four weeks depends on negotiating in good faith an end to this—" She bit off the nasty word she wanted to call the occupation. "This protest."

She turned toward their vehicles and said, "We're done here."

5

While Dolan harangued Katie Glauber and Jay Gersich about "the criminal theft of Adams County lands by the federal government," Andi and Ben and the FBI agents waited in the department SUV. Ben said, "You held your ground pretty damn good, I'd say."

"What about saying I'd consider shortening to two weeks if they negotiate in good faith and there's no more violence? Too soft? Ad Schaefer thought if I offered it, they'd think I was weak."

"Ain't soft or weak," Ben said. "Just realistic. Ain't gonna be easy watchin' 'em get hungrier. You gave yourself some wiggle room. You already said you'd shorten it up if they negotiate the endgame in good faith. You ain't losin' nothin'."

"How about not charging them with trespassing? *That* too soft?"

"What I'd do. We already got the men to charge."

The radio crackled. Andi keyed the mic. "Pelton here. What's going on?"

Static. Callie's voice: "Dispatch here. Court's going on. Crane's lawyer filed a motion for change of venue, and Dickie Flure scheduled a hearing, nine tomorrow morning."

"Damn. I told the protesters I'd be up here at eight-thirty." She looked over at Ben. "Can you do the court thing for me?"

"Been to that rodeo more'n once. Tell me what you want me to say, and I can say it good as anybody."

She lifted the mic again. "Callie, I've got to be up here. Ben'll be the one going to court. Can you call Irv and inform him?"

"Can Dolly Parton sing country?"

"Okay. Out." Andi replaced the mic. "Let's collect the media and get off this ridge."

CHAPTER TWELVE — WEDNESDAY

1

The morning negotiation session turned out worthless. As she walked back to the pickup with Ed and the FBI agents, she muttered, "That sucked. They say, 'Food,' Ed says, 'No,' they say, 'Food' again, Ed says 'No' again, and we say 'Leave' and they say 'No,' and we do that a half-dozen times and walk away. This could go on till winter."

In the pickup, she jammed the key into the ignition and twisted it hard.

Ed looked at the key. "Break that, you're the one gets to ask Dolan to let us sleep in Crane's RV."

"Screw you," Andi said. But she smiled.

From the back seat, Joe Mitchell said, "Actually, I think it went okay."

Before she turned the car around, Andi looked at him in the rearview and said, "How can you say that?"

"Because they're learning you won't cave," he answered, "and that'll pay off. Their position stinks—hungry, stuck up on that mountainside, bored shitless. I'd bet half of them or more would pay hard cash to avoid arrest and go home, which is just what you're offering."

Ed said, "And there's another thing. Did you notice how angry Carl Jenkins was? He wasn't glaring at us, either. He's pissed at Dolan."

"You're right." Joe said. "I saw it and it's a good thing. For us."

Andi said, "Yep. And it's just a matter of time before it boils over. Hope we don't get burned."

2

Andi and Ben met in the parking lot behind the station and walked to the door together. "How'd your palaver with Dolan go?"

She snorted. "He said *Food*, we said *No*, he said *Food*, we said *End the occupation*, he said *No*. The End." She shook her head. "Joe and Ed think it was good for our side, though."

Ben patted her on the shoulder. "No use worryin' yet, Andi. These things take time."

Andi stopped at the door to the station. Coming from Ben, the words felt, what? Assuring. She nodded. "So, how'd the venue hearing go?"

"Full of surprises. First surprise, Crane's lawyer announces he's now representing Stenborg. Dickie asks him why, and he says in his opinion the first lawyer ain't competent. Dickie has Stenborg brought, swears him in, and asks him. The little squeal says the same exact words. Rehearsed as hell. Then Anwalt requests change of venue for *both* cases. Claims the jury pool here in Jefferson is 'too emotionally invested' to give either defendant a fair trial."

"Could be true. What'd Dickie do?"

"He agreed. They'll be goin' over to Missoula this afternoon. Highway Patrol's movin' 'em."

"What about Crane's bail? Could the Missoula judge set Crane loose?"

"Dickie said his order changin' venue would include askin' the new judge to refuse bail for Crane, and that it'll include details about the damage Crane's done in the valley and the likelihood of his returnin' here if freed. Gotta give Dickie credit, he thought it through."

Andi nodded. "Truth to tell, I'll be glad when Crane's out of the valley."

Ben held open the door. Andi said, "I'm going to stand out here in the sun for a few minutes. I'm hoping the heat will loosen my shoulder muscles. See you in a bit."

"Suit yourself. Sure is damn hot, though."

"And getting hotter."

3

She stood in the parking lot, her back to the sun, letting the sun pour over her and the heat from the asphalt radiate up her back. Her neck and shoulders were tight, a sure sign she felt in over her head. But after two or three minutes in the heat, the muscles began to loosen, as if her shoulders were wrapped in a warm shawl. A *very* warm shawl. After a few more minutes, and sweating freely, she returned to her office and sat at the big desk, looking south down the valley at Mt. Adams and the Coliseum. The sight of the big mountain and its cirque always comforted her. This time, though, the comfort gave way to chills—after the sun, the AC was cold.

Twenty-eight years a cop, she thought. *So why so unsure of myself?*

The answer came instantly: *Twenty-eight years a deputy. No time as a sheriff.*

She was pondering that when the buzz of her intercom interrupted. She swallowed quickly, lifted the receiver, and punched the button. Callie said, "Got a call for you, Doc Keeley, line two."

Her shoulders stiffened again. "I'm on it."

She punched line two. "John? Andi Pelton here."

"Andi, I have very bad news. Sheriff Ordrew died this morning at nine-twenty-four. The cause of death was a third massive cardiac arrest. He never responded."

Dead. Not shot. Dead. She tried to react, to muster something to say. All she found in herself now was empty space. And somewhere in a dark corner of the void, a spark of fury.

4

Immobilized, she sat at the desk for many minutes. Then she began listing things to do. The first thing she wrote was *Find Brad's family*. Not knowing if he had family or relatives chilled her as much as the air conditioning. She realized she had come to know very little about him.

She jotted, *Message the department. Plan the funeral.* Then, *Visit Brad's house, find contact information, will, insurance papers, etc.* That seemed intrusive, but she saw no alternative. *Check legality with Irv Jackson.* Who will bring Brad's body back? Might he have made burial arrangements? *Check with Bayless Funeral Home.* Then, after another moment, *Upgrade Stenborg's charge to murder one.*

Her heart sank. Upgrading the charge would require another hearing. If she didn't get that done this afternoon, before the state police arrived to convey Stenborg to Missoula, she'd have to drive over there—six hours, round trip.

She grabbed the phone and dialed Callie's extension. "Dispatch and Reception."

"Callie, grab a pen, I have a bunch of things I need you to do. First, get on the phone to Judge Flure. Tell him—"

Oh, God. She stopped. *Don't tell her this way.* "Callie, I'm sorry to drop this on you. Bad news." She paused. "Brad died." She waited. After a minute, "Callie?"

"Hold on." Sounds of hard breathing came over the line. After a moment, Callie said, "I never made no effort to like that man." She ended with a quiet cough.

"Yeah, me neither." Andi gave her a moment longer. "Look, there's a lot we need to do. You okay?"

"One more minute." Andi listened to Callie's ragged breaths. Waited. "Now. I'm ready."

"I need you on the phone to Dickie Flure right away. Tell him Sheriff Ordrew has died, we need to up the charge against Stenborg to murder, and I need it done here before he's taken to Missoula. I can't afford the time to go over there for another arraignment."

Callie was silent.

"I'm sorry to tell you this way, Callie."

She heard soft weeping.

"Callie?"

"It ain't you, Andi. Bradley could be three kinds of dick, but ain't nobody deserves to die shot in the back." Andi waited while Callie blew her nose. "Okay, done. I'll call Dickie right away. What else you need?"

"Pull Brad's personnel file. We need to locate next of kin." It hit Andi hard. "I don't even know if he has any. If there's nobody listed in his file, we'll have to go to his house and try to find a will or something."

"None of us knew him, did we?"

"Looks that way." The loneliness of the man seized her. Her eyes burned. "So, call Dickie, get Brad's file, and I'll call Rick Bayless."

Callie said, softly, "Sometimes bad just don't end."

5

As Andi hung up the phone after talking with Rick Bayless at the funeral home, Callie buzzed her. "I got Paddy Malloy on line three for you. He's been waiting five minutes." Paddy was chief of the Adams County Volunteer Fire Department.

"Paddy, Andi Pelton here. Thanks for waiting." Words caught in her throat and she waited a moment. "We just learned Sheriff Ordrew died of his injuries."

"Dear Lord above us, worse news I've not been told in a month o' Sundays. His wounds, then, were extreme?"

"Yeah." She focused. "Sorry to keep you waiting. What can I do for you?"

"Moments ago, it's Judd Norbeck, over in Carlton, I was speakin' with. Ye'll be rememberin' him, their fire chief. It appears they've two small wildfires on the Carlton side of Mt. Adams, behind the Coliseum. He's thinkin' and I'm agreein' they were set by lightning during Friday's dry storm."

Wildfire. Straps of iron seemed to clamp her chest. "How big?"

"For the moment, mere specks on the mountain. Their chopper pilot assures us each covers no more than a few acres. Still, ye know, this God-awful heat could speed them up. Forest's dry as a farmer's throat after the last beer's gone."

Andi, despite her upset over Ordrew's death, smiled; Paddy's brogue and his way with words always tickled her.

He fell silent a moment. "Sure, and there's an old service road nearby, and Judd wants to attack both fires today. The lad's got high hopes of containin' 'em both."

"Let's hope so." She relaxed. "So, we're not involved?"

"Aye. We'll be the shirttail relatives on this one—informed, but uninvited. Carlton County get's this dance."

Through her office window, she again looked south toward the Coliseum, gouged out of Mt. Adams. She couldn't see any smoke, but over the mountain she made out a brown haze against the sky. *Damn.* Down below where the haze seemed thickest was St. Brendan's Monastery. Brad Ordrew's death came back to her, an ache.

Paddy was saying, "You'll forgive me, I misspoke about invitations. Judd wants us to join the incident management team—so we can move swiftly if it comes over the mountain into our county. Are ye up to meetin' tomorrow mornin'?"

"No, I've got a protester meeting. How about I send Ben?"

"A finer choice couldna be made. He's been a stalwart on the IMT for years. It'll do me heart good to work with him again."

Andi thought of all she had to do. "Okay, keep me posted, Paddy. There's a lot on my plate."

"That I will, lass. Sure, ye've a big plate. And my deepest condolences on the death of our departed sheriff. When I learn more about these burns, I'll be callin' ye."

As she hung up, she looked south toward Mt. Adams. Last summer, the wildfire on Hunters' Peak had come down in the night like a necklace of shimmering orange destruction. She shivered, remembering. She could envision this new fire descending on the monastery, voracious, unquenchable.

She shook herself. *One disaster at a time.*

PART THREE

CHAPTER THIRTEEN — SAME DAY

1

Wildfire! Andi straightened her back, swallowed. She scanned the desk. *Where's Ed's picture?* A flash of panic—she needed Ed, or at least his photo, and where was it? Everything personal on the sheriff's desk belonged to Brad. In the uproar since his shooting, she hadn't brought anything other than case files from her cubicle. She hurried to the squad room, grabbed Ed's picture from her desk, and carried it, tight against her chest, back to Brad's office. Put it on the desk.

For a moment, she gazed at his face. *The more shit hits the fan, the gladder I am you're with me, big guy.* After her divorce back in Chicago, she'd believed she'd never be secure with a man again.

Wrong.

2

Outside his camper, Carl Jenkins sat with the eleven other Monastery Valley ranchers. Alan Burns was saying, ". . . is hopeless. These guys are hardliners, totally impractical." As he spoke, one of the other men pointed south. "Is that smoke?"

They all stood, peering into the yellow sky above Mt. Adams. Carl nodded. "Looks like smoke to me. Small fire, but fire."

"Damn it," Alan said. "We gotta get our butts outta here. If we got us a wildfire, Paddy's gonna call us out."

Carl said, "Let me go talk to Jack."

• • •

He was back in ten minutes. "We leaving?" Alan demanded.

"Nope. He said, this is a professional protest movement, and nobody's leaving until we win."

"To hell with that! We ain't professional anything." said another rancher. "This here's a joke, starting with Crane picking this trap to protest in. It's a goddamn free country and if I want to leave, nobody's stopping me."

As he spoke, Jack Dolan sauntered over to their gathering. "Afternoon, boys. Carl tells me you're worried about a fire."

Alan Burns squared off with him. "And he tells us you're saying we can't leave if we want to. Since when—?"

Dolan interrupted him. "Calm down, Alan. What I told Carl was, we're a democracy here. Nobody's voted on whether to let anybody leave. We have to get the sense of the full group."

Jenkins slapped his thigh. "Goddamn it, Jack, you never said that to me."

Dolan shot him a cold look, but then shrugged. "I'm calling a camp meeting in twenty minutes. We'll debate it then, and vote. Majority rules."

• • •

Carl's argument for the valley men's leaving died a fast death. Earl-somebody stood. "We're not here to run home to mama. We're here to rescue stolen lands from the federal government. Until and unless we get the sheriff's pledge to restore the county's ownership of this ridge, we're staying." His look dared the valley men to complain. "And you whiners will stay with us."

Alan Burns yelled, "This valley's our home. There's a fire at the south end. Would you stay if you knew your homes might be in danger?"

Earl-somebody shook his head and addressed Dolan. "I knew it was a mistake to recruit men afraid to do men's work."

The valley men erupted, and suddenly, they were surrounded by outsiders, guns at the ready. Carl yelled, "Stop! No violence!"

Everyone froze.

Jack Dolan said, "Good decision, men. We don't need trouble like that. So, we vote, and the majority will decide."

It was inevitable: Thirty votes for staying, twelve for leaving.

Alan muttered, as he walked to his camper, "*Démocracy* my sweet ass. This is a prison camp."

3

At Freedom Camp, a little after one, Andi's team, less Ben who'd gone to the firefighters' incident management meeting in Carlton, approached Quinn and Nameless. Quinn said, "It's not the time."

She said, "We're here with information you need. Would you please get Carl and Jack?" Quinn narrowed his eyes, then walked to the RV.

While they waited, Andi walked over to the water tanker and peered at the gauge. When she came back to the entry, she said to Greg, "About two thousand gallons left."

He removed his cap and ran his fingers through his curls. "They're using what? About fifty gallons a day per man?"

"We'll have to refill it tomorrow."

Jack Dolan returned with the guard. "Quinn says you have something to tell us?"

"I'll wait for Carl."

"Carl won't be joining us. He and your valley men are sulking because we won't let them leave to go fight some forest fire."

She looked at the men crowding behind Dolan; there were quite a few missing. *How many valley men are up here?* she wondered. "Why won't you let them leave?"

Dolan ignored the question. "So, what's this news? Are you ready to provide us food?"

In turn, she ignored his question. "We're here to inform you of a few things. Before that, I need to know why you won't let them leave. You're playing with legal fire there."

"Are you threatening us, Sheriff?"

"Sharing a fact. False imprisonment's a crime. One I can't ignore."

"And I can't overlook the fact those men are part of an important movement."

Andi decided to let it play out for now; Jenkins and the valley men would figure out how to get home. "We'll deal with the valley men's issue later," she said. "I've got three things to tell you. First, this morning, Judge Flure ordered a change of venue to the U.S. District Court in Missoula; Crane and Stenborg will be transported there later today, and won't be returning."

When she paused, Dolan said, "What did you mean, the reverend isn't returning?"

"I told you. He was denied bail, and that will stand in Missoula." Again, shouts erupted. Dolan turned and lifted his hands. It took a few moments for the men to quiet.

"The next thing, Sheriff Ordrew died this morning, so the charge against Stenborg will be first-degree murder. We call it deliberate homicide in Montana."

This was met with silence. She watched the men in the crowd glancing at one another; a few looked angry, but more looked like they'd heard a threat, or a warning. Andi waited until Dolan asked, "And the third thing?"

She pointed to the water truck. "The tanker contains seventy-two hundred gallons of water, which should last you a week. You're using about twice that much. We'll be coming up tomorrow to pick up the truck and refill it, but after tomorrow, keep your usage down to twenty-five gallons per man per day. Understood?"

Santa's rosy face almost glowed with fury. "Outrageous! Grown men need between eighty and one hundred gallons a day."

"True enough. But they take long showers, which you can't. You don't have to flush toilets or run dishwashers or do laundry or water the lawn. I assume you don't need water for cooking, since you're out of food, so for hydration, washing up, and brushing teeth, twenty-five gallons is plenty. Anything else?"

"You bet there is." He turned toward the camera. "We have learned you are feeding the FBI agents down below, but you still refuse to provide us with food. This is unjust and inhumane. I demand you provide food for Freedom Camp immediately."

Andi grimaced inwardly; he had a point. Was it unjust to withhold food? But she too raised her voice for the camera. "Jack, inhumanity is shooting a man in the back. Inhumanity is refusing water to thirsty men. We're not doing either one. The longer you stretch out this occupation, the harder it's going to be on your people. Don't talk to me about *inhumanity.*" She turned away. "News delivered. Let's go," she said to the team.

Ignoring the renewed shouting from the protesters, the back of her neck tingled. She wondered: Would she hear the shot?

4

On the way back to town, Andi asked the team, "What do you make of Dolan saying the valley men are, what was it, pouting?"

"'Sulking,'" Joe said.

"Seems blatant," Greg added. "The locals want to leave, and the outsiders won't let them. Like you told him, Dolan could be flirting with false imprisonment."

Joe grunted. "So, here's the sixty-four-dollar question: *How* are they keeping them from leaving? *Everybody* up there's armed to the gills. Have the outsiders disarmed the locals?"

"Here's *my* question," Greg said. "What can we do to influence how this goes?"

Andi said, "I decided to let the conflict heat up."

"Sounds to me like it's already plenty hot," Joe said. He chuckled. "Nice choice of words, with this weather."

Andi said, "Well, we need to stay on top of this. It could be real trouble." As she said it, she remembered. "Jesus," she said. "I've almost forgotten about Brad. We've got to tell the community and plan a police funeral, invite Missoula's and Carlton's departments."

No one spoke for a couple of miles. Then Greg said, softly, "Those men up on the mountain, they've got binoculars. So, when they look out and see a line of police cars, lights blazing, driving down Highway 91 for the funeral, what do you imagine they'll think?"

Joe said it first: "That we're starting a war."

5

They walked into the station, and Callie signaled to her. "Andi, just in time. Dickie Flure scheduled the hearing on the murder charge for two-thirty. You've got twenty minutes. And the second thing, Brad has a relative in Oxnard. Name's Brit Ordrew. I'm guessin' she might be a sister." She handed Andi a slip of paper. "Here's her number."

"If we're lucky, she'll know the rest of Brad's family." She returned to her office and closed the door, then sat a moment, collecting her thoughts. She gazed at Ed's picture. Then she dialed.

"Hello?" A woman answered, which relieved Andi—this was no news to leave on voicemail. The woman's voice was gentle, friendly.

"Am I speaking with Brit Ordrew?"

"You are. Who is this?"

"I'm Acting Sheriff Andi Pelton from Adams County, Montana."

Brit Ordrew gasped. "Acting sheriff? My ex-husband is the sheriff in Adams County. Has something happened?"

Andi flinched. *Ex-wife, not sister.* "Yes, I'm afraid so." She took a breath. "Brad died this morning, of wounds received in the line of duty. I'm very sorry."

Silence drifted down the line, then the sound of quiet weeping. Andi waited. Then, "Forgive me, Sheriff. Bradley was a hard man to love, but I still love him."

"Then this is extra tough." Andi looked again at Ed's picture on the desk and felt a surge of tenderness. "I hate calling you like this, but . . . We would've called you when he was shot, but we didn't know, and didn't want to enter his home without permission. Turns out your name was in his personnel file. We thought you might be his sister."

Again, silence from Brit. Andi waited, imagining getting this call about Ed. Finally, Brit said, "Brad believed I was ashamed of him when he was fired from the LAPD, and he hated that my job supported us. He had a lot of pride. I wasn't ashamed of him, but when he got an idea in his head, he held it real tight. We argued a lot, which I chalked up to stress and his perfectionism. I told myself it would pass, but our arguments convinced him I resented him." Brit took in a long, shaky breath. "Do you have plans for a funeral?"

"That's something I wanted to talk with you about, and—"

Callie opened the office door and tapped her wristwatch. Andi glanced at hers. Ten minutes till the Stenborg hearing. "I'm sorry, Ms. Ordrew, I have to get over to court to charge Brad's killer with murder. May I call you when I get back?"

"Yes, please do. And what did you say your name was? I'm sorry, I'm upset."

"No problem. It's Andi Pelton. Please call me Andi."

"Thank you, I will."

As Andi put the phone in its cradle, she heard Brit Ordrew wail.

6

Andi got to court just as Dickie Flure gaveled them into session. "Ready, Prosecutor?"

Attorney Anwalt, standing beside Leroy Stenborg, interrupted. "Your honor, before we begin?"

"What?"

"Your Honor, this is highly unusual. You ordered the change of venue this morning, so this court no longer has jurisdiction."

The judge looked at Irv Jackson, who stood and said, "*Subject matter* jurisdiction requires that the court be empowered to deal with the type of crime in question, and that is the case here. Similarly, *personal* jurisdiction is assured given that Mr. Stenborg shot Sheriff Ordrew in Adams County and until he is handed over to the Highway

Patrol, he is still in Adams County's custody. On both counts, this court retains both forms of jurisdiction."

Judge Flure nodded. "Mr. Anwalt, do you wish to argue further?"

Anwalt shook his head. "No, Your Honor."

"Very well, let's proceed, Mr. Jackson."

Andi was sworn in. Jackson asked her if she had new evidence in the case, and she answered, "Yes. Sheriff Bradley Ordrew died today, at twenty-four minutes after nine this morning, of damage from gunshot wounds received on June eleventh last. In the past two hours, an autopsy has been performed, and the bullets taken from his body have been examined by the Division of Criminal Investigation in Missoula, and found to have been fired from the defendant's rifle, which was confiscated on June eleventh and is in custody as evidence. In addition, fingerprints taken from the rifle match Mr. Stenborg's fingerprints, and no other fingerprints were found on the rifle." She hesitated. "Except FBI agent Greg Haney's, placed there when he retrieved Mr. Stenborg's weapon from the ground."

Irv Jackson said, "Thank you. No further questions, Your Honor."

"Mr. Anwalt?"

"No questions, Your Honor."

"Very well. Mr. Stenborg, please rise."

Stenborg did not move until Anhalt leaned down and whispered something. He stood, glowering.

At that moment, two troopers from the Highway Patrol entered the courtroom and stood at the back.

Judge Flure said, "Leroy Stenborg, in light of the evidence presented here, the charge against you is changed from attempted homicide to deliberate homicide. Your attorney will explain the difference and the penalties for deliberate homicide. You pled not guilty to the charge of attempted homicide. Do you wish to change your plea to this charge of deliberate homicide?"

Stenborg looked at Anwalt, who shook his head. "No, I ain't changin' it. I ain't guilty."

"Very well then. The bailiff will escort you to the holding pen until the Highway Patrol is prepared to take you and Mr. Crane to Missoula."

He tapped his gavel. "We are adjourned."

7

At the station, people spoke in hushed tones, as if Brad Ordrew's body lay in the next room, not on a gurney in the Medical Examiner's lab in Missoula. No one joked. Ben was in Andi's office, working at the long conference table against the north wall. She touched his shoulder, and he looked up at her.

"Workin' on funeral plans. We ain't had but one police funeral, my dad's back in '91. Dickie's hearing go all right?"

She nodded. "Deliberate homicide. Did you call Rick Bayless?"

"Sure did. The ME's ready to release the body, so Rick'll go collect it in the morning."

"I'm going to call Brad's ex-wife and see if there are other family members we need to notify. Then we can talk funeral arrangements."

Ben looked kindly at her for a moment. "Leave the funeral plannin' to me. You got yourself enough on the plate."

The kindness in his voice touched her and she leaned down to embrace him.

"Well," was all he said, and cleared a thickness in his throat.

• • •

"Ms. Ordrew? It's Andi Pelton. How are you doing?"

"Not real good. It's been six years since he left, but it's all comes back. You know, I never really let go."

"Do you, ah, have somebody . . ." The big clock above the conference table ticked louder than she had ever noticed. Outside, she knew the afternoon heat had passed beyond brutal. Clearing her throat made a sound like sorrow. From his work table, Ben looked over at her.

Brit was saying, ". . . somebody close? No. Yeah, sure. Girlfriends. My mom is still living, but she's ninety. And my sister's in Spokane. We talk on the phone. But this is hard." She coughed. "Did Brad ever . . . *mention* me?"

How deep the ache must be inside that question, Andi thought. "Uh, I can't quite say. Not to me, anyway—he and I weren't friends, more like competitive siblings. He might've talked about you with some of the others when he was a deputy. I'll ask around."

"No, please don't. I need to let him go now more than ever. And I couldn't bear knowing he never told anyone about me."

Now Brit was sobbing. Andi's own tears tracked down her cheeks, and she let them. Ben, hunched over his work, glanced at her, his eyes soft. Like Ed, Ben was there for her, she knew. *All I need to do is ask.*

Brit said, "Andi, I'm sorry. You must have your hands full—I saw TV coverage of that occupation and even saw Brad talking to the protesters. He looked angry. Anyway, you don't need a grief-stricken ex-wife crying on your shoulder, so . . ."

Though Brit couldn't see her, Andi shook her head. "To tell the truth, Brit, you're just what I need. I've been letting the stress of the protest twist me up instead of realizing how lucky I am. I'm sitting in Brad's office with our previous sheriff, and my husband and step-daughter are worrying about me, and I'm—" She took a moment to regain her voice. "I'm surrounded by love. You telling me about your love for Brad wakes me up to that."

For a moment, silence. Then, "Thanks for that." Brit paused. "And please, as soon as you know, call me about the funeral. I want to be there."

"Good. I will do that. And I've got a question. Does he have any other family we should notify?"

"Not that I ever met. He had no brothers or sisters, and he'd been estranged from both his parents since college. His father was an LA cop, but he was terrribly abusive, and Brad's mother never protected him. Both parents died in a car crash after a night of drinking. Brad never mentioned any relatives."

"Good God. Your husband lived a tragic life. And none of us knew a thing." How can you work side-by-side with a man and know so little? After a moment, Andi whispered, "Thank you, Brit. Call me anytime. Please." About to end the call, she stopped. "Wait, Brit. This morning when we learned of Brad's death, we all realized nobody here knew anything personal about him. He must've been very lonely here. It breaks my heart to find out you still love him and he never knew it."

"My heart too," Brit Ordrew managed before she began softly weeping again.

CHAPTER FOURTEEN — THURSDAY

1

Up at Freedom Camp next morning, while Xavier Contrerez and Felix Maslow escorted Tony, the driver, from the squad to the water tanker, Andi waited with Ed and Ben to talk with Jack Dolan. Greg and Joe waited at the SUV. Katie Glauber and Jay Gersich were set up, already filming. Jack Dolan arrived alone.

"I'd like Carl to join us, Jack," Andi began. "It's time we talk about ending this."

"Carl's no longer on our leadership team. He and his men staged a mutiny when they lost the vote."

"Vote? Vote on what?"

Dolan smiled. "You're surprised that we're a democratic group?"

"Were you *elected* leader to replace Crane? He appointed you both. That doesn't sound like democracy to me."

Dolan's smile faded. "That was an agreement between Carl and me. We were co-leaders, I was the spokesman. When Carl objected, we put it to a vote. His group lost."

The small group—Andi, her team, and Dolan—moved away from the entry as the big tanker backed up, then, ponderous, it drove around toward the access road. "He'll be back in a couple of hours," she told Dolan as Ben and the deputies took positions behind her and Ed.

"Tell us more," Ed said, "about the vote that Carl and his men lost."

"It's a private matter among the men, Ed. I'm not free to discuss it with you."

Carl Jenkins appeared behind him, flanked by several men familiar to Andi. "I am. Those of us from Monastery Valley wanted to end the occupation, the outsiders didn't, and they outnumber us thirty to twelve. That's the damn 'vote' we lost, and this is no democracy."

Dolan swung around toward Jenkins, his eyes fierce, but he said nothing. Andi watched him finger the grip of the Glock at his hip. She'd already seen that the local men weren't armed.

Ed, his voice easy, said, "Jack, if the valley men leave, you don't have to end your protest, do you?"

Jenkins said, "That's right. Me and my men, we're hungry, we're angry, and we want to go home in case we're needed on that fire." He pointed south, to Mt. Adams, where the smoke was visible. "There's no good reason to keep us here."

Angry mutterings and curses erupted from the men crowded behind Dolan. Andi figured they were the thirty who voted to stay.

This time, Dolan let them shout. Gradually, they quieted. Dolan said, "All of us swore an oath to support one another until we achieve our goal. We have not achieved our goal yet, but that oath was taken in good faith. These men wish to violate it, and that is unacceptable."

Jenkins spit on the ground. "That oath was bullshit. The Rev gave a speech. He told us we were all going to stick together until we win, and made us raise our right hands and swear to support our comrades and everybody did and cheered and nodded and clapped each other on the back. It was a party, not a damn oath."

"It sure as hell was," Dolan shot back. "Nobody had to raise his hand, and the Rev would've let him leave that minute. You gave your word to all of us, Carl, and we expect you to honor it."

Andi interrupted before the argument could go any further. "I have a question, Carl. Why haven't you just left? You're free men."

Jenkins shook his head. "No, we're not. They've made it very clear that if we try to go, there will be bloodshed."

Shouts of "The hell you say!" and "Damn wrong!" and "Liar!" flared like flames in dry thatch.

Again, Jack Dolan didn't silence them. When the shouting ended, he said, "There have been no threats from my men. That's a bald lie."

Andi said, "Obviously, you men disagree." She looked at Dolan. "I need to remind you, Jack, that any threat of force to keep these men in camp could be false imprisonment. That's a crime."

A man jeered. "What're ya gonna do, Sheriff, arrest the whole camp?"

Andi smiled. "That'd be a trick, wouldn't it?" The couple of chuckles surprised her: She hadn't made her comment to ease any tension.

"Carl, you and your men give it a day to work this out." To Jack, she said, "You see to it that there's no threat—or use—of force. Deputies will escort the tanker driver when he returns, and—" she gestured toward her team. "—we'll be back in twenty-four hours. If you guys have talked through to a solution, fine, and if not, anyone who wants to go we'll escort off the mountain. Acceptable?"

Dolan was silent. Jenkins said, "No. We want to go now."

Andi said no. "We need the rest of the day to prepare to escort anyone who wishes to leave. We didn't come prepared for that today."

Jenkins scowled. But Dolan said, "We'll talk."

2

After the sheriff and her team drove down the mountain, Dolan called six men, the ones he knew best and trusted most, which to begin with wasn't a lot, into Crane's RV. "Close the door, Quinn, we gotta talk." He hesitated. What he had to say could turn out risky. "Okay. We're over a barrel. If we continue to threaten Jenkins's people, she'll broadcast an accusation of false imprisonment all over the country. Between Stenborg murdering the sheriff and a false imprisonment charge, our credibility goes out the window."

Quinn made a growling noise, and the others glared, their eyes dark, angry. *At me?* he wondered. "Look, I need ideas. If we're not able to swing the valley men to our side before tomorrow, the sheriff will be up here with twenty-five armored SWAT agents, and we won't stop anybody from leaving."

A bald young man named Carter, his arms and shoulders black with tattoos, said, "Let them go, for God's sake. They're a distraction. You saw it—instead of negotiating for food, the meeting was wasted because Jenkins wouldn't shut up."

Quinn slapped his hand on the wall he'd been leaning against. "We gotta stop talking bullshit. If we let these guys go, how do we keep others from leaving when the hunger gets to them? That girl sheriff'll keep whittling us down till we won't have the firepower we need to protect ourselves from the FBI. I say keep the cowards in camp. They took the oath like the rest of us. Let's get back to what we came for: seizing the federal lands."

Dolan shook his head. "As long as they want to go, they won't fight with us. They'll most likely oppose us. Be realistic. They're a time bomb waiting to go off. With them gone, we'll be united and a lot more effective."

Quinn shook his head. "We've got their weapons," he said, his eyes hard, "and all we've got for security is the vehicle ring. If twelve trucks pull out, our security's blown."

Carter made a sour face. "Security, hell. Think, Quinn. Say we let them move their vehicles outside the camp tonight. When they do, we tighten the ring before the sheriff gets here in the morning. When she comes up, we give the assholes their weapons back and let them go, and the ring's already tight." He looked around the room. "Quinn and Dolan are right about one thing, though. We gotta keep our focus. Holding those twelve men is a huge distraction. We didn't come to play jailer, but to take back this benchland for the county sheriff."

Another man grunted. "Who doesn't want it and won't negotiate with the BLM to get it."

Dolan paused. *Should I tell them?* Quinn started to speak, but Dolan raised his hand. "Wait, Quinn." He decided to end the charade. "Look, guys, there's something you don't know. Reverend Crane realizes that taking back federal lands through county sheriffs won't happen." He held up his hands when all the men in the RV began talking at once.

Quinn's voice rode over them. "What? Then what in the fuck are we doing up here?"

"Come on, settle yourselves down and pay attention. The Rev teaches the Posse's principles, sure—the county sheriff's the only valid constitutional authority, the income tax is illegal, you know the drill. But to take back federal land was never his real plan. His goal was to recruit into our movement as many men here in Monastery Valley as he could. Geez, guys, think about it. You can see that's happened— Jenkins and his friends buy into the core values. If we force the locals to stay now, we'll turn them against us. No way José, we need them to hold steady to the core teachings, so they can be the nucleus for our movement here. The Rev wants to use them to disrupt Adams County."

The silence was charged. A small fellow toward the back of the RV said, "What? Why does the Rev want to disrupt Adams County?"

"Five years ago, he was promoting the movement here. One of the valley men betrayed the Rev to the sheriff, and when they raided a meeting, Pelton shot and killed the Rev's half-brother Michael. He's never forgiven her."

"So, rescuing the land from the BLM hasn't been the real reason we're here? We're here because the Reverend wants revenge?"

"Hold your horses, that's important, but it's a side issue. Think. How'd you develop your loyalty to the Rev?"

The man said nothing, but Quinn spoke. "I'll answer that. I got committed to him when you and me and him traveled to support Cliven Bundy. I've never been prouder of anything I've done and I'm in with the Rev for the long haul."

"Exactly," nodded Dolan. "That's what the Rev wanted for the valley guys, that experience, so they'd be loyal. If we don't let them leave, they'll end this thing mad and distrustful, so we fail the Rev's goal."

Quinn leaned toward Dolan. "You fucked us! We're sitting ducks up here, and for what? To make these valley jokers loyal to Crane? No wonder you're wasting our time talking with that girl sheriff about food. We should be delivering our message a hundred-percent. I say, let's get back to the Posse's real work, damn it. If those weasels don't like it, the hell with 'em."

Dolan shook his head. "Quinn, I'm sorry you feel that way. But I'm in charge here, and we do it the way the Rev wanted. The valley men go." He surveyed the men. "Are you men with me?"

The men looked to Quinn. He was rigid with anger. Everyone could see the muscles in his arms quivering.

Finally, the smaller man in the back said, "I am."

Quinn shook his head. "Hell no."

Two more, almost guiltily, said "Yeah."

The last two said no, and looked at Quinn.

Jack Dolan saw those looks. Narrowed his eyes, locking those two men who'd sided with Quinn into his memory.

3

Grace fine-chopped fresh basil and worried. Beside her, Lane was dicing chicken breasts rubbed with peanut sauce, before sprinkling them with the cilantro chopped by Estrella Contrerez, Xavier's wife, who was grating mozzarella now. They were prepping Lane's signature Thai chicken pizza.

Grace looked at Lane. "Andi told me the protesters know we're bringing food to the FBI, so they're demanding we do the same for them. We don't have enough volunteers for that, do we?"

He stopped dicing. "Is Andi going to do it?"

Grace scooped the chopped basil into a bowl and handed it to Lane. "I asked her. Not yet. But she said if they're showing signs of getting sick, especially the old ones, she'll agree to provide field rations. I'm worried we don't have enough volunteers for that."

Lane smiled. "Field rations—they're called MRE, Meals, Ready-to-Eat—come prepackaged. The police will manage that. They don't want us out there—we'd just be in the way."

"That's a relief. I was getting nervous we couldn't help enough." She rinsed off her knife. "What's next?"

Lane pointed to the pile of red peppers. "Dice those big boys for me. No bigger than a baby's thumb."

Bobby Place came into the kitchen. He still wore his handgun, and he still looked angry. "The truck's ready to go," he said. "We've got the big Yeti all set for the pizzas and the second one with ice for the water bottles. Jen took the silverware and plates and stuff out in our pickup."

"Thanks, Bobby," Grace said, looking up from the pile of peppers. "I'm glad you decided to help us."

He looked away. "I didn't decide. Jen blackmailed me into it." His voice sounded sour.

"I'll bet she did," Grace wiggled her eyebrows at him. "Like, as in no coochie-coo if you don't?"

Bobby's face turned as red as Grace's peppers. "Shut up, Grace. It's none of your damn business."

4

Ad Schaefer crushed his cigarette, twisting his boot vigorously to be sure it was out. Fire in the woods was almost as hateful as the government. He rested on the bole of a limbed ponderosa he'd buck after his second cigarette. The heat, even up this high on the mountain, was a burden. "Kinda ruins a man's break," he muttered.

Behind him, the satellite phone rang in Davey's backpack. He lit his second Camel. A moment later, the crew chief yelled to him, "Ad, the boss's on the phone. For you."

He whispered, "What the hell now?" Weaving through the debris from the morning's work, he took the phone. "Boss, Ad here. What's goin' on?"

Magnus described the conflict between the valley men and the outsiders at Freedom Camp. Ad listened, staring down the valley toward Mt. Adams. He enjoyed watching the Monastery River come down the mountain and run along the east side of the valley for a few miles, before beginning its long westward arc to flow along the foothills of the Monastery Range, just below where they were working.

"What's the question, boss?"

"Her question is, she wants to bring the SWAT team up and extract the men who want to leave. How do you think these people will react to that?"

Ad stared into the distance. Was that a plume of smoke, just south of the Coliseum? Well, not a plume, but like a smudge across the sky. He stared, trying to make it out.

Mack's voice came over the phone: "Ad? You there?"

"Sorry, boss. I'm seein' some smoke down south, Mt. Adams way. Leastways, I'm thinkin' it's smoke. Distractin'." He collected his thoughts. "Groups like these, they fracture," he said. "One bunch gets cold feet or decides the action ain't workin', the other gets pissed and tries to beat 'em back in line. I seen it go violent. Happens fast, like lightning strikes." *Or a wildfire starts.* "This case, though . . ." He thought. "How many Fibbies she got?"

"Thirty-five, I think. Thereabouts."

"And the protesters?"

"Forty-two, now."

"All armed?"

"Heavily."

Ad drew on his Camel, blew smoke and watched it curl and thin out in the breeze, then said, "My money says they got theirselves a plan for defendin' their camp. Don't know these guys, but they'll put up a fight. Sure of that. She brings the Fibbies up to break up their quarrel, she'd best expect serious trouble."

"Any ideas what else she could do?"

"I'm guessin' the outsiders ain't ready to leave—the longer they can talk to reporters, the longer they'll stay. I'd tell her, isolate 'em. At some point, they'll run out of food and water. Don't—"

Magnus interrupted. "They've already run out. She's providing water, but no food."

Ad sat up straighter, impressed. "Whoa. That's hardass. Here's what I'd do. No more talkin' to the press, keep 'em locked up tight and hungry—after a time, they'll break."

"And the locals who want to leave?"

He stretched his back, working the soreness out. "Ain't her problem, and if she's serious about no violence, steppin' into their feud would be her worst move, bar none."

Ad looked south again. Watched the smoke-like smudge a moment. "I'm bettin' we got a fire, boss."

"We do. It's on the south side of Mt. Adams. No threat to us."

Ad studied the smoke. "From your lips to God's ears."

5

Andi ended Magnus's call. Pete was scheduling duty assignments for next week on the computer at Andi's desk.

He looked at her. "What'd Mack say?"

"Ad Schaefer says we should cut off the protesters' contact with the media, but stay out of what's going on between the valley men and the others."

"That could bite us. The protesters will yell about their First Amendment rights, and we'll look bad."

She nodded. "Yeah, but without access to media, who'll they yell it to?"

"Hell, the *media* will yell, which makes it national news."

"Which hurts us and gives the protesters—*and* the media—a reason to distrust me, without any benefit to us." She flexed her shoulder muscles. "So, we keep the pool media. Not sure I agree with Schaefer about staying out of the conflict, though. We've got to help the valley men if they're being held against their wills."

Callie buzzed Andi from Reception. "Line 1 for you. Paddy Malloy."

She put it on *Speaker* so Pete could listen in. "Hi, Paddy. Pete's with me. How's the fire?"

He told them the fires had not been contained or controlled, and had stopped moving south on Mt. Adams' lower slopes and started moving up the southwest flank toward a saddle just below the Coliseum.

Andi stood at her window, looking south, and could just make out the saddle Paddy described. The tension in her shoulders tightened. St. Brendan's Monastery lay below that saddle. She asked Paddy what he thought the fire might do.

"Ah, sure and it'll be a crawler for a time, but it's caught the edge of the old Cougar fire drainage, so God knows what might happen; I'm told, though, He's mum on the matter. The weather forecast is na helpful. We'll be havin' at least twenty-four hours more of this infernal heat, but the northeast winds are mild as sheep, so we're in hopes it shan't climb far. Still, the direction gives me willies."

"What should we do?"

"For now, prepare, and we're all about that, what with the firelines and hose lays. And pray if ye've a heart for it. The incident management team's on the docket tomorrow mornin' at eight, if ye'll be so kind as to let Ben know. And ye might alert Abbot Timothy. I can't foresee it, but if this devil comes over the mountain, it could take the monastery, God forbid. The monks may need to evacuate."

Instead of goodbye, Paddy said, "Whisper a wee prayer, will ye?"

6

She dialed St. Brendan's and asked for the abbot, then put the phone on *Speaker* for Pete, but he said, "Have to go. Say hi to the abbot for me."

While she waited, she looked again to Mt. Adams, recalling her last trek up to the Coliseum. So many fine memories of that summit, hikes with Ed and Grace, the day they married each other under the soft sky. She wondered whether this new fire could threaten the Coliseum, and her breath caught at the idea.

When Abbot Timothy answered, she told him about the fire and mentioned the possibility of evacuating the monastery. Timothy was silent a moment, then said he doubted that would be necessary, because the monastery was stone. "I'm sorry, Andi. I should've asked about Sheriff Ordrew. How is he?"

Andi grimaced. "Sad to say, he died yesterday. We'll have a funeral next week."

"That's terrible. Please, let me know when it'll be and the brothers and I will come down for it. Will you accept the gift of one of our caskets for his burial?"

"Thank you, Abbot. We will. That's very generous." She remembered the beautiful caskets from St. Brendan's in which Grace buried her mother and Ed buried his patient, Beatrice John.

"It's the least St. Brendan's can do. And we'll keep you and your department in our prayers. It must be hard on all of you."

The memory of Brit Ordrew's wail filled her mind. "If I were Catholic, I'd need absolution for the thoughts I've been having."

"Any priest on earth would grant it."

7

While she was driving to Freedom Camp to oversee the water delivery, Andi brooded over Brit Ordrew's futile love for her ex-husband. *What did I miss in him? He must've been so lonely.* She blinked to clear her vision.

Everything was ready when she got to the FBI camp. The big tanker was waiting between the mess tent and the access road, the SWAT team had already taken the APCs up, and deputies Lanny McAlister and Bud Gilman climbed into the back seat of her squad car, laughing about something.

"Somebody tell a joke?"

Bud laughed again. "Yeah, the driver, Tony. He's a hoot."

"You going to tell me?"

Bud blushed. "Lanny, you tell it. I'm lousy with jokes."

"Nah, you're just afraid of the punch line."

"Tell me! We got water to deliver." She put the squad in gear and started up the rutted access road.

"Sorry, Sheriff, the punch line's kinda embarrassing."

"Hell, I'm a cop, not a nun." But both deputies stayed staring out the window and said nothing, so she let it go. In her rearview, she saw the big tanker pull onto the access road behind her.

• • •

On the ridge, she parked off to the side so the tanker could pass them. The SWAT teams had formed a line from their APCs to where the tanker would park. Andi and the deputies watched Tony maneuver the big truck into place.

She walked over to talk to Jack Dolan. "Water's back. Like we said this morning, you need to keep your use to twenty-five gallons a man per day. We won't be refilling for seven days." She turned and watched Lanny and Bud escorting Tony to the squad car. "Are you resolving the conflict in your camp?"

"I told you we'd talk. I'll tell you tomorrow how that turns out. Meantime, I want to put food on the agenda sooner. I've got some old guys here who are already getting weak, and—"

"Hate to interrupt your speech, Jack, but we're delivering water, not negotiating. We'll be back in the morning. I expect you to resolve the problem."

Quinn muttered, "Bullshit. Utter bullshit."

She ignored him.

Dolan barked, "We *will* resolve that issue. You'll have nothing to do with it."

Despite his harsh words, Andi sensed hesitance in his voice. "Whatever you say. But remember, if Carl's men still want to leave and you won't let them, I'll have to consider a charge of false imprisonment."

Dolan's eyes narrowed. "Are you threatening me now?"

"No. I'm stating a fact, so you know what the stakes are."

"You're not going to arrest me, Andi. We saw the trick you pulled on the Reverend."

She smiled. She'd said she'd consider a *charge*, not an arrest. That could wait.

She turned and walked toward the squad, where Lanny and Bud stood, watching intently. Tony was already in the back seat. She stopped and faced the protesters. "We'll be here at eight-thirty," she called. "And we'll bring the SWAT guys with us to escort Jenkins's men. Just so you know."

She turned back toward her deputies and smiled grimly. "Lanny, up front. Let's go." She greeted the driver. "They say you tell a good joke."

Tony, she noticed, not remembering it from the other time she'd seen him, wasn't just gimpy and fat, he had ears like wings. He shook his head and she could've sworn they flapped. "Uh-uh. Ain't any of my jokes fit for a lady's ears."

8

Before Andi got home, Ed dialed Lynn Monroe's cell phone number. It was time for Grace's plan. Lynn picked up on the first ring.

"Hey, Lynn, it's Ed."

"I saw your name."

Lynn's voice trembled. He almost asked about it, but decided it wasn't his business. "Thanks for answering. I just wanted to know if you'll be coming to work tomorrow. You've got three patients on the book and if you're not coming, I'll have to, uh, make arrangements."

"I wouldn't do that to you, Ed. Or to my clients." Her voice sounded cold.

"Didn't think so. And I've got something I want to run by you. What time will you be getting in?"

"Twelve-thirty. My first client comes at one."

"Okay, I'll be there."

Before he could end the call, her voice quavered. "Ed? Our last conversation, uh, ended badly. I'm sorry. Is that what you want to talk about?"

"Not about the conversation, but about Rachel's problem. I might have some ideas for you both."

"Tell me now?"

"I'd rather do it in person, if you don't mind. I think you'll be interested." *I hope.*

"Oh. Well, okay." She paused. "Yeah, I'll see you tomorrow."

Ed hung up. *This'd better work,* he thought.

CHAPTER FIFTEEN — FRIDAY

1

"Action's starting early," Andi said, leaning on Callie's reception counter, holding keys to a squad.

Callie said, "You going up now?"

Andi nodded, her stomach tight. "Big day up there. We're hoping they'll let our valley men leave without a big hassle, but you never know. Pete'll handle things here. Did you round up the guys I want with me?"

"Did Lincoln give the Gettysburg Address? They're waiting in the SUV."

"Thanks. Ben's going to the fire incident management meeting—"

Callie nodded. "On his way. I saw the smoke driving into work. Already got one call from a nervous citizen this morning. Do you want me to set up another community meeting?"

"Good idea. Talk to Mack. We'll brief everybody on both the protest and the fire."

"You got it. And you stay safe up there, hear?"

2

At the FBI camp, Andi was surprised to see only Katie and Jay in the media tent. She walked over. "Where is everybody?"

"Most've gone home," Katie said. "A few are sleeping in. My station manager's pissed that Jay and I think we should stay, because the coverage is boring. We asked around if anybody from another station might be willing to take over, but nobody volunteered." She sighed. "I'm getting tired of that motel bed, too."

"Not sleeping too well?" Andi patted her arm. "I know how *that* is. But things are going to get interesting this morning."

Katie pulled out her cell phone and tapped the *Record* app. "What's happening?"

"This is on background, okay?"

Katie's face fell. "I identify you as 'a person familiar with the situation' and quote you."

"Right. As you know, the valley men want to leave, and we're hoping the outsiders will let them go this morning."

Katie brightened. "So, Jay and I will get the scoop."

Andi nodded.

"This'll make my station manager happier. When should we get up there?"

"I'd go now. That'll give you plenty of setup time and you can cover the SWAT team arriving. The party starts at eight-thirty."

3

Andi, Ed, and the FBI agents approached the entry. Four deputies waited beside the SUV. The Posse guards were already in position— the arrival of the SWAT team no doubt triggered them. Jack Dolan, looking weary, walked toward them. Andi again looked at his ruddy face, big stomach, and white hair and beard and thought, *What's Santa got in his sack for us this morning?*

Jack said, "Right on time, Andi." He pointed to the SWAT team. "You brought your army."

They'd agreed earlier that Ed would speak for the team. He said, "They're here to escort those who want to leave."

Dolan feigned surprise. "We're not there yet. I think we'll have an answer for you this afternoon." Dolan looked at the deployed deputies and SWAT personnel and grinned. "Sorry I couldn't notify you not to bother with the army, but we have no means of communication."

Andi hid it, but the manipulation angered her; she was glad when Ed spoke sharply. "Baloney, Jack. The media were up here in plenty of time for you to have told them so they could drive back down and we'd have known not to bring the agents. We're looking for some good faith here—and not finding a hell of a lot."

Dolan's face reddened more than usual. "Hold on there, Ed. You're worrying about good faith, and we're worrying about starving." He turned to Andi. "As long as you're here, we want to talk about food for next week."

"Jack, when Ed's with me, he speaks for the sheriff's department," Andi said.

Ed asked, "Do Carl's men still want to leave?"

"They do. We'll come up with a solution today."

"But in the meantime, they're not free to leave?"

Dolan turned to the camera. "It's not a matter of freedom, it's a matter of honor and faithfulness to our cause."

Andi spoke up for the camera, but looked Dolan's square in the face. "Jack Dolan," she said, "I'm charging you with false imprisonment. When the valley men leave, safely, I will consider dropping the charge. Until then, this charge will hang over you, and you'll be subject to arrest when you step outside this camp."

"Fine, fine," Dolan said. "So, let's get past the theatrics and talk about food. I am proposing that you begin providing food for my camp on Monday."

Andi deferred to Ed, who shook his head. "We're not talking food till two weeks—and that's with good faith. Showing good faith is *how* you'll get closer to food."

Andi said, "We'll be back at five this afternoon." She looked at the SWAT team. "All of us."

4

Ben called her cell phone as she was driving back to the station. She handed it to Ed in the passenger seat beside her. Ed chatted with Ben while Andi pulled onto the shoulder and braked. She reached for the phone. Ed said, "Okay, here she is," and handed it to her.

Ben told her that the Carlton firefighters hadn't contained the fires and that they'd merged into one, much larger. He thought it likely that the Missoula Interagency Dispatch Center would upgrade it to a Type 3 incident and send an incident commander and staff, and a handcrew. "We might even get hotshots," he said. Meantime, Paddy Malloy was bringing his volunteer department up to St. Brendan's to get a head start on building a fireline around the monastery. "If I were you . . ." Ben stopped.

"Finish, Ben. If you were me?"

"It's early, but better early than late. I'd call a stage one evacuation for the monks."

"Which means 'Get Ready.'"

Ben grunted. "Yeah. Let's hope we ain't gonna need 'Get set,' and 'Go.'"

5

Andi looked through the messages. Mack's was on top, but she decided to call the abbot first. The monastery voicemail took the call. *Probably at prayers,* she thought. "Abbot, it's Andi. Please call me back, as soon as you can." She left her number, hung up, and dialed Magnus Anderssen.

He was expecting her call. "Andi, Callie said you want another community meeting. I've already called Dick Harrod at the high school. We're on for six."

"Good. Let's make it seven, though; we've got a meeting with the protesters at five, and I might have good news to announce. And we need to include information about the fire. Can you get Paddy Malloy there too?"

"I'll call him. What's the status?"

"Not contained, and the two fires have merged. Hotter conditions tomorrow. It's not moving fast up the Carlton side of Mt. Adams, but it is moving up, and its speed could change if the wind does. Paddy's building a fireline around the monastery, but half his crew is trapped in the protest. I'm wondering if the county can rent your logging team to help his crew."

"No."

Andi wondered if she'd misheard. "Mack, I'm—"

"Andi, I'm saying no to the rent idea. My guys have cleared fire control lines before, they know what they're doing. I don't want the county paying anything."

"God, Mack, what would Adams County do without you?"

Mack was silent. Then, "My father was a selfish jerk who did nothing for anybody without being paid. The valley people did just fine. They'll do fine after I'm gone too."

"Not so sure about that. But thanks for all you do."

6

Andi dialed the monastery number again. This time, a monk answered. "Yes, Sheriff, the abbot got your message. One of the brothers is ill, so he's checking on him in the infirmary."

"Can you get him for me? It's urgent."

"Of course. But it'll take a few minutes."

While she waited, the phone on *Speaker*, she filed through the phone messages again, reprioritizing the order of Callie's stack. She buzzed the desk. "Callie, the community meeting's at seven in the high school auditorium. Notify Bud Groh to get it on the radio, please? The topics will be the protest and the Mt. Adams fire. Then call all my messages back and tell them about the meeting—we can answer their questions there."

"I didn't figure any of them was something you needed to jump on—except Mack's."

"You were right."

The abbot came onto the speaker phone. "Hi, Andi, it's Tim."

"Thanks for taking my call, Tim. I'm announcing a stage-one evacuation order for the monastery. This means you should be collecting whatever you need to take, arrange transportation, that sort of thing. It's called the 'Get Ready' stage. The second stage's 'Get set,' meaning make sure everything's packed up and ready to go in a few minutes. And the third stage is 'Go!' which is obvious. You don't have enough vehicles up there. What will you need?"

"Honestly, Andi, I think we'll be safe in the monastery. It's stone and—"

"You're may be right, Tim. But if you need to evacuate, I want to be sure you and your monks have time to prepare."

The abbot was silent for a moment. "I see your point. So, if we go, we'll need a school bus for the monks and a full-size moving van."

Andi had been jotting a note, but at the moving van, she said, "Really?"

"We have to save the library, the liturgical vessels and vestments, and our caskets."

Andi remembered Grace's visit, years ago, to the reliquary in the abbey chapel. "What about the relics and their containers? They must be worth a fortune."

"Given the circumstances, the living are more important than the dead. If we have time and space, sure, we'll save them. But if not, we take the people, their clothing, liturgical materials, the library, the caskets, and our tools. Whatever we'll need to continue living the monastic life." He fell silent again. "Somewhere."

"Okay. How much time do you think you'll need?"

"Four, five days. Do we have that?"

"At the moment, we do. But the fire could explode if the wind changes."

Another pause. "Well, we'll be praying that it stays away. But we need the bus and the truck here a.s.a.p. The rest is God's business."

7

"Ad, you're at home?"

"It's where you called me, boss," Ad chuckled.

Magnus laughed. "Right. I forgot you don't carry a cell phone. Look, I have a question for you. That fire on Mt. Adams is moving toward the monastery, slowly, but moving. Paddy Malloy's scraping a fireline around St. Brendan's, but half his guys are tied up in the protest. The sheriff's trying to spring them, but no luck so far. She's worried."

"Forget what we do here, boss?" Ad chuckled again. "We're loggers. But I got me a question too."

"What's that?"

"Why call me? Why not call Davey?"

"I called Davey. You didn't want to be involved with the sheriff, so I wanted to give you a chance to stay out of it."

"Ain't doin' it for the sheriff. Doin' it for the monastery." Ad's throat filled. "My ma raised me a Catholic boy, sent me to school with monks. Loved 'em." His voice roughened.

"I didn't know that," Mack said.

Ad smiled to himself. "Nope, you just knew my furious side and my work. Anyway, boss, I'm in. Davey can get us up there in the morning."

"That's right. Thanks, Ad. I appreciate it."

"We'll get the line built, boss. Tell your sheriff not to worry about it."

8

Noon. Lynn Monroe stepped into the waiting room, red-faced, looking drained.

"Hey, Lynn," Ed said. "You look miserable. Hot drive?"

"My AC's on the fritz, so yeah, hotter than hell."

"Oh, man, I can imagine. It's gotta be ninety degrees."

"Ninety-six. Not good for your wildfire." She dropped her briefcase on a chair. "Give me a few minutes in the ladies' to freshen up, then we can talk."

"Go for it," he said. "I'll be in the office."

While he waited, Ed rehearsed. A lot rode on this. If Lynn didn't buy into his idea—well, *Grace's* idea—his plan for working less would go up in smoke. Speaking of which, through his office window, he spotted the smoke haze hovering above Mt. Adams.

Lynn knocked, then came in before Ed could say anything. On Tuesday and Friday afternoons, the office was hers. In fact, during these summer months when Lynn didn't come to the high school, Ed had hoped she might fill in some morning hours, giving him two days off each week. Fishing time.

Except for the occupation. And now the fire. And Rachel's problem.

"So, what's your idea?" Lynn started them off.

"Well, I got this idea from Grace, my daughter." *Plunge right in,* he told himself. "What if Rachel joined our practice?"

"What?!" Her hand touched her mouth. "Ed, I—"

He stopped her. "Why not? You know the research. Therapy is more effective if the patient makes lifestyle changes along with it. I've often wanted to refer patients to a wellness counselor, but there's nobody in the valley. And you've told me her wellness business in Missoula isn't growing, so it's possible she could do better here, with both of us referring folks to her. Suppose Rachel came down with you Tuesdays and Fridays, and we expand our services. You'll have more time together."

He watched her face. At first, she looked shocked. But gradually, her lips, which had gone tight, relaxed. After a moment, she said, "Yeah, more time. But I'm not sure it'd be quality time, hanging out in the Jefferson House."

He nodded. "The Jeff House isn't quite a resort, is it? Look, I've thought about that. I'm willing to rent you a small house. And for fitness training, she'll need a studio, I'm guessing, and the house I'm thinking of would be perfect. It's right on Division Street, and the first floor could be remodeled into a studio, and you guys could live upstairs."

She gasped. Her hands covered her cheeks.

Before she could say no, Ed said, "It'll save your dream and Rachel's. And mine."

"Ed! My coming into your practice was supposed to be your way to work less and someday retire. If you do this, you can't afford to work less!"

"Not so, Lynn. My retirement problem isn't the money, I've got plenty of that. My problem is I work too much and no matter how hard I try to cut back, there's always somebody who needs help. You—and Rachel—are my solution to *that*."

Lynn stared at him.

"What do you think?"

"I'm stunned. Just numb. I don't know *what* to say."

He ignored his fear that she—or Rachel—would say no. "Then don't say anything," he said quickly. "Think it over, discuss it with Rachel, and we can talk more about details when you've decided."

"Ed, I don't need to think it over. I've decided."

His heart fell. "Please, Lynn, give it some time first. I—"

"Ed, I've decided. My answer's yes. All that's left is convincing Rachel to take the plunge."

He jumped out of his chair and pulled her into an embrace. When he could speak, he whispered, "That's the best news I've had this whole damn summer."

9

At five p.m., the team deployed at Freedom Camp. Dolan stood between Quinn and Nameless, arms folded.

Andi nodded to Ed.

"I'm speaking for the Department, Jack. Have you resolved the conflict in your camp?"

Dolan's eyes flashed. "We've got no conflict here. We—"

Ed interrupted. "Pardon my skepticism, Jack. Carl and the men from Monastery Valley want to leave. You and your men have been preventing that. That's a conflict."

"Whoa Nelly, it's not. It means we're negotiating the terms of their leaving. We'll get that done tonight."

Andi broke in. To Ed and her team, she said, "Let's talk."

Gathering again behind the SUV, she said, "Screw this. We're not dancing to his fiddle any more. We go down, and we don't come back until the valley men leave. They can drive down without an escort."

They fleshed out the plan and Ed said, "I'll tell them."

He walked back to where Dolan waited, looking angry at their having walked away. As he approached, he started to speak. Ed held up his hand. "No, Jack, *we're* not talking. *I'm* talking." He made sure Jay was filming, and told Dolan what the team had decided: no negotiations, no media, no discussion of food until all those who wanted to leave were safely gone.

Dolan spoke. "That's outrageous. We're trying to solve—"

"We're done, Jack. Solve it. We'll be back when the valley men come down."

10

Compared to the first community meeting, this one was a church social. Bobby Place and his friends were again in the front row, arms folded, looking tense, but to Andi's relief they wore neither jackets nor weapons. The air conditioning was purring. Murmured conversations drifted up from the seats.

Andi swallowed hard as she approached the podium. She couldn't gauge the mood of the crowd. The hard looks on Bobby's face and those of his buddies unsettled her. She hoped there'd be no replay of his outburst last time. After greeting the crowd, she told them of Sheriff Ordrew's death and that funeral plans would be announced soon. "I'd like us all to stand and give Sheriff Ordrew a moment of silence." Everyone stood, heads bowed.

After the moment of silence, she briefed them on the status of the protest. Murmurs broke out when she described the valley men being kept in camp against their will.

Bobby Place jumped to his feet. "Sheriff, all due respect, you've got all those FBI agents there. Why aren't you forcing the protesters to let our friends go? This is what I warned you about, that those of us who want this over can make that happen."

She let him finish before she spoke. "We've tightened our control of the protest. There will be no more media and no food until our citizens come down. I'm not going to allow any violence from our side. When the valley men have come out safely, the FBI and my deputies will outnumber the protesters, and we will evaluate our strategy then. And not until then."

Bobby started to say more, but Jen took his arm and pulled him back. Andi waited. He resisted for a moment, then fell back into the chair. She breathed more easily and took a few questions, none tough.

Paddy Malloy updated the people about the fire and the pending upgrade to a Type 3 incident. When he finished, Andi called for more volunteers to ferry food up to the monastery for the firefighters and the incident management team that was coming.

Before she'd even finished, people were raising their hands. "Thank you! Please see Callie Martin or call the sheriff's department after we adjourn." She gave out the phone number. "Okay, one last thing. If evacuating the monastery becomes necessary, the monks will need places to stay. They want to stay in the valley, so they can use St. Bernie's for their prayers. St. Bernie's rectory has two bedrooms, and Magnus is making his StreamSide Lodge available, but that's only ten rooms. We have nineteen monks, so if you can see your way to provide a spare bedroom for a monk until this emergency passes, please call the sheriff's department and get your name and phone number on a list."

She turned away, then turned back to the microphone. "Thanks, everybody! Let's go home!"

CHAPTER SIXTEEN - SATURDAY

1

On the bedside table, Andi's cell phone buzzed. Her groan followed Ed's. "What time is it?" she whispered.

"Five-fifty."

"Damn," she muttered, untangling herself from the sheets. "Never good news at five-fifty."

Her screen read *Haney*. "Greg? What's up?"

"Up? All twelve valley protesters. Nobody came down overnight. I'm wondering if you'd want to cancel the team meeting for this morning, since we've got nothing to prepare for."

"Good thinking. I'll call the station and let everybody know."

After she'd called the night dispatcher, she explained the cancelled meeting to Ed. He wrapped his arm around her. "Like a snow day off from school, eh?" He pulled her down onto him.

She relaxed into his embrace. "Yeah. We've got some time."

His hand slid under her T-shirt. "Let's use it well."

. . .

And they *were* using the time well when her cell buzzed again. Insistently.

Stretching for the phone, she muttered, "Fuck!"

Ed said, "Trying."

She read the screen. "It's Ben this time." Hit *Talk*.

Listened.

Ed watched her back. Saw her shoulders slump, then square again. Heard, "Be right in."

"You need to leave? Right *now*?"

She said, "Sorry, man. Fire's upgraded to Type 3, and an incident management team and a hotshot crew are on the way. I gotta get to the office and talk to Ben about what they'll need, then drive up to St. Brendan's and scout sites for the HQ."

Ed shook his head. "Your job just might do what all those years in Catholic school never could."

"What's that?" she asked as she climbed out of bed.

"Make me a monk."

2

Ben met her in the parking lot. "I'll make 'er quick, Andi," Ben said. "Wind's come up overnight, around twenty-five miles an hour, and it's swung around to the east. So, the fire's movin' —"

"Toward the monastery?"

"It ain't square on, yet. But if the wind turns southerly like they're sayin' it might, it'll aim right at St. Brendan's, movin' faster and gettin' bigger." He took off his cap and tousled his hair. "I got me a conference call with Carlton's chief in twenty minutes. You want to come?"

Come? She thought about how close she'd been with Ed; banished the thought. "No, you take it. How soon will the hotshots get here?"

"Ain't been told officially. Paddy 'n me, we figure a day or two, depends where they're comin' from."

"And how fast could the fire get over that saddle?"

"Depends on the wind."

"Lots of depends, eh?"

They talked about what the incident management team and the handcrew would need. "Okay," she said. "You do your call. I'm going to see when Mack's crew is going up to the monastery."

"His boys are drivin' up there as we speak. Paddy's meetin' 'em." Ben looked fondly at her. "Damn smart to call 'em in, girl. You're gonna make a hell of a sheriff."

"If I survive the on-the-job training."

3

When he called her back, Andi updated Abbot Timothy on the fire's movement and the upgrade to Type 3. "Magnus Anderssen's logging crew is going to build a fireline around the monastery. You'll hear them."

"I've already met them." Timothy sighed. "Andi, it grieves my monks to think of leaving."

Andi caught a touch of the abbot's sorrow. "Yeah. It's your home." When Tim didn't answer, she said, "I put in an order for a school bus and a moving van. They should be up there later today. Oh, we're bringing meals up for the crews. They'll be cooked down here, but may we use your kitchen to warm the food up and your dining room to feed them?"

"Absolutely. Monasteries are all about hospitality." He fell silent. "But what if you order an evacuation?"

Andi waited. After a moment, Timothy said, "Andi, I don't believe we need to evacuate. St. Brendan's—"

"I know, Tim, it's stone. Let's take it a day at a time. I'll call with news whenever I have any."

She'd just hung up when Paddy Malloy called. "It's a call with the Missoula Interagency Dispatch Center I've just finished. A gem of an organization, believe you me. An incident management team with a hotshot crew are what we'll be gettin', in forty-eight to seventy-two hours, is the word I'm given."

"Why so long? Ben thought it might be a day."

"It's from California they're drivin'. Should they fly, it'd be ours to provide all the gear and vehicles to carry the team from Missoula. We can't do that. So, it's drivin' that'll take the time."

"We have that much time?"

"I'd wager we do. In this damnable heat, I've no doubt the fire will grow, but it's spread rate shouldn't dismay us. It'll be the forecast for tomorrow that nags at me."

"The wind?"

"Indeed, the wind. And the heat." He sighed. "Ah, but then, tomorrow's another day."

"'Sufficient unto the day . . .' Say, Mack's logging crew needs your guidance on the fireline."

"Indeed, and we've had our meetin', before which I spoke with the crew chief, a fine lad, and him with a good Irish name. They were ready to deploy when I arrived. Next, I'll be briefing the abbot on the goings-on—or would ye prefer to do that?"

Andi sighed. "No, go ahead. I was just talking with him."

"Very good. Be well, lass. Be well."

Hardly a minute later, the intercom buzzed again. "Greg Haney for you, Andi," Gen said. "Line 2."

4

"Andi? Haney here. Look, a minute ago, shots were fired up above."

She stiffened. "How many?"

"A dozen or so. I'm going up in the personnel carrier to investigate."

"Any of our people or the media up there?"

"None."

"Greg, what if they're manipulating us? I said we wouldn't be back until Jenkins's people have left—this could be a way to draw us back." She rubbed her neck near her shoulders.

"Could be," Greg said. "But I can't wait, Andi. If—"

"No, you're right. If somebody's injured, we've got to respond. Yeah, go up—I'll send the EMTs, in case."

"I'd like to call your husband, let him do the talking if they won't talk with me."

She froze. "Ah, man, he's a civilian, and gunfire . . ." She drew in a long breath. "But we need to know what's happened, and you're probably right they'll blow you off. Yeah, give him a call."

She leaned against the wall of her office. "Greg?"

"Yeah?"

"Armor him up."

5

After ending the call, Andi tormented herself. *Have I put Ed in harm's way?* But after a couple minutes of this, she swore at herself and marched out to the front desk. *Worrying's a waste. Time for work.*

At Reception, she told Gen she was heading up to the monastery to look at the space she thought would be best for the IMT's headquarters and to check out the work being done on the fireline. "If Ed or Greg Haney call, patch them through to my cell phone."

As she drove down the valley, the smoke from behind Mt. Adams and the Coliseum drew her attention, a filmy haze smudging the hot, steel-blue sky.

• • •

Four crew cab pickups, another pickup, and a midsize work truck were parked in the small lot between St. Mary's Lake and the monastery, just past the corner of the monastery wall. The front doors of all but the spare pickup bore the Double-A logo. Three men gathered around a map spread atop the hood of one of the pickups. She recognized Paddy Malloy and one of the monks, Father Anselm. The third man was pointing out something on the map. Beyond the three, at the edge of the forest, another group was gassing up chainsaws and pulling Pulaskis out of the truck. Andi wondered which of them was Ad Schaefer.

Paddy saw her coming. "Andi, come see the plan." She joined them. To the man she didn't know, she said, "Hi, I'm Andi Pelton."

"Davey Houlihan, ma'am. I'm Mack's logging crew chief." *Ah. The 'good Irish name.'* Davey held out his hand, and they shook. His grip was firm, his hands rough, and his muscled arms were browned from sun.

"Hi, Father," she said to Anselm. "Thanks for helping with Sheriff Ordrew's funeral."

He smiled. "Pastor Evington and I had a very good conversation about it. It'll be an honor."

"Good," she said, turning to the map. "What've we got?"

Paddy pointed to the closest corner of the monastery wall. "Come. You'll be wantin' to see." They walked over. A narrow path paralleled the granite wall, then headed into the forest.

Paddy said, "You'll not see it for the trees, but Father Anselm informs us that a high granite outcrop meets this wee trail a third of a mile out. He calls it a hogback. The fathers use this trail for prayerful walks, I'm told. It'll be a firebreak when we're done." He led her back to the map on the pickup's hood and jabbed his finger on it. "We'll be anchoring the fireline here at the lake—" Made another jab. "And the other end at the outcrop."

He folded the map. Davey Houlihan had joined his crew and Father Anselm had returned to the monastery. "Davey's lads will work that line, and with my crew I'll be wantin' to wrap a second line around the monastery, for insurance if the blaze jumps the main line out beyond the hoses. It's hoofin' it around the whole monastery I'm off to, for to grasp the distance. Walk with me?"

Before she could respond, her cell phone buzzed in her pocket. The screen said, *Ed.* "Sorry, I've got to take this. Trouble at the protest." She hit *Talk.* As she answered, she walked over and leaned against the monastery wall. *Please let this be Ed, not somebody using his cell phone because he can't.*

6

"Ed! You all right?"

"I'm hot as a spud in the broiler in this body armor, but yeah, I'm all right. There's big trouble in the camp, though. They've had—"

"Did somebody get shot?"

"No. Shots in the air. To signal the start of a coup."

"A *coup?*"

"Yeah. Remember that guard Quinn?"

"Sure. The nastier one."

"Dolan wants Jenkins's guys to leave, and Quinn thinks that's disloyal to Crane. So, he and a bunch rebelled. Their plan wasn't smart—just fanning out to take control of the camp. But Jenkins's men sided with Dolan and now there's a standoff—although Carl's guys are angry at not being allowed to leave."

"Can we get them out?"

"No way I can see."

"And everybody's still armed?"

"As far as we can tell, only the outsiders."

"What's Greg thinking?"

"Let me give him the phone."

Andi shifted her phone to the left hand. Her right ached; she realized she'd been squeezing the phone. Hard. When Haney came on, she said, "Greg, anything we can do?"

"Can't see any way. If we intervene, the civil war turns into a battle with all of them against us. I'm getting my teams ready for an attempted breakout. I called Pete so he could get ready to close the highway so if anybody comes down, they'll have to turn north and leave the valley. If nobody comes down, I suggest we go up tomorrow morning, show force, but do nothing to start a fight."

"Good. I don't want them in town for any reason. Look, I'm up at St. Brendan's." She glanced at her watch. "Can we meet at Magnus's RV around, say, four o'clock?"

"Not necessary, Andi. There's nothing to do but wait and see."

She shifted her phone back to the right hand, which now trembled. She said to Greg, "Sounds like a royal mess."

"Nothing royal about it. More like a snake pit."

7

Andi leaned against the wall, letting the stones' heat relax her shoulders and back, regretting she'd sent Ed up to Freedom Camp and into danger, relieved he hadn't been hurt.

Paddy rounded the corner of the wall. He tilted his head when he saw her. "You look daunted, lass."

She stood away from the wall. "Trouble at the protest." She focused. "How far is it around?"

"Close enough to eleven hundred feet to call it that."

"Do we have time?"

Paddy scratched his neck. "Missin' half me lads? If we're blessed with luck, probably."

"And without luck?"

"Pray the hotshots arrive before the fire does." Paddy lifted his cap and rubbed his curly red hair. "God deliver us, it's hot, even up here." He replaced the cap. "It's a thought I've come to, if the wind freshens much, we'll have perhaps three days before the fire's upon us. That's *perhaps* with a capital P. That's three twelve-hour shifts, plus travel time up and down, which asks a lot of volunteers." He looked at Andi.

"I know. You need your men," she said. "I'll get them out. There's something going on that we don't yet understand, though. It might delay us."

Paddy turned and looked sadly at the monastery. "If me lads don't get out, could be this precious old home burns."

8

As she mounted the stairs to the monastery church, Andi heard a rumble behind her. *God, what now?*

A semi-trailer was turning into the monastery drive. The driver rolled to the gate, then braked and climbed out of the cab.

He was a tall man, red in the face, with blue eyes set wide apart and a long, brown beard. Below his T-shirt sleeves, his left arm was tan, but his right arm was pale. Andi smiled. *Drives with his arm out the window.* He looked down at her and grinned. "Didn't expect a lady at a monastery."

"I'm the acting sheriff, Andi Pelton. We're preparing for a wildfire."

He nodded. "So I'm told. Where you want me to park this beast?"

The abbot came through the gate. Andi made the introductions and Timothy asked him to park length-wise along the wall, with the tail adjacent to the monastery gate. Timothy and Andi watched him maneuver the truck into place.

As the driver climbed out, Andi said to the abbot, "Sonny Carter's bringing the school bus up. You have anyone who can drive a school bus, if you have to leave?"

"Two of my monks drove truck before they joined the order. They're rusty, but they tell me it'll come back."

The driver, who had joined them, laughed. "Jus' like ridin' a bike."

The abbot said to him, "Have you a ride down?"

"Yeah. Guy's on his way." He handed the semi's keys to the abbot. "If you need to get outta here before I can get back, one of your men will have to drive 'er." He said to Andi, "I'm told we'll take the bus driver back down too."

Andi nodded. "That's the plan." She checked her watch. "I've got to get going. We've got a problem at the protest I need to get under control." *As if I can.*

She looked up the mountain, straining to see smoke, but the forest was too thick.

Despite the warm air—up here, it was warm, not the unsparing heat in the valley—she shivered. Dense trees meant dense fuel.

9

At the water tanker, Dolan pushed Quinn from the spigot and took his place. Quinn drew his Glock and leveled it at Dolan's midsection. "Fuck you for that, Dolan. You move a muscle and I'll shoot. Step away from the tanker."

Carl Jenkins froze.

Dolan, his round face redder than ever, said, "You say you'll shoot me if I move, then tell me to move. Which is it?" As he spoke, though, he looked to Jenkins, almost ordering him with his eyes to get involved. Jenkins, appalled, turned away, expecting the shot that would settle the rebellion by killing Dolan. And condemn his men to remaining on the mountain.

As Jenkins looked away, he saw Mt. Adams at the southern end of the valley. Tan smoke rose above the saddle west of the summit. Another valley rancher nudged Jenkins. "Stop them."

Jenkins turned back toward the water truck. "Quinn, put your gun away. We're in enough trouble. Just stow the damn thing."

Quinn turned the weapon Jenkins's way. "You the man who'll make that happen, Carl?"

Jenkins closed his eyes, weary of the whole thing. The occupation, the feuding, the tension. He was hungry, damn hungry, and lonely for his wife. "No, Quinn, I'm not the one who'll make you do anything. I'm just sick of you people and your bullshit."

He turned and walked back inside the ring of vehicles. *Shoot me, asshole*, he thought.

A few of his men joined him at his camper. "Get the others," Jenkins said, his voice low. "We need a plan."

• • •

When his men gathered, Jenkins said, "Things are getting out of control. I want us to leave—tonight. Midnight. Keep everything normal, and be prepared to leave anything that's outside your vehicle when you bed down. At the stroke of midnight, start your vehicles, pull out of the ring, and start down the road."

"Carl," Alan Burns said, "it can't work. The first couple of guys might get away, but while the rest are waiting to get on the road, they'll bottle us up. Maybe kill us."

"I don't think so. But if anybody doesn't want to risk it, then just sit tight while the rest of us go."

"And leave us alone up here?"

Carl closed his eyes again. Quinn was right—he wasn't the man to settle this kind of tension. "It's a personal call, Alan, not mine. It comes down to the risk of leaving versus the risk of staying."

From behind them, a voice—Quinn's—said, "Or the risk of being overheard." As he spoke, fifteen men poured around the vehicle and ringed Jenkins and his eleven, their weapons ready. Quinn barked, "Five of you keep your weapons on them. The rest, disarm them."

The valley men yelled and a couple moved toward Quinn, but were stopped cold when Quinn leveled his weapon at them. "Next man who moves dies."

Something in Jenkins snapped. He stepped forward. "I'm moving, Quinn. Kill me. Then see if you can get out of this valley alive. Monastery Valley folks don't all share the Rev's politics, but we sure as hell take care of one another. Kill me. Every rancher in the valley plus the FBI'll be up here again the minute they hear I'm dead. Sooner or later, the sheriff's coming back, and none of my men will help you, so it'll be the SWAT teams and the sheriff's department against you— and you'll have my guys and Dolan's people at your back. So, go ahead, tough guy. Shoot me."

Quinn looked furious, but he lowered his gun. "No, Carl, I'll do something worse." He said, his voice commanding. "Ten of you, confiscate *all* their weapons. Every one."

Jack Dolan, panting, pushed through the crowd. "What the hell are you doing, Quinn?"

"You're late to the party, Dolan. Your pals are disarmed."

10

Andi was a mile from home, driving under a sunset-bronzed sky, when Paddy Malloy called. She parked on the shoulder and answered.

"True, and in me hand I hold tomorrow's forecast. It's in two evil words: Hotter and windier. Temps in the upper nineties, even that high on the mountain. The demon wind'll be comin' 'round and blowin' southeasterly by dawn, at a steady twenty-five miles an hour, with gusts of thirty-five or more during the afternoon."

"That'll push the fire right up the mountain."

"I'm considerin' that likely." He paused. "Andi, it's more volunteers I'm needin'. Ten of my lads will go up at first light, but I need more."

Andi gathered what he didn't say: *Free my men.* "Paddy, I've got bad news on that front too. A faction of the protesters has taken control of the camp, and they won't let your men leave. We can't risk using force to get them out. We're giving it another day."

She imagined Paddy's face reddening. "Damn it to Hades, Andi! It's me men I'm needin'. I can't save—" He stopped. "I'm sorry, lass.

Not your fault. I just don't know if there's enough time with the crews I've got." He was quiet a moment. "Sure, and that's not your worry."

"I understand, Paddy. We're all in a squeeze. Give me your opinion: If the incident team and the hotshots aren't here and the wind gets bad, can the guys you've got handle the fire if it reaches the monastery?"

"Andi, I wouldna ask it of 'em. Oh, me lads're trained well enough, but wind-blown wildfire is a demon hungerin' for your immortal soul. If we don't get the firelines built, we'll have to let it burn. I'd be wrong to risk anyone getting hurt."

"I get that. Do you think Carlton could spare some men for a few days?"

Paddy didn't answer for a moment. "Sure, and there's a thought, though Judd's hands are full too, I'll wager. I'll phone him to see what he can do. But, pardon my nag, the best is gettin' the lads back."

Andi grimaced. "I know. We've got some ideas how to get them out, but they're all based on assumptions we don't know are true."

Another silence. Then, "Well, then, best of luck with your assumptions. I need me lads."

* * *

Andi turned back onto the highway and drove the rest of the way home, weary. She slumped onto the porch swing beside Ed. Even in the gathering dark, the still-easterly breeze blew hot. She imagined the wind shifting and pushing the fire up the mountain; the image sickened her. Ed patted her thigh. "Glass of wine?"

"You bet. With ice."

Her thigh tingled where he'd touched it. As Ed left for the kitchen and the wine, that tingle spread. When he returned, she said, "One glass. Then I'm getting out of this damn uniform and we're going to pick up where we left off this morning. *Coitus interruptus* leaves a girl . . . uh, interrupted."

He grinned. "I know the cure."

"Hell, everybody knows the cure."

CHAPTER SEVENTEEN — SUNDAY

1

Just after eight in the morning, the SWAT teams and the CIRG agents converged on Freedom Camp. The protesters reacted quickly, gathering with their weapons in front of Loyd Crane's RV. To a man, they looked haggard but angry, unwashed, heat-frayed. Garbage lay in small piles scattered around the camp yard. Quinn and Dolan planted their feet in the entry, legs apart. Dolan held an AK-47, his first time armed. Both men scowled as the SWAT team deployed.

The sheriff's vehicles came last, and Andi got out and surveyed the situation. The crowd inside the ring of vehicles looked smaller to her. Much smaller. Her stomach tightened. *What's going on?* She said to Greg Haney, "I don't see as many people inside. Am I missing something?"

He shook his head, scanning the wider area. "I don't either." He leaned toward Joe on his right. "Joe, count the crowd, please."

They waited. After a moment, Joe said, "Twenty-eight, plus Quinn and Dolan."

"Huh," Andi grunted. "Missing twelve. Anybody see Jenkins?"

No one did.

"Crap. Houston, we have a problem."

2

Quinn spoke first, glancing at Jay's video camera. "Sheriff, you said you wouldn't be back until your people leave Freedom Camp. Is this a sign of what your word is worth?"

"The situation changed. But we haven't been introduced. I'm Andi Pelton." She reached out her hand.

Quinn shook his head. "My name is immaterial, Sheriff. I—"

Dolan said, his voice low, "His name is Quinn."

Quinn glared at him. "Sheriff, you gave us your word you would not come back, yet here you are. I think—"

Andi put up her hand. "Skip it, Quinn. You people fired a weapon or weapons, and we learned that you're seriously, perhaps violently, divided. We've come up to extract the men who live in Monastery Valley, to protect them from whatever violence you people may be contemplating. Please let me speak with Carl Jenkins to arrange for their leaving."

"I don't see your husband. Not letting him negotiate for you?"

Andi allowed a small, cold smile. "This isn't a negotiation, Quinn. I demand to speak to Carl Jenkins and the men from Monastery Valley." At her word, *demand*, she noticed Quinn's lips twitch. She glanced at his holstered Glock.

"Jenkins is under camp arrest. He and his group threatened our unity, and cannot be allowed to disrupt our mission. You may not speak with him."

Jack Dolan spoke to the camera. "Let the record show that I, and twelve men with me, disagree with Mr. Quinn, but I am no longer in control of the camp. I am fully prepared to cooperate with the sheriff's department and welcome their help in pursuing the release of the men from Monastery Valley."

Quinn, swift as a snake, slapped Dolan's face. He staggered back. Andi saw him grip his AK-47 hard, lift it toward Quinn. Swiftly, she said, "Don't, Jack. We'll work this out." A hand print reddened on Dolan's face, and his eyes flared, but he nodded and lowered his rifle.

Andi watched Quinn. He wasn't changing position on the locals leaving, as they'd hoped. "Quinn," she said, "I gave my word that anyone who leaves the camp will not be arrested for trespassing. I also charged Mr. Dolan with false imprisonment, but promised I would drop the charge when the men are released. I'm now charging *you* with false imprisonment of those men. The same conditions apply."

Quinn narrowed his eyes.

Angered him, Andi thought. *Good.*

"I don't give a good goddamn about your charge, Sheriff. Jenkins and his people are not leaving until I release them, and I'm not releasing them. And you guaranteed the safety of our camp. You can see why I question the value of your word."

Her jaw clenched. She turned from Quinn and Dolan and looked south, toward Mt. Adams. The smoke plume hovered above it.

Her frustration boiled over.

3

To her team, Andi swore, "Damn it, let's talk." They regrouped behind the deployed SWAT agents.

"I'm furious," she said, keeping her voice low. "And I'm tempted to go into the camp and bring the valley men out."

Greg started to object, but Andi interrupted. "I'm *tempted*, but I'm not suicidal. What I want to do, instead, is bypass Quinn and talk straight to his men."

Greg frowned. "And say what?"

"I'm wanting to jam the wedge between Dolan and Quinn harder, and a new one between Quinn and the men."

For a few minutes, they discussed her idea and how they could accomplish it without too much risk. Ben radioed the station for deputies to cover the south access trail, and Greg radioed the agents on that trail to move north to reinforce the main access road.

"Okay," she said to Joe, "Let's go." She led the way back to the entry portal, but she stood six feet to Quinn's right, facing into the camp. She never looked at him. "Men, I'm talking to you all," she said, her voice as forceful as she could make it without shouting. "Can you hear me in the back?"

"We hear you," someone shouted.

Quinn began to interrupt her, but she held up her hand. "Not a word, Quinn, or I'll arrest your ass right here and now." She turned back to the men in camp. "I want you all to know that Quinn is leading you into very serious legal trouble. Unless the men who want to leave are free to go, everyone who assists in holding them will be charged with false imprisonment and arrested when you try to leave."

Another voice shouted, "You can't arrest us all!"

"Not alone, I can't. But I'm not alone. I have thirty-seven FBI agents, nine deputy sheriffs, and the Montana Highway Patrol. The road down is one vehicle wide and our armored personnel carriers block your way out. With that force, I can arrest whoever holds these men against their wills."

She paused, expecting an outcry, but there was an ominous silence. Two men shifted their weapons so they pointed at the ground beneath her feet. Shivers ran down her back. Behind her, the SWAT team leader said, "Ready."

Quinn's face was a grimace of anger. "You're doing violence to us. I'm going—"

"No, Quinn, I'm not. I'm responding to your false imprisonment of Jenkins and his people. Release them and everything goes back to the way it was before. But until the valley men come down that road, there will be no more media coverage up here, and no more talk." As she turned away, she again saw the smoke plume above Mt. Adams. The ache in her shoulders spread down her back.

4

On the way back to the station, Ben drove so she could talk with Magnus Anderssen. She asked him to have Bud Groh at the radio station broadcast a call for more volunteers to work on the firelines at the monastery. Mack agreed.

After ending the call, she said to Ben and the agents, "I'm done playing with these protesters. I've got an idea for ending this."

Ben looked across at her. "You figurin' on tellin' us now, or we waitin' for a meetin'?"

"Now's good. Tell me what you think."

"When ain't I told you what I think?" He looked at her again, grinning.

"This wildfire could become a real problem—so I think it's time I got aggressive on ending the occupation. I want to have a sit-down with Quinn and Dolan, none of this stand-at-the-damn-door crap. They say—"

Ben grunted. "No way, too damn dangerous."

She grimaced. "But look, if we do it before the CIRG guys leave, we'd have all thirty-five plus my deputies—what're they going to do, kidnap me? That'd be our excuse to take them down." Even as she spoke, she knew it was bravado spurred by impatience.

Greg shook his head. "I'm in command at the protest, and I won't allow it. I'm sorry, but you can talk to them at the entry, like always."

"Okay, then, forget that part of it." She continued describing her proposal, as they turned the SUV around and went back to Roberts Mountain.

5

It started badly. Once again, Andi stood away from Quinn and Dolan and addressed their men. "You people want the BLM to transfer this land to Adams County, right?"

Dolan started to answer, but Quinn moved in front of her and interrupted. Dolan came to his side. Quinn snarled, "Didn't you say you wouldn't be back until your valley pussies leave?"

She nodded. "I did. But look out there." She pointed south. The smoke plume had grown, and the wind smeared the heavy brown smoke across the southern end of the valley. "That fire threatens a monastery that's been up there for a hundred and eighty-two years. The valley men you're holding hostage make up half our fire department. We need them to protect the monastery."

Quinn shook his head. "I don't care what you need. I care about our mission, and it's not to help your fire department."

"Let me ask *you* a question, then. What does Crane want to get out of this?" She asked Quinn but made eye contact with Dolan. Quinn started to repeat the lines about taking back federal lands, when Dolan interrupted him, his round face angry. "Crane needs money. He told me after we got here that he decided to do this action so the media coverage could stimulate donations to his church. Simple as that."

Quinn whirled toward him, drew his gun, and slashed Dolan across the face. The gun barrel crunched against Dolan's nose, the sound of the bone collapsing. Santa fell to the ground, his hands clasping his face, moaning. After a moment, he lay still.

Andi moved toward him. Quinn swung toward her, aimed his gun at her chest. "Not a step closer, Pelton. Dolan's disloyal. We'll handle him."

Joe had already drawn and trained his weapon on Quinn. "Freeze, Quinn. And if one of your men shoots me, I'll get one off before I fall."

Andi chilled, remembered that happening in the motel room—she was hit in the shoulder but got off the round that killed Stetson as she fell. She held her breath.

Quinn didn't move.

Andi thought, *Standoff*. Then Quinn said, "I'll put the gun away."

Joe said, "Slow."

After his gun was holstered, Andi said, "I'm taking Jack to our hospital. You men can't offer him any medical care up here. And Quinn, add this to your list: I'm charging you with assault with a deadly weapon. When your occupation is over, you'll be arrested."

Quinn glared. "Bullshit, Sheriff. You'll *never* arrest me."

One man behind him called out, "Don't push your luck, Quinn. You're screwing us all with your crap."

Quinn spun around, reaching for his pistol, but stopped: The man's rifle aimed at him.

Andi raised her arms. "Stop this. Everyone take a breath."

The man covering Quinn slowly lowered his weapon.

"Agents Mitchell and Haney are going to move Dolan into my squad, then we'll take him to the ER. Any objections?"

She scanned the men; no one answered, but many men looked down at Dolan. She saw concern on some faces, so she knelt beside Dolan, who was still unmoving. His face and white beard were covered with blood, his nose split and crushed. Joe and Greg approached, and as they lifted Dolan, he made a small groan, but remained unconscious. His mouth was open. They carried him to the SUV and laid him gently on the back seat. Greg and Ben took the rear seats.

Andi and Joe climbed into the front seats. Joe turned and looked at Dolan. "He's breathing, at least." He faced forward as Andi began the drive down the mountainside. "What's next?"

"We get Dolan to the ER and then we figure out how to arrest Quinn without someone getting killed."

6

Jack Dolan had regained consciousness in the ER, but was in such pain that Doc Keeley gave him morphine, which knocked him out again. As Andi left the hospital, she looked south to Mt. Adams. The smoke plume had continued growing, reflecting the angry orange glow of the early evening sun. The upper wind tore the top off the plume and flattened it, a brown anvil down the sky.

She dialed the station. "Gen, any word from St. Brendan's?"

"The abbot called. Let me get my note." She shuffled papers. "Here we go. He said the crews are making progress on the fireline. It's well past the monastery wall, and Bill Howard brought up his bobcat, so that's two up there now. Bill and a bunch of guys are scraping the fireline down to . . . I forget what he called it."

"Mineral soil?"

"That's it."

"Did the abbot say anything about how his evacuation prep's going?"

"Nope."

"I'll give him a call.

•   •   •

"Tim, it's Andi. Are you almost ready to evacuate?"

"I believe we're staying, Andi."

She stiffened. "That's foolish, Tim. Have you ever been in a wildfire?"

"No, but the building's stone and the roof's metal. We'll be fine."

"Seriously, I can't allow that. If anyone at Saint Brendan's were to die or be injured by the fire, I'd have failed in my duty to keep you all safe."

Abbot Timothy said nothing for a moment. Finally, he sighed. "All right, I'll do this. I will bring it to the monks and get their ideas about evacuating. I'll let you know."

"Tim, I—"

"That's all, Andi." His voice hardened. "I will let you know."

7

She called Ed from the station, told him what had happened.

"Come home," he said. "We'll talk about it. I want to see your face."

She considered it. Looked at her watch. Six-twenty p.m. "I've got a bunch of phone calls to make. I'll be home after that. Not much more I can do today."

But her calls reached no one, so she had to leave messages. Doc Keeley's nurse said he was busy. Calls to Abbot Timothy, Magnus Anderssen, Greg Haney, and Paddy Malloy all rolled over to voicemail.

Hanging up from the last fruitless call, she swore under her breath. Then she drove home to Ed.

8

He was waiting on the porch swing, moving back and forth quietly. He'd set up a fan. "Sit by me," he said. "It's hot, but worse inside."

She shook her head. "Gotta get out of this uniform first. Pour me a glass of Pinot?"

"Glad to."

She changed into shorts and a T-shirt. When she returned, he said, "You look cooler."

"I'm not, but let's talk. I need a fresh brain."

"With this heat, mine's fresh as a week-old banana. What are we talking about?"

"Tell me what you think. What if we shut off their water and offer free passage out of the valley to everyone who comes down? Everyone except Quinn. Him I'm going to arrest."

"Other than the word *inhumane*, I like it. Two, three days without water, my guess is most of those men will drive down and leave."

She sipped the wine. After a moment, Ed said, "I say something wrong?"

"No, you're right about that *inhumane* thing. We earned political capital at the first community meeting from talking about the protesters as human beings."

"And meaning it." Ed frowned. "But things have changed, no?"

"Does that justify cruelty?" She hesitated. "Is keeping the camp quarantined until they decide to leave morally right?"

"What about the valley men?

She nodded. "They're a reason to intervene, for sure."

"How's this? Shut off the water until they release the valley men, then turn it back on."

She thought about it for a moment. "*Quid pro quo*: You deprive men of freedom, we deprive you of water. You free the men; we free the water." She paused again. "I like it."

"What does Haney think?"

"I haven't talked to him about it yet." She looked at her watch again. "Five after seven. Let's go talk to him."

"Just call."

"Nope. If he agrees, I want to turn the water off tonight."

9

Haney agreed.

Andi rubbed her hands together. "All right, let's do it."

Greg's eyes widened. "Now?" He looked at her shorts and T-shirt.

"Now. All we need's a good padlock—" She pointed to Ed, who held one. "We just walk up to the tanker, lock the spigot, tell them the new rules, and leave. Simple."

Haney clapped his hands and called to his agents, "We're going up. Battle gear!"

"Greg, let's not do that. Just you, Joe, Ed, and me. While Ed and I talk to Quinn, Joe can saunter over to the spigot and padlock it. No fuss. You can stay off to the side and cover all of us. Once it's locked, I tell them the new rules."

"At least we wear armor."

She argued, but lost. The borrowed armor she wore was too big, but Greg was adamant. Andi was sweating before they got in the FBI crew cab.

• • •

For once, it worked without a hitch.

When Joe rejoined them at the entry, she said, "You men, listen up," she shouted. "Your water is off. It will remain off until the valley men—and anyone else who wants to go—have left safely. No charges will be brought if you leave. But if you hold the valley men longer than twenty-four hours, you will be charged with false imprisonment and arrested when you try to leave. When all the valley men are accounted for below, we'll turn your water on again. How long this takes and whether you are charged is up to you."

Ignoring the outraged shouting, the team turned and climbed into the SUV and there was nothing to do but leave.

On the way down, Andi said to Greg, "That came out okay. But when we go back up to turn it on again, they'll be expecting us. And they'll be pissed."

"And thirsty. When that time comes, we tie the key with a nice ribbon to one of Vic Sobstak's cows and let her deliver it to Quinn." He chuckled. "Uncle Sam can afford another padlock."

She snorted. "And another cow."

Chapter Eighteen - Monday

1

As of five-forty a.m., when she woke, Andi hadn't gotten a call from Greg Haney. No one, apparently, had come down during the night. She wanted to sleep a bit longer, but knew she wouldn't. First, she called the hospital and left a message for Doc Keeley; he hadn't returned her call last evening.

She stepped out on the porch. Dawn light graced the western mountains, but the air hadn't cooled much overnight. She walked around the corner of the cabin to see the sun, which had risen fifteen minutes earlier. Hot wind staggered her. She caught her breath and stepped back into the shade of the house. "Damn," she muttered. She watched the taller pines north of the cabin swaying in the wind. The wind came from the southeast now. *It's shifting*. Paddy's forecast was right.

Ed was brewing coffee when she came back in. "Morning," he said. "Couldn't sleep for the heat."

"It's a furnace already. At six in the morning, for God's sake! And the wind's blowing from the southeast."

Her cell buzzed. *Haney*. She answered. "Hi, Mark, what's going on?"

"All's quiet on the western front. They've gone twelve hours without water, so I'm hoping we'll see results today."

"You all set up?"

"Everybody and everything. I do need two deputies for traffic control, though. I want to close the southbound lane."

"They'll be on the way as soon as I hang up."

She ended the call and stepped back onto the porch and down into the yard. The sun blasted her again, and the hot southeasterly wind reddened her face. She looked toward Mt. Adams and the monastery. *God help us if it swings all the way south.*

2

The morning meetings done, Andi stood on the highway shoulder where the dirt road around Vic Sobstak's pasture met the highway. "You got to work early," she said to Greg, who stood with her.

"Four a.m. I figured nobody was dumb enough to drive down at night—that access road's too dangerous. We got the APCs in place at four-thirty, so now we wait. By the way, how's Dolan?"

"In Missoula. He needs serious facial surgery, and the doctor thinks he'll be disfigured."

"That sucks. Bastard didn't deserve that."

They watched Xavier Contrerez, standing with his STOP/SLOW sign on the southbound shoulder, in front of the big personnel carrier blocking the lane, its light bar flashing red and blue. Felix Maslow waited, also with a STOP/SLOW sign, beside the northbound lane, fifty yards south. There was no traffic for them to manage. And no one coming down from Freedom Camp.

"All right," she said to Greg. "If you don't need me, I'll head up to St. Brendan's. The wind's changing direction, which will speed up the fire."

"We're good here, Andi. It's hurry-up-and-wait for thirst to do its magic. You go. I'll keep in touch."

"Fingers crossed there's something good to keep in touch about."

• • •

She parked in the monastery lot beside St. Mary's Lake. Smoke hung in the air, not too dense yet, but if the wind continued to move toward the northwest, it'd thicken. She surveyed the two school buses—one for ferrying volunteers up and down, and one, she hoped, waiting to evacuate the monks. Pickup trucks were scattered along the shore of St. Mary's Lake. The semi-trailer stood by the monastery wall. In the distance, chainsaws whined, so she walked along the fireline toward the sounds of work.

The line had grown—both in length and width, wider even than the twenty feet Paddy wanted. It looked naked, the understory and the brush cut down and piled on the far side of the line, opposite the side the fire would attack. And on the fire side, the taller timber had been limbed up, and thirty feet into the forest, the larger brush had been removed, leaving the bigger trees and the scrubby undergrowth of grasses and low shrubs. The nearest crew members were just visible perhaps eight, nine hundred feet from her; they'd progressed well beyond the large woodworking shop. The shop, unlike the monastery itself, was built of wood, not stone. It had a metal roof, though.

That didn't comfort her.

As she approached, she listened to the scraping and chopping of Pulaskis. Dings as the iron struck stone, thuds as dirt moved. Ahead, beyond this line of men bent over the ground, chopping, she heard the drone of chainsaws and the growl of the Bobcats. She walked past them to where the fallers were bringing trees down, extending the line. Paddy Malloy was watching the work.

"Top of the mornin', Andi. It's good progress you'll be seein', both here and on t'other side of the monastery."

"I can see it." The chainsaws' screams echoed from the monastery building.

For a moment, they stood silent, watching the men work. Without looking at her, he asked, "Have me lads left the protest?"

"Not yet, but we've got reason to think it'll be today."

"Ah, that'll be in me prayers."

3

Andi walked the fireline back to the parking lot and into the monastery. Boxes, stacked high, filled the vestibule of the church. She slipped into the church itself and sat on a pew in the back. She rested her hands on her lap and looked around. *Peaceful*, she thought.

After a few quiet moments, she returned outside. Her cell phone beeped, and she saw she'd missed a call. *Blocked by the stone walls*, she thought as she pulled up her messages. The call was from Greg Haney.

She punched in his number. "Greg? It's Andi. What's up?"

"They're coming down the mountain. So far, we've cleared seven. Apparently, most of the protesters opposed Quinn's order to keep the valley men."

Relief flooded her. "The water's working."

"That's what they're telling us."

"Okay," she said. "Look, I can't be there for an hour and a half. When they're all down, can you unlock the water?"

"I can, but I'd recommend you do it. We won't move anyway until the last five get out, so it could be awhile before we unlock the tanker. I think you should be the one. Display your authority."

"Got it. I'll get there as soon as I can," she said. "So next we deal with Quinn and twenty-eight protesters. Progress."

"It is," Greg said. "And I've got an idea for how to do that."

4

As she drove down the mountain, the smoky air cleared a bit and Andi allowed herself a small smile of relief—seven valley men already on their way home, could be all twelve by now. At last, something was working.

For a while, as she drove down through the Narrows, a canyon almost five hundred feet wide, spacious enough for the highway and the river and a band of forest, she let herself enjoy the ride. This narrow ravine was beautiful, and the now creek-sized Monastery River ran sparkling and fast alongside the road. Red and brown and yellow striations in the rimrock walls made a miniature Grand Canyon. The road wound down in tight curves and switchbacks for two miles, then flattened and straightened as it neared the valley floor. When she emerged from the gorge, her cell phone beeped again. She glanced at the screen. *Greg Haney, twice.* She sighed, and pulled over at the first wide spot. *Vacation's over.*

"Greg. Sorry, I didn't have a signal."

"No worry, Andi. All twelve of our guys are down and safe. And hungry. Are you still at the monastery?"

"No, I'm on my way back." She did a momentary calculation. "Give me an hour."

"An hour it is. We'll be ready to go."

5

Andi drove onto Vic Sobstak's field and parked beside the FBI mess tent. Stepping out of the squad, the heat stunned her. Greg and Joe came out of the mess tent. "My God, it's got to be a hundred degrees!" she said.

"One-oh-three," Joe said, wiping his face. A few SWAT agents came out of the tent, inside which the fans blew furiously. Everyone dripped.

Greg waved. "Right on time. You got your armor on?"

"Just the soft, but give me a minute for the plates." She reached across to the passenger seat and grabbed the plates and slipped them into the inner pockets, then put it on. "Okay, ready. Ready to suffocate. What's the plan?"

"I'll brief you while we drive."

• • •

The ring of vehicles had shrunk. The vehicle spaces left empty by the twelve departures had been filled, so the circle was tighter. Andi said to Greg, "Think there's room inside for the ones who are left?" Crane's big RV and the trailers parked beside it left little open space. The SWAT and CIRG teams, ahead of Andi's squad, had deployed at the water tanker, and the protesters had jammed themselves into the remaining space inside the camp.

Joe said, "Pretty crowded in there. That should help us."

Andi stepped out of the squad and raised her voice. "We're turning the water back on."

The protesters stood shoulder to shoulder, literally, almost up to the entry portal. Although the heat was not quite as ferocious as down on the valley floor, the men were sweating, their faces dirty, their beards ragged. Quinn pushed his way through the crowd and stood in front of them. They pressed against his back. Frowning, he stepped outside the ring.

Andi called to him, "Step back inside your camp or I'm going to arrest you for your assault on Jack Dolan."

He said nothing, and didn't move for a tense moment. Then, looking furious, he turned and ordered his men to make space, then stepped back inside the ring.

Meanwhile, Greg had removed the padlock from the spigot.

Andi said, "Men, we'll be back tomorrow morning at 8:00 o'clock. We'll have the media with us, and Doctor Northrup, and we'll resume negotiations."

Quinn barked, "We demand food. Now!"

She waited a beat. "Tomorrow morning, Quinn." They left.

6

Inside the mess tent, overheated air eddied around. Andi tore off her armor. Her shirt was soaked through. Like Greg's. Like everyone's. From a cooler, she grabbed three cold bottles of water. *Grace and her people are doing a great job.*

"So, Greg, you said you have some ideas."

"I do. Let's change our stance on food. We tell them we'll allow four men to drive their pickups into town and buy food. Then, at the highway, we use the APC to send them north, out of the valley, and warn them if they try to return, they'll be arrested."

"So how do we explain that they don't come back?"

Joe smiled. "We say, 'When your friends got to the highway, they turned north and left the valley.'"

Andi thought about that. "Well, it's the truth—just not the whole truth."

"Exactly."

Andi stood. "I have to get back to town. Let me think about it, and we'll talk it over at the team meeting in the morning. Six-thirty."

"Think hard," Greg said. "I want to get my men home."

• • •

During her drive back into town, her radio sounded. "Sheriff, Dispatch here. Incoming call. Over."

She grabbed the mic. "Sheriff here, Callie. What's happening?

"I'm patching Paddy Malloy over to you. Hang on . . ."

Paddy's voice, a bit thin, came over the radio. "Andi, it's bad news I'm bearin'."

Andi interrupted. "Hold on, Paddy. Your men are free."

"Thank the Dear Lord in His Heaven, lass! Now on to the bad. The Carlton pilot called. The fire's near the top of the saddle and he's saying it'll be crossin' onto our side within the hour."

"*Damn.* How much time do we have before it gets to Saint Brendan's?"

"On that note, I'm unclear. Fire moves slower downslope, as I've said. Our wild card's the wind. Strong gusts are the order of the day, unfortunately—I'd wager thirty miles an hour, and it all could worsen during the night. I'll not be relaxing until the incident management team and the hotshots arrive, and they can't do that fast enough to suit me."

The alarm in Paddy's voice, something he almost never showed, chilled her.

"The monks plan to load the truck tomorrow," she said. "They should do it tonight. Can any of your men help?"

Paddy didn't answer for a moment. "Sadly, no, I have need of them workin' on the firelines till dark." He paused. "Wait. I'll roust the twelve protesters to drive up here this evening. Whatever they've been through, they're firefighters, and this precious monastery cries out for them."

PART FOUR

CHAPTER NINETEEN — THAT EVENING

1

Back at the station, she called the abbot. "Tim, I hate to bother you with this, but I've got serious news. The fire's crossing the saddle above the monastery and we don't know how fast it's going to come down the slope."

"Do you have an estimate?"

"It depends on the wind, but no, I don't. I'm raising the evacuation order—level two, 'Get Set.' I need you and the monks to load your truck tonight, and have everybody packed and ready to go by morning. If I need to raise the order to level three, you'll have only minutes to leave. I'll send a few of my deputies to help you load up, but you've got to get it done tonight."

Again, he was silent. After waiting, Andi said, "Tim, you there?"

"I'm here, Andi. Our walls will protect us. We don't need to leave."

And sighed. "I get it, Tim. It's your home. But it's my responsibility to protect you."

"I realize that, I do. But . . ." He paused. "We'll load the truck tonight. You don't need to send your men up, we can manage. As for leaving, let me pray on it overnight, and we can talk in the morning."

Andi closed her eyes. "Tim, listen. if I raise the order to level three, it's mandatory. If I think your lives are in danger, I'd be derelict if I didn't order an evacuation."

Timothy cleared his throat. "And if we refuse to obey your order, what happens?"

That's the question, isn't it? "Somebody could be injured, somebody could die, or nothing could happen. Don't risk your men's lives, Tim."

"I'll pray on it, Andi. Let's talk in the morning."

As she ended the call, she muttered to herself, "Pray on it? Good God."

2

Looking south, Ed saw the fire, a string of red-orange pearls just below the saddle. As the dying evening light faded behind the western mountains, the blaze glowed brighter, feeding on darkness. From his porch, Ed watched, fascinated. Such beauty from such a terrifying element. As the evening darkened, a car turned into the long drive up, and in a moment, headlights swept the yard. Andi was home, at last.

When she climbed the porch steps wearily, he said, "You look exhausted. It's almost ten."

"Way past exhausted." She stood beside him, watching the fire for a moment. Then, "Let me get out of this uniform. Mind waiting while I take a cold shower?"

"Nope. A glass of wine? It's not chilled much."

"Put ice in it, would you? And I've got two things I need to talk about after I shower."

Ed smiled in the dark. "Still on duty, eh?"

"Things are happening fast."

• • •

Andi returned from the shower in ten minutes. "The fire's coming down."

Ed pointed toward Mt. Adams. "Yeah, I've been watching it. Hate to say, but it's beautiful at night."

"The abbot's being stubborn about leaving. Any ideas?"

"It's mandatory if you order it, right?"

"People ignore mandatory evacuation orders all the time. I can't see arresting all the monks, or even Timothy. But if something happens to one of them, I don't know how I'd live with it."

Ed nodded, then said, "Don't lay that on yourself. They're adults. Make your best case, then let it go."

Andi watched the flames burning on the mountain. From here, forty miles north, they *were* beautiful. "Okay. Next topic. Greg Haney is suggesting a tactic to end the protest." She described the turn-them-north idea. "I think it could work, but I hate lying, even to that asshole Quinn."

"Well, if you tell him his people turned north and left the valley, it's not a lie, is it?"

"Don't you Catholics consider pale lies as much a sin as full-blown lies?"

"Number one, it's 'white lies,' not 'pale lies.' Number two, I'm not a Catholic anymore. Number three, this bunch occupied property that doesn't belong to them, killed six cattle, murdered the sheriff, ruined Jack Dolan's face, and held twelve men hostage—and you're balking at a little white lie?"

"Well, put that way . . ." She chuckled. "I'm maybe taking this job a little too seriously?"

"You think?"

"Okay, I'll lighten up. Some." She took a sip of wine, then stood. "I need to call Ben about the plans for Brad's funeral tomorrow—he told me it's at eleven, but that's all I know."

CHAPTER TWENTY — TUESDAY

1

Eight-thirty. The wind was blowing steadily at Freedom Camp. Andi guessed at least fifteen miles per hour. Ed spoke for the department. Quinn listened to the proposal—that four men drive their trucks into town for food—though he kept his back turned on Ed. When Ed was finished, he faced Ed and Andi, and rejected it. "Our demand is that the *sheriff* provides food."

Ed answered loudly enough that Jay's camera and mic couldn't miss a word. "That's your answer? You're rejecting food?"

The angry muttering behind Quinn grew louder. He snapped, "I'm not rejecting food. I'm demanding that you provide it."

Ed shrugged. "The sheriff's department isn't a caterer." He looked back to Andi, who said, "Well then, I guess we're done here."

She started to turn, when one man in the back of the crowd yelled, "Damn it, Quinn, you blow this and we starve. I'm sick of your hard-ass shit."

Curious at this rebellion, Andi turned back toward Quinn and watched his face turn crimson. But he said nothing. The tension built. Finally, he muttered, "Fuck all!" He swung around and faced his men. One by one, he pointed at four men. "You four go into town and buy food. Enough for a week. Take two pickups."

Andi, alarmed, looked at Greg. His eyes had closed, and he'd bowed his head. The plan required that all four drive their own vehicles.

The grumbling began again. Andi watched the men. Their anger was focused on Quinn, not at her. She kept her face neutral, thinking furiously.

"Money, Quinn," one of the four said. "I don't have money for that much food."

Quinn stiffened. He stared at the man, then glared at the crowd. "All right. Any man who wants to eat, fifty dollars. In my hand. Now." Some reached into their pockets for wallets. Others hurried to their tents or campers to get the money.

Andi gestured to the team. They huddled. "We're screwed," she whispered.

Greg Haney agreed. "The passengers won't want to leave their vehicles behind. And if we let them hike back up here, they tell Quinn our trick and we lose any credibility we still have."

"Damn," Andi swore softly. "No way around it, we have to let them go into town. I can't think of a pretext to call the whole thing off."

They heard Quinn say, "Here's your damn money," and they looked back. He was handing a sheaf of bills to the driver who had asked for it.

Greg, keeping his voice low, said, "I need to alert my guys to let them go to town."

Andi nodded. "I'll follow them and radio ahead to have two guys meet us at Art's Fine Foods. I'll be damned if I'll let these men do anything other than shop."

2

One of the protesters, young, shirtless, long greasy black hair and beard, and a swastika tattoo on his bare shoulder, yelled at Quinn. "I want my damn money back. I don't trust those pricks you appointed. I'd rather go hungry than give them an excuse to run home."

The driver with the money shouted, "Up yours, Conners, we're not going to steal your precious cash." The other driver lowered his AR-15.

Andi shouted, "Stop! I'll escort the drivers into town and make sure they buy food for the rest of you."

Before anyone could answer, an older man, white stubble on his cheeks and his almost bald scalp, stepped forward, shaking his head. He called out to Andi, "So if we leave, we won't get arrested?"

"That's the deal. Except for Mr. Quinn here."

The man turned to Quinn. "I'm done. I'm loading up my RV and getting off this goddamn mountain. If the Rev was here, none of you jerks would get away with all this ruckus."

Some men screamed obscenities at the old man, others roared back at them, other men yelled they wanted to leave, others called them cowards. The bearded man with the swastika tattoo, his face fiery with rage, started pushing the old man, then he was set upon by five other guys, fighting, everyone yelling, guns being dropped in favor of fists. Quinn raised his voice above the fray, but no one stopped. He lifted his rifle and fired into the air.

Quinn roared into the sudden silence, "Traitors. Go. We don't need cowards in the Church."

Andi yelled, "Quinn, add reckless endangerment to the list." Then she turned to Ben and Greg. "I'm going with the shoppers. You guys take charge of this, so it isn't chaos. Ed, come with me back to town."

Greg nodded. The two pickups with the four shoppers eased out of the vehicle ring and moved cautiously across the grass toward the access road. Andi stopped them, made a rolling gesture. The men opened their windows. "I'll be right behind you into town. When we get there, pull aside and I'll guide you to the grocery store. Clear?"

"Clear."

Andi and Ed climbed into the squad car and followed them into town.

• • •

As soon as the shoppers had gone, Ben shouted, "People, listen up. Me and Agent Haney, we'll be up here. Anybody wants to leave, you'll go down one at a time, three minutes apart, so there ain't no bottlenecks on that road. All you do is tell us your name and repeat it to the agents at the bottom, then go north when you get to the highway. We'll radio your name down, so the agents know who's comin'."

It took forty minutes, but eleven men left with their vehicles. The remaining trucks and campers looked scattered and random on the grass. Quinn had disappeared into Crane's big RV. Eighteen men remained in Freedom Camp.

Ben said to Greg, "Now, I ain't sayin' that's enough, but I'd call eleven a good day's work." He pulled his old timepiece from his pocket, looked at it. "Time to go bury me a sheriff."

3

After she'd parked at St. Bernard's church, Andi called Paddy. "Your scouts back yet?" she asked.

"Indeed, they are. The fire's moving about sixty-five feet an hour. Bless the steep downslope, the wind shadow, and sparser undergrowth for slowing it a trifle."

"How long until it reaches the monastery?"

"Sure, and this is pure guessin' on me part, but if that spread rate continues, we have perhaps twenty-six hours, so—"

"That puts it between noon and one tomorrow afternoon."

"It's me best estimate, unless conditions change. Which, Lord knows, they always do."

As she started to answer, a second call came in. She glanced at the screen: *Sheriff's Dept.* "Got another call, Paddy. I'll be up after the funeral. A couple hours." She hit the *Talk* icon. "Yeah, Callie?"

"You got company, girl. Lots of it."

"Who?"

"The incident management team and twenty real good-lookin' young men."

"The hotshots." She looked again at her watch. "They're early." She thought for a moment—which was more important—paying her respects to Brad Ordrew or getting the fire crew up to the monastery?

No-brainer.

. . .

A crowd had gathered in the shade of the old cottonwoods behind the department lot. Two green crew carriers lined one side of the lot, Forest Service logos on their doors; "Harlan Mountain Hotshots" was stenciled on the side. A crew-cab pickup, and a twenty-six-foot truck were parked close to the station door.

In the shade cast by the crew carriers, three men and a woman were talking with Pete as Andi joined them. Pete introduced everyone. First, the incident commander, Del North, round-faced, blond, a confident smile on his lips. Next, Chuck Abruzzi, the captain of the Harlan Mountain Hotshots, a rail of a man, with a mop of curly black hair and two-days' black stubble on his chin. He smiled at Andi. "Not actually a *captain* captain. Assistant Superintendent's the full title. But 'captain' has a cooler ring."

Andi laughed, then turned to the woman. "Acting Sheriff Andi Pelton."

Del North said, "Sheriff, this is Mary Ogilvie, my logistics chief, and Colin Pearse, operations." Mary was as tall as Andi, five-eight, with an easy smile. Colin, shorter and stout, looked tired, with sad eyes.

Andi shook their hands. "Glad to meet you." She looked around. "Your whole team's not here yet?"

Del nodded. "On their way, a half hour behind. Along with Mary and Colin, I've got two other chiefs—planning and finance." he said. He wiped his forehead with a kerchief. "Man, you folks have some serious heat going here. And wind."

Pete said, "Hottest June on record. It's cooler up the mountain."

"Not much cooler," Andi said, and asked Del, "What do you need?"

He said that usually he'd meet with the mayor or county leaders to find out what they expected, but given the size of this fire, he thought those meetings could wait. "I need to be sure I'll have legal authority to take command of local fire and law enforcement operations on the fire scene. We'll get you the forms when we set up. Otherwise, all we need at this time is directions to where our HQ will be. Mary, Colin, and I will start setting up the HQ while Chuck and his crew scout the fire."

"You guys can follow me up there. Del, if you ride with me, I can brief you on options for siting your HQ."

"Good idea, Sheriff."

"Oh, please call me Andi."

"Andi it is." Del North clapped his hands and called out, "Let's roll."

4

Andi led the way. Additional IMT people and their gear meant the Coliseum trailhead parking lot wouldn't be big enough for the vehicles, the HQ tent, and the hotshots' tents. If Del chose that site, she'd have to close the road. The hotshots could camp on the east shoulder.

As they drove, she filled Del in about the fireline work and the monks' preparation for departure—including Abbot Timothy's hesitation—and then outlined the two options for siting his HQ and the camp—Webber's Creek or the trailhead parking lot. He decided on the parking area. "Fifteen miles is a bit farther away than I like. You say there's a decent-sized lake between that parking lot and the monastery?"

Andi described the layout: the highway ending at St. Mary's Lake; St. Brendan's Monastery on the western shore, with its parking lot between the monastery wall and the lake; on the lake's eastern shore, the trailhead parking lot. North agreed the monastery, its lot, the lake, and the highway were adequate firebreaks.

When they arrived at the monastery, she pulled in behind the big truck holding the monastery's valuables, and Del said, "Thanks, Andi. Point me to the fireline."

She pointed toward the south corner of the monastery wall. "Starts right at that corner."

He turned and walked there, fast. The hotshots poured out of the personnel carriers and followed him. She fell in behind them and called Paddy as she walked.

"I'm a quarter-mile along the fireline," he said when they connected. "I'll be comin' toward you."

"Perfect."

. . .

After she introduced Paddy to Del North and Chuck Abruzzi, she said, "I need to see the abbot, so I'll leave you guys. Paddy, check in with me later."

"Aye, lass, that I will." Paddy turned to Del North. "What's first?"

Del said he wanted to see the wood shop Andi had described. Between the rear wall of the monastery and the shop, thirty yards or so, grew a small orchard. Apple trees, ancient and healthy. Paddy's crew had begun laying a sprinkler line through the orchard. North said, "Good call. Can you get the water on the back wall of the monastery too?"

Paddy said, "Sure, and it's already in me plan."

Del smiled at the brogue. "You're from Ireland?"

"Indeed, and proud of it."

"What brought you?"

"'Twas 1961, and I was all of eighteen years, so wet behind the ears you could wash your hands there. John Fitzgerald Kennedy had just been elected, and don't ya know I wanted to live in a country that elected an Irish Catholic lad president."

Del chuckled. "Doesn't Ireland *always* elect an Irish Catholic president?"

"Aye, lad, they do, but they haven't a choice. You Yanks had a card-carryin' WASP runnin' and you took the Papist. I had to come."

He pointed to the rows of windows that looked as ancient as the apple trees. "It seems those are the monks' bedroom windows. I'll have you note that glass is fragile. A wind-blown ember or two might shatter some."

Del and Chuck looked up at the windows. "You're right," Del said. "That glass looks old as God." He asked Paddy, "Did you count the windows?"

"Ah, did I now. There's all of fifteen on each floor of the dormitory and eight big windows for the wood shop, two in each wall."

"Thanks." Del radioed Colin Pearse, who was in the trailhead parking lot setting up the command tent, and told him to order enough plywood to cover the monastery's rear windows and the windows of the wood shop. He said to Paddy, "Plywood's on the way. Show us the shop."

He and Abruzzi saw right away that the shop was a frame structure, not stone. The door was unlocked.

They stepped into the cleanest, most orderly workshop any of them had ever seen. Two rows of seven workbenches stretched front to back, like pews in church. Each bench bore a casket in varying stages of construction, and beside each bench a pegboard wall held tools, each tool hanging atop its painted silhouette.

The caskets farthest back were mere frames. Those nearest the front door were complete, gleaming, beautiful, their exquisite finishes shining in the afternoon light. Against the outer walls, finished caskets rested on industrial shelves, radiant.

Chuck said, "Gotta hand it to them. This shop's cleaner and more efficient than mine, and mine's a beaut."

"Aye," Paddy said, "But I'll wager yours has but one workbench, not fourteen."

Chuck laughed. "What's that door at the back?"

Paddy led the way into a second room, a room as big as the workshop itself. Inside, racks held carefully stacked lumber. Dried, ready-to-work boards nearest the shop itself, boards still curing farther back. Del grimaced. "Fire gets to this, nothing will stop it."

As they moved back into the shop, Chuck said, "We gotta build a control line around this place. It's nothing but wood waiting to burn."

"It'll be already half complete," Paddy said. "Me lads have been wrappin' the whole monastery and this shop in a grand fireline."

Del frowned. "Good. I'm a hell of a lot more worried about this shop and all the wood in it than about the monastery. That building's stone. This building's nothing but fuel."

5

Before she entered the church and rang the abbot's bell, Andi stopped outside and called the station. Callie relayed what Ben had reported on his way to St. Bernie's for the funeral: Eleven men gone, eighteen left.

Andi savored the fact that something unplanned had worked so well. Eleven seemed so much better than four. She said, "Callie, I need a deputy to drive up the man who'd delivered the semi to the monastery. I want this rig down as soon as possible and so far the monks aren't budging."

After Callie found his name and contact information, Andi added, "And say a prayer I can convince the abbot to leave."

"You're kidding. He wants to stay up there and roast?" Callie snorted. "Well, I suppose priests ain't as afraid of hell as the rest of us."

6

Andi pushed through the big monastery doors into the vestibule of the church. To the left, she saw the door to the dormitory. To the right, the door to the offices and other monastic spaces. She pressed the button beside Abbot Timothy's name on the bell list. While she waited, she opened the door to the church itself. The stacks of boxes that had lined the vestibule and the halls of the monastery were gone, no doubt onto the truck.

Abbot Timothy opened the door. "Hi, Andi. I suppose you're here to learn our decision. Let's talk in my office."

When she sat down, he took a long breath. "I'm sorry, Andi," Timothy said. "But we're staying. We had chapter and all the brothers agreed."

Damn. "Chapter?"

"It's what we call our community meetings. Anyway, the brothers voted to stay, unanimously."

You're the damn abbot, for Christ's sake. She started to argue, but he held up his hand.

"Please. St. Brendan's our home. The whole building is stone, and—"

She interrupted back. "Hold on, Abbot. We're at evacuation Level 2 right now, and when I issue the 'Leave now' order, it's mandatory. Your safety is my responsibility, and I—"

The abbot interrupted her. "Andi, with all due respect, the safety of the monks is *my* responsibility, and I believe the monastery will protect us. If my brothers had voted to leave, we'd leave. But we are going to protect our home."

Screw this. Time for the big gun. "Tim, will you talk to the incident commander, Del North?"

"Yes, of course."

They left the office. Passing through the vestibule, Timothy said, "But we're not leaving."

• • •

The debate began. After Timothy had argued that the stone wall and stone building and metal roof would keep the monks safe, Del shook his head. "I'm sorry, Abbot. Stone can be good protection, but wildfire is unpredictable, and the windows on the back side of your building—"

"That's our bedroom wing."

"Right. In a wildfire, things can turn very bad very fast. When the fire gets here, I won't have time or personnel to help you escape. You need to go now."

The abbot shook his head. "We're staying, sir." He waved his hand, indicating the camp and the road down the mountain. "There's nothing for the fire to burn between the monastery and your camp, you're protected by the lake and our parking area and the road. If something goes bad and we're at risk, we have the school bus. We'll drive down the road till we're out of danger."

Andi grunted. "We're saying you're *already* at risk, Tim."

But the abbot, like his monastery, was stone. "It's my understanding," he said, "that you can't force us to leave."

"No. I can't, but I—"

Timothy turned to the commander. "And I can assure you, sir, that my monks and I will not require assistance. If things turn bad, we'll get out and you won't have to worry about us. Until then, we're staying."

North shook his head, turned to Andi. She could see anger in his eyes. "It's in your purview to arrest them, and I could order you to do it if the danger were imminent." Del said. "Call it protective custody."

Andi realized arguing was useless. She wanted to drag them to safety, but more, she wanted done with this. She said to Timothy, "I'm sending the truck down as soon as the driver gets here. I won't be responsible for losing St. Brendan's treasures, even if you seem determined to risk your lives."

The abbot sighed.

CHAPTER TWENTY-ONE — WEDNESDAY

1

Six-fifteen a.m. In her office before the morning's first meeting, Andi called Paddy Malloy. "How do things look up there?"

Paddy described the day's work ahead, completing the fireline and setting the hose and sprinklers around the monastery and wood shop. He told her the wind had died overnight, so the fire's spread rate appeared to have slowed. But stronger wind and gusts were expected by evening, so Del North wanted to start backfires before they rose.

"You're aware the monks aren't leaving?" she asked.

He was. "And didn't I have an argument with the abbot about just that? He's bankin' on God protectin' 'em. The last I knew, God's no firefighter."

She sighed. "Well, give a call if anything changes or you need something."

"What I'll be needin' is the wind to stay low."

"Tell the abbot to talk to God."

• • •

She joined her team in the conference room. "Okay, let's make a plan to end this thing."

Greg Haney glanced at Joe for a moment, then said, "Andi, I got a call from Salt Lake. The special agent in charge wants her CIRG guys back. Which tells me my SWAT teams will be called home soon."

Her stomach clenched. With the protest shrunk, losing the ten CIRG agents might be workable, but to lose the Missoula and

Bozeman SWATs would shut down most of her options. "Think we can get another week?"

"I can't say. But I doubt we've got that long."

Ed said, "The camp's got, what? Eighteen guys. Without CIRG, we've got twenty-seven, plus the deputies. Can we close down the protest?"

Ben shook his head. "They still got firepower, and hungry men ain't thoughtful men. We'd get us a battle. Complete with dead people."

Andi said, "So. Alternatives?"

Ben grunted. "I ain't seein' any, tell you the truth."

Greg stood up, running his fingers through his hair. "Both sides are in a bad place, but ours is better than theirs."

When the realization hit her, Andi gasped. "You know what? Quinn attacked Dolan before I told them our plan to talk to the BLM. What do you think? I offer to propose to the BLM that they deed the land to Adams County. This is on camera, so Quinn can claim a win. In return, they agree to leave."

Nobody spoke. After a moment that, to Andi, seemed an era, Ed said, "I like it. It lets Quinn and the protesters save face. I'd refine it, though. Offer to get a BLM official up there so Quinn can pitch the idea himself. Directly. On camera."

Andi looked around. "Objections? Problems?"

Greg Haney said, "Not a problem, I like the idea, but we'll need a couple days to get somebody from the BLM here. I'll make some calls."

Joe Mitchell chuckled. "Hope whoever comes is a good actor."

Andi started to laugh, then remembered the fire. What new disaster would it bring today?

2

Freedom Camp was a skeleton. The remaining vehicles had been rearranged into a smaller circle, but gaps separated them. The former fort now resembled a circular parking lot. Jay's camera panned the changed perimeter, then focused on Quinn when he met Andi's team at the usual place, although it was not much of an "entrance" now, with all the gaps in the ring of vehicles. "Your protest is shrinking, Quinn."

"It's not a protest. We're here to return federal land to the citizens of Adams County."

She said, "You and your people leave. They'll have safe passage out of Adams County and this will be over." She didn't add, *And I won't have to concede anything.*

"We refuse to leave until our demand is met. Those who ran away were weak. Those who remain here are not. We will prevail."

"In your dreams. Adams County has no interest in owning federal lands. I'd suggest again that you leave and call off the charade."

In the silence, the wind hissed in the trees on the upslope behind the camp. She tensed and looked south. The smoke plume was leaning northwest. Toward the monastery.

A man, his eyelids red, his acned face stubbled with black whiskers, stepped out of the crowd, said, "I'm out of here. Ain't no good comin' outta this bullshit, not no more."

Within seconds, five other men had joined him. Andi called out, "Anybody else want to leave? Safe passage, food, home."

Quinn growled at her. "Shut up! Inflame my men against me and I'll . . ."

"You'll what, Quinn? Kill me? Hit me in the face with your pistol? You're losing this. Make it easier on yourself."

"You've promised to arrest me. I'm not leaving here."

"Have it your way then." She turned away and spoke to the men, some of whom had already started packing their gear into their vehicles. "Same plan as before. One vehicle every three minutes. We get your name before you go down, then you leave and don't come back into this county."

Even before the sixth truck had gone over the ridge and down toward the valley floor, Quinn had stormed away and slammed the RV's door. "No one to announce the BLM scheme to, I guess," Andi said. They all piled into the squad. Pushing the key into the ignition, Andi said, "Twelve men to go." As she backed the vehicle around, she saw the smoke above Mt. Adams, looming over where the monastery waited.

She shivered, despite the heat.

3

Driving to the station, Andi kept glancing south to the smoke. It looked like a malignant gray-brown fist shaken at the sky, obscuring the summit of Mt. Adams. After parking in the lot behind the department, she called Paddy again. "From down here, the smoke looks dense, but seems not to have come much farther down the mountain. What do you see?"

"Ah now, that'll be nothin' of substance from down here. Merely smoke and trees." He told Andi that Chuck and one of his hotshots had gone up to scout it, and saw it was moving, slow but steady, on the downslope. The plan, he said, was that when the fire had reached the flat leading to the monastery, they would drench both sides of the firelines. "And won't it be our fondest hope that thirty feet will be enough."

"Why both sides?"

"Ah, yes, a fine question. Our plan's to wet the walls of the buildings and the apple orchard on the monastery side, and thirty feet into the forest on the fire side."

"Got it. A favor, Paddy? Double check that the abbot has the school bus keys in case they have to leave."

"That I can do, and will. I'll be calling if anything changes. The forecast's the same, congenial wind at least today, and this cursed heat. There's rumor of another dry lightnin' storm, sometime tomorrow. Blown embers scare me, though."

"Why? You've got hose and sprinklers there."

"Though it's a broken record I'm soundin' like, the wind's the wild card. If gusts build up, they'll change the picture. To be sure, the incident team seems persuaded that our firelines will hold, seein' as we've got good water. I'm of like mind, but fire's unpredictable. No doubt I'm wrong, but I still worry."

"I see why."

"By the way, the incident commander has some paperwork you need to get signed by our commissioners."

She remembered that from their regular training for incident command situations. "Authorizing me to speak for the county and the incident commander to take charge of our departments at the fire." She found herself short of breath. "This is getting real, isn't it?"

4

Smoke clogged the air around the monastery. St. Mary's Lake lay gray and sick beneath it. The Harlan Mountain Hotshots, using drip torches, had set brush on the forest floor afire from the inside edge of the fireline. The back fire had burned maybe twenty feet toward the wildfire, which hadn't yet reached the flat.

She saw Paddy approaching along the main fireline. She stepped carefully over the three supply hoses and waited for him, watching the backburning operation. The hotshots were moving methodically, fifteen feet between men, each watching his section of the backfire intently.

When Paddy reached her, he said, "Me lads are behind the wood shop. Del's needin' that fire break back there widened." Together, Andi and Paddy walked through the parking lot and crossed the road to the HQ.

"How's the food operation going?"

Paddy smiled. "Splendidly. The women have dubbed themselves Operation Square Meal. Chuck Abruzzi informs me the hotshots love the food, which is so much better than MREs." He stopped and looked back toward the fireline. "Del told Grace and the women to complete lunch and dinner today, then to stay away until he calls them back."

"Because?"

"The fire arrives tomorrow."

She and Paddy stepped into the command tent.

Del North looked up from his table, on which was spread a detailed map of the mountain. "Afternoon, Sheriff." He grinned. "I mean, Andi."

"Hi, Del. Need anything from the county?"

"Two things, a.s.a.p. One, these forms need signatures from each of your county commissioners—they authorize you to speak for the county when fire issues arise, and me to take command of local law enforcement and firefighters here on the scene. And two, try to talk some sense into that damn, excuse me, *darn* abbot. Those men need to evacuate. With no extra stone wall between the workshop and the bedroom floors, that apple orchard between them scares the hell out of me."

"There's a sprinkler line in the orchard, no?"

He nodded. "We always hope we've got what we need to knock down a fire. But things go wrong."

Paddy had said much the same thing. Andi whispered, "Jesus."

"We can use his help, too." Del grinned.

"I'll tell the abbot to put in a word."

"And then get him the hell off this mountain."

• • •

"Abbot, here's the plan: If the fire jumps the control line, it could take the wood shop. If it does, you and your monks leave."

"No, Andi, I'm sorry to be stubborn, but no. We're staying."

"Tim, listen to me. If the fire takes the wood shop, it'll move into your orchard. Once it's there, it attacks the back of your building where there's no extra stone wall. The heat might not destroy the stone walls, but the commander said the old window glass could explode and embers blow into the rooms and ignite what's inside. Are you willing to expose the brothers to that danger?"

Timothy blanched. "We hadn't thought of that. I have to meet with everyone and get their opinions."

"Decide, Tim! You're the *abbot*. This isn't a democracy."

The abbot looked surprised. "No, it's not. But this is a decision I will make only after conferring with my brothers."

She bit down her frustration. "Okay. You've got half an hour. Tell the monks if you still refuse, I will consider arresting you all and busing you down." But she knew she wouldn't.

5

Andi left the monastery, fuming. Paddy was returning to his crew on the rear fire break. "And are the good monks leavin'?" he asked her before going.

She cleared her throat. "They're *conferring* about it, for God's sake."

"Am I detectin' a tone of indignation?"

"You are. They could be risking their lives."

Paddy shrugged. "It's sometimes remarked that the faithful yearn for the next life. I'd not be shocked if there's a whiff of that in their reluctance to go." He smiled. "No doubt, they will in the end do the right thing. I must go." He turned and walked to his crew.

While she waited for the monks' decision, she watched the hotshots monitoring the backburn, standing in their usual single file. A few men knelt on the scraped fireline, the others stood, resting on their Pulaskis. Chuck saw her, waved, and came over. "Hey, Sheriff. How's it going?"

"We're making progress on the protest." She gestured toward the backfire. "This looks like it's going well."

"As long as the wind stays low, we're in good shape. This is the way most fires are—ninety percent boredom, ten percent sheer terror. Right now, we've got boring."

"I'll take boring any day." She and Chuck watched the backburn quietly. As the minutes ticked away, her unease grew. What would she do if the monks refused to go? Once the fire hit, it might be too late for escape. The worry fueled more irritation. She slapped her thigh.

"Okay, I have to move these crazy monks to safety. See you later." Going through the monastery gate, she ducked into the building, and rang the abbot's bell. After a moment, the door to the cloister opened and Timothy came out, followed by a solemn line of men. They all carried backpacks and suitcases.

"Andi, we're leaving."

She sighed with relief. "Good decision. Thank you."

"Do we have an hour to bless the house?"

She hesitated. She wanted to check this problem off her list. Now. "I'm sorry, Tim. Your prayers in the bus will bless the house."

He nodded, tears coming to his eyes.

6

When she got home, close to six-thirty, the late afternoon air was stifling, and smoke from the fire had settled in the valley. Andi's chest clutched, like a cough that wouldn't come. The sun, high over the western mountains, was an angry red disc. She wondered where Grace and Ed had gone.

Andi stripped, stepped into the shower. Turned the hot water low. Let the cool water run over her shoulders and breasts, down her body. After five minutes, she dried off, put on shorts and a T-shirt, and flopped onto the porch swing.

Ed drove into the yard and came up the steps. He stared out into the smoky air. "Don't think I'll run today."

"Don't blame you," she said. "I just took a cold shower and I'm already too warm."

Grace's PV had followed Ed's truck into the yard, but she hadn't gotten out yet. Music pounded from her radio, and Grace's body was bobbing in rhythm. Ed sat beside Andi on the swing. In a moment, Grace jumped out of her car and ran up the steps. She sprawled on the porch chair across from them, her arms draped over the chair, legs splayed.

"I've never been so tired."

Andi nodded. "You've been working hard. How's it going?"

"Well, I'd say really well. Lane's amazing. He can keep a million things in his head, never forgets a thing, cooks like a real chef—"

Ed laughed. "He *is* a real chef."

"I know, but it's so fun to watch him do everything. And the ladies are awesome. They come in early and stay late, and when I thank them, they all say, 'Well, it's the least we can do, with those boys protecting us.'"

"Good people," Andi said. She thought of the twelve protesters who'd broken free and had gone to work on the fireline without rest. *Not happy with their politics*, she thought, *but they're good citizens.*

They talked about the wildfire for a while, then the protest. Finally, Andi said, "How about a glass of cold wine?"

"Perfect," Ed said. Then he said to Grace, "You too?"

Her eyes sparkled. "Northrup, sometimes you make me really happy you adopted me."

Ed faked a frown. "Just *sometimes*?"

• • •

Near dawn, Andi woke, startled by a new sound. The alarm clock read 4:48. Ed was at the window, peering out. "Wind," he said. "Big wind."

Andi jumped out of bed. In the dim dawn twilight, the jack pines around the yard were seesawing, dancing in the wind. "Crap," she whispered. "That fire's going to explode."

CHAPTER TWENTY-TWO - THURSDAY

1

After the morning's briefing, Andi took the first step in her plan to end the protest. She called Doc Keeley.

"John, Andi Pelton here. I have a question about Jack Dolan."

"You remember he's over at Saint Pat's?"

"I do. That's my question. Who's his surgeon? I need to ask him a question."

"Her. Her name's Alison Strand. Just a minute." In a moment, he came back and dictated Strand's number.

When Andi's call connected with Dr. Strand, she said, "Thanks for coming to the phone, Doctor. I know you're busy, so I'll keep it brief. I need to know if Jack Dolan can talk. We have something urgent and I need his input."

"We intubated him, so he's got a very sore throat and some damage to his vocal cords. The tube's gone, but I don't want him to talk for a few days. Is this urgency about the protest Mr. Dolan was part of?"

"Yes."

"Okay, I'll get one of the nurses to go to his room and she can relay his answers to you. Ask 'yes' or 'no' questions so he can nod or shake his head. Give me five minutes, then ask the operator to connect you to room 407."

"I can do that."

She waited the five minutes, looking out at Mt. Adams. The smoke boiled higher into the sky, driven by the wind, now blowing hard out of the southeast. A brown smudge lay over the valley. Watching it made her want to cough. After five minutes, she called St. Pat's and asked for Jack Dolan's room. As planned, a nurse answered, who said she was putting the phone on *Speaker*.

"Thanks." She waited a beat, then said, "Jack, can you hear me?"

The nurse said, "He nodded yes."

"Good. I'm so sorry for what happened to you, and I hope you'll have a good recovery."

"He wrote, 'Thank you.'"

"Jack, there are only twelve men left on the mountain. The rest have gone. Your pickup—or whatever vehicle you came in—is still up on the mountain. Are the keys in it?"

The nurse said, "He nodded yes. Wait, he's writing something." In a moment, she said, "He wrote, 'I came in the RV with Crane.'"

"Ah. Well, we'll be impounding that until Crane's able to retrieve it, so—"

The nurse interrupted. "He's shaking his head and writing again." Andi waited. The nurse said, "He says, 'Big RV mine, not Crane's. Keys top drawer bedroom dresser.'"

Surprised, she said, "Oh. We all thought it was Crane's. Okay. I'll make arrangements to get your RV over to St. Pat's when the protest is over."

Callie popped her head in the office door, waving a note. Andi took it. *Haney called, says BLM coming tomorrow late morning. Details later.*

She nodded. To Jack, she said, "One other thing. You don't need to press charges against Quinn. I witnessed the assault so we'll arrest him. But I'd like to give him an incentive to leave the camp by telling him you won't press charges. Is that all right with you?"

The interval before the nurse spoke was longer. When she spoke, her voice was hesitant. "He wrote, 'Go ahead. I will punish Quinn my own way, own time.'"

2

Andi had just ended a call to Magnus Anderssen, asking him to call KEMT-TV in Missoula to send Katie and Jay back tomorrow morning. He'd asked her why.

"I need them to cover an important negotiation that could end the occupation."

Magnus said, "I'm on it," and a moment after ending the call, her cell phone buzzed in her hand.

The screen read *P. Malloy*. When she answered, he said, "Andi, I regret to say, we have a bother."

So much for success. "What?"

"Let me begin with the weather. The wind is expected to grow much stronger, perhaps twenty-five miles an hour. In addition, regretfully, there is a thunderstorm on our doorstep, arriving after noon."

"Are you ready for the fire?" She gripped the edge of her desk. Hard.

"Is one ever prepared for wildfire? But yes, I believe we, ah, have done our due diligence." But trouble laced his voice.

"What's wrong, Paddy?"

"The plywood for the windows is what's wrong. They didn't deliver enough for the second story."

His tone scared her. "How about sprinklers?"

"Ready. But consider, should the wind blow hard, the water mayn't reach the second story. It's conjecture, of course, and I'll wager of little value, since there's naught to be done in any event. I'm thinkin' we'll pull through."

"That's your opinion?" She held her breath.

"'Tis, and of which I'm all of ninety percent confident. The ten percent is up to the wind. I must say, a helicopter doin' water drops from the lake would be welcome; Del called for one, but none are close enough or can be spared. We're cursed with too many fires in the Rockies. Del is still hopeful, bless his heart, but aerial support for this small a fire is unavailable until tomorrow evening, earliest.

Unfortunately, this fire's timetable is uncooperative—we're expectin' it this afternoon. Right on time for the lightnin' storm."

Andi breathed through her mouth, nauseous.

3

A half hour later, on her way up to the fire HQ, Andi met Abbot Timothy in the meeting room of Anderssen's StreamSide Lodge on the Monastery River. He and his monks had converted it into a makeshift chapel. The room felt closed in, the air stifling. "Can we talk outside?"

"Of course." They walked together down the sloping lawn to the river. She briefed him on the situation.

"It will work out, Andi. I trust God." He smiled. "And our firefighters."

She winced. "Paddy's worried about the wind, and—" Even as she spoke, the wind gusted in the tall cottonwoods lining the river, startling them both.

Timothy looked down at the water eddying over river rocks. "Our caskets . . ."

Andi could imagine the pain losing those caskets would cause Timothy and his monks.

"And you said if the fire takes the shop, embers might attack the monastery windows and the glass could explode . . ." His voice trailed off.

She said, "Paddy's crew put plywood—" when her phone buzzed. *P. Malloy.* "It's Paddy, Abbot. May I take it?"

"Dear God, yes!"

"Andi," Paddy said immediately. "I'll be sharin' the thunderstorm forecast Del relayed to me. Sure, and they'll be callin' it a dry storm, loads of wind and lightnin'. It's two hose teams Del's wantin', one ready to attack the wood shop and one ready to attack the fire in the bedrooms if they ignite. Sure and those upper story windows are where we're needin' more plywood, but it's got to come from Missoula and we haven't the time for that. My call, though, is for somethin' else. The doors to both the monastery and the shop are locked. We'll have to break through 'em. I'm needin' ye ask the abbot—"

"I'm with him now." She hit *Speaker*. "Repeat that for the abbot, Paddy."

Malloy did. Andi watched Timothy's face carefully. He might have been watching a crucifixion. Then his eyes narrowed. "Yes, we locked the buildings before we left. Andi told me the main risk to our home would be the windows—that's the part of the monastery the fire would attack first."

They discussed the threat to the second-floor windows. After Paddy repeated his request to break through the doors, he asked, "Will ye be needin' to have it from Commander North's lips, Abbot?"

"No, no. But can you give me, say, a minute?"

"Without question."

Andi stepped aside as Timothy moved toward the river. He knelt at the bank, and leaned over, his back rounded, his shoulders low, and reached his hand into the water. For a long moment he held it there, its wake widening as it flowed downstream. He lifted his wet hand to his forehead, made the sign of the cross, then closed his eyes for a moment. Praying, Andi thought. He got to his feet and turned back toward her. His voice was steeped in sadness, but firm as stone. "Do whatever you need to, Paddy. Just save our house."

4

On the drive to Freedom Camp, Andi pondered the moments with the abbot. To lose your home and livelihood, everything. Unbearable. She set it aside. *Nothing I can do about it now.*

Far off, a rumble of thunder. The heat was putting a heavy load on the air conditioner in the van. Opening the door for Greg and Joe to climb in brought the heat in with them. Andi thought of the fire.

As they crested the ridge and drove across the grass toward Freedom Camp, now a scattering of vehicles rather than a fort, she said to Greg, "Remind me the agent's name."

"Sam Lander. He's special agent in charge in Billings."

Everyone got out of the van and walked toward Quinn, who stood alone, though no longer in an entry to anything but a pasture with randomly parked vehicles on it. Eleven men stood in a row behind him.

He snarled, "We demand more food. The food our men bought has run out."

She ignored him and launched her plan. First, she told him Jack Dolan declined to press charges. Quinn grimaced. Andi hoped he thought he'd not be arrested for his attack on Dolan. She repeated her threat to arrest Quinn for false imprisonment and reckless endangerment—unless he cooperated, starting now. He turned his back. "You'll never arrest me, bitch."

She ignored that too. This next piece was the seed of success. She planted it. Told the men Special Agent Sam Lander of the Bureau of Land Management was on his way to Adams County. "I'll allow you to make your argument to Special Agent Lander, on one condition."

When Quinn turned back and said, "No fucking conditions," another man yelled. "Shut your trap, Quinn! She's giving us more than any other sheriff ever offered. Wreck this and I'm leaving." Other voices echoed him.

When they quieted, Quinn said, "All right, name your condition."

"After you make your pitch to Special Agent Lander, you men will have three hours to clean up all your garbage and then leave this mountain."

Quinn said nothing at first. Andi saw two men behind him edging closer to Quinn's back, but Quinn seemed not to notice. "We will not leave until we have the word of the BLM agent that our demand will be met."

Swiftly, the first guy reached around and pulled Quinn's Glock from its holster. He jumped back. "No, Quinn, you're wrong about that."

Quinn had swung around violently, his fist raised, but the second man—taller and heavier—wrapped his arms around Quinn, immobilizing him. A third man approached with a length of rope and tied his wrists behind his back. Done, he said, "All of us are together, Quinn. And we all will be talking to this special agent tomorrow."

To Andi, he said, "And we accept your condition, Sheriff. We'll be gone."

"Good. Agent Lander will arrive around noon. Be ready."

As she turned to go, another rumble of distant thunder rolled up the valley.

5

Andi parked at the monastery ninety minutes later. As she climbed out of the squad car, she checked the wind. *Not so bad up here. Mountain's casting a wind shadow.* Beyond the fireline, through a screen of trees and undergrowth, she saw flames, orange and angry, writhing and whirling. The fire was almost down to the flat.

Thank God, no fire in the crown. She saw the ground blackened by the backfire. Small flames danced on its far side, facing the big fire. Smoke made breathing hard. And a touch of fear added to the tightness in her chest. From the other side of the mountain, thunder sounded. Closer now.

This heat wasn't the oppressive heat of the summer air. *This* heat she experienced as living, hungry, searching. She shuddered.

Making her way along the fireline toward the lake, she shivered, breathless, bracing herself at the edge of fear.

She forced herself not to run, not to turn, not to look back. She imagined the fire searching for her, stretching to devour her. She was sure the flames were closing on her back, like a bullet from hell. The roar of the fire was growing, still in the woods at the base of the steep mountainside, but coming, its hiss and crackle closer. She shivered again.

The evil in people like Crane she understood, knew, could deal with. But this?

Another burst of thunder; she walked faster toward the HQ tent.

• • •

Inside, Del stood behind his management team working at their tables. He held his two-way radio close to his ear. Chuck was saying, ". . . take down those two ponderosas near the wood shop? As a precaution?"

Del said, "No, leave them. The wind's down a bit, they'll be okay. And that thunderstorm's near." He waved Andi in. She couldn't make out Chuck's next question, but Del's answer was clear: "Turn the sprinklers on when the thunderstorm gets here. Out."

He clipped the radio to his shoulder strap and moved toward the rear tent flap. To Andi, he said, "Join me," and stepped outside. Thunder rumbled behind the mountain. They'd seen no lightning before it. Across the lake, the fire was on the flat now, a red-orange boil under the trees. Smoke blotted the sky. Andi watched beside him. Del cropped his words. "So far, so good. None up in the overstory, wind's moderate. Best guess, it stays on the ground."

Andi watched the twisting flames, transfixed. She'd been in the valley for four wildfires, but never this close. She looked across the lake to St. Brendan's. And never with so much to lose.

Stan Russo, the incident planning chief, came to the back-door flap. "Forecast just in, Del!"

Del hurried to Stan's table, Andi behind. "Tell me."

"The storm's two miles behind the fire and moving fifteen miles per hour toward us. Abundant cloud-to-ground lightning and microbursts up to fifty-five miles an hour. Rain unlikely. This one's a boomer."

Del grimaced. "It's coming fast."

"Yeah, and we won't see it till it hits because the smoke's between us and the storm."

Andi did the math. Apparently Del did too. He raised his voice. "Listen up, everybody. That thunderstorm's coming right over us in eight minutes. Abundant lightning and wind. No rain."

A few team members groaned.

"I want all the teams into their vehicles. Wrap up here and be inside them no later than six minutes from now. You know the drill."

Murmurs of "Roger" and "Got it" circled the tables, and people began shutting down and unplugging electronics and moving papers into folders and folders into metal boxes under the tables. Fast.

Andi said to Del, "I just—"

Del unclipped his radio. "Sorry, Andi, this storm's a crisis. I need to call the men."

．　．　．

Del radioed Chuck, then Paddy, ordered their crews into the vehicles for the duration of the storm. "Stay on my frequency." He looked at his watch, called out to his team, "Six and a half minutes to go. Remember to tie down the door and window flaps. Leave the front flap for me." The headquarters was a tornado of people packing up, tying down, and dashing to vehicles.

Del grabbed his pack and stuffed his papers in it. Andi saw the flash, counted silently: one and one-half seconds, then the crash. A mile and a half.

Del closed his pack. "Okay, Andi, let's go." He called to the remaining two staff, "Let's *move*, people!"

Andi glanced at her own watch.

Mary Ogilvie was the last staff person to leave, running. Andi followed her ahead of Del, who as he tied down the door flap, said, "Okay, we're out of here."

Del ran to the driver's door of the van closest to the HQ tent. Four people sat in the back seats. Andi ran toward her vehicle parked in the monastery lot.

Del shouted over the wind, "Andi! With me. Take the front passenger seat!" He watched as the other vans' doors slammed shut. Andi checked her watch—two minutes—then turned and looked at the mountain above the fire, saw only smoke. But flames jumped and twisted on the flat, closer to St. Brendan's. Ravenous. She ran to Del's van and climbed in.

Del was punching his radio again. "Hotshot lead, Command here. Come in, Chuck."

Her watch read, *Fifty seconds.*

"Roger, Del."

"Status of your teams?"

"Valley men and hotshots are all in vehicles. Everybody's accounted for. Sprinklers are on around the perimeter."

"Affirmed. Stay safe. Out." He repeated the call to Paddy Malloy.

After Paddy reported, "Sure, and everybody's safe," Del, looking sideways at Andi, said, "So now we wait. Should be here in a few seconds."

Those seconds passed.

No lightning.

Del chuckled. "Don't ever trust a weather forecaster."

Andi watched the tops of the trees nearest the monastery. They were waving. She said, "The wind's—" Her voice was lost in a crack of thunder that slammed her chest. Del said something, but Andi couldn't catch his words. Black clouds darkened the air.

Del said, "I didn't see lightning, did you?"

She shook her head. "On the backside of the mountain?"

"Or hiding in the smoke."

Another crash, closer, then two more. Still no visible lightning. They waited. Someone in the back said, "What's this, the third or fourth lightning storm we've been in this year?"

Thunder drowned the answer.

Andi watched the tops of the trees waving more wildly now across the lake. Behind the trees, the fire itself was closing on the monastery. "Is the fire moving faster?" she asked.

Del watched it for a moment. "Sure is. The wind's driving it now."

Andi was about to ask how the storm would affect the firefighting plan, when a bolt of lightning flashed high up on the mountain, followed fast by a peal of thunder, then by another enormous flash, then another. Thunder buried them. A gust of wind rocked the van. A cup fell out of its cup holder.

Someone in the back muttered, "Christ have mercy." Then, they saw it.

6

A shaft of lightning, wide as a man, flashed down, split in two, and blasted the two Ponderosa pines closest to the shop and orchard. They flared, torches tossed in the wind.

"My God!" someone whispered.

Andi couldn't breathe.

Del said something. Another blinding bolt blotted his words. He didn't repeat. The two flaming Ponderosas swung fast in the gusts. Inside the van, the air stifled, tinged with a sting of ozone. The interior was suddenly bright, raked by two white flashes. Winds rocked the van. No one spoke under the relentless booming.

Flames flashed in the two pines, their crests drawing long red arcs against the dark clouds. Embers flew out of the torched branches like rivers of fire, landing in the orchard and on the shop. *Thank God for the metal roof.* Del shouted, "Andi, take this!"

He handed her binoculars. He yelled above the clamor. "See if you can make out whether the sprinklers are working. I'm afraid the pumps could short out."

She scanned near the shore of the lake as lightning lashed the church steeple. She flinched. Then, as she shifted the scope to focus on the sprinklers, an enormous bolt struck just beyond the wood shop. Magnified through the lenses, its brilliance blinded her. She recoiled, eyes stunned. "Damn, that hurts!"

"You okay?" Del asked.

"Don't know. Seeing black." She heard the crashing thunder, but saw only darkness. A chill of fear—was she blind?—jolted her just as another detonation exploded above them. "Here," she said, holding the scope toward Del. He handed it across the seat to Stan on the passenger side in back. "Try to spot the sprinklers."

In a few seconds, she could make out a shape: the HQ tent.

After a moment, Stan shook his head. "Negative. Too much smoke."

Del radioed Chuck. "Can you see if the pumps and sprinklers are working?" He listened, but a huge boom engulfed them. "Say again, Chuck."

Static. Then, Chuck's voice from the radio: "I can get close enough to see."

"Good. Let me know."

Across the lake, the hotshots' personnel carrier crept along the shore to the pumps. The driver's door opened.

Del swore. "Stay the hell inside!"

But no one got out, and the door shut. In a moment, Del's radio crackled. "Everything's working. Want me to check the north pump?"

Before Del answered, a string of bolts tattooed the forest on their side of the lake. Andi jumped. Thunder stormed the van, crushing them in an avalanche of unbearable sound and the smell of ozone. "Right on top of us," Del shouted "Hang on!"

Wind rattled the van again. Andi, eyes closed, braced herself. Another volley of lightning attacked behind them. Enormous sound buffeted her chest and jerked open her eyes; her vision was clearer, but she gagged on the ozone.

Across the lake, the blazing ponderosas swung madly, untamed gusts twirling the trees as if they were twigs. Embers poured toward the wood shop and the monastery and as she watched, both burning trees bent impossibly far.

Del yelled above the thunder. "Microburst! Pray those trees don't fall!"

A massive cracking sounded over the water, slow at first, then faster, louder, drawn out, as if the gates of hell were splitting. In seconds, another ear-piercing crack, monumental in its threat of devastation. Andi's breath caught in her throat. Someone in back yelled, "Can't see. What the shit's happening?"

She called, "The ponderosas!" The giant trees slanted violently toward the wood shop, leaning, falling, then crashing. Embers billowed up, blown by super-heated air toward the back wall of the monastery. Toward the bedrooms.

Del's radio sounded. "Command! Come in, man!"

Thunder deafened them. Del waited. "Del here! You all okay?"

"We can't see! Sounded like two crashes. Trees down?"

"Those ponderosas fell. I don't know how they could've missed the shop, but we can't see where they landed."

Two successive lightning strikes deeper in the forest lit up the interior of their vehicle. Thunder crashed even before the light faded.

"Chuck, work your way along the monastery wall to see where they came down!"

"Second carrier's in the way. I'll send them. Quicker."

Static snarled, then a lightning bolt slammed into the forest ten feet to Del's left. Someone screamed. Thunder's roar drowned it. When it stopped, Del radioed, "Everybody stay in the vehicles. Pass the word. No one outside."

A wave of fear gripped her spine. *No one to fight the fire. No one to save the shop.*

From the heavens, thunder fell on them like wrath.

7

It took twenty minutes.

They knew the shop was burning—new smoke poured into the sky from behind the monastery. They waited, enduring the thunder as it moved away, watching the lightning depart, eyeing the smoke. The wildfire had almost reached the blackened ground of the backburn. Lightning flashed high on the Coliseum, but the storm seemed to have passed the monastery.

Del spoke into his radio. "Chuck, Command here. Come in, Chuck."

"I'm here. I think we're clear, Del. Permission to inspect."

"Affirmative. Two-in, two-out, inspect the situation and report. Everybody else remain in vehicles till I give the all clear."

. . .

After three minutes—Andi had timed the wait, her vision normal— Chuck's call came back. "Both trees took the shop—it's engulfed. The east tree took most of the apple trees, but no fire there. Sprinklers working fine all around. Glass is gone on the second floor and some bedrooms inside have ignited. I don't know the situation on the first floor, but the plywood isn't burning. The outer stone walls look good, but contents inside second floor are burning. I'd recommend attacking it."

Del repeated it. Then, "Clarify: What about the shop?"

"We can't save the shop. The trees destroyed the roof and collapsed the orchard-side wall. All the wood inside has ignited."

Andi clenched, thinking of the abbot's tears. *Those beautiful caskets.* The ache in her throat, the near-nausea in her gut, reminded her of her grief on the night her mother died.

She bore the burning of the caskets in her heart.

8

After another five minutes, she itched to move. "Okay to join Paddy?" she asked Del. "I need some action." She tensed, expecting a "no!"

But instead, he said, "Ordinarily, no. But Paddy says the church and the rest of the monastery are in good shape, and you'll be safe enough there. Wear one of the Nomex suits and a helmet from the back of the van, and stay with Paddy so I can reach you by radio." He looked at a sky brown with smoke that sucked the blue from it, but no black clouds. "If you see lightning, get in a vehicle, any vehicle."

Across the parking area in front of St. Brendan's, two fat hoses snaked from the portable pumps on the shore of St. Mary's Lake, one through the gate and into the monastery, the other around the monastery wall toward the wood shop. Paddy and most of his crew had gathered near the front door of the church. He saw her coming and waved her toward them. When she got there, he said, "So here's the situation: We have two men on a hose on the second floor, and two men"—he pointed to firefighters standing in the doorway to the dormitory—"behind them for rescue if they get in trouble. It's twelve minutes they're inside, so I'll be calling them out straightaway. 'Tis smoky as Hell's kitchen in there, and they'll be out of air in their bottles. They—"

A familiar voice came from Paddy's radio. *Carl Jenkins*, she thought.

"Chief, Carl here. Come in. Over."

"Got you, Carl. Talk to me. Over."

"Visibility is bad up here. Lots of flame everywhere. Heat's intense. Oxygen bottle's getting low. I think we should withdraw to the first floor and wet it real good, try to save it that way."

'Try to save it?' She pushed the thought away.

Paddy was saying, "Affirmative, Carl. Withdraw to the first floor. I'll come back to you in a minute. Over." Andi noticed his clipped and elided speech. Radio language, not brogue.

Carl repeated the order.

Paddy frowned. "If the second floor comes down, and if this wall is wooden" —he waved toward the wall between the vestibule and the dormitory— "don't we have a complete pickle on our hands. Wait here." He turned to one of his men. "Danny, with me. Bring an axe. No need for a mask and bottle, this will be a mere moment." Putting on his own helmet, he said to Andi and the men, "I'll be wantin' to check that wall. Pray it's fine old stone." He and Dan entered the monastery vestibule itself.

Andi said to one of the firefighters, "Because stone won't burn."

"Yep. If it's wood, we fight it right here in the vestibule, or we lose the church."

She suffered another stab of grief, and watched Dan chop holes in the old pine panels every foot or so along the top of the wall. After he'd hit stone behind pine with every blow, Paddy and he turned, Paddy reaching for his radio. To Andi, he called, "The wall's solid stone." He keyed his radio. "Hose Team Lead, this is the Chief. Come in, Carl."

In a moment, Carl responded. "We're coming down, Paddy."

"Carl, new order. Withdraw from the building. Repeat: Withdraw from the building. Keep water on everything as you come out. Reply."

"Copy, Paddy. Withdrawing. Watering everything."

Men backed the water-gorged hose out through the big doors into the courtyard. In a minute, Carl and his partner emerged into the courtyard, and Paddy radioed the engineer at the pump and ordered the water off.

He holstered his radio. "'Tis our prayer now that that old stone will lock the fire in the dormitory."

One firefighter said, "If God built this church right."

Paddy nodded. "Or absent a deity, if we're lucky."

Andi forced her breathing to slow.

As Carl removed his SCBA, helmet and hood, his eyes were wide. *Fear*, she wondered, *or something else?* He avoided her eyes. His hair was matted to his skull. She pictured Death.

Then came the explosion.

9

Almost immediately, Paddy's radio crackled. "Chief, this is Command. Paddy, what the hell happened?"

"Second floor collapsed. Fire's much more intense. Smoke's invadin' the church vestibule now. A hose team I'm sendin' in, attackin' the fire to protect the church."

"Do it. Be safe. Keep me posted."

Paddy holstered his radio and ordered four men to attack the fire in the dormitory, two on the attack hose and two for rescue. To the hose team, he yelled, "Take position at the entrance to the dormitory, check for any fire above, open the door, hit the fire, and push it back from the door. Don't go inside the dormitory, just keep the fire away from the door."

The men carried the stiff hose into the church's vestibule. The rescue team stayed back a few yards, standing inside the big monastery doors, which were propped open to allow the hose in.

Andi looked toward those doors, carved from beautiful yellow pine, polished to a gleam, every bit as beautiful as the glorious caskets in the wood shop. She turned to Paddy. "It's so sad, all those caskets, burned in the shop."

Paddy looked at her a moment. "Sure, and with the dormitory door open, you're not to go into the church through the vestibule, but I'll be showin' you a thing." He turned to another of his men. "Boyo, you're command until I return. Keep contact with the lads on the hose. Second team goes in in ten minutes, should I tarry. Any problems, radio me." He turned back to her. "If you'll follow me, lass?"

Confused, she trailed him around the church and along a narrow drive inside the courtyard wall. "Where are we going?"

"Now that you'll be seein' in no time." He opened a double door at the back corner of the monastery. "Deliveries they take through this door. Next it's into the kitchen you'll be steppin'. It all connects." He gestured her inside. "Follow the first hallway. It'll take you into the church."

"And I want to go into the church why?"

"You'll see soon enough, then."

She entered what she saw was the kitchen. Beyond, the dining hall. She found the hallway to the church, walked along, and entered it.

What she saw stole her breath. And gave her a moment of solace.

• • •

"My God," she whispered, looking at the rows of gleaming caskets lining the aisles.

She spent a few minutes walking among them, caressing them, her throat thick. Then she made her way back around to the monastery doors.

"You saved the caskets," she said to Paddy.

He grinned. "It warms me heart to know it. Me lads moved 'em last night."

"I thought they were lost." She turned to him, her eyes gleaming. "Thank you, Paddy. Thank you more than I can find words for." Then she surprised them both by hugging him, smoky Nomex suits and all.

10

At day's end, Andi drove down the mountain, reeking of smoke, exhausted, but relieved. The firelines had held and although the wood shop and the bedroom wing were lost, no one was injured. The fire had jumped the main fireline where the sprinkler hose ended, blown by the thunderstorm, and was moving north down the mountain, but the monastery was safe. As she drove out of the Narrows and the wide view opened, the setting sun cast a red glow over the valley.

Monastery River glimmered in the ruby light, a rope of color laid along the valley floor.

Despite her fatigue and smoky stink, she turned into the drive to the StreamSide Lodge. She found the abbot in the converted dining room, on his knees with nine other monks. She waited while the men finished their prayers.

Timothy turned, startled that she was there. "My God, Andi, you look exhausted."

"Getting there. I can report how things turned out."

"Thank you. We've been praying for the firefighters and our home."

Her gut churned. She remembered the falling trees, the monstrous flames, the roar as fire devoured the dormitory, the horrifying sound of exploding glass, then the detonation when the second floor collapsed. "Tim, I hate to tell you, but the fire destroyed the wood shop and the bedrooms. The rest of the monastery is safe, but all that's left of the dormitory are the walls and smoldering debris."

The monks seemed to shrink into themselves. A few looked at their brothers, but most stared at her, their eyes wide. A few had tears.

"Tim?"

"The shop and the dormitory, gone?" His voice cracked. "And our church?"

"Is fine. No damage, although there's a bit of smoke, but not bad."

One of the monks raised his hand. "What, Anselm?" the abbot said.

"Sheriff, what about our caskets?"

She smiled. "Saved. Paddy and his crew moved them all into the church. They're perfect." This seemed to revive them; a few even smiled. A silence stretched out. Andi looked past the men out through the open doors to the river. The cottonwoods on the bank were alight with the day's last sun, which glowed red through the smoky air.

Then, his voice soft as a prayer, Timothy said, "Our caskets saved. Perhaps there actually is a God who loves us."

Chapter Twenty-Three — Friday

1

Next morning, eleven-thirty, Andi stood with her team and four deputies on the northbound shoulder of Highway 91, at the gate to Vic Sobstak's pasture. Their vehicles waited on the shoulder behind them, light bars flashing.

Greg pointed north. "Here he comes."

A white crew cab pickup with the BLM inverted triangle logo on the door slowed and Andi waved. The truck pulled onto the opposite shoulder. The Adams County team crossed the highway toward it.

A tall, brawny man with a shock of white hair got out, his big hand outstretched. "Sheriff Pelton?" A small woman climbed down from the front passenger seat, and a swarthy man with a wide smile and jet-black hair got out of the back.

"Agent Lander?" Andi took the big man's hand.

He didn't shake hers, he crushed it. "Sam Lander, BLM special agent. My men are Carlita Muñoz and Rocco Mancini, both rangers."

Andi looked at Carlita, who rolled her eyes. "Your *men*, Agent Lander?"

Lander grinned. "Figure of speech." He pointed south. "I looked up your town. Not much there."

Andi bristled. "It's small enough, that's true. But we've got our share of big problems."

Lander interrupted. "Don't get your shorts in a bunch, Sheriff. Just observing." He reached out and shook Greg's hand. "Haney, you Fibbie dog." He slapped him on the back. To Andi, he said, "Greg here's a good guy, you should be so lucky he's on your side. But the

BLM's been on the dance card with plenty of these *nudniks*. Haney's the best guy for this *tsuris* you got on your hands. Except for me."

"*Tsuris?*" She couldn't get the t-sound onto the front like Lander did.

"Aggravation. It's Yiddish." He reached out to Ben. "You look like the old-timer on this crew. Sam Lander."

"Ben Stewart." They shook. "I'm the former sheriff, a deputy now. Greg's told us you're the best man for our plan."

Sam Lander folded his arms and looked fierce. "I'm the best *mentsch* for any plan." He turned to Andi. "So, *nu*, tell me this plan, honey."

Testing me, she thought, amused. "My husband's daughter hates it when we call her honey. Almost as much as I do."

"*Oy*, I'm *verklempt*." But his gray eyes twinkled.

Carlita laughed. "Sam, knock off the playacting and let's figure out how to help end this shindig."

Lander laughed, a big bellow, and looked at her fondly. Carlita said to Andi, "This dope's the best damn special agent I've ever served with. And you've got him on your side in three minutes. He adores tough babes."

2

Andi looked around the scene; everyone at the ready. Jay's red camera light glowed. She looked at the twelve men, standing in a line facing her team. *Apprehensive*, Andi thought. The air was hot, and the men were sweating. Their hands, their faces, and their hair were filthy. She looked at their hands.

"Didn't want to waste water," one of the men said, looking embarrassed at the grime.

Quinn, his hands no longer tied but still angry, half-turned away from her, radiating contempt.

She said, "Gentlemen, we're here to listen to your proposal for the disposition of this federal land you've been occupying. The Bureau of Land Management has sent Special Agent Sam Lander and Rangers

Carlita Muñoz and Rocco Mancini to receive your proposal. We've agreed to broadcast this meeting live. You've agreed, in turn, that you will end your occupation. Shall we begin?"

Quinn stepped out of the line. "*Acting* Sheriff, I never agreed to that. My position is that we will remain here until we receive word that the BLM has met our demand."

Sam Lander snorted.

Another protester said, "Sheriff, Mr. Quinn no longer speaks for us. We have agreed to the conditions you outlined. I'm prepared to speak for our group."

Lander walked into the camp—what was left of it—his hand extended to the guy who'd spoken. Quinn shouted at him. "Stand back, Agent. This is our camp and you are not welcome inside."

Lander turned and approached Quinn. "Nix to that, *nudnik*. This land belongs to the government of the United States. I got a tip for you, buster—play nice, give your speech, then get the hell out of here before I arrest your sorry butt." He extended his hand again. "Now shake hands with me and let's get this show on the road."

"Fuck that, you federal pig. I don't shake hands with cockroaches."

Lander's bellowing laugh shocked everyone. "Never in a long and action-packed career have I been called both a pig and a bug in the same sentence." Still laughing, he went over to the other eleven and asked their names. "Just your first name, though. If I were you, talking to a federal pig and cockroach should caution you to keep your last name to yourself."

The man who'd spoken smiled. "I'm Norman." They shook.

Andi relaxed a little.

Lander said, "Okay, Norman, give your pitch. I'm listening."

Norman pulled a folded paper out of one pocket and a pair of reading glasses from another. "Our group accepts no authority higher than that of the county sheriff. The federal government and the Bureau of Land Management therefore must transfer ownership of this land to the sheriff of Adams County." It went on for a while.

Quinn, however, stood apart, rigid. Lander said to him, "You got a little speech, *schnuk*?"

Quinn spit on the ground.

"Okay, no speech." He turned to the others. "Yep. Real familiar ideas. Posse Comitatus, right? 'Power of the county'?"

Andi was watching Quinn, who spat again. "We don't need your translation, Lander. We need your answer. Now."

Lander stepped back to Andi's side. He said, "My answer, *boychik*, is that I'm not the one who gives answers. My bosses in Washington will get a copy of the video you folks just made and if you'll give me your business cards or let me know your mailing addresses, they'll contact you." He made a face. "With *their* answer."

Quinn shook his head. "That's total bullshit. I give you any contact information and your rangers will crawl all over me."

Lander laughed. "Now that's a reasonable assumption, bud. So, if you want their answer, you'll have to watch the evening news." He turned to Jay and Katie. "Turn off your recording devices." He turned back to Quinn as soon as the red light on Jay's camera winked out. "Off the record, bud, my personal and completely unofficial answer is: *Schtupp* yourself and the horse you rode in on." He walked back toward Carlita and Rocco, "Let's get back to Billings."

Andi said, "Thanks for your help, Sam."

"Always glad to give a pretty *shiksa* a hand."

Andi and Carlita rolled their eyes.

• • •

When the BLM crew cab had left the ridge, Andi said to the protesters, "You've got three hours to finish cleaning up your camp. To help, I've ordered a truck sent up. You can put all your garbage in it, and we'll take it down later. Have you found the keys to Dolan's RV and Stenborg's car?"

Norman nodded, pulled them from his pocket, and handed them to her.

"Okay. We'll be back at—" She looked at her watch. "—three this afternoon. Any questions?"

Quinn shook his head angrily. "This was a fucking sham. I'm leaving now."

"You'll leave your friends to do the clean-up?" She could see the anger on their faces. "Well, no, you're not leaving now. You're staying here until the camp is clean. If you try to leave before I come back, the FBI will arrest you at the bottom. That clear?"

"I'll sue you for false imprisonment."

Andi laughed at the irony. "Do that, Quinn. I'd love to testify about everything you've been up to here." She turned and said to her team, "We're done."

3

Thirty minutes later, Andi stood with Greg and Joe, watching the FBI camp being dismantled. The SWAT agents worked steadily and the tents were being loaded into the equipment truck fast. The guys wanted to get home. Greg had okayed moving the personnel carriers closer to the tents so the guys could load their duffels and personal belongings into the storage bins.

Greg told her the teams would be gone by three-thirty this afternoon, just after the protesters came down. She was about to say she'd be in the shower by then, when they both heard a vehicle on the access road, pounding down fast. They whirled to see. A pickup, speed way too high, dust billowing behind, rocking and bucking as it hit potholes and dips, thudding and crashing down the access road.

"It's Quinn!" Andi yelled. Running toward the road, she unholstered.

An agent ran ahead of her to the base of the road and held up his hand. Quinn never slowed. Last minute, the agent leapt to the side of the road. Quinn's left front bumper clipped his leg. He fell to the ground with a painful grunt.

Andi jumped away, so the agent wasn't in her line of fire, and shot at Quinn's rear tire.

It blew out. Even she was surprised. But Quinn kept driving, slowed by the flat tire.

Joe Mitchell yelled to another agent, "Robert, with me in the pickup!" The two men ran to the FBI crew cab, jumped in, and roared down the dirt road after Quinn, who had reached the highway and turned north.

Andi called to her deputy, Xavier Contrerez. "Xav, go! Back them up!" The deputy sprinted to his vehicle and roared after the agents.

Andi and Greg ran to the injured agent, who lay on the dirt, his face pale. "I think it's broken."

Andi said to Greg, "Help me get him into the squad and I'll run him to the hospital."

She and Greg gently helped him to the vehicle. Greg said, "I'm going with you."

Andi said, "Stay here. We need to close the access road again, and I want you here if somebody else up there makes a break."

"Got it. You coming back at three or do you want me to let them go?"

"Wouldn't miss it."

4

Joe drove, and Robert rode shotgun. They caught up to Quinn in no time.

A half mile or so north on the highway, Joe said, "The tire's exploding." He backed off for safety, and watched with Robert as rubber flew everywhere and Quinn lost control, swerving at fifty into the ditch. His pickup flipped ninety degrees, then rolled again, coming to rest on its roof. Joe left the road and pulled in behind Quinn's truck. Xavier Contrerez sped into the space right in front.

The upside-down driver's door opened and Quinn rolled onto the grass, lifting his pistol toward the agents behind him. Joe yelled, "Down!" and he and Robert dove below the dashboard. Quinn fired into their windshield, showering them with glass, then jumped up and ran toward the highway.

Xavier yelled, "Stop!" He slammed open his door and jumped out, unholstering his pistol.

Quinn whirled toward Xavier and fired. Xavier fell. Joe yelled to Robert, "Deputy down!" and fired at Quinn. Missed. Fired again. Another miss. This time, Quinn turned to fire at joe, and Joe hit him, saw blood bloom on his left shoulder. Quinn fell, his gun in his right hand.

Joe approached cautiously, his Glock extended, his heart pounding. Loud, he said, "Quinn, if you move, I shoot."

Quinn roared, swung his gun arm up toward Joe. Both fired.

Robert, running from where Xavier had fallen, fired. Quinn screamed, fell back against the asphalt. His head bounced; his eyes closed. Blood spread in two places on his chest.

Joe, angry now, heart pounding, ran in and kicked Quinn's pistol out of his hand into the grass beside the highway, rolled him over, started cuffing his wrists. Quinn tried to pull away, but cried out from the pain of the two gunshot wounds and fell back. Joe finished cuffing him.

Joe said, "Nice shot, man. Let's hope he doesn't die before we arrest him." He looked back toward where Xavier lay in the grass. "How's Xavier?"

"I don't know—he's hit in the chest. I called for an ambulance."

"Is he conscious?"

"In and out."

"Look, I'm going to see how he is. I'll call another ambulance for this asshole."

Joe, starting to come down from the rush, ran over to Xavier, who lay in the grass. Joe saw the blood on the side of his chest. Not good, but Xavier's eyes were open.

"You . . . get him?" Xavier asked, breathing hard.

"Got him. Two wounds to the chest."

Xavier said, "You're hit."

Joe shook his head. "Naw. Just Quinn. I—"

Xavier pointed at Joe's sleeve, now red with blood.

"Oh."

5

At three o'clock that afternoon, Andi and Ben left their pickup and walked to the broken camp, followed by three deputies who'd driven the SUV. "God, it's hotter'n hell even a thousand feet in the air," Ben muttered. The protesters were sweating heavily and looked miserable and filthy. There was no semblance of a camp, just the RV and Stenborg's pickup, the protesters' campers or pickups lined up ready to leave, and the department truck loaded with trash. The row of toilets that had stood behind the camp looked forlorn, out of place, a row of miniature green rooms standing alone in a field, one of them overturned. The water tanker sat isolated on the grass.

Andi said, "My deputies are going to inspect the area before you leave."

"It's clean, for Christ's sake, lady. We bagged every lousy piece of trash," Norman said. "It's all in your damn truck."

She let slide his angry tone—from hunger, no doubt. "Good." She nodded to Felix, who, with two other deputies, walked around all the remaining vehicles, looking for any garbage left behind. Andi told the protesters what had happened with Quinn. "When Quinn escaped, the FBI caught him half a mile up the highway, and there was a firefight. He wounded one of my deputies and FBI agent Mitchell."

"Quinn's dead?" Norman said, his voice raspy.

Andi wondered what he hoped the answer was.

She let the question hang in the air for a moment. Then, "No. He's under arrest in the hospital. He's lucky, his wounds are serious but won't kill him. Once he's out of the hospital, he'll be arraigned."

From behind the water tanker, Deputy Felix Maslow yelled, "Sheriff, you'd better see this."

On the back side of the tanker, someone had spray-painted "Hang the sheriff!" Andi's fury rose in her chest, so she calmed herself before she walked back to the protesters. "Who painted that?" she demanded.

A man who hadn't spoken before said, "Quinn. Before he made his break."

She shook her head. "I have two choices. I can arrest all of you for vandalism and try to find a way to prove it—"

The men began to shout and swear. "You fucking said you wouldn't arrest us." "Damn you, bitch!" "The goddamn hell—" "Hey, it was Quinn!" Their voices ran together.

She held up her hand, and they quieted. "Or, I can let you go. I want you men out of my county, so that's what I'm doing. Get the hell off this mountain, drive north, and never come back, or I'll arrest your butts faster than you can wipe them."

$$\bullet \quad \bullet \quad \bullet$$

When they were gone, Andi and Ben surveyed the area. The toilets stood—or lay, in the overturned toilet's case—abandoned in their lonesome green row. All that remained were Stenborg's beat-up pickup, Dolan's RV, the department's garbage-laden truck, the toilets, and the tanker. She said to Ben, "And all for what? A lousy speech to a camera."

She studied the trash in the county's truck: piles of black bags stuffed with throw-away cups and paper towels and God knows what else; boxes of empty liquor and beer bottles; soiled sheets crammed into paper grocery bags; a torn American flag. She shook her head. "Freedom Camp."

Ben spat on the ground. "All the work, all the trouble, Brad's death—at the end, it don't amount to more'n a pile of crap."

She nodded and tried to smile, but her face was too tight. "All right," she said. "Let's be done with this."

6

At the foot of the access road, Andi, her squad car the last vehicle down, pulled aside and parked. For a minute, she watched the agents taking seats in the personnel carriers, then climbed out of the pickup into the heat and walked toward Greg Haney sitting on the tailgate of the FBI pickup, writing. Sweat darkened his armpits. Greg looked up at her as she approached.

"Have you had any word from Joe and Xavier?"

"Joe's sitting in the truck," he pointed behind himself. "Joe, come say goodbye to Andi."

Andi saw the heavy bandage on his forearm. "Sorry I can't shake. Hurts when I move my hand."

"Bad?"

"Naw, just a scratch," he said. "I didn't feel anything till Xavier pointed it out. Hurts some now, though."

"Thanks for all your help, Joe. I appreciate your work for us."

Joe blushed. "Oh, I forgot. The ER doc said he'd call you about Xavier."

"Good. I—" She pulled out her cell. Doc Keeley's number appeared. One voice message. To Greg, she said, "He called. I'd like to take it,"

"Of course," Greg nodded as he slid his notes into a briefcase.

Keeley's message said, *Andi, Xavier will be all right, although I'm keeping him a couple days to jump on any infection. I expect, he'll be up and about in a week or two, but at home. He should be recovered in six or seven weeks. If anything changes, I'll call you stat.*

She relayed the news.

"Good," he said. He reached out his hand. She shook it. "I've been impressed with your work, Andi. You've shown professionalism and courage. This could've gone very badly, but your restraint made a big difference."

It caught her off guard. "We, uh, we all, that is, everybody . . . did their part." *Get a grip*, she told herself. "I couldn't have handled this without you and Joe. You leaving now?"

Greg nodded. "We'll be on the road within ten minutes, home by six-thirty. The Salt Lake guys left just a few minutes before you and your team got here. Everybody's itching to see their families."

She laughed. "And itching from all the sweat."

7

As soon as Ed picked up Andi's call, she said, "Hey, big guy! They're gone!"

Ed, standing in his office doorway, could sense the satisfaction in Andi's voice. "Fantastic, kid. That's a load off your shoulders."

"A hell of a load. Look, I've got a report to write and then I want us to—"

Ed's phone gave triple beep. He held the phone away, scanned the screen. "Andi, hold on. I've got a call. It's Lynn. I have to take this."

"Good luck," she said as he ended the call.

• • •

His chest tightened. "Wish me luck!" He opened the other call. "Lynn! Have you and Rachel—" He reined himself in. *Let her lead.* "How're you doing?"

The line was quiet. Ed held his breath. Released it.

Lynn said, "Ed, this is hard."

He sagged against the doorframe. "You're saying no."

She exhaled. "Rachel said no, then told me if I stayed on with you, she'd leave." She sniffed. "So, I lose either way."

Ed forced a calm he didn't feel and took refuge in technique. "So, you lose Rachel if you stay with your dream or you lose your dream of private practice—"

She broke in, "—if I stay with her." She sobbed softly. "I could lose her anyway. What if I get another chance and she still says no? Can I trust her not to?"

Ed shook his head. *Don't go there.* "What do *you* want, Lynn?"

Her silence stretched out. Ed held his breath, but had to release it before she finally whispered, "I'm giving you two weeks' notice, okay?"

CHAPTER TWENTY-FOUR — SATURDAY

1

Abbot Timothy wept.

He stood in the monastery parking area with Andi, gazing at the desolation. Trees, their lower trunks and branches sooty, stood over blackened ground still smoldering around his monastery. "It took everything," he whispered. For a moment he looked in silence at the destruction, then pulled out a handkerchief and wiped his eyes. "Show me the orchard and the wood shop."

Andi led the abbot to the main fireline along the monastery wall. The black soil, the emptiness of the once-dense forest, and the silence, thick as smoke, were eerie. As they rounded the corner of the wall and stepped onto the fireline, still muddy from the sprinklers, the abbot stopped. The two huge ponderosas, charred and denuded, lay amid the ashes of the wood shop. Smells of wet charred wood came from the debris.

"Dear God in Heaven," Timothy whispered. He walked closer, close enough to see the broken apple trees in the orchard. He turned to Andi, his eyes brimming. "Why didn't they burn?"

"Sprinklers," she said.

The abbot nodded. He walked along the broken trees and looked up into the second-floor windows, all shattered, their frames scorched. Looking up through the smashed windows, they saw blue sky.

The fallen ponderosas blocked their way to the ash pile that had been the wood shop. "If we walk around the monastery, we can get there. Do you have time?"

Before she could even say, "Of course," he turned back toward the main fireline and circled the monastery with long strides. Andi kept up with him. When they reached the shop, the abbot stood quietly. Andi stayed behind him slightly. Mounds of ash, some of it giving off small curlicues of smoke, piled around charred beams and jagged slabs of wall. The ruins lay beneath the huge trees. Andi made out nothing of the inside other than ashes and scorched wood. Timothy stepped closer, onto the edge of the ashes.

"Wait, Abbot," Andi said. "Your shoes'll be a mess."

Timothy sighed. "Shoes can be cleaned."

He stood silently, then folded his hands, and Andi saw his lips moving softly. Tears wet his cheeks. After his prayer, he made the sign of the cross over the ruins.

• • •

They returned to the monastery gate. Timothy held back a moment. "Where are all the firefighters?"

"They're down at Webber's Creek. The creek runs through a wide flat for a long way. They're building a new fireline to stop the fire there."

"Ah." Timothy took in a long breath and looked up at the gleaming monastery doors. "I guess I need to go in."

Andi said, "It's still too dangerous to go into the dorm, but you can see enough from the door."

But someone had nailed up a sheet of plywood over the dormitory entrance and spray-painted *DANGER!!! DO NOT ENTER!!!* on it. Andi examined it. "Do you have a Philips screwdriver, Tim?"

Tears came to his eyes. "All our tools were in the wood shop. No."

She reached for her cell phone. The smell of wet burned wood was too much. "Let's step outside so I can call Paddy."

Paddy answered. "Ah, lass, it's surely a mixed outcome we're havin'. Where are ye?"

"At St. Brendan's with Abbot Timothy. He needs to see the dorm. Can you send one of your guys up to take away the plywood over the door?"

"Ah, as to that, I'll be discouragin' it. The danger—"

"Not to go in, just to see it."

"Oh, now that'll be another kettle of fish. I'll send a lad now. Give him twenty minutes."

•   •   •

It took closer to a half hour, which Timothy spent in the church, praying. When Andi, waiting outside, saw a pickup pulling into the monastery drive, she entered the church and said, quietly, "Tim, he's here." In a moment, the fellow came into the vestibule, carrying a toolbox.

"Carl?" she ventured.

Jenkins saw her, stopped, froze. After a tense moment, he cleared his throat. "You said we wouldn't be arrested. Are you—?"

"Not arresting anybody," she said, smiling. "The abbot—" She stopped. "Abbot Timothy, this is Carl Jenkins, a rancher from the north valley. He's one of the volunteers who fought the fire." To Carl, she said, "I need to tell you guys how grateful everyone is to you. You've gone way beyond the call of duty."

Jenkins looked surprised. "Those of us up on that mountain, I think we all feel a little foolish. Made us want to work harder." He glanced at the abbot. "You know, redeem ourselves."

Andi thought back to the magic teddy she used to "redeem" herself with Ed. "Tell the others there's nothing to worry about. People's politics are their business, until they force them onto others, which makes it my business. You men paid your debt here on the fire."

Carl looked at her for a moment, nodded, and turned. "I'll see to that plywood."

Ten minutes later, Timothy stood at the doorway, staring into the devastation. The air was foul with the smell of wet scorched wood and fabric. Nothing remained but the soot-stained stone walls surrounding a piled jumble of charred and broken lumber, fractured chunks of flooring at all angles, collapsed and burned wallboard. More than half the roof had caved in and fallen on top of the interior debris. Andi stood close enough to sense the abbot's trembling.

Scattered in the ruins were burned fabrics, clothing or bedclothes or curtains. Charred books and hulks of chairs and tables. Very near the door, a twisted metal crucifix lay face-down. Timothy stepped into the ashes and retrieved it. The Christ figure had melted into a slender ingot. The abbot shook his head. "The fires of Hell."

Andi moved slightly closer to him. After a moment, she said, "I'm sorry, Tim. So sorry."

The abbot straightened his shoulders, nodded. "I am too, Andi."

2

Turning from the door, Timothy said, "I'd like to spend more time in prayer, if you don't mind, and then check the offices and the refectory. Can you give me a half hour?"

"Take all the time you need," she said. In the courtyard, she saw the delivery van. "Grace and the women running Operation Square Meal are here to do lunch—Del North gave them the green light. I'll wait with them."

Timothy looked back at the doorway to the dorm. "This is so much worse than I'd imagined. I'm worried now whether our insurance will be enough to . . .." He sighed again. "I need to pray."

• • •

The van carrying Grace and the women with the food for the firefighters had pulled into the parking area. Andi waved.

Grace jumped out and ran to her, anguish on her face. "Omigod, Andi! This is horrible!" She pointed at the darkened ground surrounding the monastery. "I had no idea."

Andi gave her a hug. "Yeah, it's terrible. But thank God, nobody was hurt."

The church lady in charge of the food prep approached. "Sheriff, I don't see nobody around. How many men we fixin' lunch for?"

Andi told her to prep for two separate groups. "The HQ team is in their tent, that's seven, and the hotshots and Paddy's crews are down on Webber's Creek digging another fireline."

"If I remember right, that's forty-four, then, on Webber's?"

"Yeah, that's right." Andi glanced at her watch. And the abbot and three others from the valley should be here at lunch time, so if you have enough for them . . ."

"Of course we do," she said, smiling. "Always enough." She rubbed her hands together. "Okay, then. We'll feed the folks up here first, then take lunch down to Webber's Creek on our way home." She walked to a wide side gate in the monastery wall where the delivery van was parked and opened the gate. The driver eased the food truck through. Grace said to Andi, "We unload right into the kitchen. I gotta go."

"Come with me first."

Andi opened the big door to the church. "Be quiet," Andi whispered, "the abbot's praying."

When she saw the caskets lining the aisles, Grace whispered, "Oh my God." The late morning sunlight filtering through the stained-glass windows bathed the yellow and blue pine caskets in dappled beauty. "It's like the fire never happened," Grace whispered.

They made their way to the kitchen, where the women were already assembling prime rib sandwiches on the counters and warming rhubarb pies in the oven. Andi watched, listening to their quiet chatter, the gossip and jokes and small-town talk. For the first time since the Posse showed up in her county, Andi felt at ease.

3

Andi left them to their work and walked around to the front of the monastery. As she stepped outside into the heat, she saw Ed's pickup in the parking area. Walking toward her with Ed was Jack Conrad, the county commissioner.

"Hey, Jack. Come to see the damage?"

"That, and plenty more. But before anything else, let me extend the commissioners' gratitude for your management of the protest and the fire."

"Thanks, Jack. I had no role in managing the fire. Thanks for that go to Magnus, Paddy, and our volunteer fire department, and the hotshots and Del North's team. The protest, well, without Ben and Mack and Ed and the FBI teams, we'd have been in another kind of hell."

Conrad nodded his approval. "Praising the team. Right thing for a politician to do."

Andi flinched inside. *Politician!*

Ed grinned.

"All right," she said. "What's next?"

Ed said, "We're here to see the abbot. And Mack should be here any minute."

4

They found Timothy in his office, scribbling intently on a yellow pad. When they knocked, he looked up, startled, then stood. "Jack, Ed. Welcome to St. Brendan's." His eyes were red.

Jack shook his hand. "Abbot, the county's very sorry about your losses. I know you're very busy and I'll be brief."

Abbot Timothy pointed to chairs. "Please, have a seat."

Jack spoke as he seated himself. "The county considers St. Brendan's an important part of our community. We want to help you rebuild your dormitory. The commissioners voted a donation of twenty-thousand dollars, and . . ."

Abbot Timothy fell back into his chair. "Good Lord, Jack, how did you know? I spoke with our agent. Our policy will cover some rebuilding, but the limits of the policy are minimal. She doubts we can rebuild the dormitory to anything like its previous quality."

Another knock came at the door. Magnus Anderssen appeared in the frame. "May I join you?"

"Of course, Mack," Timothy said. "Come in. Jack has just made an unbelievable offer from the county."

Magnus pulled up a chair and sat, nodding. "I know. We discussed it yesterday."

Conrad said, "There's more, Abbot. I'm friends with a major contractor back in the Twin Cities, a good Catholic guy. His firm does skyscrapers, so he's got whatever you'll need. He's talking to his board about dedicating a crew to your project. He'll bring an architect and a structural engineer."

Timothy looked stunned. "This could cost—"

"A few million," Conrad said.

Timothy folded his hands. Little tremors rippled on his lips. Andi thought, *Praying?* "There's no way St. Brendan's can afford millions, Jack. I know we'll get support from the other monasteries in our congregation, but they're poor too."

"You won't have to afford millions, Abbot."

Timothy looked at Jack, then at Andi, his eyes wide. "You just said . . ."

"That's what my friend is talking with his board about. He wants them to donate the work. At no cost to you."

Timothy could say nothing, a look of disbelief in his eyes.

Jack laughed. "I told you, he's a good Catholic boy. Not to mention that it'll be a heck of a tax deduction for his firm."

5

Andi, sitting at the side table away from the men, glanced at Ed. His eyes were red, a small sign of the grief he'd shared with her last night, after Lynn Monroe had given her notice, his "retirement plan" up in smoke, like the dormitory and the wood shop. But he looked collected.

"My turn, Tim," he said. "You know a disaster like this can take a massive psychological toll. Even on monks." He smiled. He told the abbot he was prepared to offer his services *pro bono* if any of the monks—or Timothy himself—showed signs of stress.

Timothy's already red eyes glistened. "Ed, I can't ask you to accept that expense, I—"

"Tim, you don't need to ask. I'm telling you I'll do it."

Timothy's head bowed. For a moment, his head stayed low, then he looked at Ed. Andi saw something in his eyes that hadn't been there since the evacuation: a flicker of hope.

Magnus Anderssen cleared his throat and looked at Ed. "Are you done, my friend?"

"I am."

"So," Magnus smiled, turning to the abbot. "We haven't talked about your wood shop and your casket business. May I assume that your insurance on that building won't cover a full rebuilding?"

Timothy, looking stricken, nodded. "My agent doubts we'll be able to replace it."

"I thought so." He told Timothy that one of his loggers, the old fascist named Ad Schaefer, had given him an idea. At Magnus's copper mine, there stood an old unused workshop, larger than St. Brendan's had been. Vacant for years, it would need refinishing, but its structure and roof were sound. "I'm willing, when you're ready, to disassemble it and move it up here and reassemble it. You and your monks are wood workers, so I'll leave the interior renovation to you, although Ad asked me if he could work on it with you—seems he's got a soft spot for monks. Anyway, it'll make a fine home for your casket business."

The abbot, tears by now streaming down his cheeks, rose. Everyone else stood as well. Unable to speak, with his fingers tented on his desk, he looked at all three, one by one.

Then he spoke, his voice soft. "In a monastery, you look for signs of love in the little kindnesses that make living with other men bearable. I'm told it's the same in marriage." He looked at Andi, then Ed. "Monks know that the age of miracles is over. We don't look for them, don't believe in them, and pretty much don't hope for them. We try to find hints of God in the small things. But today, you have given my brothers and me a miracle."

Ed smiled. "Tim, that's what the folks of Monastery Valley do, as you know because you do too. We take care of our own."

Andi raised her hand. Her stomach had been growling. "Abbot, may I say something?"

"Please."

Her stomach growled again, audibly. She chuckled. "At this very moment, Operation Square Meal is taking care of us all with prime rib sandwiches and rhubarb pie. Let's go get some."

6

Eight-fifteen. Ed sat on the porch swing, Andi in the chair facing him, looking south, watching the smoke billowing into the sky. Sunset was an hour away. She watched the westering sun shining on the smoke plume, although its light would soon pass behind clouds boiling over the Monastery Range. "I hope the Webber's Creek fireline stops the fire. If it jumps there, there's nothing to stop it reaching Mack's southern fields. It'll burn through all his hay in no time, right north into town."

Ed smiled. "Won't happen. He's got his crew scraping a fireline a hundred yards wide inside his south fence line. He said losing a half-percent of his hay profit was worth protecting his apple orchards."

Andi chuckled. "I should have known Mack'd be a step ahead."

The screen door burst open and Grace rushed out. Andi held up her hand. "Whoa, girl. Where you off to?"

"Town. Jen and Dana's husbands are having boys' night out, so we are too."

Ed said, "Having boys' night out?"

Grace just looked at him, one eyebrow arched. "Girls' night *in*. There may be drinking, so Dana and I will sleep at Jen's."

Andi said, "Good thinking. Otherwise, it'd be two misdemeanors."

"Two?"

"Yeah. Underage drinking and driving drunk."

"Ah." Grace skipped down the porch steps and headed for her PV. "See you legal eagles tomorrow."

Ed watched her drive out of the yard. "A night to ourselves, and no Posse or wildfire to interrupt us."

Out of nowhere, she thought about Brit Ordrew, then about Brad Ordrew's isolation and loneliness. About how grateful being married to this man made her.

Ed said, "I've got something on my mind."

She laughed. "You've *always* got sex on your mind. Shouldn't you be slowing down a little? You're sixty, right?"

"Actually, I wasn't thinking of sex, but if *you'd* like to discuss it—"

She remembered her magic teddy. "You were thinking about *what*, exactly?"

"How about we reschedule our honeymoon? I called our travel agent today. We can get set up in a week."

Inside, Andi tightened. "Ah, man, that'd be, uh, great. But . . ."

Ed smiled. "Don't stick your 'but' in my face."

"I'm sheriff now, and—"

"Whoa, Andi! Being sheriff doesn't mean you can't have a life out of uniform."

He's right, she told herself, and took a moment to collect herself. "I suppose that's true."

"Let's take charge of this job right at the start. I don't have any problem with you laser-focusing when something bad is happening. But in between crises, I want us to have a life together."

She tried to hold back her annoyance. "*Enough*, Ed. I *said* you're right."

"No, you said you *supposed* I was right."

"Damn it, I—" She stopped. "Do you sense something wrong?"

"Such as, we're arguing on the first evening we have to ourselves with no serious worries to deal with?"

"That too, but no. Something else. I just felt kind of . . . I don't know. Something physical."

"Could be your body's just catching up with the mention of sex."

Then she realized what it was. "Ed, the temperature's dropping. I feel a *cool* breeze."

They looked at the Monastery Range in the west. Over its peaks, clouds were pouring into the valley, obscuring the sun.

Andi whispered, "Good God, this better not be another dry lightning storm."

Ed stood, alarmed. "Let me check the forecast."

A minute later he came back out, reading his cell phone. "Fast-moving cold front and heavy rain starting . . ." He studied his watch. ". . . any time now."

Andi jumped up, stood looking at the clouds spilling into the valley. "How heavy?"

He frowned at his phone's screen and scrolled down until he found something. "Wow. Half-an-inch an hour, and it's forecast to last through 4:00 a.m. That could mean three-and-a-half, four inches."

The breeze freshened, delicious, cool, and moist. Fat raindrops splatted on their vehicles and the porch steps.

"Think it'll be enough to put out the fire?"

Ed shrugged. "No idea. But we can hope. It'll sure slow it, though."

Andi stood. "Ed, let's start that out-of-uniform life now. Take off your clothes."

As Ed just stared at her, she unbuttoned her shirt and removed it. Took off her bra. Stripped down to her skivvies, slipped out of them. "Come on, old man. Get the clothes off."

In seconds, Ed got naked, grinning.

She took his hand and led him off the porch. "Out into the rain, bucko," she said. "I want to feel it on my skin."

THE END

AUTHOR'S NOTE

Here's to Freddie Manton, former host at Brit's Pub in downtown Minneapolis, a fine watering hole where some of my best writing was done before we moved to north Idaho. I'm going to let you in on a little secret about Freddie at the end of this; but I'd also love it if you'd read the tribute to Freddie on Brit's Pub's website: https://britspub.com/about. It's a hoot. Just like Freddie.

When I lived and worked in Minneapolis, an evening or two a week I'd walk the five blocks from my office on Loring Park to Brit's on the Nicollet Mall, and Freddie always greeted me cheerily at the door. He was intrigued that I wrote fiction—"Ah, Bill Percy, you've the gift of gab!"—and I was enchanted by his enormous appetite for flirtation. No longer a rock and roll drummer in Liverpool, now aging but still spry, Freddie was everyone's favorite raconteur, man of the world, and incorrigible flirt. No young lady ever went to her table unescorted by Freddie (her husband or boyfriend trailing behind). I enjoyed watching it, then leaning down to my laptop and my next paragraph.

Freddie used to say, "Bill Percy, aye, you're the scholar and I'm the scoundrel." You can see his phrase on Brit's home page: *Serving Scholars and Scoundrels since 1990.*

On my last visit to Minneapolis, I'd gone to Brit's to spend a couple of hours, down a pint, and work on a very early draft of *The Fury Before the Fire.* When I asked after Freddie, the manager gave me the sad news: Freddie had died just the night before. A hole opened in my heart. Without thinking, I tapped on my laptop screen and said, "Stuart, I'm going to dedicate this book to Freddie." In earlier drafts, I had named one of the deputies after him, but realized that after reading the dedication in the front matter, readers might be distracted from the story by knowing the name belonged to a real person. So, here's the secret I promised: I renamed F̲reddie M̲anton "F̲elix M̲aslow." While I gave Freddie's initials to Felix, I gave the fire chief, Paddy Malloy, an Irish accent (because Liverpool's accent is said to resemble an Irish brogue) in honor of Freddie. "Felix" is Latin for "happy, lucky," and believe me, I don't know anyone who was more *felix* than Freddie. He is missed.

• • ••

The Posse Comitatus (Latin for "power of the county") is a radical right-wing organization that combines an anti-government and anti-taxation ideology with Christian Identity beliefs and virulent anti-Semitism and racism. (You can read more about the group, if you wish, at http://tinyurl.com/ybdds447.) Posse members believe that the sheriff is the highest legal authority in the land. The spray-painted phrase, "Hang the sheriff" on the water tanker in the closing pages of the book, refers to an infamous injunction in a pamphlet written by one of the earliest members of the Posse, back in the mid-20th century. He wrote that if a county sheriff doesn't do his duty and protect the values of Christian Identity, anti-Semitism and racism, anti-taxation, and resist encroachment by the federal government, Posse members should take that sheriff "to the most populated intersection in the township" and hang him at high noon (https://tinyurl.com/ybdds447). This was written in the mid-20th century.

In writing the story of Reverend Crane's occupation, I decided not to focus on the Christian Identity, sovereign citizen, anti-Semitic/racist, and anti-taxation dimensions of the Posse's core beliefs, but on their anti-federal government politics, their adherence to unrestricted gun ownership, and their willingness to use violence to achieve their ends. The Posse appeared to have faded away after the 1990s, but it has come roaring back in the last decade. Cliven Bundy's

2014 occupation of federal lands over his refusal to pay federal grazing fees, and his son Aamon's 2016 occupation of the Malheur National Wildlife Refuge in Oregon, are two recent examples of Posse activities.

Given the surging energy of right-wing terrorism over the last decade, I wanted to study the phenomenon and tell a story that affects every American, no matter how distant it may seem—and to tell it as a story-teller, not as a scholar (or a scoundrel). I hope I succeeded.

. . .

Finally, readers familiar with police radio protocols will notice that the first few times someone communicated over radio, they used standard structures to ensure clarity and understanding. For example, they identified themselves by their roles and repeated information concisely to ensure that they'd gotten it correctly. There were plenty of "overs" and "outs."

After a while, though, you may have noted that I let them speak more normally. Why? In those instances, I wanted the tension high and the pace fast. All the standard communication rules interfered with both, so they flew out the window. My apologies to my radio-savvy readers.

ABOUT THE AUTHOR

Award-winning author Bill Percy writes vivid, engaging tales of people confronting painful and challenging mysteries. His novels in the *Monastery Valley* series, *Climbing the Coliseum, Nobody's Safe Here, The Bishop Burned the Lady*, and *Standing Our Ground* have all won awards in multiple book award competitions. The *Monastery Valley* series tells the stories of life, love, mysteries, and crimes in a small-town community in fictional Monastery Valley, Montana.

NOTE FROM THE AUTHOR

Word-of-mouth is crucial for any author to succeed. If you enjoyed *The Fury Before the Fire*, please leave a review online—anywhere you are able. Even if it's just a sentence or two. It would make all the difference and would be very much appreciated.

Thanks!
Bill Percy

Thank you so much for checking out one of Bill Percy's novels.

If you enjoy this book, please check out our recommended title for your next great read!

Climbing the Coliseum

Foreword's "Book of the Year" *IndieFab* Finalist

Big Book Award's Distinguished Favorite

View other Black Rose Writing titles at
www.blackrosewriting.com/books and use promo code
PRINT to receive a **20% discount** when purchasing.